THE GRASSHOPPER FILE

Mary Barr

THE GRASSHOPPER FILE

Vanguard Press

VANGUARD PAPERBACK

© Copyright 2024
Mary Barr

The right of Mary Barr to be identified as author of
this work has been asserted by her in accordance with the
Copyright, Designs and Patents Act 1988.

All Rights Reserved

No reproduction, copy or transmission of this publication
may be made without written permission.
No paragraph of this publication may be reproduced,
copied or transmitted save with the written permission of the publisher, or in accordance
with the provisions
of the Copyright Act 1956 (as amended).

Any person who commits any unauthorised act in relation to this publication may be liable
to criminal prosecution and civil claims for damages.

A CIP catalogue record for this title is available from the British Library.

ISBN 978-1-83794-227-5

This is a work of fiction. Names, characters, businesses, places, events and incidents are
either the products of the author's imagination or are used in a fictitious manner. Any
resemblance to actual persons, living or dead, or actual events is purely coincidental.

Vanguard Press is an imprint of
Pegasus Elliot Mackenzie Publishers Ltd.
www.pegasuspublishers.com

First Published in 2024

Vanguard Press
Sheraton House Castle Park
Cambridge England

Printed & Bound in Great Britain

Dedication

I dedicate this book to my fabulous niece Esther Barr-Richardson. Like the women born in these pages, you have grown into a strong, talented, independent and amazing adult! I will always be proud of who you are and who you will become. Like the many Barr-Richardson women before you, remember you can achieve anything you wish and become anyone you want to be. Stay as beautiful as you are! You live in my heart, always.

– Aunty Mary –

Contents

The Boozeman 9
His Rights as a Grasshopper 14
Evil Anger of Siobhan Burke 20

Getting Signed On 26
Removing Sheffield Hollingsworth 36
Attachments and Love 40
Staying Cautious 43
Spying on Brock Burke 49
Hopeless Existence 59
Organizing Love 63
Preposterous Saffron 70
Poor Gus 86
Evoking Brock 95
Replacing Love 98

Finally, Leaving Bankers Securities, Inc. 104
Instant Lover 116
Loot Honor Whimsy-Sparrow 123
Eternity Happens 136

Baggage of the Dead 165
You're Now in the Family 176

Moments with Jon Riddley 192
Absolutely — I Do! 201
Remnants of a Life 217
Yonder Swims a Microfiche 226

Baby Charlie 242
Another Mother 253
Realizing There's More 264
Renewing Acquaintances 275

The Grasshopper File 302
About the Author 303
Read a sample chapter from Mrs Dolymauchers Daughters 304
Chapter Two 304
Bethony Smith 304
Synopsis 307
Mrs Dolymaucher's Daughters 307
Character Sheet 310
The Grasshopper File 310

The Boozeman

Gus Boozeman hurriedly entered the dilapidated apartment building situated near the Lincoln Tunnel in New York City. He slammed the old door loudly as he entered the shabby room he called home. He was bone tired and he knew he'd be in trouble for being late – it had been a bad day and an even worse evening. If the old man had been dozing, he wanted to wake him up. Why should he rest anyway?

"Could you be any noisier, boy?" the old man scolded as he moved slightly to a more comfortable position and wiped the dribble from his chin. Gus didn't answer.

"You're late. I'm hungry. Where you been?" the old man reprimanded moodily.

"Yeah, I know I'm late, Pa, and you know where I've been," Gus answered, throwing his dirty working jacket on the chair and missing it completely. He removed his filthy boots, one at a time, and threw them, too, toward the chair, again missing it. Instead, they landed heavily on the floor with a loud thump. The overwhelming smell of sweaty feet invaded the small room.

"I haven't eaten all day and you don't seem to care. How do you think I feel, stuck here every day, just sitting and waiting for you to come home?" the old man ranted. Gus had heard it a thousand times before. It was the same every time, except tonight his Pa really did sound tired.

"Yeah, Pa, I know it ain't fun for you stuck in that chair day after day, waiting for me. But I gotta pay the rent and if I don't work, you won't eat. I do me best, Pa," Gus replied wearily, relaxing a little now that he was home. He scratched his balding head as he searched the almost empty cupboards for something to make into a meal. He didn't see the assortment of things that fell from his dirty scalp as he scratched. Still scratching, he moved to the old refrigerator. Gus was pleased it continued to function; there was no money for a new fridge, and precious little for food.

Finally seated at the small rickety table, both men began hungrily devouring their plates of runny red spaghetti and cheese. They each had two slices of toast and a dirty chipped mug of pale, watery tea from a tea bag that had already been reused several times. Pa rolled his wheelchair slightly toward Gus as he handed him his second slice of toast.

"'Ere, you need it more than me, boy," he said, dropping it onto Gus's plate with hands almost as dirty as those of his son.

"Yeah, thanks, Pa," Gus said between bites.

"I was watching TV tonight while I waited endlessly for you to come home," Pa began, eyeing his son carefully, his congealed spaghetti momentarily forgotten. He watched Gus devouring hungrily every scrap of his food as he wiped his dirty plate with the last of his soft toast. He saw a fifty-five-year-old man. No taller than a boy, Gus stood just five feet tall. Grayish red, thin, greasy hair, which needed a cut, as the longest pieces stuck together and almost touched his shoulders. His worn-out face looked more like that of a seventy-year-old. His deep-set, pale blue eyes had once held a twinkle many long years ago. Gus had a strong jaw, broad shoulders and thin lips. His teeth were yellow and chipped at the front. Gus again wiped up the remains of his meal with the very last piece of his toast – the old man sat and continued to stare at his son as he observed him for the first time in quite a while. The old man was thinking he needed to choose his words carefully if he was going to get an answer to his next question. Soon he continued, "Saw the footage of them taking away a girl's body from the Fraser building. Isn't that where you were cleanin' tonight – those corporate offices of yours, Gus?" Pa asked, holding his breath as he waited for an answer. Gus was a part-time janitor by night, and during the day he worked for Jimmy, a known criminal who had supposedly done his time and was now going straight. Jimmy owned a second-hand shop, and he seldom paid Gus regular wages, so Gus relied heavily on his janitorial job for a regular income. He mightn't do anything important, but he took his work seriously. The old man knew that Gus seldom discussed anything to do with work; he knew his son kept all his worries tightly inside. Gus didn't answer, so the old man slid the remains of his dinner toward his son.

"No, Pa, you've hardly touched it, really I couldn't," Gus said, eyeing the barely warm red spaghetti hungrily.

"Go ahead, son, I've done nothing but sit all day, and you look like you need it," Pa said in a gruff, throaty voice that sounded about as kind as it ever did.

"What else can you do, Pa, but sit? I know it's hard for you and the days are long. I'll take you out for a walk the first time I'm home before dark, I promise," Gus said, tucking into his Pa's now congealed plate of spaghetti and small piece of leftover toast.

"I want an answer, Gus. You were at the Fraser building tonight workin', weren't you?" Pa asked again. Gus took his time answering, but finally decided to tell him some of the truth. What would be the point in lying completely anyway – his Pa had obviously already seen it on the news.

"Yeah, Pa, but it ain't nothin' to be worried about."

"You see her?" Pa asked. Gus had hoped he wouldn't ask and he'd hoped Pa hadn't been watching TV. Gus knew the police would want to interview him again soon, so he thought it best to tell his Pa almost everything.

"Yeah, Pa, I found the body. She was lying face down on the white carpet of the President's office. I've seen her once or twice before. Very pretty, tall, slim brunette, in her mid-twenties, I would say. I came 'bout eye level with her boobs – very nice, too. I think her name was Marlene Brice, or that's the name on the front of her desk. She is or was Brock Burke's secretary. Didn't see no weapon, Pa, but there was one other thing," Gus said, stopping to finish his meal as he tried again to erase the horrible sight from his mind.

"Yeah, go on... what, Gus, what?" Pa asked. This was the most exciting thing that had happened all year and he wanted to know every tiny detail; he needed a good story to tell old Tom, his neighbor, when next he called in. He was worried about his son being involved and finding the murdered girl, but he still liked the idea of hearing the details firsthand.

"Well, Pa, it was her hand, her left hand. I found it first in the trash bin in the basement; long deep pink nails. That was when I called the cops. I was only cleaning the first floor at that point. So, they never found her body till I opened up the 7th floor." Gus was interrupted by a loud pounding on the door.

"Bet it's the police now, Pa. They said they might be needin' to talk with me again," Gus said, taking several steps towards the door.

"Special Agent Bow Grismold; may we come in?" the detective said, not waiting for an answer as he pushed his way into the small, grimy room. A uniformed officer followed but remained discreetly inside the door. Bow Grismold was a large man, both in stature and presence, and he immediately dominated his surroundings. His eyes fell briefly on the old man, before resting intently on Gus.

"Disturbing your dinner, are we?" the tall detective asked, not caring or wanting an answer. "Mr Boozeman, just a few questions about tonight's deceased person."

Gus nodded, feeling completely dwarfed by the six-foot-tall man who invaded his domain.

"My son's a good boy, hard workin' and a good son," Pa put in, thinking he needed to.

"I'm sure he is, sir. However, we have some further routine questions, as it was your son who found the body."

"I already answered the policeman's questions earlier."

"I understand that, sir. If you could just be patient with me, if you please. Now, did you touch the body or anything in the room before we arrived?"

"No, sir, just the phone when I called security," Gus replied. He hadn't mentioned the security guard asking him if he had scrambled the closed-circuit video cameras that surveyed the 7th floor, nor had Gus mentioned how he'd thought he saw a lithe figure dressed entirely in black leaving by the stairs as he exited the elevator. Gus knew the less he said the better. He briefly remembered the money he'd taken from the girl's handbag. She wouldn't need it now anyway, and he'd only touched the fifties. Gus didn't want it to look suspicious, so he'd left the twenties, tens and fives, and she'd had a lot of those also. He needed that money, and so he'd helped himself to her wallet; her handbag was just lying there on the floor beside her, begging for his attention. Gus would never have touched it if she'd held it in her other hand. There was lots of blood where her hand had been sawn from her wrist. It was a sickening sight.

Gus often took things from the offices he cleaned, either from the trash or things he didn't think people would need. He'd then sell them at Jimmy's second-hand store, sometimes with Jimmy's knowledge, but usually without; it really depended on whether Jimmy was around or not. Gus never intentionally hid things from Jimmy. There had been several things Gus had thought of lifting on the 7th floor before he'd discovered the girl. But, like always, he would go back and get them last thing before he left. Now Gus realized it really did pay to be careful.

"Did you stay in the room when the security guard arrived?"

"No, sir, I had to continue my cleanin', as I have to get home to me Pa. He's all alone, he relies on me."

"Yes, yes, so I see," the taller man replied, briefly eyeing the old man in the wheelchair with a look of disdain.

"You're quite sure you didn't touch anything? Either in the room or on the body of the deceased before the police arrived?" the detective persisted.

"Yes, sir, quite sure," Gus answered, mentally recounting how he wiped her handbag with his cloth in case he'd left fingerprints.

"Your prints were on the door handle leading into Mr Burke's office, Mr Boozeman."

"Oh, yeah, I forgot. It was locked, so I had to unlock it to get inside. I wanted to empty the trash, and I didn't see her until I was halfway inside the room."

"Okay, Mr Boozeman, we'll leave it at that for now. My card, if you think of anything further, anything at all you'd like to add to your statement." Agent Bow Grismold took two large steps to the door. Gus observed his shiny black patent leather shoes; his clean, neatly pressed black trousers, crisp white shirt open at the neck, black leather overcoat and neatly groomed dark hair. The guy was not only raggedly good looking, but he was tall as well, Gus thought. This guy had it all. How can life be so unfair!

His Rights as a Grasshopper

"Al darling, are you coming to bed? It's almost two a.m. – remember, I have to work in the morning. I'm already feeling that delicious rush of excitement, darling. The anticipation is building inside me. I hadn't realized, but I've been missing the challenge, the power, the thrill. I really can't wait to get started!" Hugo called excitedly to his wife, who was still working frantically at her desk.

"I'm excited, too, sweet cheeks; just give me a few moments longer. You know I'm a perfectionist. I'm just making sure everything's perfect; nothing less will do now, will it?" Al called back, almost singing her words, her excitement easily matching her husband's.

Hugo sat and waited. He loved hearing the anticipation in his wife's voice; it mirrored his own – they thought alike, they understood each other and he adored her for it, almost as much as he loved her. He sat alone in the large king-size bed; he smoothed the pale blue satin sheets with his left hand, while he held his martini in his well-manicured right hand. He sat looking out over Manhattan. It twinkled before him like a vast, sparkling, moving quilt just daring the dawn to steal its splendor. Hugo looked around their opulent apartment with its polished floors, expensive furniture, three spacious bathrooms and huge walk-in closets. Finally, he knew they had really made it. An apartment of this size on Park Avenue was not cheap, but they had the money, and working in Manhattan had been a dream for both of them for a very long time.

"It's all done, perfectly. No one would ever know. Well, Hugo Grasshopper, you are now officially Alastair Rasnic. When I've finished with you in the morning, you'll look more like the dead man than he did himself," she said, laughing as she dropped her satin gown to the floor and walked seductively toward the bed. She moved slow and sensuous like a panther prowling, perfectly naked. Her curly shoulder-length, red hair bounced loosely around her slender neck, her perfect oval aqua eyes sparkling seductively in the dim light, she continued walking slowly towards him. Hugo knew without a doubt she was an elegantly stunning and very sexy woman. Alberta was forty-nine years old, soon to be fifty. Over the years she'd had some very expensive work done by some of the best cosmetic surgeons available, and Hugo thought she looked even better now than she had twenty years ago. She didn't look a day over thirty. He enjoyed watching her approach, with anticipation. She was, in fact, two years his senior. Hugo had also used several of the best cosmetic surgeons and would do so again when they left New York in about eighteen months – if all went to plan, and he knew it would.

Hugo had met Alberta Fisher when she was twenty-five years old and he was just twenty-three. She was a makeup artist with Twentieth Century Fox, and one of the best. Hugo had a small part in a movie, which required an extensive makeover. Art imitated life, and Hugo excelled at his acting. A perfectionist at all things, he was cast quickly in two more movies at the same studio. Finally, he was offered a contract. However, by that time they knew they were destined for bigger and better things. Hugo thought her the worldliest person he had ever known, and he was so in love with her that he would have followed her to the moon if she'd asked. Fortunately, Alberta thought the same way and all she asked for was a wedding. Hugo quickly learned she was expecting their son Zax.

Alberta was an only child. Her parents were elderly and very rich, so the wedding was a grand affair and organized at break-neck speed by parents who didn't wish to be socially embarrassed.

Hugo and Alberta quickly completed their family with their daughter, Neve, who arrived one year after Zax and was followed shortly afterwards by Alberta's first visit to the plastic surgeon. Zax was now the same age as Alberta had been when she'd first met Hugo. Their lives were by no means parallel; in fact, there were no similarities at all. He was nothing like a Grasshopper. Zax seemed to favor Alberta's parents' conservative and mundane lifestyle.

Zax met Molly when he chose to do a year's exchange at Eton from Harvard. Lady Molly Win-Stanley was also studying accountancy – she thought it the most prudent thing to do with her family's ailing monetary situation. The Win-Stanleys were not only an old, aristocratic, English family, they were also landowners. Real estate-rich and money-poor was how Zax described them. However, thanks to Zax becoming part of their family, financially things were turning around. He was organizing new buildings on some of their land and bringing new growth to the vast estate. It not only helped generate jobs for the struggling villagers, but also brought much needed wealth to the Win-Stanleys. Zax hadn't a lot in common with his parents, but he did have their desire to achieve; however, unlike them, he liked to stay on the right side of the law. He viewed the large acreage owned by the Win-Stanleys as a vast untapped area of wealth, and he saw it as a financial challenge making the land yield profitably.

Married for only nineteen months, the Hoppers, as Zax preferred them to be called, already had two children. They wasted no time, both feeling a family of their own was important. Bobby had arrived nine months after their marriage, almost to the day, closely followed, ten months later, by Elizabeth. Due to their ancestry, both children were titled: Lord Robert Hugo Hopper and Lady Elizabeth Florentine Hopper. Although Zax had chosen to forego his parents' lifestyle, and his life in America, he still chose to receive his substantial allowance from the Grasshopper Family Trust, as did Neve. Somehow, the fact that most of the funds came from illicit means didn't seem to stop Zax from accepting a generous amount of money each month. The Grasshopper children were well taken care of and would continue to be so, no matter what.

Ten years into Alberta and Hugo's marriage, her parents had mysteriously died just two weeks apart, and Alberta Grasshopper became even wealthier than before. Unlike Alberta, Hugo had no parents. They had died when he was in his teens, doing exactly what Al and Hugo were doing now. It was a dangerous occupation, Hugo had learned from the loss of his parents, unlike his brother, Felix, who had not.

Although supportive of each other, the Grasshopper brothers were very different. Felix ended up in jail soon after he graduated. Felix had held up several 7-Eleven stores and was also busted for assault. After serving time, he'd remained free for less than twenty-four hours. When last he was released, Hugo and Alberta had not yet rescued him when he was involved holding up a large prominent bank in the middle of the day. Again, a long sentence followed. Hugo and Alberta had been minutes away from arriving at his place when the news broke on the radio. They both thought they were lucky to escape involvement, and it shook them to the core. Felix would be up for parole in another year, and this time Alberta and Hugo would have the limo waiting at the prison gates. Neither of them felt comfortable getting that close to the lockup, but they both knew it must be done if Felix was ever to be set up in a regular life. He was now in his mid-forties and couldn't afford another misdemeanor. He wrote often, telling them he'd found God and that he had been born again and was now reformed. They both agreed that this time he must stay clean!

Alberta and Hugo never again had an orthodox job; they hadn't needed to ever work again. They could easily retire and live the good life while enjoying their children and living in luxury. Had they chosen to do so. Instead, they chose to use all their skills and intelligence and pursued a life of embezzlement and danger. They felt it was what kept them vibrant, alive and fresh. Their sex life also couldn't have been better! Never had they thought of getting caught, but they never took any of their successes for granted and pretended each job was their first. They were a great team, both meticulous perfectionists.

Alberta slinked softly into bed that evening – tomorrow was briefly forgotten. Her body molded perfectly into his, tightly, touching. His passionate kiss, like his arousal, was mounting rapidly with every second their bodies touched. Both fired on by the thought of what was to begin in the morning. Maybe there would be no sleep at all tonight!

The ringing of the phone on the table directly beside the bed intruded on their love-making. Slowly they drew apart and wondered just who would be calling at two forty-five a.m. on a Wednesday morning.

"Daddy, have you read this morning's paper?" It was Neve. She sounded her usual happy upbeat self, no matter what time of the day or night it was.

Alberta grabbed the phone. "Baby Girl, how did you get this morning's paper so early? And what on earth does it say that would make you call us at this hour?"

"Gee, Mom, you weren't sleeping, were you?" Neve asked, surprised. She never thought of things like the time of day, she felt them much too unimportant. Hugo grabbed the phone before placing her on speaker.

"Okay, Baby, what you got?" Hugo asked.

"Well, Dad, I was just thinking of our family motto – *'A Grasshopper always looks after its own'* – so as I read page three of the *New York Times*, I knew it was my duty to call. A murder at Bankers Securities Inc. – it's located on the 7th floor, I checked. That's where you'll be working tomorrow as Alastair Rasnic."

"Is this a good thing, Baby Girl? You sound excited!" Al asked, as she quickly switched on the huge TV screen situated above them on the ceiling. Al and Hugo knew Neve was smart and wouldn't be sounding this excited if she didn't think they could all benefit. Unlike her brother, Zax, she shared their penchant for living dangerously. Surfing the channels, they soon arrived at the item she was referring to. They listened intently for a few seconds before Neve's impatience interrupted them. Already they'd seen enough to know why she was excited.

"So, there will be a secretarial job immediately available – secretary to the CEO and President, Mr. Brock Burke. I've already checked him out and he likes slim, intelligent blondes with long hair and a sexy elegance. I've made a booking on the first flight in the morning, Mom, and you can make me over immediately," she finished. Al and Hugo rapidly forgot their rising ardor.

"Baby Girl, it's way too dangerous," Alberta said, trying to convince herself as well; although, like Hugo, she knew it could easily work.

"The time to get to know Brock is when he's at his weakest, and he won't be getting much sleep at the moment with this scandal about to break. Bankers Securities will be heavily in the news tomorrow and for a few days to come, and he'll need someone competent to handle it immediately. The merger is about to happen with the Asian bank, and the Columbian clientele don't like to be kept waiting – $370 billion is quite a bit of money. With me in the president's office, we can get in and out a lot faster!" Neve finished convincingly.

"What do you think, Hugo?" Al asked.

"Well...," Hugo began, but before he could say anything further, Neve continued.

"Okay, I've already spoken to the employment agency; she owes me anyway, so when my girlfriend arrives, she'll be looked after. She'll never know it will actually be me. I'm packing now; see you in a few hours. Sleep tight, love you..." and the line went dead.

Hugo and Al looked at each other, and together they said, "Well, she's your daughter...," and turned off the light.

Evil Anger of Siobhan Burke

"Brock, I'm not allowing you to do this anymore. No! I want it to stop. I wouldn't even have found out if I hadn't accidently picked up the extension while you were talking. I'm not allowing this, not anymore, do you hear me…?"

"Darling, please calm down. It's not like I'm doing anything wrong. Look at the lifestyle you have, we have. Darling, please be reasonable."

"No, Brock, it's wrong and we both know it. Hiding money from the tax man in my name is very wrong. I'm not going down with you. And don't call me Darling. It's the fact you hid it from me that I despise most. If it's not wrong, then why haven't you discussed it with me like you used to when we were first married?"

"Siobhan, a lot has changed since then. Look where we are now and where we've come from. I'm at the top of my game. Why, you're now married to the CEO and President of Bankers Securities Inc. Come on, Darling, you wouldn't want to jeopardize any of this, surely, would you?" he pleaded, trying to give her the look which used to make her melt, although it certainly wasn't working at the moment; it seemed to Brock the more people he had under his control at work, the less he could control his own wife. She had the perfect life, so why didn't she trust his judgment?

"You want to talk about a lot changing, Brock? Like the hours you arrive home, like the perfume I smell on your shirts and the lipstick I see on your collar, when you say you've been working late or in a meeting. The type of meeting you're involved in usually includes just two people, you and your latest secretary, in very close proximity for a very long time. I hate it, I hate it all. The very first time you cheated on me, you lost my love, my trust and my respect. No, Brock, marriage is about a lot more than being members of the same élite country club, showing a united front while you're playing golf and I'm enjoying tennis. Do you honestly think I'm that stupid?"

Brock didn't answer; he turned and walked quickly away before slamming the bathroom door and turning on the shower. The hot water on his back always soothed him. Siobhan briefly wiped away a stray tear from her cheek as she sat quietly on the edge of the bed. She kicked off her satin pumps, one at a time. She usually didn't bother confronting him, but she'd only arrived home thirty minutes before he had. The little restaurant he so often frequented must have been almost empty for him to get home so quickly. She bit hard on her bottom lip as she again tried to hold back the tears. She should be way past this after all these years and she knew it.

Siobhan hated the times when Brock was enjoying an affair with yet another woman, the late nights, his coldness toward her, his lack of communication. However, she also understood that once he'd won them over and they were madly in love with him, he would quickly grow tired of them. Brock loved the chase. A diamond bracelet and a letter of termination would soon follow. Then he would again love only her. She lived for these times and they continued to be as good as ever. She'd always go on hoping that one day he would love only her. Slowly she removed her satin dressing gown, before turning down the sheets of their king-size bed. At times like these Siobhan wondered again just why she still slept with him; at present she liked nothing about him, least of all his manipulating and devious ways. How strange it was that after all he did to her, they still shared a healthy and loving sex life, if only between affairs. Although tonight she'd be on her side of the bed by herself, of that she was sure.

Siobhan sighed deeply. She was clad in thin silk pajamas, and was quite unaware of how devastatingly beautiful she looked as she got between the sheets. All day she'd had a feeling of foreboding; at times it had been so intense she was relieved to see Brock arrive home safely, even if it was late in the evening. It was about twenty minutes later when she heard the bathroom door open and the light momentarily pierce the darkness of the room. Then she felt the bed dipping as Brock gently got into his side. He briefly turned on his bedside lamp and then immediately turned it off again quietly so as not to disturb her. As she lay in the darkness with her back toward her husband, he made no effort to comfort her. Within minutes, his rhythmic breathing told her he was asleep. Siobhan lay where she was, staring up into the darkened room, as large hot tears rolled unchecked down her cheeks and onto her long blonde hair that cascaded over the pillow and around her – she had learned long ago how to cry silently. Why should Brock feel the triumph of knowing he had hurt her yet again? She often wondered how she could continue loving him. Siobhan often wished she knew how to make it stop.

Brock always kept his cell phone beside his bed, and he kept it turned on. When the phone rang in the darkness, it seemed louder than usual. Instantly, he reached for the light switch before answering it.

"Brock Burke." He paused.

"Yes, detective. Are you sure… in my office? Not Marlene, I can't believe it!" Brocks face turned ashen as he paused while the person on the other end of the phone spoke for some time.

"I can't answer that right now, detective. I'm on my way…" Then a brief pause before he hung up.

"Siobhan, I'm sorry, Darling, I have to go back to the office. Something needs my urgent attention," Brock said, appearing to have forgotten their earlier disagreement as he kissed her briefly on the cheek.

She watched through teary, half-closed eyes as he quickly dressed in a clean business shirt and his navy pinstriped suit. She briefly noted that he had not chosen one of his best suits. He randomly chose a tie and thrust it in his jacket pocket, then grabbed his briefcase from inside the door in one hand, his cell phone and shoes in the other and raced down the stairs. She faintly heard the car tires screech as he headed out of the circular driveway onto the street. Brock had decided to take the Porsche. Siobhan realized the reason Brock was dragged back to the office was the same thing she had been dreading all day. Somewhere deep inside, Siobhan knew exactly what that was; it was something she chose to ignore. She took several slow deep breaths to steady her inner turmoil, before reaching over and turning off the light. She felt like a weight had lifted off her shoulders. A slight smile touched her lips. Alone in a bed made for two, she waited for sleep to find her.

Brock headed out of the driveway. He didn't care which car he drove, but the silver Porsche was directly outside the front door. It was the closest. Brock's mind was in turmoil: he couldn't believe the call he'd just received... murdered... in his office? But she'd been so alive when he'd left her. Well, he thought, at least the autopsy won't find any traces of him. She'd made sure of that. Marlene Brice had repeated the same four little words to Brock, which minutes before she'd said to her husband over the phone.

"We need to talk." Those four little words sent chills down his spine and all thoughts of their anticipated torrid love-making quickly vanished. Then she'd chilled him to the core by gazing at him with her purple blue eyes and dropping a bombshell that could potentially change his life.

"I'm pregnant...," Marlene Brice had uttered as cool as a cucumber, "and it's probably yours..."

Brock could clearly see her sitting across from his wide mahogany desk, her dark chestnut hair perfectly framing her face, looking devastatingly cool as she spoke. Brock had always wanted children of his own, but Siobhan hadn't wanted to compromise their lifestyle and her body. Looking back now, Brock knew, the moment Siobhan had told him she never wanted children of her own was exactly when he'd started having affairs.

"I have some things to finish in my office, Brock. I'll give you a few minutes alone, and thank you for not yelling at me. By the way, I am thinking of getting rid of it, whoever it belongs to; but, Brock, I am pretty sure it's yours, as Borg was away working on the oil rigs three months ago." She'd said no more and graciously got up and walked back to her own office, closing the door behind her.

Brock sat for a long time, staring into space and thinking. Finally, he decided he wanted this baby, and if it was his, he'd leave Siobhan and marry Marlene if she wanted him to. This was a life-changing decision, and one he needed to think some more about. Just as he was about to call her back into his office, he thought he'd heard her talking to someone. He briefly checked to see if any of the phone lines were being used, but noticed they weren't. The quietness of the offices at night was obviously playing tricks on him; he must have been mistaken.

Brock's mind immediately raced back to the baby. He was secretly delighted with the news. Naturally he was shocked at first, but he'd often wondered if he had fathered any other children. Lord knows, he'd had enough affairs.

The moment Marlene walked into his office, he scooped her into his arms, before wrapping her tightly in his embrace and kissing her passionately. He felt her pull away slightly and apologized for being so cool when she'd told him the news. Brock said he just needed time to think. Soon he told her what he proposed to do and said he would let her sleep on it and they'd talk tomorrow.

"Marlene, you've rocked my world and I think I like it. We should celebrate. Let's dine at La Maison. Darling, please give them a call and tell them we're on our way. It's one of your favorites, isn't it?" Brock announced, getting up and putting on his jacket. Then he noticed she hadn't moved.

"Brock, I appreciate your enthusiasm, but I really need to be up to date with the paperwork for the pending merger tomorrow. Why don't we wait and celebrate both things when the papers are signed?" Marlene had always been both practical and cool; she was also one of the best secretaries he had ever had. She was also the only married brunette as well. Brock was a little disappointed and surprised by her lack of interest in spending the evening with him and quite taken aback with her answer.

She then quickly got to her feet, kissed him lightly on the cheek and returned to her office, before quietly shutting her door. It was a strange thing for Marlene to do – one she had never done before. Seconds before the door closed, Brock had the distinct feeling she was not alone. Could Marlene Brice have had another person with her concealed in her office? Brock knew now she may have, as he thought of her nervous behavior, her rejection of dinner, and the light kiss she had given him on the cheek. Brock may not know everything about Marlene Brice, but he knew she was a passionate woman, and he now knew something had been very wrong when he'd left the office earlier in the evening.

Marlene Brice was dead. Brock Burke was in deep shock. He knew he should never have left her alone, late at night, on the 7th floor of the Fraser building on Wall Street. Brock asked himself again, *'Had Marlene Brice been alone…?'*

Getting Signed On

Alberta and Hugo Grasshopper had very little sleep, but from the moment the alarm sounded they were both wide awake and out of bed. It was four thirty a.m. and Al had a lot of work to do on Hugo before she could send Alastair Rasnic off to work at Banker's Securities, Inc. Al had worked hard on the rubber mold her husband would wear to change his appearance, and now she must make sure it would fit perfectly and look completely natural. Hugo Grasshopper was a tall, slim man with a physique any man would wish for. Hugo seldom exercised and didn't need to. His hair was light brown with a touch of white at the temples; Al described it as distinguished. Soft and wavy, it seldom moved from where it was combed. Al always hated covering Hugo's perfect skin with her mold, but she had done so many times before and would no doubt do it again in the future.

    She briefly gazed into his light brown eyes before kissing him on the tip of his nose. Attaching the mold and the dark hairpiece took a lot of time, especially the first time. Next, she placed thin silicon ends over each of his fingertips, before strapping on the extra twenty pounds he would carry around his stomach. The clothes Alastair Rasnic would wear were not nearly as elegant, stylish or expensive as Hugo's own. They had been purchased off the rack at Brookes Brothers and were perfect for the head financial officer of investment holdings at Banker's Securities, Inc. Alastair wore a burgundy and gray striped tie, a white shirt and a subtle dark gray business suit for his first day at work.

    At six thirty a.m., 'Alastair Rasnic' and his wife 'Sylvia' were seated at the kitchen table enjoying a large breakfast, not because they were hungry, but because Al had to make sure Alastair's new face was working properly. She watched him closely as he ate his toast, before making a small adjustment behind his left ear.

"Perfect, Alastair darling," Al said, kissing him, toast and all, on the lips. Al then produced a black leather wallet from her desk and went over its contents with her husband. Credit cards, American Express Platinum – of course – Barclays Visa card, driver's license, the necessary membership cards, including one to a 'gentlemen-only club', Al said, winking at him.

"I believe Brock Burke also belongs to this gentleman's club, although it is not common knowledge around the office. Keep it to yourself until you know the time is right. Then she showed him a tiny button hidden on the inside of his wallet. "This will record anything from the computer; it's wireless and cannot be traced. You have the usual wires in the extra pounds you are wearing, so, as always, I can hear everything; along with the usual camera concealed in your tie pin."

"Is it all the same as last time, Alberta darling? If so, it will work wonderfully."

"It sure is, sweet cheeks. You know we're now Al and Al," Alberta said, laughing as she winked at him.

"No, we're not, Sylvia," Hugo corrected her, laughing. It was at that moment the doorbell rang.

"Neve!" Al yelled excitedly, racing to the door. Neve burst into the room, her short auburn hair looking completely unkempt and badly needing a brush. Her olive skin was flawless and made her eyes appear to shine in her pretty pixie-shaped face, which had seldom seen makeup. She wore a tight pair of holey black designer jeans, a black t-shirt which once had large metallic writing on the front, but most of it had vanished in the wash. Her t-shirt was mainly covered by a pink cashmere bomber jacket with large gold buttons.

"Indeed it is me, Mom. Your next client has arrived!" Neve burst into the huge opulent room, briefly surveying her surroundings. She let out a low whistle before immediately hugging both her parents tightly. She quickly held her father at arm's length as she said, "Mr Alastair Rasnic, I presume?" Giggling, she looked him up and down.

"You presumed correctly, young lady. Do I know you?" Hugo asked, laughing as he twirled his beautiful daughter around several times.

"Apparently not – but I have a strong feeling that you soon will," Neve replied, keeping the banter going. Still heavily in work mode, Al brought the moment back to work.

"Do you see anything familiar about this man, Neve?" Al asked, referring to the way her husband looked.

"No, Mom. Nothing. I've never seen this man before in my life, and I would have no reason to give him a second glance should I pass him on the street." They all laughed as Hugo retrieved his briefcase from the chair, tucked his wallet into the inside pocket of his jacket and kissed both women on the cheek.

"What time will you be starting, Miss Amanda Dolman?" Hugo asked his daughter, as he walked toward the door.

"Around lunchtime, Daddy," Neve replied.

"I hope Amanda Dolman won't be looking too sexy. I know you're all grown up, but in my eyes you'll always be Daddy's little girl, Honey," Hugo said, using Neve's new name for the first time as a small frown appeared on his rubber face.

"Go, Alastair, off to work with you. Leave us girls to do whatever we think is necessary," Al replied, opening the door.

"Nothing too sexy," Hugo warned, heading for the elevator.

"Enjoy, Daddy; see you later!" Neve called, as the apartment door closed. Alastair silently passed the entrance to the other apartment on their floor – it was apartment 7B. He walked down the carpeted hallway to the elevator. Just like every other time, he didn't hear the soft click as he passed and the camera lens blinked quickly into life.

~

Hugo decided to walk the seven blocks to his new Wall Street office. The weather was fine, and it would give him time to truly become Alastair Rasnic.

From the moment Alastair walked into the Fraser building, it was a whirl of activity. Police cars lined the street and the Fraser building was partially cornered off. Plain-clothes detectives hovered as early morning commuters bustled along the street and hurried to their respective offices.

It was eight fifteen a.m. when Alastair arrived at the reception desk on the 7th floor. Moments later, he was greeted by a lady in her mid-fifties, who introduced herself as Mrs. Berry Pye. She wore a conservative light gray knitted suit over a pale pink satin blouse, tied at the throat with a large silver brooch. She had neat, short brown wavy hair, small brown eyes and a small mouth with wrinkles around the edges accentuated by her bright rosy pink lipstick. Alastair had expected better of Brock Burke's staff with his reputation for enjoying gorgeous women. So far, the receptionist was the most attractive woman Alastair had seen.

"Your office, Mr. Rasnic. Please make yourself comfortable. You may call me Ms. Berry or Mrs. Pye. I shall bring you your morning coffee if you will instruct me as to how you take it."

"Black, thank you, Berry," Alastair answered, watching as she frowned slightly, before saying in her controlled monotone voice, "Ms. Berry or Mrs. Pye, if you please, Mr .Rasnic."

"I shall call you Berry, and I shall be pleased to do so. Your quaint name suits you well," Alastair replied charmingly. Berry rewarded him with a tight smile and left the room. Moments later, she returned with his coffee in a pristine white cup and saucer. Hugo was standing at his floor-to-ceiling glass window, legs slightly apart, hands clasped behind his back. He was looking out over the Hudson River and Statue of Liberty.

He commented on the magnificent view, saying it certainly took one's breath away, to which Berry replied coldly, "I wouldn't know, Mr. Rasnic. I have no time to waste observing the view. My small office has no windows." She was turning to leave when a plain-clothes detective poked his nose in the door. Berry was most annoyed. "I do beg your pardon. Do you have an appointment with Mr. Rasnic?"

"No, ma'am, I don't. But I'll need one if an appointment is required. I need to speak to you also when you have a moment. I am Special Agent Bow Grismold." He briefly flashed his ID card as he introduced himself to Berry. Hugo could clearly hear all they were saying and almost spilt his coffee. The door to his office was open, so he continued listening to the short conversation taking place outside.

"I shall look in my diary and let you know. Mr. Rasnic is just starting with the firm and has a very busy day of introduction scheduled."

"Good, I'll just sit here and wait until either of you can speak to me, Mrs. Pye. Is your name really Berry Pye?" Agent Grismold asked, almost laughing as he thought she was one person who didn't fit her name.

"I will let you know when I am available. You may leave now if you please," Berry said, firmly standing up behind her desk.

She's a tough nut, Hugo thought, knowing he had better get her on side and keep her there. He continued observing the view and listening.

"No, Mrs. Pye, I will not leave. You may sit down while you answer my questions. This is a murder investigation and no one in this office is above suspicion, even the new guy in there. Do you understand?"

Hugo didn't hear Berry answer, but he sure heard her object again as they fingerprinted her and asked her all manner of questions – personal and not so personal. Within moments, the detective's tall frame was standing in the doorway of Hugo's new office.

"Got a moment, Mr. Rasnic? Your secretary seems to think you may have an opening – better now before everyone arrives than later, when you have to stay behind after work, I would say, wouldn't you?" Detective Grismold said, taking a seat without being asked.

"Certainly, detective, whatever I can do to help, although this is my first day on the job…"

"Indeed, so I've been told, several times. Your full name, date of birth and place of birth, sir?" the detective asked, staring him straight in the eye. Alberta had briefed him well, although he had forgotten his middle name. At that exact moment his cell rang.

"If you'll excuse me, detective?"

"Yes, but make it brief."

"Alastair Rasnic speaking." Alastair knew it would be Al, giving him the answers he needed, and he was grateful for her call. He knew that not remembering your own middle name can look a tad suspicious!

The detective kept his questions general as Alastair was new to both the city and the work place. Finally, as the detective stood up from his chair and was about to leave, he turned back. "Any chance of a coffee? It's been a long night and promises to be an even longer day," he said, eyeing Alastair's half-empty steaming coffee.

"Certainly, detective. Berry will bring you one," Alastair replied charmingly.

The detective's uniformed assistant then appeared to take Alastair's fingerprints. He found it all rather unnerving, but didn't let it show. He knew Al would be sitting at home watching and monitoring his racing pulse. This was something that had never happened before, and Alastair didn't like it one little bit. The uniformed officer assured him it was merely routine. Outwardly, Alastair remained calm, but inside he was thinking of his brother Felix and already rethinking his plan to work at Banker's Securities.

The moment the detective left, Alastair asked Berry to take him a cup of coffee. For a moment he thought she was about to refuse, but without a word she did as he asked. Moments later, she was in his office again, sitting across the desk from him, her spectacles on and her diary open. No fun here, Alastair thought. Just then, his cell rang and Al instructed him to compliment her on her blouse and brooch, ask where she shopped, as his wife would adore both the blouse and the color. Alastair immediately did as Al instructed, and before long they were talking like long lost friends. Berry almost offered to go shopping with Sylvia and show her around… almost, but not quite.

Berry then got back to the business at hand, but appeared to have a softer approach than previously.

"First, I shall take you down to Human Resources. You need your security pass, company credit card, entry key, business cards. They will also need your bank details, so you can get that large salary of yours paid directly into your bank account. They will also set up your laptop. And show you your company car and parking space. Then I shall introduce you to the people you need to know around the office. Please note, I will not waste time with people I don't think you should bother with. Then a meeting with Mr. Burke, firstly on his own and then in a board meeting where the Board of Directors will briefly outline each of their expectations of the pending merger. I'll brief you on each one first, save you concerning yourself with incidentals, etc."

Again, Alastair nodded; she was nothing if not efficient, he thought.

"Then, if the Board members like you, they will invite you to lunch, and if not, I will bring you lunch in your office and you can meet the people who you will be directly responsible for. And then…" She went on and on. Alastair just watched her rosy pink lips talking and talking as she neatly and efficiently ticked off each item after she discussed it with him. Finally, she stopped talking and was looking hard at him. Alastair knew it was time to tune back in.

"I'm sorry, Berry, I missed that," Alastair said charmingly.

"Oh, it's quite a lot to take in all at once, I know. I shall print you a schedule of what is expected of you today. I asked you if you would like to look over the files now. I suggest you do briefly as it's a great deal of money and one of our largest mergers ever. If Banker's Securities is successful, and I'm sure they will be, it will place us in another league altogether," Berry finished. She was obviously proud of the company's pending achievement.

"Yes, Berry, bring me the files and give me thirty minutes to quickly get up to speed."

"Yes, Mr. Rasnic, but that won't be nearly long enough. You see the files are sub—"

"Berry, the files, if you please," Alastair instructed, cutting her off. He was already more than familiar with the merger and probably knew more than anyone in the company. After all, the money it created was the reason he was here.

"Well, lucky you. You got the Berry Pye while Brocky gets the lady in red," a tall, pale guy joked to Alastair some time later as he washed his hands in the men's bathroom. "He doesn't allow us guys to enjoy anything attractive, says it takes our mind off work. Sorry, I know you're Alastair Rasnic, the new guy. I'm Phil Monkston, and this skinny guy is Ross Moss."

Alastair nodded as he dried his hands before Ross said, "Hey – not so much of the skinny guy thing. Did you dudes get a load of Brocky's new secretary? Man, is she stacked! Only the best for Brocky... classy, too!"

"He sounds like a lucky guy," Alastair said, taking a deep breath. He knew they were talking about his daughter.

"Yeah, dangerously so. Hey, let's walk past her desk on the way back, Ross," Phil said, grabbing the smaller guy around the shoulders.

"See ya, Alastair, enjoy your Berry Pye. We're off to see the goddess in red," Phil joked sarcastically, as the two younger guys left the bathroom laughing. Alastair wondered just what Neve looked like. Did he really want to find out? Somehow, he knew he soon would. She had worked only one other job with him and that was in Minnesota several years ago. He'd hated the way the guys looked at her then, too, although he had to admit it had shortened the length of time he'd needed to stay. Neve had proven a very efficient asset then, and he felt sure she'd do so again.

The morning raced by as Berry followed him around meticulously ticking everything off her list as they walked. At twelve o'clock he was shown into Brock Burke's office after meeting Brock's new secretary, Miss Amanda Dolman. As Alastair looked at Neve, he could see exactly what the guys were talking about. Al had turned her into a total knockout; she looked like a movie star. She wore a fitted red woolen dress with three-quarter sleeves and a huge, soft, floppy collar. It wasn't too low, but Alastair knew the suggestion was certainly there. She had a low-slung wide suede belt on her hips studded with large red and blue rhinestones. Her stilettos were thin and tall and also in red with high black heels. But what made Alastair stare the most was her face. Her beautiful eyes shone, surrounded by dark lashes, and her straight, long platinum-blonde hair fell almost to her waist and glistened with health. Her lips were full and moist and they sparkled with a soft red gloss; her perfume was so sexy, Alastair had to remember she was his daughter. He briefly recalled smelling the same intoxicating perfume on Al. The night that followed vividly flashed through his mind, before he quickly gained control, remembered where he was, and entered Brock's office.

"Welcome, Alastair, glad you're on board and part of the team. Things are rather crazy around here, but I'm sure they'll soon settle down. Most unfortunate business," Brock said, trying to hide his shock. He was still unable to think of anything but Marlene Brice. The only moment she'd been out of his mind was when Amanda Dolman was introduced to him. She was a knockout and presented as a very efficient secretary also.

"Glad to be here, Mr. Burke."

"Brock's the name. Please, take a seat," Brock said, raking his hand through his disheveled brown hair. Alastair noted Brock was a man of average height and build, with brilliant blue eyes and an overly handsome face. Alastair noted he looked like he'd been up all night and then realized he probably had.

"Mrs. Pye gave you the files required for today's board meeting?" Brock asked, still pacing the floor as he tried to focus on Alastair.

"Yes, sir. I believe I'm up to speed."

"Any questions at this stage?"

"Well, only on the Columbian influence. I'm unsure as to their depth of involvement, Brock?" Alastair asked. From just one question, Brock realized this guy was not only up to speed but also sharp. He would need to phrase his answer carefully. But at that exact moment the door was flung open.

"Mr. Burke's in a meeting. I told you, you can't—" Amanda said loudly, as a scruffy young man burst into the office. Alastair immediately got to his feet.

"You – you bastard! You crazy, fucked-up bastard! You murdered my wife… you crazy bastard, I'm going to kill you!" screamed the younger man as he lurched for Brock, flying over his desk and grabbing Brock's throat before both men fell heavily to the floor. Alastair only just managed to pull the newcomer from Brock's body as he continued to yell obscenities, threatening Brock loudly. Alastair held fast to the smaller guy as he continued to kick, punch and try to pull free. Seconds later, two uniforms pushed through the crowd of employees gathered at the door. They quickly restrained Borg Brice, dragging him still kicking and screaming from the room. He never stopped accusing Brock of murder until he was out of earshot.

Alastair lifted Brock to his feet and helped him into his chair. His face was badly scratched and bleeding, his suit was torn and crumpled and he was clutching his right shoulder, wincing with pain. It was then Alastair looked at Amanda, still standing several feet inside the doorway; she motioned to him to check his hair piece. He subtly did so, quickly checking himself in the large wall mirror; he immediately realized it had moved slightly during the tussle. He knew it would have been enough to give him away had anyone noticed. Berry was busy getting everyone away from the doorway and back to work. By the time Alastair righted Brock's desk, plus several other pieces of furniture, and retrieved most of his papers from the floor, the paramedics arrived.

"Brock, sit tight, we'll have our meeting another time," Alastair said, heading for the door. He knew Brock was in shock and hadn't expected him to say anything further, but he did.

"Alastair, I want you in that board meeting this afternoon. Save your questions for later. This is not a normal day around here." Alastair nodded, retreating, as he left the paramedics to their task…

Things may not be going too well for Brock Burke, but Alastair thought everything was going very nicely in his direction. Alastair smiled at Amanda Dolman, before returning to his office and shutting the door.

Removing Sheffield Hollingsworth

Ali Singh held tightly to the dirty steering wheel of the truck with one hand, while, in the other, he held his old cell phone. He half listened to the annoying voice of his third ex-wife rant about needing more money for their son. She must be the worst of all his wives, he thought. This was how he felt about each of them until the next one called. Ali was hauling rocks from the quarry; the work was dirty, the load heavy and, for him, the truck moved much too slowly. Ali continued arguing with his ex-wife, until he became aware that he was no longer on the truck route. He was, in fact, suddenly in the main street of a small town. There were people and cars everywhere. All moving in slow motion, as if time didn't matter, they appeared to go about their day. The road was much too narrow for his huge rig, and Ali was, as usual, driving the heavy truck just as fast as it would go.

"Well, I don't have it… won't have any money 'til payday, and that's not 'til next week." She wasn't listening, he could tell by her response. He placed the call on speaker: he needed two hands on the wheel if he was to maneuver his way down this bustling narrow street.

"Don't you give a damn about the boy? He needs it, and he needs it now. Surely you don't expect me to work any more hours than I do and raise your son. No wonder you can never stay married, you perverted creep. I agree with your other wives; all the signs were there, I was just too in love with you to notice…"

Ali put the phone back up to his ear; he wanted her to hear him clearly when he said, "You in love…? You wouldn't know the meaning of the word, bitch…"; and so, it went on. Again, Ali thought about getting back on the truck route as this town was crazy with people all walking anywhere they chose, while the parked cars made the road impossible to navigate. He remembered that his brake pads needed replacing, so if he had to stop in a hurry they would probably let him down.

~

Sheffield Hollingsworth was a retired FBI agent; he'd been retired for nearly twelve years. That didn't mean he wasn't still working. He had just taken one case with him when he'd left the force. It was the one fascinating unsolved case, and it was the one that had really gotten under his skin. Every time he thought he had it solved, it would take another crazy turn and end up going nowhere. Sheffield Hollingsworth had never had a case he couldn't solve; some took years, while others just a few weeks. What made Sheffield a legend in the force was his dogged tenacity and ability to check every clue, every lead; once he focused on anything, he couldn't let it go. If a case went cold, he'd start over. The second time round he looked harder and noticed every tiny detail as he searched for anything he may have missed before. He always found something, and it was these small clues that often ended up leading somewhere.

Now, twelve years into his retirement, he'd never given up. The trail had led him all over the country and even to Europe and back several times. His only son had recently left the force and was setting up his own Private Investigation business. Sheffield was very proud; he thought Chuck even more meticulous than he was himself. Chuck's record had also been exemplary.

Sheffield had been on this case for eighteen years three months and fifteen days, and as he disconnected his cell he felt like jumping in the air. This time he was sure he had them. Yes, he thought to himself – Sheffield Hollingsworth had finally solved the one case which had stopped him from truly retiring. He called his son, as he headed over the road to Starbucks, where his patient wife sat in their usual corner booth and waited with his favorite coffee. They would be celebrating tonight. Sheffield was overjoyed.

"Chuck, you won't believe this, son. I've finally solved it! I've finally solved the case; they were using the identities of recently deceased people – that was what I'd been missing. I knew all the pieces would finally fit into place, I just knew it. Son, can you believe I've actually solved it? Now I can retire properly, take your mother on a cruise, travel, take up golf. Once this is wrapped up and they're safely behind bars – I'm free!" Sheffield yelled into the phone. Chuck had never heard his dad so elated, and he was genuinely pleased for him.

"Wow, Dad, I always knew you'd do it. After all, you're the best there is. Where are you, Dad? Have you told Mom?"

"No, son, she's waiting at Starbucks. I'm headed there now. This feeling is better than winning the lottery – I've solved it after all these years. I've been so close so many times, but some key pieces were always missing," Sheffield said excitedly.

"Dad, congratulations! I'm just on the other line organizing my business license, and then I'll join you," Chuck promised. Sheffield hardly heard him. He was so intent on telling his son the missing link that he stepped out onto the road without looking.

Ali Singh didn't see anything. He heard a slight thud, but he kept driving. Further up the street, he gazed in his rear mirror and saw people swarming into the street behind him. He then turned the corner and continued arguing with his ex-wife about the money he couldn't give her.

Rita Hollingsworth sat in their usual booth on the corner. She had a clear view of Main Street. She saw Sheffield more animated than she had ever seen him. He was waving his arms in the air to make his point to the person he was talking to on his phone. She saw him step into the road without looking. She saw the large truck moving much too fast toward him down the narrow street. Rita Hollingsworth stood up and screamed, before racing outside.

Sheffield was barely alive as she gathered him into her arms. He was bleeding profusely. In no time the ambulance was gathering her husband off the dirty street. She wouldn't let him go – she was going into the ambulance with him. Rita was just about to climb inside when she saw his private and confidential file, and the papers scattered over the road. She jumped out of the ambulance and gathered the closest papers, before quickly stuffing them back into the old, dirty, worn file, which had a large tire mark right across the front and was covered in mud. Rita creased it even more as she tucked the thick file folder into her shoulder bag and climbed again into the waiting ambulance. She hadn't even sat down when the siren wailed and they started moving. Sheffield wore an oxygen mask over his face and already there were tubes coming out of everywhere. With shaking hands and tears flowing freely down her cheeks, she dialed Chuck's number.

Sheffield was in the operating theatre for five hours while Rita and Chuck waited and prayed. Finally, Rita got to see her husband through the glass partition as he lay unconscious inside the intensive care unit. He was in critical condition and his prognosis wasn't good. Chuck stayed until the early hours of the morning, before going home to sleep, saying he would return around nine so Rita could get some sleep also. Rita knew she couldn't leave, no matter what. She was finally allowed to enter his room. Rita was holding Sheffield's hand as she dozed in the chair beside him; all around her the attached monitors beeped and clicked.

The moment she felt a movement, she was alert. One of Sheffield's eyes was covered with a bandage, but to her amazement his other eye was open and looking straight at her.

"Sheffield, my darling, you're awake," Rita said, moving closer as he gripped her hand tightly.

Looking straight at her, Sheffield Hollingsworth whispered, "The Grasshopper file, do you have it?"

"Yes, my darling, I do. Please don't concern yourself with it until you're feeling better."

The moment Rita uttered those words, the alarms Sheffield was hooked up to sounded loudly. Then he appeared to slump deeply into the bed. He seemed to grow smaller before her eyes. In seconds the room was filled with doctors and nurses, all knowing what needed to be done and working fast to do it. Sheffield Hollingsworth did not respond to their efforts to resuscitate him. He had peacefully passed away.

Attachments and Love

Siobhan Burke lay face down on the massage table at the spa. Her mother lay on the next table.

"Where you from, Mrs. Esmeralda?" the Mexican masseuse with the magic hands asked Siobhan's mother.

"I was born in the United States, of course," Esmeralda answered none too kindly.

"Yes, but Mrs. has dark skin, like us."

"I use a tanning room. Now rub lower back again. Mrs. Esmeralda has ache," she easily replied following their lingo, before quickly changing the subject.

In the past, Siobhan had often wondered the same thing about her mother, as she had such fair skin and hair, while her mother had olive skin and bleached brown hair. Siobhan sometimes thought her mother had slightly oriental features. Esmeralda, like her daughter, was a beauty, but their looks were very different. Both took great pride in their appearance and worked hard to keep their perfect looks. They met every month at the spa and enjoyed four wonderful hours of being completely pampered, before going to lunch at any of the expensive restaurants where you're seen by anyone who counts.

"So, where your mother born, Mrs.?" the persistent girl asked. She was a new girl, while the other girl was Siobhan's regular masseuse. Siobhan had been waiting for the right moment to ask her mother for the name of a private detective. She knew the question wouldn't be received well, but she wasn't ready to discuss such a delicate matter with any of her girlfriends yet, although she would if she didn't get what she wanted from her mother.

"Momma, I need to ask you something, but I don't want you to get angry," Siobhan began.

"Of course, nothing can make me more annoyed than the stupid questions this girl asks me. Why, it's not even worth an answer. No big tip for you, young girl," Esmeralda said curtly.

"Well...," Siobhan began, not feeling this was the perfect time, but knowing there may never be one.

"Momma, I want to contact a private detective. Do you know anyone?"

The two masseuses were now working on their clients' legs, and both winked at each other as they heard the question.

"Siobhan, honey, don't even bother. Just get a good lawyer; only the best will do. Pack your things and move back home. Your rooms are ready and waiting for you any time of the day or night. Why, you've been gone almost eight long years, and I've missed you every single day. I don't want any more talk about you staying with that beast. Let's visit the lawyer this afternoon," Esmeralda said, animated. She could hardly contain her excitement at the thought of her only daughter moving back home.

"Momma, I know you have my rooms ready, but I want to do it my way. Right now, all I want is the name of a good private investigator – discreet, thorough and reliable. Momma, please listen to me," Siobhan begged as she saw the look she knew so well on her mother's face. Esmeralda was about to blast her daughter with her thoughts on Brock, when one of the masseuses spoke.

"If Missus don't mind, my sister got card of good P.I. She say he very good – he starting own business. My sister cleans for his parents. She was given his new business card. She give one to me, maybe I have in my handbag. Just wait, I look."

"That won't be necessary, girl, just keep rubbing my legs," Esmeralda replied immediately.

"It okay – no trouble. It only take minute to find."

"Yes, I would like the card," Siobhan said, as again the girl headed toward the cupboard where she obviously kept her purse.

"Just keep rubbing my legs. Why don't you do as you're told? I want my old girl back next time!" Esmeralda whined.

"Sorry, Missus," the girl replied, returning immediately as Esmeralda continued.

"You can't honestly expect a masseuse would know the name of anyone respectable, let alone reliable. You want someone first class, if you really need anyone at all. Why won't you do it my way? You know I'm right. Remember, Momma's always right. I can make an appointment with the lawyer's office now – the one I have in mind specializes in divorce. Honey, it will be quick and painless and you can take him for every penny he's got. You won't be super-rich, but until you find your next mega-rich husband, you'll be very comfortable. Just give Momma the word, Siobhan. I think the number is in my phone. I've had it there for a while, just in case you needed it. It would be just like old times having you home again, darling," Esmeralda cooed sweetly.

"No thanks, Momma, now let's relax. The massage is almost over," Siobhan said, turning her head away as she pretended not to hear her mother's loud nasty remarks. Fifteen minutes later they were putting on their fluffy white robes and preparing to leave. Esmeralda left the room first, and just as Siobhan was about to leave, the girl pushed a business card into her hand. Siobhan quickly read the card:

– Chuck Hollingsworth –
Private Investigator to the Stars
By appointment

Just what I need, Siobhan thought, as she winked her thanks quickly at the girl and followed her mother into the steam room.

Staying Cautious

Hugo found his first day at work to be long and tiring; he had not worked for the past year. When he arrived at the apartment, Al had prepared a special dinner and it had been waiting for him for over an hour. However, she knew where he was and what he was doing as he was wired, so she could see everything he saw through the camera he wore. There had been a lot going on today, and even Al felt exhausted. She wanted to start planning their next project in San Diego, but there was no time. Al was almost unable to keep up with the many things happening in Banker's Securities, Inc.

Al also closely monitored Neve, and that was proving a job in itself. Brock Burke's office was wired, and Al was rather concerned with some of the things she had heard. One of her greatest concerns was the amount of drug money being filtered into the company from the Columbian drug lords, but not by Brock Burke directly. Al had no idea if Brock Burke was aware of all the happenings inside his own organization. However, Saffron Moffit had been in Brock Burke's office when he was safely in a meeting, and Al learned an enormous amount of information from her. Al was horrified that with all the research she had done on Banker's Securities, Inc., she had never come across anything that led her to believe the company was anything but legitimate. If it was in the past, it was about to change rapidly. If the pending merger was not headed up by Brock Burke, the president and CEO, then it must be none other than his vice-president – Saffron Moffit. Al recently instructed Hugo to wire her office, but she seemed constantly in residence. Al knew that was the reason Hugo was still not home, and it was now almost nine o'clock. Hugo must leave soon or it may raise unnecessary suspicion. The janitor was already starting his cleaning rounds.

It was now dark when Hugo walked the seven blocks home. He needed to clear his head. He would pick up his company car tomorrow. The car, he knew, would mainly be for Al's use anyway, as parking in Manhattan was almost impossible.

By ten p.m., Al and Hugo, still dressed as Alastair, were seated on the wide balcony with the lights of the city laid out below them like a twinkling carpet at their feet. Al had many candles lit. It was the only light they had on their balcony. They dined on caviar, a leafy green salad with tender chunks of venison covered in crumbled goat's cheese. They ate slowly as they sipped their Moët champagne. There was much to discuss, although neither wanted to break the ambience of the moment. It was unlike Hugo to be tired, but tonight he couldn't wait to remove his face and take a shower. He always kept his face on until bedtime, as in the past, on occasions, people had called unexpectedly. Finally, Hugo finished his meal and sat back to enjoy the last of his now slightly warm champagne. Then he said something that Al never expected to hear.

"Darling, I think it's almost time to retire. This game is for the young. I know you handle all the technical stuff, but today when I was asked to give my fingerprints, it scared me. What if you'd forgotten to put them on this morning? What if they check them out in their database? Al darling, there are so many 'what ifs'. Yes, I think we shall do only a couple more jobs, then we'll just fade into the background, enjoy our wonderful family and each other's company as we always have. We should spend more time with our rapidly growing grandchildren and continue to travel the world. What do you say, Al?" Hugo asked, looking at her with a serious expression she seldom saw.

"What if, Hugo darling, you're just very tired? What if you try retiring between the satin sheets and let me handle the worrying? I know there's a lot going on and they should have let you start much earlier if they wanted you completely in the game. We need to wire Ms. Moffit's office. I really believe she may be the dark sheep in the company, and as such, definitely the one to watch. Someone's feeding the drug lords' info, and it has to be someone quite high up to have access to the kind of information they require. We both thought it must be Brock Burke, but he appears to be badly grieving for his last secretary, Marlene Brice. Why... I'm not sure. With his reputation, she wouldn't have been any different from all the others, and he's had no difficulty in letting them go. Hugo, Ms. Moffit must surely be the one to watch. The quiet ones usually are. What do your instincts tell you about her, darling?" Al asked.

"I hardly saw her. I shook her hand, and she never even spoke to me, just nodded and answered her cell before moving away. You're right, she could be dangerous. She certainly is quiet; in fact, she hardly makes her presence known. Although I felt the guys at the board meeting either don't like her or were afraid of her, but I don't understand why."

"Hugo, there's one last thing that I find very strange," Al commented, knowing she had Hugo's full attention now.

"Another problem?"

"Well, not a problem yet. I am waiting on some of the latest technology to arrive in the morning to make sure it doesn't become one."

"I'm still listening, darling,"

"Actually, Hugo, I shall know more tomorrow night. I shouldn't tell you anything yet," Al said, knowing Hugo hated being teased.

"Oh no you don't, my beautiful wife. You tell me everything you know, right now. I hate it when you know something and don't tell me. Remember our pact when we married, darling?" Hugo gently reminded her, raising his right eyebrow higher than his left.

"Okay, Hugo. I suspect that we're not the only ones who have Brock Burke's office wired. I also suspect at least one hidden camera. I will have the equipment to do the trace tomorrow. Neve will have to place the trace; she has so much more access to Brock's office than you do."

"Who do you think would want to have Brock Burke's office bugged, darling?" Hugo asked.

"I wouldn't be surprised if it was Ms. Moffit herself. But, Hugo, there's three wires inside Brock's office – three including ours."

"Wow," Hugo said, letting out a long, low whistle, as he finished off the last of his champagne and sat quietly contemplating the latest information Al had just hit him with. Deep inside he knew he was not comfortable with any of it. It just didn't ring true.

"I will find out just what is going on inside Banker's Securities, Hugo. Anyway, it looks like Alastair and Sylvia Rasnic are going to be invited to cocktails on Friday night. I'll have to visit the store sooner than I thought so I can become the sufficiently dowdy wife of Alastair…," Al said as she was interrupted by the phone; it was the cell they kept for contact with Neve.

"Hi, Mom, Dad. Long day, wasn't it? So much happening. Amanda Dolman is going to be a very busy girl," Neve said in her happy, upbeat voice.

"She sure is, Baby Girl. I've had a rather long day also, so I'm off to bed, unless you want to talk to me."

"No, nothing much to talk about, yet, Daddy. Good night. I'll see you at work tomorrow and at the cocktail party tomorrow night?" she questioned.

"You've already been invited, Baby Girl?" Hugo asked, astonished.

"Sure, Daddy; I've got a date, too!"

"Not Brock Burke?"

"No, Daddy. He's far too discreet, and he certainly hasn't been living up to his reputation so far. He's told me twice that I look familiar to him. He never told me who he thought I looked like, but, whoever it is, I don't think he likes it either."

"Neve, that's a strange comment. You must ask him again who you remind him of. As for his reputation, you really shouldn't be thinking like that."

"Daddy, I might be your Baby Girl, but we need to move fast on this one. Way too much is happening. A man like Brock is always at his weakest between the sheets. And no, he's not going to tell me who I look like. Good night, Daddy," Neve replied, completely disregarding his question as she sent him good night kisses over the phone.

"Not so fast, young lady. You've avoided telling me just who is taking you out Friday night. Are you trying to stop me from sleeping altogether?"

"No one of importance, but unless I get a better offer, I'll go with him. His name's Phil Monkton, and he's from accounts, I think. He'll be very tame and very boring. So, no need to worry about me. He's no match for the fabulous Amanda. So good night again, Daddy."

"Well, actually I've met Phil and his sidekick, Ross Moss. Now, Neve, not too sexy on Friday night… all right, ladies?" Hugo warned, getting to his feet as he kissed his wife. He knew his girls would be talking about work and everything else for a very long time.

It was some time later, after Hugo had enjoyed a long hot shower and easily slid between the sheets, that he heard Al finally finish her conversation with Neve. Hugo was vaguely aware of Al entering the bedroom and walking through to the bathroom. She must have just entered the bathroom when the front doorbell rang and then rang again – someone was being very persistent. Instantly, Hugo became awake and alert, and he jumped out of bed and into his bathrobe. Quietly, Al walked to the door before looking through the peephole; Hugo was peeking out from inside the bedroom when she mouthed the words… "It's the police." Her words sent fear through Hugo again for the second time that day. Al told him to hide.

"Good evening, officers – rather late to be calling, isn't it? Can I help you?" Al asked, answering the door sounding as calm as a cucumber.

"We're looking for a Mr. Alastair Rasnic… this is the address we were given. Are you Mrs. Rasnic?"

"No, actually I'm her cousin. They're out for the evening. I'll be staying with them for a few days. Can I give him a message, officer?" Al asked as sweet as apple pie, speaking with a heavy southern drawl.

"Yes, ma'am, can you ask him to contact Special Agent Bow Grismold? Here's his card," the young officer said, producing a white business card.

"Can I say what it's concerning, officer?"

"Why, I don't rightly know, ma'am. I don't think it's anything of real importance. We were supposed to contact him at his office late this afternoon, but we got called out."

"Why thank you, officer, I'll be sure to pass it on. You all have a good night now, officers."

"Good night, ma'am. Sorry for disturbing you," the young officer said, clearly smitten. Hugo breathed a sigh of relief before again getting back into bed.

Spying on Brock Burke

Chuck Hollingsworth sat at his shiny new desk. He looked out the window onto Main Street. All around him his new office was neat, organized and comfortable. The desk for his secretary/assistant remained unfilled. His degrees, diplomas, awards and commendations lined the walls, just as he imagined they would – beside them hung those belonging to his dad, Sheffield Hollingsworth. He knew he should take them down – but so far, he couldn't. No clients had yet sat in his new, elegant, deep purple leather chairs or placed a new white coffee mug on the Italian glass coffee table.

Chuck sat, like he had sat every day for the last month in his new office chair, staring out the window. From this angle, he could almost see the place where his beloved dad was hit by the negligent truck. One day he would bring that bastard to justice – but not today. Today was another day when the computer would not be turned on. Today, his over-full voicemail would not be cleared, and today no one would enter the office. It would probably be the same today as it was yesterday and would be tomorrow.

In the top drawer of Chuck's desk sat a crumpled file bursting at the edges. Inside were many sheets of paper, some still showing signs of being roughly retrieved from the road and stuffed quickly back into the file. Chuck knew the wind had taken a lot more pages of valuable information – to who knows where. The Grasshopper file had sat on top of his desk until yesterday. Many times, he'd thought of opening it and reading, but just as many times he'd decided not to. Yesterday, Chuck had taken the thick, dirty old file folder and placed it roughly in his top drawer – he decided it didn't matter now anyway. He knew it had mattered, and mattered a great deal to his dad, but sitting here now, with his sorrow, he wanted to convince himself that he would never read the Grasshopper file, that it was not important and no longer mattered. It was his father's dream to solve the case, it was his father's case and not his. Right now as the deep sorrow gripped his soul, he had almost convinced himself, that nothing really mattered. What he needed to know was where the blame lay for his father's death. Was it the truck driver or the Grasshopper file – which one?

The phone rang again. Chuck slowly turned in that direction, knowing the message machine would pick up. But it didn't, it merely said, 'Please call back, this voicemail is full'. Chuck sat looking out the window, staring into space, and he saw nothing. He missed his dad so much. He had been his mentor and best friend – the person who'd taught him everything he knew. The man he went to for advice, the one he talked to when he needed a problem sorted. Sheffield had listened closely to his son's wishes to get out of the force and make something of his life using his many skills and talents. Sheffield had said he must do whatever was in his heart; he'd promised he would always be there for him, support him and even work with him if that's what he wanted.

Sheffield had agreed to help him start his own business if that's what he decided to do. Sheffield was looking forward to proudly introducing his son to the many contacts he'd made over the years, and Chuck knew this would prove invaluable in his success as a top Private Investigator. In his mind he could hear his father's voice so clearly talking to him, encouraging him. Then he heard his mother's voice agreeing with her husband, always supportive of each other, backing the other up in perfect harmony and still so much in love. Just the thought of his mother sitting alone at home made the tears he had been holding back finally flow. He was thinking of renting out his house and moving back home to be with her. He'd call her now. Chuck picked up the phone to call his mother when a woman's voice on the other end startled him.

"Hello... hello, Mr. Hollingsworth?"

"Oh yes, yes, who is this?"

"I'm sorry, I didn't know you'd answered. My name's Siobhan Burke and I left you a message yesterday. I was told you were the best, so I expected you to be busy. I'm two blocks away from your office and I just wondered if you would have a few minutes to see me?" Siobhan asked. There was silence on the other end of the phone and she waited.

Chuck wanted to hang up on her... he didn't want to talk to anyone, especially a prospective client. He wasn't ready and didn't know if he ever would be. Without his dad, he didn't know if he could follow his dream, he didn't think he could do it. He'd always thought his father would be right beside him at this moment and they'd listen carefully together, taking notes they would later compare. His first case was supposed to have been shared with his dad. On his own, Chuck knew he wasn't ready. But he also knew he couldn't turn a client away now that she was on the phone.

"Certainly, Ms. Burke, I will see you in about an hour, if that's suitable?" Chuck said, sounding professionally confident, and not feeling it at all.

"Yes, thank you. I will enjoy looking in some of your quaint little stores in your town and then I'll walk over to your office. I'll look forward to meeting you, Mr. Hollingsworth; see you soon."

The moment the phone went dead, Chuck Hollingsworth knew he was not ready for even one client, and really didn't know when he would be. As he sat staring out the window, his body trembled at the thought of his first client walking through the door. Maybe she would instinctively know he wasn't yet open for business and leave before she entered. Slowly, he moved to the door and turned the new silver lock. At that moment he felt like he was opening himself to the world. He didn't have a secretary or an assistant – but it was too late now, and Chuck hurriedly searched his desk for a notepad and paper.

The phone rang again and, this time, he instinctively answered it.

"Mr. Hollingsworth, you still haven't gotten back to us about your choice of assistant and the applicants tell me you haven't yet interviewed them. Mr Hollingsworth we are not in the business of wasting time, either yours or mine. This is Carole Lind, in case you haven't guessed."

"Carole, I'm sorry, I've been rather busy. I will get onto it later today."

"Mr. Hollingsworth, I just called to inform you that both Fredrick Blook and Blue Satine are about to accept other positions, but I'm holding off making a decision as they have so much background in your area. I know they would be perfect for your new venture. Blue has previously worked for a prominent private investigator in the city; she has her police training certificate and book-keeping diploma. You'll find she also has excellent people skills. Her references are impeccable. While Fred has already chalked up considerable hours as a P.I. and wishes to cut his hours back once the new baby arrives. You did say you wanted to start your assistant on a 'work as necessary basis' if I recall, Mr. Hollingsworth?" Her raspy voice went on and on until it grated on his nerves. He glanced at the hundreds of messages on his machine and for the first time in his life, Chuck lied and made his decision based on nothing but raw emotion and a momentary need to move forward.

"Carole, I have looked at Blue's résumé," Chuck lied, "and you can get her to start in the morning or even later today if she prefers. Please send Fred in later today for an interview. I also think he'll work out just fine."

"Very good, Mr. Hollingsworth, I shall do as you instruct. I am glad to have been of service, and if you are not completely satisfied with either of them, please don't hesitate to contact me again. Good day," she said, as the line disconnected. The phone continued to ring as Chuck watched a new pale gold Mercedes sports car draw up to the curb right in front of his office window. A long, shapely leg and black suede stiletto soon touched the sidewalk. Chuck watched, transfixed, waiting for the other leg to follow as he anticipated the whole beautiful woman she must be. Chuck was excited that his first client would be a classy lady – he knew his dad would have approved. Chuck watched and waited, then he faintly heard what must be her cell phone ringing somewhere in the car. He knew she was speaking, but exactly what she was saying he couldn't tell. He watched the black suede stiletto leave the sidewalk and the car door close. Moments later, the car silently drove off.

Chuck sat watching out the window until the tail lights disappeared around the corner. Maybe it hadn't been his client after all; she did say she would be "walking over" – but he had felt sure it was. Then the phone rang and confirmed his suspicions. Siobhan Burke informed him she was running late and would see him within the hour if he still had time. He assured her he did and somehow felt disappointed that he had to wait another hour. Knowing he didn't really want a client, Chuck decided his anticipation was weird, and he knew it must be due to his recent isolation and grief. Chuck was not what you'd call an emotional person, but things change and circumstances make people different. Chuck knew he had to pull himself together, and fast.

Chuck sat as before at his desk, looking out the window; the only change was that he now held a pencil and had several sheets of paper on his new desk. He decided it was time to try his new cappuccino machine, so Chuck got to his feet. He walked several steps towards the sparkling new coffee-making machine, but as he stood looking at it, he realized it was harder to operate than it looked. He read the instructions. Then he read them again. He did exactly as they instructed and waited. Finally, he placed one of his new white coffee mugs under the nozzle and filled it with coffee – so far so good. Next, he tried for the froth on top, and that was when it all went wrong. Chuck was just cleaning up the mess the machine had created when the door opened and a short, strange-looking girl walked into his life.

"Well, I'm here and ready to start. Came as soon as she called. Hi, I'm Blue, Blue Satine, from the agency. This is completely great! I just live around the corner, so I can walk here in less than ten minutes. Why, I really love life when things work out so well, don't you?"

Chuck nodded and briefly took her outstretched hand in his, before he realized he was covered in milky froth. Always the detective, he looked her over... she was short with curly, dark brown hair, some of which looked as though it had missed the comb as it was heavily matted into a frizzy ball. She had huge liquid brown eyes and a small rosebud mouth. She was petite and dressed completely in black. It looked like she'd tried hard to get it right, but somehow it just didn't happen. Her lips were lined with black lipstick, and her nails were freshly painted black. Chuck thought he might just like her. Her happiness was infectious and he realized he needed some happiness.

"Here, let me do that. Guys are never as good as girls when it comes to anything technical. Oh, cool office by the way, real cool. I really like it a lot," Blue said, moving him out of the way as she expertly made them more coffee.

"You have cookies? I'm starved. It took me a while to get ready. I was just sitting around in my bathrobe waiting for the phone to ring, and then it did," she continued, giggling with delight.

"No, Blue, I don't have any food in the office. Do you think we should?"

"Why yes, I should say so! What about your clients?" she continued wide-eyed. "Private investigation is delicate and intimate work – food always soothes the nerves – works every time! Where's the petty cash? I'll go to the best bakery in town. It's only a short walk. I know a shortcut, so I can get there real quick. I'll go right past the liquor store also." Chuck got a fifty from his wallet and pointed at the petty cash tin in her third drawer.

"Back in a jiffy," Blue said, as the door closed behind her. By the time Chuck managed to get his head around her, she had returned and was drinking her coffee as she went through her new desk. She expertly began filing away some of the large piles of files into the new tall filing cabinet. She then switched on her computer and quickly familiarized herself with it as she asked him many programming questions that he didn't know the answers to.

"Never mind, I'll get it all sorted. Now, shall I start on your voicemail? Looks like your mailbox is full. Guess you've been really busy. I can see you really need me – feels good to be needed. Too much time sitting around in my bathrobe never does my mind or bank account any good," she commented, checking her nail polish as Chuck nodded.

Chuck hadn't noticed the sleek gold Mercedes again pull up to the curb. He was completely startled when Blue spoke to him on his new intercom and informed him that his next appointment, Mrs. Siobhan Burke, had arrived.

Moments later, Chuck looked at the same black suede stilettos and perfect shapely long legs, but this time he noticed the whole woman. She was quite something! Willowy and on the tall side, with immaculate blonde hair and skin so flawless it didn't look real... beautiful eyes, the kind of eyes a man could drown in. Her makeup was subtle, delicate – hell, she hardly needed any, Chuck thought. Once Blue took her coat, Chuck couldn't help but notice she had curves in all the right places. He suddenly realized he was staring and hoped his mouth hadn't fallen open – he needed to get a grip. It was then Blue popped her head around the door.

"Excuse me, Mrs. Burke, may I offer you coffee, Moët & Chandon champagne, anything?" she asked. The other woman declined.

Champagne, Chuck thought. *Why, I didn't even know we had any. How could she make fifty dollars go so far?*

"I'm Siobhan Burke and I'm sorry to have kept you waiting. My mother called and said my father wanted to see me as he had something important to tell me. She told me he was just around the corner, but when I got there he was having coffee with his guy friends and couldn't talk. I really sometimes worry about my mother's state of mind," she said, dazzling Chuck with her smile.

"How do you do? Please, take a seat. I'm Chuck Hollingsworth."

"Well, Mr. Hollingsworth...," she began.

"Chuck, please."

'Well, Chuck, my mother is totally against me visiting you, and for the life of me I don't understand why." She paused briefly as she again dazzled him with her smile.

"I'll get right to the point. I want my husband followed. I want to know exactly what he is doing twenty-four hours a day. I want photos, recordings and I want to know all about the women he sees. I understand you're both thorough and discreet, Mr. uh... Chuck," she concluded.

"Oh, indeed we are discreet and thorough. We always check our clients out before we take them on. Yes, Mrs. Burke, I understand what you require. Did I mention I am also expensive," Chuck concluded, hoping to discourage her, and then, looking her over again, he realized money wouldn't be a problem.

"How much is your retainer, Mr.... er... Chuck?"

"Fifty thousand as a retainer, plus expenses – the balance when you're satisfied with the results. I always deliver on my promises, Mrs. Burke."

"If you supply me with all I want, it will be money well spent."

"Am I to understand you suspect your husband of cheating on you?" Chuck asked, looking at her and not believing any man could.

"Yes, and he has been for a very long time, I think...," Siobhan answered, not feeling so confident now she finally said it out loud. She knew Brock had cheated, but how often she had no idea.

"We will need a recent photo, his social security number, and the address of his office and any other places he visits frequently – plus the registration numbers of his cars and cell phone numbers. I'd also like you to tell me what you think his daily activities are, as far as you know. I would also like the same information about you," Chuck finished, trying to remember if he was doing everything correctly and by the book.

"Chuck, I'm not the one I want you to investigate. I don't need to know anything about myself," she answered, holding back the annoyance she was feeling at his last question.

"I understand, Mrs. Burke, but we must safeguard ourselves also and make sure you legitimately want the kind of information you're asking for, and also that you're not involved or have ever been involved in any criminal activity. Also, a marriage license, so I know you are legally married, you wouldn't believe the stunts some of my clients go to. My reputation is potentially on the line when I represent you." Chuck mentally went over everything he knew he must ask and with a quiet sigh thought he remembered it all correctly. He watched the beautiful woman in front of him as she obviously thought it over. Her cheque lay on the desk between them. Several minutes passed, and as Sheffield had taught Chuck, after the cards are played you say nothing until the game is set – so he waited and continued to wait as Mrs. Burke stared at the floor. Finally, she agreed.

"If that's the way you work, I don't have any problem with it. I have nothing to hide, nor do I have a police record. Just so you know, Chuck, I have been faithful to my husband for the extent of our marriage." Chuck nodded, feeling he was invading her privacy by hearing her answer.

"When and how will you contact me, Chuck?" she asked.

"I can give you a report in person once a week or I can call you every time I find something of interest, Mrs. Burke. It is your choice."

"I think I should prefer both. I recently purchased a cell to receive only your calls. Here is the number; please use no other. I intend to check it several times a day. Here is all the information you'll require," Siobhan said, retrieving a large brown envelope from her handbag.

"You have come prepared I see, Mrs. Burke. I think it will be a pleasure working with you," Chuck said, standing when she did.

"I expect results, Chuck. I expect you to have my husband covered twenty-four/seven, or until he returns home at night. It will be a pleasure doing business with you when you achieve all you say you can. Good day, Chuck," she said, heading for the door; but before Chuck could open it for her, Blue held the door wide.

"I'll show you out, Mrs. Burke," Blue said professionally, as Chuck wondered just how she had known Mrs. Burke was about to leave.

"Well, how did it go?" Blue asked, as she poked her head around the door before opening it wide.

"Well, I think it went well, Blue. How did you know she was leaving?"

"I sure wasn't spying or listening, that's your job. I heard her move her chair as she got up. That's how I knew," Blue replied as she bounced back to her desk that was now covered in files.

"Oh, by the way, Fred Blook called and he will be here in about ten minutes. I said it would be okay, but I took his number if you want to change it."

"That's fine, Blue," Chuck said, as a smile played on his lips. She was certainly efficient, and so far, she was fun to have around. Chuck realized it was the first time he had smiled in a while. He decided to call his mother. He then realized how his life had suddenly changed since his last call to her.

As he spoke to his mom on the phone, he watched Blue racing around the office doing all the things he should have done before her arrival. She never seemed to stop moving. Later that day, Fred Blook became his part-time associate P.I.

As Chuck closed the office door later that evening, he realized his life had been kick-started and now it was in motion. He didn't know how to stop it. Maybe this was just what he needed. 'Chuck Hollingsworth, Private Investigator to the Stars' was now officially open for business.

Hopeless Existence

Lately, Potter Moffit had been questioning many things. His life, his wife and just whether he wanted things to go on the way they were. He'd married Saffron Moffit when he was just twenty years old and Saffron had been twenty-one. Saffron had chased him until finally he gave in, thinking he couldn't live without her. Saffron had shown him the benefits of dropping out of school and making money while she stayed on to finish her business degree before advancing onto her master's. She had convinced Potter that chemical engineering would not bring them in as much money as her career in finance.

At the time, Potter had been young and naive enough to go along with her, and now it was too late. It was just months before she was to graduate and he was to return to school and finally finish his degree that Saffron discovered she was pregnant. Saffron was not happy. When Saffron Moffit was not happy, no one else could be happy either. She blamed Potter, she didn't want a baby. She felt a baby would ruin her chances of climbing the corporate ladder. She wanted to get rid of their child. So, again, Potter needed to forgo his dreams. He had to stay home if they were to keep the child, while his wife pursued her career. By the time the baby was due, she was already employed in a high-profile company. Saffron had merely taken two weeks' holiday from work, given birth and returned to work as if nothing had happened.

Potter hoped his parents would embrace their first and only grandchild. Hoping his son, Cox, would bring them some of the joy they had lost when their own daughter was abducted at the age of three. And it had. It had certainly brought them back together as a family, or more so than in the past. Potter knew they still blamed him for the disappearance of his sister and their daughter and always would. They couldn't seem to move forward, and he finally realized they never would. He'd married Saffron to get away from the continual sadness surrounding his parents and their home. He'd thought Saffron would give him the love and affection he so craved. And she did to a point, but she used love as a reward for him doing whatever she wanted, and she used affection in much the same way. It didn't take Potter long to realize he had gone from one bad situation to another. Only his parents didn't like Saffron, and so he saw less of them as the years went by.

Potter knew at just thirty-eight years old and with Cox, his seventeen-year-old son, now in college, his time had passed. He had no skills other than being a house husband and a constant fixture in Saffron's life. He was also her drug runner, and several times a year he went to Europe to drop off money and collect drugs. It had taken him several trips to realize just what she was asking him to do, but now he was pretty sure she was stealing money from Banker's Securities and purchasing drugs. They lived in a mansion in an élite gated community. As if Potter didn't have enough worries, Saffron had been playing both sides of the fence during the merger of Banker's Securities. He had found out she was double-dealing with a huge company based in Columbia headed by some of the most notorious drug lords in the world. Potter knew she was helping exchange important and damaging information. Potter was disgusted with his wife and scared for them both, very scared!

Cox Moffit was a straight 'A' student. Potter had high hopes for his son. He had his mother's ruthless personality and Potter's charm, either a winning combination or a very dangerous one. Just recently, Potter had reason to suspect his son may have discovered the drug trafficking happening under his nose. Potter always hid the packages carefully, but last time he went to make the exchange, he was sure one of the packages had been tampered with. And sure enough at the weigh-in, one came up light.

As Potter had been a reliable courier for many years, it was noted but overlooked. However, the incident greatly added to Potter's numerous worries. Today, he stood in his giant closet in the master bedroom. They had his and hers closets. Saffron's closet was overflowing with designer suits, dresses and shoes, while his closet held her evening dresses and cocktail wear. Potter had only a few clothes and always wore the same suit to every event he accompanied his wife to. Saffron had ordered him to get a new wardrobe, and now he realized he had again forgotten to do so. He knew she would be angry. As he stood surveying his meager options, Cox bounced up the stairs and into the bedroom behind him.

"Yo, Dad! The guys and I are thinking of taking off to Vancouver and attend the Olympics. We want to see the men's downhill skiing. Pete's dad got us all tickets. It's no problem, is it? We'll be away about a week, okay?" Cox asked, knowing his father probably hadn't heard a word he said.

"What... Oh, the Olympics? Aren't they in Canada or somewhere?"

"Yeah, Dad, wake up old man, they're in Vancouver, Canada. Pete's family has a house at Whistler, not far from the Games. It'll be cool!"

"But aren't they in Canada?" Potter asked again, finally tuning into what his son was saying. Potter looked up at his six-foot-tall, blue-eyed, dark-haired son and as usual he felt the same sense of pride as he always did. Cox had his blue eyes and Saffron's dark features. It made for a handsome combination, but just where he got his height from, Potter had no idea.

"C'mon, Dad, my grades have been great and I have enough money."

"Just where are you getting all this money from, son?" Potter asked, trying to get an easy confession from his son.

"My allowance; remember how Mom increased it when I turned seventeen? I'm at school nearly all the time, so I hardly use any of it. Why do you ask, Dad?" Cox asked, looking curious.

"No reason, son," Potter replied, thinking that his son was either a very good liar or he was as devious as his mother. Potter had never known Cox to lie to him before. But who else could have taken the drugs?

"So, Dad, is it okay with you? Will you drive us guys to the airport tomorrow, then?"

"It's okay with me, so long as you call in every day. But the final word belongs to your mom. You'll have to call her and check."

"Gee, Dad, do I have to? We both know she doesn't give a damn what you and I do or where we go."

"Now, Cox, don't speak like that about your mom," Potter replied, trying to sound stern.

"Oh, come on, Dad, we both know it is…" Cox knew it was pointless to finish, so instead he looked hard at his father. Cox knew his dad had once been a handsome man of medium height with a well-muscled build and shaggy light brown curly hair, but time had not been kind to him, and now Potter had many tiny lines on his face and around his eyes. His hair was turning a slight gray at the sides and his shoulders no longer seemed to straighten. Cox secretly thought his father had been nagged to death.

"What you got to wear, Dad? Is it the cocktail party tonight? Mom said for you to look good. I heard her yell to you from downstairs before the door slammed this morning at five a.m.," Cox said, still looking hard at his father and wondering just how he put up with her.

"I know, son, my side of the closet is almost empty. One day I'll have to go spend some of that dough your mom makes so much of," Potter said, laughing.

"How about right now, Dad? Rundle's dad owns all those high-end men's clothing stores. I can call him up?" Cox asked, eager to please.

"No time, son. I have to be ready by seven."

"Dad, it's only one thirty and you've been standing here for half an hour already. C'mon, Dad, it'll be fun," Cox coaxed. When Potter shrugged his shoulders and didn't reply, Cox made a quick phone call, before dragging his dad downstairs and into his black Range Rover.

Organizing Love

Siobhan Burke was feeling pleased with herself and her meeting with Chuck Hollingsworth when she finally arrived home. She still had the smile on her face when the front doorbell rang.

"Mrs. Burke?" the delivery boy asked. Nodding, she accepted the huge bouquet of flowers. Siobhan knew immediately who they were from; it was always the same. Over the years, Siobhan knew each time Brock's affair ended he would again pursue her, and for several months they would have a blissful and happy marriage. Siobhan loved these times, and she knew they were, in fact, the only thing that kept her faithful. Brock was a fabulous lover; he had a special way of making her feel as if she was the only woman in the world. Brock would lavish her with gifts, adoration and attention every minute they were together; every minute, that is, until his next affair started. Each affair usually corresponded with yet another new secretary. Brock was boringly predictable – however, it hadn't always been so; for the first five years of their marriage he would organize a surprise exotic holiday destination for her and her mother, saying he would soon follow; but, of course, never did.

Esmeralda, Siobhan's mother, had Brock pegged from the start, but Siobhan had chosen to believe in him, and had done so for many years; comfortable instead to remain in the safety and security of her fairytale. Siobhan put her nose deep into the blooms and inhaled. As usual, they were all her favorites. She then removed and read the note.

To the love of my life,
My one and only,
I know I have neglected you,
Please forgive me,
I shall love you always,

B

Moments later, as she was about to head into the kitchen, the doorbell again sounded. This time she was presented with a package from Tiffany's. She closed the door before opening the box. There was no note, but she knew instinctively it was from Brock the moment she saw the sparkling diamond tennis bracelet. Siobhan had always loved tennis bracelets, and this time Brock had outdone himself. The bracelet was simple with a minimum amount of gold surrounding each huge diamond. Dropping the box on the hall table, she fastened the bracelet around her slim wrist. It fitted perfectly and rewarded her with its dazzling brilliance. This must really have cost him, she thought, answering the phone on the second ring.

"Darling, did I do well?" Brock's mellow, deep voice melted over her like silky smooth, velvety chocolate.

"It's beautiful, darling. By far the nicest one you have chosen," Siobhan cooed into the phone. She felt like she was talking to her absent lover for the first time in ages. Brock was unable to see the way her blue eyes sparkled and her cheeks took on a pretty pink glow. She couldn't wipe the smile from her lips, but she knew he could easily sense it in her voice.

"… and the flowers…"

"… are just perfect, all my favorites," Siobhan finished for him, knowing somewhere deep inside how their game was beginning all over again.

"Good. I'm getting out of here at around six. I've booked us your favorite restaurant for tonight. May I suggest you wear that stunning red Chanel dress, darling, and no, I don't care if you also wear it tomorrow night to the cocktail party."

"Oh, Brock, are you sure you want me to wear that dress again?"

"Quite sure, darling. It makes you look even more stunning than you already are, if that's possible," Brock said as he put his hand over the phone to speak to someone who had just entered his office.

"See you tonight, Brock darling," Siobhan cooed, caressing the phone lovingly.

"Love you, see you tonight," Brock replied smoothly, and just as he was disconnecting, Siobhan heard him say, "Saffron, I'm the president and CEO, not you..." Siobhan wondered for the hundredth time just why he didn't fire her. She knew Brock held the majority of shares, and she also knew Banker's Securities could easily afford to pay her out and be rid of her for good. Siobhan then made an urgent appointment with the spa, before grabbing her handbag and racing outside to the Porsche. She intended to not only feel completely loved, but also totally pampered before her date with Brock this evening. Siobhan knew she looked like a beautiful woman, but after the spa she would again begin to feel like one also.

"Missus, you back so soon?"

"Yes, I need you to work your magic. I have just two hours, girls," Siobhan said, relaxing onto the table. Just thinking of Brock and the way he would touch her intimately later gave her butterflies in the pit of her stomach. It was always the same. The anticipation, the excitement, the longing, the attraction, the desire, and finally, the best lovemaking she had ever had. Siobhan shivered with anticipation.

"You cold, Missus, you want I turn up heat?"

"No, I'm fine."

"Missus call P.I. guy from card?"

"Yes, I did," Siobhan answered, wishing they would stop talking so she could relax. She needed to feel the tension leave her body; when Brock was having an affair, she was tense the whole time. Intuitively she always knew. Each time she worried he would leave her.

"Where's your old Momma?"

"My mom is not with me; this was a spur-of-the-moment decision, and my mom wouldn't appreciate you calling her old, so if you value her as a client, I suggest you don't think of her that way again," Siobhan reprimanded the girl.

"Your Momma, I know, from Philippines, she has same look as my uncle's wife. I know they brought me up in Philippines for ten years, before I went to Mexico to be with my father's family. I know her, she say she from the USA, but she not."

"Yes, she is," Siobhan answered, beginning to get annoyed at the girl's constant chattering.

"How you be her daughter, you fair skin, she not."

"I am her daughter; now please be quiet. Missus need to relax."

"Okay, Missus, you want to relax. I give special Filipino massage, you like?" the girl asked, easily changing her technique. Siobhan had never felt anything like it. Forty-five minutes later, the girl was trying to wake her up by saying, "Massage over, Missus, you sleep all through." Siobhan felt so relaxed she could hardly stand. Whatever the girl had done, she felt more relaxed than she had ever felt in her life. Maybe she'd keep this new girl, after all. Siobhan grabbed her handbag and tipped the girl $50 before leaving the room. As she walked down the hall behind the girl towards the steam room, Siobhan suddenly noticed her bracelet wasn't on her wrist. Surely the girl hadn't stolen it.

"My bracelet..." she yelled as the girl turned around to look.

"Never mind, we find. No one else use my room. Come back, Missus, we look together," the girl said, not missing a beat. Siobhan had just had the best massage of her life. She wanted the same massage next time, so she didn't want to believe the girl was a thief. Upon entering the room, she quickly checked to see if her cash was still in her wallet. She was relieved it was. Siobhan was feeling very upset at the thought of losing her bracelet so soon. She eyed the girl suspiciously. The moment they entered the room, the girl tore off the white sheet covering the bed, and to Siobhan's relief her bracelet fell to the floor. It was not broken, and the girl helped to place it on her left wrist.

Brock and Siobhan enjoyed the perfect evening. He never took his eyes off her and told her a hundred times how beautiful, sexy and lucky he was to have her as his wife. The dinner was long and leisurely, with not much eating and many martinis. On the ride home in the back of the limo, Brock pulled her close.

"Darling, I can't wait a second longer to have you in my arms. All evening your eyes have seduced me, your body has tantalized me and your erotic perfume has held me powerless against your charms. I am just a man and only so strong..." He never finished his words as he kissed her long and deeply, before together their passions mounted. They were in a world of their own and nothing else mattered. All too soon, they pulled into the driveway.

The Jacuzzi was hot and fragrant. Together they sipped champagne from long crystal flutes as they looked out through the full-length glass windows of the bathroom over a thousand glistening lights of the living city below. The bubbles tickled their bodies as the warmth of the water caressed and invaded every part of them. Later, Brock's lovemaking was long and slow, continuing for hours until they reached a crescendo of bliss enhanced by the familiarity of being with the one you love. Several hours later, they repeated what they loved doing, and as the early rays of dawn melted the dewy earth, they slept. For Brock, it was a short sleep until his alarm alerted him to another working Friday morning. Brock tried in vain to arouse his sleeping wife before kissing her on the cheek and bounding out of bed. Siobhan didn't hear him as he sang softly in the shower. His mind was already awake and active as he thought over the day ahead – it was then he realized Marlene Brice was almost a memory. As always when an affair ended and he again moved back into the arms of his loving wife, he wondered just how he could ever have been unfaithful to her in the first place…

At almost eleven o'clock, Siobhan greeted the day leisurely. She felt fabulous, as she, too, sang softly under the warm shower water. Her housekeeper was already working downstairs. Siobhan, still in her satin gown, wandered into the kitchen. As she sat enjoying her strong, black coffee and remembering last night, she called Brock's cell to leave a love message. Then she remembered Chuck the P.I. and hurried back upstairs to find his number and the cell phone she had purchased to call him.

"Hello, can I speak to Chuck?"

"Sure, you can. Is that Mrs. Burke?"

"Yes, it is. Is he in?"

"One moment, ma'am."

"Chuck Hollingsworth."

"Siobhan Burke speaking. Good morning to you, Chuck."

"Good morning to you, Mrs. Burke. However, we haven't anything to report to you this soon, I'm afraid. We only picked up on your husband this morning as he left the house and trailed him to his office. So far, everything is as you said it would be. We'll need a little more time and even then, you must understand it is up to your husband's discretion as to when and if he cheats on you, Mrs. Burke."

"Yes, I understand…" Siobhan began as he continued.

"We have not yet completed our background check on you, but so far it is proving very interesting…"

Siobhan wasn't listening. He was ruining her happy morning, and she just wanted to stop it right now. "Mr. er… Chuck, I want to cancel the investigation on my husband, as of now."

"I'm sorry, Mrs. Burke. I thought you said you wanted to cancel. But just yesterday—"

Again, she cut him off. "Yes, yes, I know what I said yesterday, but circumstances change and so do people, Chuck."

"Yes, I agree that circumstances often do change, but people, never."

"Anyway, I want the investigation to cease immediately, do you understand me?"

"Yes, I understand you, and it shall be as you wish, Mrs. Burke. I shall, of course, mail the return of your retainer in full."

At Chuck's words, Siobhan suddenly remembered she didn't want any mail arriving here – it certainly wouldn't do to have Brock find out.

"Chuck, there is no need to return my retainer. Please keep the retainer with my file. I feel sure I shall be in need of your services at some stage. Thank you again and goodbye," Siobhan said. She had only just hidden the cell phone when her housekeeper advised her that her mother was on the phone. Siobhan sighed deeply, knowing now her happy feeling was just a thing of the past.

"Hi, Mom."

"Honey, when are you coming home? We've been waiting and waiting for your call. Shall we come and get you? Your father will order the moving truck. We've both been worried about you still living with that monster. We are here for you… waiting."

"Mom, I'm not coming home and never said I would. I love Brock and he loves me and he is my husband. I was probably feeling a little neglected, that's all. Perhaps it's because you brought me up to be such a diva. I've turned into a diva just like you, Mom," Siobhan said, her claws out and sharpened.

"Well, of all the ungrateful things to say to your mother, when we've been just sitting here worrying about you," Esmeralda replied, obviously sharpening her claws also.

Siobhan's dad immediately took the phone. "Sweetheart, just as long as you're happy and safe, that's all we care about…"

He was cut short when Esmeralda grabbed the phone. "No, it's not! I want you home, where you belong," Esmeralda screamed into the phone as Siobhan quickly silenced her screaming and hung up. That was exactly why she didn't want to go home…

Preposterous Saffron

Hugo and Alberta were up very early the next morning. Hugo had not slept well. He didn't like the way this job was progressing; he felt uneasiness in his soul. It wasn't anything he could actually put his finger on, but it was nibbling at him like a mouse nibbling your toes in the dark. He knew something very serious was happening, and he didn't want any part of it. When it came to feelings, Al could not understand; she was totally practical in business matters and very analytical. As he allowed the hot water to wash over his body and cleanse his mind, he tried to banish his night-time fears. He told himself it was just the thought of the police sniffing around that had him feeling so anxious.

Yes… this morning Hugo Grasshopper was not as confident as usual, nor was he looking forward to the day ahead. As he toweled himself dry, he thought again about this being his last job – in his bones he knew it was time to retire. Al spent longer than usual on Alastair's appearance and checked and rechecked the silicone imprints that covered the tips of his own fingers. Finally, she was happy that everything was as close to perfect as she could make it. She started preparing breakfast when Al said, "Just juice, darling. I need to get to the office early. Maybe I can get into Saffron Moffit's office before she does. Surely she won't be at the office at this hour."

"You don't think she has it locked?" Al replied.

"Knowing her, yes. She seems to have a lot to hide, but I have to get into her room sooner rather than later, otherwise you'll think I'm getting soft on you, darling," Hugo replied, chuckling as he expected his wife to laugh also; but instead, she turned to him, and with a serious look on her face she reminded him.

"Hugo, please don't forget to use your scrambler. I know I have said this many a time before, but it is an invaluable piece of equipment. In fact, I really think you should use it in every office, including your own, before you add or remove any equipment," Al concluded. Hugo looked at her long and hard, wondering if she, too, was feeling uneasy about this job.

As Hugo walked slowly to work, he was deep in thought. He had left the keys to his new car with Al so she could take it out of the city to shop. Hugo was hoping to get into Saffron's office before she arrived; he had sensed urgency from Al. Hugo entered the building through the high, glass front doors, and unlike his first day, there were no police or police cars, nor was the place swarming with Crime Scene Investigators. He briefly introduced himself to the doorman while he shook his hand. This practice had proved invaluable in the past, so Hugo understood the necessity of it now. As Alastair Rasnic alighted from the elevator on the 7th floor, all was quiet. There was no sound anywhere, no chatter, no computers and no phones. Alastair trod silently on the polished floor as he walked down the wide, brightly lit hallway to his office; his was the fourth office from the elevator. Several offices further along, Brock Burke resided. Brock's office was much larger than his – the size of a small apartment. Then down the far end of the hallway was Saffron Moffit's ultra-modern and very spacious office. Saffron's office door faced the long passageway, so Alastair knew she could see anyone from a distance if she was seated at her desk. He noticed her office door stood wide open.

Alastair moved quietly behind his desk. He placed his briefcase neatly under his desk to the right of his chair. Sitting down, he swiveled the chair around so he could watch the sun rise over the sleeping city as it slowly came alive. Everything remained quiet for several more minutes as Alastair sat surveying the view, then suddenly he heard a loud voice. He had thought he was alone, and he physically jumped – his heart pounded quickly in his chest, making him feel as if he almost had a heart attack. The voice was so unexpected.

"No, it will be tonight…" Then a pause as Alastair quickly got to his feet. He cautiously looked out his door.

"That is not acceptable; it was not what we agreed. Friday evening the janitor will let you in the side entrance as previously agreed…"

Alastair moved quietly, keeping close to the wall as he moved along the passageway toward Saffron's office. He knew now it must be her normally quiet voice that had startled him. She must have been yelling at someone for him to hear her so clearly. Alastair kept in the shadow as he crept toward her office.

"I need those papers back in place before the cocktail party happens. And don't think of trying anything, as I have plenty of insurance to make sure I remain safe. Anything happens to me and you go down, hard. With all the evidence that would surface, there wouldn't be any place you could hide…" And another pause. Alastair was just past the alcove where Neve sat, and he paused, staying in the shadows and listening.

"I may not be able to cancel anything, but I can and will make life hell for you for as long as you live. If you want to be constantly looking over your shoulder and protecting your family, then go ahead; a life in hiding is no life at all, and believe me, there's always someone who knows where you are…"

Alastair was feeling vulnerable; he was not a spy, nor did he eavesdrop – that was Al's area of expertise. Slowly, he crept back to his office, but he could still hear her raised voice. He knew he shouldn't be hearing any of this, and he was frightened.

"The cocktail party starts at six p.m. I will be here waiting until six thirty p.m. The janitor will only wait for you for ten minutes. Don't disappoint me. My absence would soon be noticed…" Then the level of her voice dropped, and Alastair could hear no more. Alastair needed air, and he needed to talk to Al, he would use a payphone.

Alastair sat in Starbucks until seven forty-five a.m.: it seemed like a more reasonable hour to show up at the office. He whistled as he walked from the elevator to his office. But the moment he entered, his whistling immediately ceased. Sitting waiting in the large armchair opposite his desk was none other than Saffron Moffit. She was dressed immaculately in a short Cabot blue, fitted suit, her shapely legs covered in sheer pantyhose, and high blue pumps completed her look. Alastair noticed for the first time she was not a beauty, but her makeup was perfection. Saffron Moffit worked hard to look as attractive as she could.

"Well, Mr. Rasnic, Alastair, I like a man who arrives early and shows eagerness and an enthusiasm for his job. I hope you're comfortable here?" she inquired, her soft words clipped and coated with ice.

"Thank you. Yes, I am enjoying my office and also the magnificent view. The work is challenging; however, I have yet to get to know the people," Alastair replied cheerfully, as she continued to tap her long red fingernails on his desk – click, click, click.

"Good, I'm glad to hear it. I'm sure we will get to understand each other well, Alastair. But just to help you appreciate me better, I believe there are several things you must know. Firstly, I run this company; I know everything that goes on within these walls, every spoken word. Anyone who doesn't work or who doesn't do exactly what I expect of them – I know about it. Brock and I started this company; he enjoys many outside interests, while I have full control over him and everything that goes on inside these walls. That includes you. Just so we're clear, Alastair…," she said as she stopped clicking her long fingernails and got to her feet to leave. Alastair stood as she did.

"I like a man with manners, Alastair, so already you have a few brownie points with me."

"Thank you, Saffron," Alastair replied humbly.

"Yes, thank me indeed; you will need them," she said, standing at the doorway, before she turned and added, as ice continued to hug her every precise word, "Just one other thing, Alastair. I also start the day early, and when I arrived earlier this morning your office door was shut and your briefcase was not here. Just so we are clear, Alastair, don't underestimate the power of a shrewd business woman. You will always come off second best. Enjoy your day," she said, disappearing from view.

Alastair heard her heels clicking sharply on the floor all the way back to her office. He let out a breath he hadn't known he was holding, and then felt the vibration of his cell. He knew without a doubt it was Al.

"Okay, don't say a thing, she is listening. She has been through your briefcase and drawers. You must search for a tiny camera; it will be up high and no larger than a small diamond. I don't think you are a big enough threat to her yet, but she may have planted one anyway. She is a mean one, so don't underestimate her, Hugo," Al said as she disconnected. Alastair was stunned.

He sat exactly as he had a few minutes ago, when Berry entered the office with his steaming cup of morning coffee. Alastair had already had several cups at Starbucks, but he didn't wish to upset Berry so early in the morning, so he greeted her cheerfully, hiding the many concerns he was feeling. He smiled his winning smile and complimented her on her pretty, pale pink shoes. Berry instantly blushed and rewarded him with a tight smile, before leaving the room and returning quickly with his schedule for the day. She was just presenting him with the *Wall Street Journal* and the *New York Financial Times*. Each was open at the appropriate pages, showing the many articles concerning the recent merger. At that moment, they were interrupted by a quick knock on the open door.

"Morning, Alastair, no time for a meeting today. But let's do lunch, 'Fras Gras', you and I, twelve thirty p.m., important," Brock Burke said, moving quickly toward his office. Before Alastair or Berry could rise from their seats or say a word, he was gone.

"I'll change your schedule to incorporate Mr. Burke's luncheon meeting with you, Mr. Rasnic, if you'll excuse me. Before I go, this is the list of investors you requested. The top performers for the past year through the past five years are at the back of the file. The highlighted funds are the ones we use currently or have used in the past. They will be your call from now on," Berry instructed, almost smiling as she left the room.

Alastair spent some time going through the file; he knew most of it from his research into Banker's Securities, but he found some interesting additions that had not been listed in their public portfolio. Alastair held several pieces of paper up so Al could make a copy of them at home. As the morning progressed and Alastair became more engrossed in his work, all thoughts of calling Special Agent Bow Grismold were forgotten, so when two uniforms suddenly appeared in his office, Alastair was not surprised. Forty-five minutes later, Alastair was relieved to see them leave with a new set of his fingerprints and more answers to their previously asked questions. Berry mentioned that the officers had again interviewed Ms. Moffit before leaving the building. He could tell by the way she set her mouth that she didn't approve or like Saffron Moffit, and he would have liked to know why. He knew he didn't yet know her well enough to ask, although he was working on it.

The remainder of the morning flew by, and before Alastair was aware of the time, Berry was reprimanding him for being late for his lunch meeting with the boss. He had no idea where the restaurant was, so Berry needed to give him a map. It was not far, but Alastair would never have found it without her.

"Alastair, welcome," Brock said, getting to his feet. "Thought you may have been engrossed in your work…"

"I apologize for being late, Brock," Alastair said, taking Brock's outstretched hand.

"Only ten minutes, no harm done. I've already started with a cocktail; what will it be?"

"Vodka martini, thanks," Alastair answered, relaxing slightly after his brief jog. They chatted on about work, with the merger being the lead topic. It was as Alastair knew it would be. Alastair said how impressed he was with the press coverage, and that immediately seemed to please Brock. Throughout the meal he instructed Alastair on investments, who they favored and why, which ones appeared solid long-term ventures and which ones could work short-term, and so on. Towards the end of the meal, Alastair made an excuse to look for something in his wallet as Al had instructed him to do. He accidentally let his membership card to 'Gentleman Only' slip from his wallet onto the table, and immediately scooped it up. He knew it was time enough for Brock to recognize the silver card.

"I see you're a member also," Brock inquired, leaning closer to Alastair and lowering his voice.

"Yes, Brock, discreetly so."

"Is there any other way," Brock replied, winking.

"Love the place, but seldom go there," Alastair said, knowing he had the younger man's interest.

"I use to visit also. A guy can get almost anything he wants there, and it's all so discreet."

"Membership expired, Brock?" Alastair inquired, continuing the game.

"No, Alastair, just very happily married... and you?" Brock asked, looking intently at Alastair.

"Just need to pick my moments, if you get my meaning," Alastair said, leaning back in his chair and laughing as Brock joined him.

"Glad we had this lunch, Alastair, you're all right. Think we understand each other and we'll work together well. I like your understanding of the word 'discretion'," Brock said, laughing as he slapped him on the back.

Alastair thought they must be about to leave as it was already past two p.m., but instead of standing, Brock leaned closer to Alastair and asked him to do the same.

"Now, I know you're a man of the world, Alastair. I don't think I need to tell you just how things work, but I'd like to be sure we're both on the same page. You'll have almost $400 million to invest by the close of business today," Brock instructed, leaning closer to Alastair as he checked that no one was listening.

"You know how the game's played. Here's the account number for the interest on the money before it makes it into the investors' accounts," Brock said, slipping a piece of paper to Alastair. When he didn't answer, he explained a little more. "Let the money sit overnight or a little longer, but not long enough to raise suspicion. There's a fine line, you know, Alastair. Anyway, let the money sit a while in an interest-bearing account. That's the account number where the interest is to be deposited, in my wife's maiden name, you understand. I don't see it as skimming, just a perk the boss is entitled to. Do we understand each other, Alastair?" Brock said, moving away and sitting back in his chair as he again slapped Alastair on the back.

"We understand each other, Brock. The boss is entitled. It shall be done and not mentioned again."

"Good man. Next time I feel the need to go to the 'Gentleman Only', you'll be right there beside me. I reward discretion, Alastair; I reward it in many ways. Gosh, is that the time? Well, we'd better get back before the office collapses without us. You're a good lunch partner, Alastair. We'll do this again."

"Excellent, Brock, I'll look forward to it."

"By the way, your credentials are impressive and you seem like a great guy to boot; good choice all round, I'd say!"

"Thank you, Brock, that means a great deal coming from you," Alastair replied, knowing the value of appearing humble.

They were almost back at the office when Brock stopped him and said, "Alastair, you're way too new to the company to understand the dynamics of Banker's Securities, Inc., but the monitory amount we received from our new acquisition was way underpriced. I fear we have a mole inside the organization; several important pieces of top-secret information have been leaked. I know you have just started with us, so yourself and my new secretary appear to be the only ones above suspicion, just so you're aware, Alastair," Brock said, looking at Alastair with a grave expression on his face. Alastair nodded, matching his boss's concerned look.

"Alastair, I also suggest you watch your back with Saffron. She may be my second in command, but each of us can only play on one side of the fence, if you get my meaning." Brock slapped Alastair on the back, before letting him enter the building.

"I had to cancel your one thirty appointment, due to your late return. I made it for Monday, Mr. Rasnic, so I hope that's suitable," inquired Berry none too kindly as he walked past her desk on the way to his office.

"Perfectly suitable, I'm sure. You are the most efficient secretary a man could wish for, Berry!" Alastair replied with a dazzling smile. Berry only blushed and turned away, but somehow Alastair thought he was slowly winning her over.

Then, as an afterthought, she added, "Mr. Rasnic? Mrs. Rasnic called in your absence and fortunately I was able to suggest to her several shopping malls that had the type of elegant, sophisticated garments that I feel we would both appreciate. She said to tell you she would be out shopping for several hours. I feel sure I sent her in the right direction for her new cocktail outfit for tonight's party. Women can be such critical, catty creatures, Mr. Rasnic," Berry concluded proudly.

"Berry, you're wonderful! Thank you for helping. We are new to this city, and I know Sylvia will find your suggestions invaluable," Alastair beamed, as again his secretary blushed a warm pink.

The management and staff of Banker's Securities were starting to leave the office in anticipation of tonight's cocktail party when Alastair heard a soft knock at the door. Looking up, he saw his beautiful daughter Neve standing there with a brown envelope in her hand.

"Mr. Rasnic, I believe you left this in Mr. Burke's office," Neve said. "I saw it marked *confidential*, so I thought I had better hand it to you myself," she concluded with a dazzling smile that could have melted ice. Behind her, Berry hovered.

"I'm sorry, Mr. Rasnic, I said she should be giving it to me, as you're a busy man," Berry said, giving Neve a cutting look that could kill.

"It's all right, Berry," Alastair said, dismissing her, even though she continued to hover.

"Thank you so much, Miss, eerr…?"

"Miss. Dolman, Amanda Dolman. I'm Mr. Burke's new secretary."

"Again, thank you. It is indeed an important document and I should have been more careful with its care."

"You're welcome, Mr. Rasnic, glad to help," she said, turning. Alastair watched her retreat as her long blonde hair flipped up and down as she slowly walked away. Today she wore a bronze fitted suit that came just below her knees and an attractive gold scarf tied loosely around her throat.

"Will there be something more, Berry?" Alastair asked, noticing she was still watching Amanda Dolman sashay back to her desk. Berry didn't answer; she was quite unable to take her eyes from the girl's retreating figure.

"Much too attractive, much too smart, altogether too much trouble, if you ask me," Berry muttered, her face tight.

"I can't imagine why you're not the boss's secretary, Berry. You seem to have been here long enough and you could easily do the job," Alastair sympathized, trying to take her attention off Neve.

"What? Oh yes, I should be, Mr. Rasnic. How observant of you. I certainly am more than qualified and have the necessary training and skill level, but sadly I lack the physical credentials," Berry replied coldly, and, to Alastair's relief, she turned to face him again. She was about to return to her desk when she asked impertinently, "I don't recall you visiting Mr. Burke's office today, Mr. Rasnic. Were you in there this morning?"

"Berry, I didn't know you required knowledge of my every move. I have two legs and a functioning, thinking brain. I wasn't aware I needed your permission or anyone else's to move freely around the building," Alastair replied, looking hard at his nosy secretary.

Again, Berry blushed at his words, before saying, "I apologize, Mr. Rasnic, I overstepped my boundaries. It won't happen again." She smiled a forced tight smile and returned to her desk.

"Close the door, please, Berry, so I can have some peace as I work," Alastair instructed.

Outside his office, many of his colleagues left for the day, laughing loudly as they passed. The moment the door closed, Alastair ripped open the envelope; he knew it was from Al. He partly withdrew the contents as he read her written instructions. Inside was a small listening device. Al said she had just received it. It was very powerful and the size and shape of chewed gum; it was also soft like gum. Alastair knew this was state of the art and Al wouldn't be using this unless she thought it extremely important to listen in. Al's instructions were for Alastair to get the bug planted in Saffron's office tonight before he left for the cocktail party. Easier said than done, Alastair thought.

He swiveled his chair around toward the view of the city and thought long and hard about his next move. Several minutes later, Alastair left the building and purchased two bouquets of flowers from the vendor outside the Fraser building's front entrance, then returned the way he had come.

"Berry, these are for you for being a fabulous secretary. You've done a great job; now go home early. Thank you, see you Monday," Alastair said, oozing charm as he bent and lightly kissed her on the cheek. He liked seeing her blush.

"But, Mr. Rasnic, it is my place to stay until you leave, in case you require my services."

"Indeed, it is, but I shall tell you if you are required to work late, but until then, you leave at five p.m. or earlier if you are up to date with your work. See you Monday," Alastair replied firmly.

Five minutes later, Berry popped her head around the door; she had her coat on and her handbag and flowers in her arms. "Enjoy the cocktail party, Mr. Rasnic. I know you'll be the most handsome man there, and say hello to your wife from me also. See you Monday." And she was gone. Well, Alastair thought, a compliment from Miss Sour Puss, Berry Pye, no less; he must be doing something right. Alastair hoped his next challenge would be as easy, but some-how he knew it wouldn't.

Alastair waited in his office until almost six p.m.; he had plenty to do. He knew also that Saffron Moffit had a six thirty meeting of her own. Gradually, the office became quiet as everyone headed out for the weekend. Finally, he felt alone enough to assume everyone must have left. Alastair knew, however, that one person still remained. Picking up the second bouquet of flowers he had previously purchased, he headed for the office at the far end of the hallway.

The door was partially open as he approached. He knocked softly before pushing it wider so he could enter. Saffron Moffit's office was decorated like no other. She sat behind a semi-circular ultra-modern glass desk. Its frame was made of the thinnest white steel, while the solid drawer fronts were finished in polished black aluminum with pewter handles. Her desk was neat and organized, like the woman behind it. In the furthest corner she had a tall, gray, rectangular vase; it stood around twenty inches high and matched a second taller one on her coffee table in the far corner of her office between two large white leather chairs. Both vases held long-stemmed white fragrant lilies.

"Saffron, I felt we may have gotten off on the wrong foot this morning. These are my peace offering that I hope you will accept; perhaps we may start over..." Alastair began, looking into the hardest, most hostile eyes he had seen in a while. He cautiously approached her desk and placed the flowers on the furthermost corner with one hand while he appeared to grasp the edge of her glass desk with the other. However, he was actually fixing the gum-like substance under the frame in the front corner, where no one would see it. He quickly pressed it hard while his eyes never left hers. He knew she had no idea. He continued to cautiously stand while he waited for her to offer him a seat. She did not.

"Shouldn't you be at home getting ready for the cocktail party? Or actually shouldn't you already be at the cocktail party? I disdain tardiness in anyone, Alastair."

"Just about to leave. I was wondering if I may accompany you this evening, if you have made no other arrangements. In fact, isn't it most likely a woman such as yourself would have left for the day and be relaxing at the beauty parlor? After all, you are the vice-president of Banker's Securities, Inc.," Alastair said in his most charming manner.

Alastair watched, as first her nostrils flared, before she turned very red in the face, and when her anger was at boiling point, she stood up to her full five feet three inch height and bellowed at him, "Alastair, firstly, I am a happily married woman and I take great offense at your proposal. Secondly, when I think it is necessary for me to visit the beauty parlor as you so quaintly put it, I shall do so. Thirdly, I am aware of my position here, and I resent your intrusion into my office!" As her face turned an even brighter red, she screamed, "If you continue working here – and I do mean *if* – I suggest you get the hell out of my office and never again return without an invitation."

As he slowly backed out of the room, he kept looking her in the eye for fear she would throw the nearest object at his head and that object would probably be the solid gray vase. He watched her hands inch toward it – he knew exactly what was on her mind – this was not a woman to be trifled with. As he continued moving backwards out of her office, she screamed again.

"You have just five minutes to leave the building. No, Alastair, not my office, the building, before I call security. Now get the hell out!" she yelled, beginning to sit again. She then saw the flowers. She quickly grabbed them, before hurling them across the office; they landed outside her door. Alastair took a few fast steps back towards her office and retrieved them. Then he walked casually away down the hall to his own office. He felt her eyes burning into his back with every step he took. Fortunately, she could no longer see his face as he could hardly contain his laughter. Alastair Rasnic felt it had all gone very, very well indeed. He had not gone more than halfway back to his office when her cell caught his attention.

"Potter, now is not a good time." Then a pause. "Well, just deal with it. Later," Saffron said, disconnecting as she got up to slam the door.

Alastair took a cab the seven blocks to his apartment building. He knew he was late. He whistled as he walked from the elevator toward the door of his apartment, and like so many other nights, he didn't see young Fran Fillimoore in Apartment 7B as she sat in her wheelchair facing the door. She clearly saw everyone and everything who passed her door through the one-way glass she had had installed several years ago. Her Uncle Tom enjoyed a hot leisurely bath before he, too, would sit in his wheelchair, and together they'd make dinner. Uncle Tom visited her most weeks, sometimes twice a week. Fran would like to imagine it was because he liked her or felt sorry for her being all alone; but she knew the real reason was because he lived in a rat-infested apartment building, and he couldn't afford the hot water to bathe, much less decent food. Fran forgot about Uncle Tom as she casually noted the time of the man's arrival at 7C. She listened for the automatic click of the camera that would take his photo.

Fran Fillimoore was fourteen years old, and she had all the time in the world. There were many things she was unable to do, but taking accurate records and photos was something she thought she did very well; she thought of it as her hobby. Fran Fillimoore was a young girl with a lot of time, a lot of money and very few friends.

When Alastair opened the door, he was greeted by a rather homely looking Sylvia Rasnic. She had short black bobbed hair, a rather square face, and carried, like Alastair, an extra twenty or so pounds around her middle. She was dressed sedately in a cream cocktail dress that fell just below the knees. It had multi-colored sequins on the bodice and a neat bolero jacket. Her shoes were conservative cream pumps with a small, thick heel.

"Darling, you're late," she said, kissing him lightly on the cheek, before continuing. "But it was worth it, darling. Everything went very well. I must say she's a tough cookie. I'll tell you about her meeting later. Your clothes are all laid out. We really must hurry," Sylvia Rasnic said encouragingly.

Alastair had seen his wife in many disguises over the years and he never warmed to any of them. They only served him to love and desire the real Al all the more. Alastair changed into his dinner jacket and in just five minutes he was ready. Before they left, they both stood arm in arm in front of the tall hall mirror and surveyed themselves.

"Well, are you ready to meet the company executives, Sylvia Rasnic?" Alastair asked, laughing.

"Certainly am, Mr. Rasnic," she replied, laughing also.

"I am told you will be with the most handsome man there tonight," Alastair teased.

"Oh yes, darling, I heard Berry say that. I think you are beginning to chip away at the ice. I wouldn't yet say your hard work has completely paid off, but I think some of the ice is beginning to thaw, my handsome husband. If she only knew!" Sylvia said, as together they laughed and headed for the elevator.

Fran watched as they passed, observing for the first time the new woman on the man's arm. She noted the time and wondered how she had got into apartment 7C without being seen. Fran blamed Uncle Tom's appearance for taking her mind from her work. Her camera was set to automatically adjust to any movement before it took the photo. Obviously, she had missed the woman's arrival, but it would be on the camera and she'd check it later. She left a blank line in her book. Fran listened for the faint click as the camera automatically recorded the movement – yes, Fran thought, the camera is still working.

The cocktail party was in full swing at the Waldorf Astoria when they arrived. It was a grand affair. As they entered, flashbulbs popped and reporters asked who they were, what they were wearing and the position Alastair held at Banker's Securities, Inc. They had only just got their first martini when Sylvia tapped Alastair's arm, drawing his attention to Brock Burke. He stood about five feet away with his back to them. On each side of him stood a beautiful, tall, slim woman with long blonde hair. One was dressed in an emerald green satin dress that was figure-hugging and off the shoulder. It highlighted her smooth perfect skin and well-proportioned body. The dress was rather short. A single strip of sequins slashed across the bodice, but otherwise the folds of fabric made for one of the most gorgeous creations Al had ever seen. On her wrist a diamond bracelet caught the light and sparkled brightly.

The other woman wore a short, blazing, orange dress that was equally as stunning and also hugged her slender figure. It was strapless and enhanced perfectly the wearer's long, slim legs while highlighting her every curve. A cluster of diamantes set off the bodice, while a long thin strand of diamonds fell from each ear.

Alastair was mesmerized.

"Which one's Neve?"

"They look so alike, I'm not sure which one is our Neve; but I do remember she was going to wear red, darling," Sylvia whispered as several people came over and introduced themselves. As they moved through the room, they became aware they were not the only ones talking about Brock's beautiful ladies. Alastair could hardly focus on the conversation as they continued talking. The moment they could move closer to Brock they did, so they could angle themselves for an introduction. But as they stood facing Alastair's boss, Sylvia and Alastair were shocked by what they saw. One of the girls was indeed their beautiful daughter, but the other was a stranger. Although she was several inches taller than Neve, the resemblance was undeniable.

Alastair and Sylvia both knew that Neve was in heavy disguise, as they were themselves, but even in her natural state, the resemblance could not be overlooked...

Poor Gus

Gus slowly unlocked the outside door leading to the stairs and the 7th floor. For some reason he felt uneasy. He often felt uncomfortable way down inside, but lately it was increasing. Now it was more than just discomfort and the uneasy feeling was now ever-present, Gus constantly tried to ignore it. Today, he tried harder, but it persisted. Gus assumed it was because of the murder and the body he had found. He still had nightmares about the girl's body just lying there, with lots of blood around her wrist. Clearly, he could remember how her left hand had been so brutally cut from her arm. He decided that was probably all it was, although he had had the same feeling before the murder.

    He usually only cleaned the 7th floor on Mondays, Wednesdays, and Fridays, and had been doing so for the past two weeks. Gus enjoyed the steady money, but he was still looking forward to Joe arriving back from holidays so he would only be required to clean the Fraser building occasionally. He had his regular cleaning round in three hardware stores and his day job at Jimmy's Secondhand; even though he barely made enough money to support himself and his Pa, he was happy with that. Although the extra money was sure helping – he had almost managed to pay all their bills. By the time Joe returned, the bills would be up to date and he would no longer need to fear every knock at the door.

    This time he wouldn't let Jimmy at the secondhand store talk him into placing his merger wages on a horse Jimmy always promised was a "sure thing". Gus was beginning to realize that some-how they never were. Gus had wised up recently and even admitted to Pa what he was doing. Gus thought Pa was the wisest person he knew. He may not say too much, but when he did, you had better listen. Pa may be old and in a wheelchair, but Pa had fought with the best of them – he still knew men from his time in the Marines, and Pa had seen the bad side of life and his comrades firsthand. They were the reason he was in a chair, and he had never forgotten it. When Gus had finally admitted his weakness, Pa quickly told him that Jimmy had never put his money on no horse, "sure thing" or not. Pa said he'd better get some money coming in and fast or they'd both be out on the street, and it was even colder there in winter than in their tiny apartment with heating that seldom worked. That was when Joe had gone on holiday, and Gus was sure glad he had.

All was quiet on the 7th floor. It was Wednesday night. Gus quickly began emptying the garbage bins as he kept an eye out for anything worth nicking. As he progressed toward the end of the hallway, he became aware that the large office belonging to the vice-president was still occupied. He hated the woman; she made his skin crawl, but it was too late now, she had spotted him.

"Hey you, janitor. Get in here!" she yelled, her harsh Brooklyn accent no longer hidden. Gus was still two offices away, so he turned in the hope she was talking to someone else. He hadn't been making much noise and he was pretty much on time. It wasn't her accent so much as her tone that scared him. Slowly, he walked toward the light and half-open door. Wishing he could run the other way, he told himself there was no reason to be scared. He had done nothing wrong; not anything she could know about anyway. Finally, he peered around the half-open door.

"What's your name?"

"Gus Boozeman, ma'am," Gus replied, still with only his head inside the door.

"Gus, take your filthy hand off my door and stand straight, and stand right here," she said, pointing to a spot just inside the door. "Why do janitors always have to be such filthy, smelly people? Just because you're a janitor, doesn't mean you can't bathe or wash your hands and hair or even clean your teeth occasionally..." she ranted as Gus remained quiet.

"Do you need something, ma'am?" Gus asked, more eager than ever to get back to work.

"Yes, I do need something, but I think you do also, Gus," she said, standing up and pacing back and forth behind her large glass desk. Gus knew she was staying as far away from him as possible, and he didn't mind at all. She reminded him of a boa constrictor about to strike or a prowling leopard before it attacked. Back and forth she prowled, her hands behind her back. Gus didn't know whether to answer her or not, so he waited until finally she asked, "You need this job, Gus; I know you do. Any man as short as you obviously has few opportunities in life. The world easily over looks you, doesn't it? Always has, hasn't it? For a short guy like you, this may well be your lucky day…" She paused, obviously trying to read his expression, but Gus remained silent he was just plain scared, and his expression never changed.

"Gus, one phone call from me and your job could be history; do you understand? What is the name of the company you work for?"

"Hendricks Cleaning, ma'am." Gus thought perhaps he shouldn't have told her, but he quickly understood that by not answering it would only make her even angrier. Gus had never liked anything that prowled, and watching her he knew he would rather be inside a closed cage with a prowling animal than taking his chances with her inside her office.

"One phone call would be all it takes, mean nothing to me, wouldn't change my day; but for you, it would mean you could no longer afford to eat or drink or gamble or whatever it is you do. No job, no money, nowhere to live," she said quietly, still prowling the floor.

"Ma'am, it's not me regular job."

"Not your regular job? What are you, multi-skilled or something? Well, I thought it wasn't, Gus. You know, one phone call could make this your regular job – would you like that, Gus? Regular income; money you can rely on; knowing exactly what's expected of you each day. Regular income means you could pay your rent on time and have food on the table for your wife and kids. Just in case you don't understand. How many filthy brats do you have anyway? One phone call, Gus, that's all it would take."

"None, ma'am, I ain't got no brats."

"So, you're going to play tough with me, are you, Gus?" she responded, raising her voice slightly. Gus knew immediately he should never have answered her, she didn't require an answer and it only served to make her more annoyed with him. Gus could hardly stop shaking and he didn't know why: she was only a dame at best, and certainly no lady at that.

"I need you to do something for me, Gus. I'll make it worth your while, of course."

"No, thank you, ma'am. I don't need anything, just want to get back to me work."

"But, Gus, I think you do need something, you need to keep your job, don't you?" she asked again as she continued to prowl.

"I don't rightly care, ma'am. I ain't done nothin' not to keep it."

"Well, that's just your word against mine. And guess who they'll believe? Not you, a grimy little janitor. Now, Gus, let's all be truthful here, shall we?"

"I am, ma'am."

"No need for you to speak unless I ask you a question, Gus – are we clear?" she asked, and he nodded, wanting more than anything to get out of her office.

"I want you to do a little something for me, Gus. You can tell the time, can't you?" she asked, and he nodded.

"Well now, Gus, Friday night at exactly six thirty p.m., I want you to be at the west door with your key. You'll hear three short knocks. You are to unlock the door and let the three men inside – you are not to look at them. They will follow you up the back stairs and you will bring them to my office. Is that clear, Gus? You must make sure no one, and I mean no one, sees you."

"Ma'am, I don't want to get mixed up in nothin'."

"I said don't speak, just nod your head if you understand. Here, take this now, and when you have shown the gentlemen out the same way they came in, exactly ten minutes later, there'll be the same amount again under my garbage bin for you on Monday evening. More money than you make in six months, Gus, yours for a few minutes' work. But if you should screw up or open your mouth – why, I'll personally track you down and cut your balls off myself," she said, almost snarling at him, before she took a deep breath and continued in a kinder tone. "But, Gus, I must have your word that you will never tell anyone about this. If I can trust you, there may be more money where this came from. Do I make myself clear?"

"Ma'am, I really don't want to get mixed up in nothin'."

"Why, Gus, that's okay, you have choices, of course we all do. I'll just make a quick call to the local NYPD and tell them about the little items you've been lifting from the offices here in the Fraser building. Remember that murder, Gus? Why, of course you do, it was you who found the body, wasn't it? I guarantee the police will be very pleased to learn about what you took from the poor victim, now won't they? What's it to be, Gus? A life behind bars, or money in your pocket?" Saffron asked, a small nasty smile on her lips; she knew by the look on his dirty scared face she had him exactly where she wanted him. Slowly, she reached for the phone and began punching in the number.

"Okay, ma'am."

"Good boy, Gus. I knew we'd understand each other. Here, take this and get your filthy arse out of my office. Forget this meeting ever happened. It's your word against mine anyway. A company vice-president and a filthy little janitor, now who would they believe?" She picked up the brown envelope he hadn't yet taken and thrust it into his dirty hand and quickly shut the door the moment he was outside. Gus was shaking. He didn't know if this was his lucky day or his worst nightmare.

The moment he was free of her gaze, he opened the envelope. Five one hundred-dollar bills! Gus could only ever remember seeing a hundred-dollar bill once or maybe twice in his life, and now, in his hand, he held five of them. He didn't really want to get mixed up in anything, but what could he do? He knew she would call the police if the whim took her. He never actually said he had taken anything – in fact, he hadn't said much at all – she hadn't let him. She must have hidden cameras all over the building. How silly he had been not to realize this sooner. Gus knew it was the end of him helping himself to things. He would tell his boss he didn't want to clean the Fraser building any more tomorrow. But would that mean he would lose the hardware stores also? If that happened, they'd only have the small income from Jimmy's Secondhand, and that was not regular or nearly enough.

Gus was glad to finish his work that evening and was thinking of how he could start work at the Fraser building by six thirty p.m. when he always found it hard to get there by seven. Then he remembered Jimmy was working Friday and he wouldn't need to go in. A slight smile curled his lips. He had solved his immediate dilemma.

"Hey, Pa," Gus said, pushing the door wide; he liked to make sufficient noise to wake his Pa, who was usually asleep in his chair by the time he came home. But as he entered the small dirty room, Gus saw the fridge door had been left wide open and Pa was cleaning up the last of the frozen macaroni and cheese dinner. He was busy wiping the side of the foil dish with his chunk of stale bread.

"Pa, what the hell ya doin'? That was for both of us tonight; we ain't got no more food. Pa, ya gone crazy or what?" Gus said, taking two large steps over to the small table.

"Fridge broke this morning, smoke started coming out the back and then poof! Had to open the window to let the stink out. That window ain't been opened in a while; nearly fell off it did, and nearly took me with it."

Gus couldn't believe this had happened, but he was sure pleased his Pa was okay. He inspected the fridge; he could still smell the smoke. "You okay, Pa? Sorry I wasn't here for ya," Gus said, forgetting his anger.

"Sorry I ate ya dinner, but it was spoiling. I thought it best one of us had something good out of that old useless fridge."

"Yeah, Pa, you're right. I'm glad you ate it," Gus replied, remembering the many times the old man had given him his own dinner and gone hungry. Then he had a thought.

"Here, Pa, look after this. I'm going to get us both hamburgers," Gus said, handing his Pa the brown envelope as his yellowed cracked teeth broke into a huge smile.

"How ya goin' to do that? You got money?" Pa asked, his dish clean and his full attention on his son.

"Yeah, Pa, just look after that. It's the money for our new fridge. Won't be buying it from Jimmy's this time. I'll take you with me in the morning, Pa. You been wantin' to go for a walk, and Jimmy doesn't want me in until three tomorrow," Gus replied as the old man looked in the envelope and let out a low whistle at what he saw. Twenty minutes later, Gus returned with two Big Macs and large fries.

"No, son, I'm done eatin'… you can manage the both of them. I'll just nibble on these," Pa said, taking a handful of fries. After the meal, the empty bag and containers stayed where they were. Gus told his Pa the story of his meeting with Saffron. The old man listened and said nothing; he only shook his head several times with the concern he felt for his son.

As Friday afternoon drew to a close and Gus hurried toward the Fraser building, he thought again about their good fortune the day before. Together, they'd found the perfect fridge, just six months old and exactly the right height. It even had a separate freezer compartment, not that they needed it. They'd delivered it free of change seeing they lived so close, and Gus even had $145 left over. The fact the fridge was purple didn't worry either of them in the least; in fact, Pa said it added a sort of upper-class ambience to the place, whatever that meant.

Now that the money was mostly spent, Gus knew he had to go through with the arrangement. At exactly six thirty p.m., Gus was waiting discreetly inside the west door. He had all the lights off except one. It gave them just enough light to see their way, but it was still dim enough for them not to see Gus' face. He thought it was a stroke of genius as he waited for the knock on the door in the semi-darkness. At 6:34 p.m., Gus was beginning to worry. Maybe he was at the wrong door, maybe they had already knocked and he hadn't heard them; after all, the emergency door was made of heavy steel. Maybe it had been cancelled and he'd have to give the money back? That thought scared him the most; then he'd be even more in debt than he was before. Just then, he heard three distinct knocks on the door. Gus felt relieved. He opened the door a little as he checked for three men. Three tall, dark figures stood outside in the fading light. One of them nodded to open the door and Gus did so. They followed him up the several flights of stairs to the 7th floor, then followed him down the hallway and just before he got to the end, he pointed the way and disappeared as fast as he could. He really didn't care whether she left his money or not, he just didn't want to deal with her any more.

Gus waited at the end of the hallway for just under ten minutes, before the men again appeared and he showed them out. Gus checked the exact time, as he expected the police to tap him on the shoulder at any moment, and he wanted to be a believable witness. Soon, Gus continued his cleaning on the first floor, and by nine thirty he was approaching the 7th floor. He could have moved faster tonight, but he hadn't wanted to enter it again until he felt sure she had left. Upon entering, Gus was relieved to see the light at the end of the hallway was off and the door shut.

He didn't want to appear eager as he knew he was probably being watched. So, he started emptying the bins at the far end of the hallway, unlike his usual routine. Discreetly, he lifted her garbage bin, and there on the floor was another envelope exactly like the first. He quickly hid it in his hand and then transferred it carefully to his pocket. He hadn't thought she would leave it for him until Monday night. All the while he was aware of the hidden cameras wherever they were, watching him.

Gus didn't check the envelope until he was out of the building, and sure enough she was as good as her word and there was another five hundred greenbacks in hundred dollar bills inside.

Gus knew he was later than usual, but he knew Pa would be sleeping, as his neighbor Tom had visited him today and his Pa would be all tuckered out from talking, or whatever they got up to. Gus whistled as he walked, and several times he tapped his pocket just to make sure the money was still there. He raced up the stairs two at a time. He had intended to go to the market tonight before they ate, but he would look in on Pa first and leave the envelope with him. He wanted it to be safe. Gus swung the door wide, certain Pa was dozing, but the scene that met his eyes was far from tranquil. Pa's chair lay on its side and the old man lay on the floor, his leg trapped heavily by the chair. He had blood oozing from a large cut on his forehead and another on his arm. He was groaning loudly. Next to him, Tom was also on the floor with his ankle twisted at a very strange angle. Tom could move around without his wheelchair for small amounts of time and he looked like he had tried to get to his feet and knocked the table over in the process. Gus stood in the doorway and stared, seeing the checkers scattered across the floor. Could these two old men have gotten into a fight over checkers?

"Gus, help us. I think I've broken something. Ya sure are late home, son," the old man admonished while he groaned in agony.

"What happened here?" Gus asked as he approached his Pa. When he tried to move him, the old man screamed with pain. So, he left him where he was and tried to help Tom back into his chair. Tom was a large, overweight man. Gus could hardly move him, and he knew his ankle was, at the very least, broken.

"Come on, son, you can do it. All that cleaning, you're a strong boy, try to lift Tom again," Pa encouraged through his pain. But it was no use. Tom was just too large. He was almost twice as tall and twice as heavy as Gus, and he just couldn't lift him more than a few inches from the floor.

"It ain't no use, Pa. I gotta call someone," Gus finally admitted.

It was almost four a.m. when Gus finally returned from the hospital where he'd left both Tom and Pa. Pa had a broken hip and a broken toe. His cuts were stitched and he was showered and cleaned up before they let him rest. Tom had several breaks in his ankle and lots of bruising. It appeared they had fallen from their chairs chasing checkers, but Gus really didn't know. He may have money in his pocket, but without his Pa it seemed pointless. Gus had never been away from his Pa before and it seemed weird… maybe it was time to stop being a son and become a grownup, he thought as he finally dozed off into a troubled sleep.

An hour later, Gus woke with a start. He wanted to check the money was still here and that they hadn't been burgled or anything. Gus knew it was a weird thought, but it wouldn't hurt to check. His Pa would have hidden it safely somewhere. And that appeared to be exactly what he had done – Gus couldn't find the money anywhere…

Evoking Brock

Amanda Dolman and Siobhan Burke looked amazingly alike. Many people commented or used the topic to begin a conversation. Everyone, that is, except the two girls. However, as they stood on each side of the president and chief executive officer of Banker's Securities and chatted to each other and the many guests – something strange began to happen. Very gradually, during the course of the evening, they became aware of the many things they had in common. Each time someone asked them for a drink, their choice of cocktails was the same. Every time the *hors d'oeuvres* came past, they chose the very same one. When they commented to Brock about a particular guest, one would speak exactly what the other was thinking. Each time a coincidence happened, they'd look at each other and giggle.

Brock was beginning to feel somewhat uncomfortable. Siobhan had never had any kind of connection with any of his secretaries. Maybe she was trying something new; if she was, it was working. Being part of two women bonding was spooky. Brock realized that if he'd ever had any desire for the beautiful Amanda, it was rapidly cooling. He had always thought Siobhan quite smart; not out standingly smart, but she had passed her college degree with honors and she was able to stay with most conversations about business, politics and current affairs. She had a mild sense of humor that was usually overshadowed by her dazzling smile. Brock knew many men would gladly climb over broken glass just to be in her circle and see her smile. But now she seemed to be enjoying a new way of challenging him and keeping him by her side. Burke remembered the old saying, 'Keep your friends close, and your enemies closer'. Perhaps that was indeed Siobhan's strategy, he thought, tuning back into their conversation.

"… and then I used to climb trees. That was not lady-like at all. And I loved it. The higher the better. I loved looking down…," Amanda was saying.

"I would sit up there for hours and watch my mom and nanny get into an awful frenzy looking for me. It was only when Mom started yelling at Dad or the nanny that I would suddenly re-appear. So, I know exactly what you mean about the higher the better," Siobhan concluded, giggling as Brock introduced them to a late arrival.

As the evening progressed, Brock's comfort level decreased even more, but he seldom moved away from the two beautiful ladies at his side. The envious glances from every male in the room was enough for Brock to know he was in a sought-after position. Most everyone thought it was a media stunt, and even the media seemed impressed. Brock knew he was certainly with two of the most stunning women in the room. Each time Amanda went to leave his side, Siobhan would coax her into staying.

Brock knew she was an incredible, sexy, charismatic young woman, and quite probably the most beautiful secretary he had ever had. She was proving super-efficient, discreet and precise in her work, and, best of all, she never intruded. What more could he ask for? But for his secretary to become friends with his wife was unthinkable; although the thought of firing Amanda was also unthinkable. After the murder of Marlene Brice, Brock knew he was being watched closely by the police, so to fire Amanda without good reason would only draw unnecessary attention to himself. He needed to find out what perfume Amanda was wearing, because it was driving him wild; he wanted Siobhan to use the same one.

When, finally, the evening came to an end, Siobhan suggested they take Amanda to dinner with them. Brock had been hoping for a quiet romantic dinner just for two at such a late hour. When she graciously declined, he was secretly pleased, but Siobhan proved unrelenting in convincing her to stay. Dinner that evening was a fun occasion, with both girls taking turns at being the center of attention. They were funny, charming, witty and sexy all at once, and the many admiring glances that came their way did not go unnoticed by Brock.

As the night drew to a close, it was voted a success by all. Siobhan again shocked Brock by extending an invitation to Amanda to join them at their country house this weekend. Brock hadn't even known they were going to the country, but he smiled politely, agreed and said nothing. Siobhan asked for Amanda's address and told her the limo would arrive at nine o'clock the next morning to take her to Brock's private jet. When it was time to say good night, the girls hugged each other tightly.

Brock didn't kiss Amanda on the cheek until he was instructed to do so, and then it was merely a light whisper of a kiss. However, it was enough for Amanda and Brock to feel the immediate electricity shoot through them. Unknowingly, they both decided it must never happen again.

As they watched Amanda head toward the taxi, Siobhan and Brock entered the limo. Brock was more confused than ever with his wife's current behavior. Was she playing with him, toying with his emotions, testing him or just teasing him? Whatever game she was playing, he didn't much like it and wanted it to stop. Maybe she just needed more of his constant and undivided attention. As they put out the light later that night, his undivided attention was exactly what Siobhan Burke had…

Replacing Love

Potter Moffit was taking a few days' break on his way back to the United States. He had again been running errands for Saffron in Europe, only this time he'd decided it would be the last time. His awakening had finally come during the cocktail party.

Cox and Potter had spent a busy late afternoon shopping so he could update both his closet and his look. Potter had never thought shopping enjoyable, although just being with his upbeat and happy son Cox was a pleasure. Cox had gone to great lengths to make sure Potter got the immediate attention he deserved at each designer store they visited. Potter estimated the money they were spending and thought they must have unloaded at least seven thousand dollars on his clothes, and probably more. Cox was a great help, and instead of trying to guide his dad toward his favorite young designers, he steered Potter into the more sophisticated and elegant stores. Potter not only had a new cocktail suit, shirt, coat and scarf for the evening, but also some rather elegant casual clothes. Cox had then taken him for a haircut, which cost more than most people earned in a week; this was followed by a manicure and pedicure. Then he experienced a facial, Potter's first, although it was not unpleasant. Potter found it interesting to see so many masculine men having facials, treatments, pedicures and manicures in the 'men only' spa!

It was when Potter arrived at the cocktail party and greeted the many people he knew, that he really started to feel good. They all commented on just how great he looked. With each compliment, Potter gained a little more confidence. He enjoyed himself as usual, even if Saffron arrived much later and barely spoke to him; in fact, she failed to acknowledge him at all. As the evening progressed, and for the first time ever, her attitude toward him began to annoy him. She was just using him, using him in the same way she used her many employees, who clearly couldn't stand her either. He finally got it.

He was just around for her use. Several martinis later, Potter walked outside onto the balcony and after standing alone for some minutes, he decided, right there and then, that he was going to put an end to his charade of a marriage. But first, he would play her at her own game. She was so smug, so self-assured, so confident, and she thought she had everyone securely under her control. He knew it would be easy for him to just disappear. He would, of course, tell Cox, so he could follow if he wanted to.

So, Potter took a few days off and enjoyed the sights and sounds of Europe. Something he'd never taken the time to see before. He booked his return flight to New York with a stopover in London. He then called his old Aunt Adele and asked her to meet him at Heathrow. Once in London, he would tell her of his plans. He'd open a bank account for himself in her name.

He sat at the little sidewalk café in Paris with a small smile on his lips, thinking how everything was so easily falling into place. He would make one last run for Saffron, but wouldn't make a return trip. He simply wouldn't take the package with him.

"Well, hi! You look like an American lost in Paris?" a friendly, bubbly, feminine voice asked. Potter was lost in thought and didn't realize anyone was speaking to him. He looked up, but the sun was behind her and he couldn't see her face. All he could see was her silhouette, and from her shadow, he knew she was tall and slim with short, light-colored hair, maybe blonde. But her face was hidden in shadow.

"Yes, you! Do you speak English?" she asked again as he stared up at her, still not believing she was talking to him.

"Yes. Yes, of course I do."

"May I sit down? I've done too much shopping and need a café au lait now. There are no other tables, do you mind?" she asked sweetly.

'No, not at all," Potter answered, about to rise and pull out her chair, when a young Frenchman beat him to it. Before briefly raising his beret, he continued on.

"Forgive me, I was deep in thought," Potter said, focusing on the girl. Now he could clearly see her face – he was liking what he saw.

"Yes, I could tell."

"May I get you a coffee?" Potter offered, not knowing what else to say.

"I have already ordered, thank you," she said, smiling a broad open smile. She had laughter in her voice and now that she was sitting opposite him, he couldn't help but notice the sparkle in her light blue eyes. Her nose was thin and straight, her mouth full and her teeth white and perfect. She had an oval face with a very cute dimple in her chin. Sitting at the sidewalk café on the Champs-Élysées, Potter had no idea what to do or say to this mischievous nymph that had chosen him to share her coffee time with.

"Oh," she said. "Forgive me," she continued, stopping briefly to wipe the froth from her top lip as she giggled, and for some reason her giggle was so infectious that Potter joined her. He then handed her his clean napkin.

"My name is Loot, Loot Honor Whimsy-Sparrow," she finally finished as she held out her hand to him over the table. Potter thought it a very strange name and he giggled as he took her small, delicate hand in his.

"So, are you laughing because I introduced myself first or because you think I have a funny name? You are such an attractive man, I know you must be used to girls wanting to sit with you. But if you are waiting for someone, I can share. The table is small, but so am I," she finished in her soft, airy voice, before she giggled again. Potter was so captivated he wasn't even listening to what she was saying, just the way she spoke. Her voice held in it the most magical sound he had ever heard.

"Oh yes," he replied, never taking his eyes from hers.

"Yes? Yes what? You actually don't like my name or you are waiting for someone or you think I am rather forward?" she asked again. Just seeing his confusion made her eyes sparkle brightly and she giggled.

"No, no. I am not waiting for anyone, or maybe subconsciously I am waiting for you. I think your name is very different but perfect for you, and so is your adorable dimple."

"So, will you share yours then?" she asked, ignoring his last comment and unable to stop her laughter from over-flowing.

"I have no dimples to share. But, yes, here," he said, pushing his half-empty coffee towards her just as the waiter arrived and re-filled their cups.

"Oh no, silly, I don't want to share your coffee or the dimple you don't have. I want to know if you would share with me your name. After all, we are sitting together at a very small table at a café on a Paris sidewalk, are we not?" she said, giggling again. Potter immediately felt foolish and quickly slid his coffee back in front of him, as she said, "Oh, here is a vacant table. I will move over." She got to her feet and began gathering together her many shopping bags.

"No, please stay. I'm sorry if I appear rude, and I do like your name," Potter added as she started putting her bags down again beside the small black wrought-iron table, before gingerly sitting.

"Only on one condition," she replied, teasing him openly.

"Anything," Potter replied, knowing they were flirting but loving it anyway. He knew he was wearing his heart on his sleeve.

"I cannot have coffee with a stranger in Paris. Why, my mother strictly forbids it. So, let's start over. I am Loot Honor Whimsy-Sparrow, how do you do?" she began again, offering him her hand. This time, Potter rose slightly from the table and took it in his own, before lightly kissing the back.

"Oh dear, you are such a tease; must I ask you outright? Who are you – and what is your name?" She giggled as Potter finally understood what all this was about. He blushed very red in the face as he comprehended his foolishness and replied.

"I do apologize, I was so taken by you, I forgot my manners. I am Potter Moffit, actually Potter Moffit the Third," he said, and this time he extended his hand toward her as she again giggled before shaking it soundly.

"I'm so glad to finally meet you, Mister Potter Moffit the Third. How strange that your name sounds familiar to me." She paused as a serious expression briefly clouded her pretty face; then, smiling again, she continued, "I do think you owe me a coffee, as mine is only half-finished and already cold, due to the time it has taken you to introduce yourself." She giggled, and he was completely unable to not chuckle also.

They talked on as afternoon turned to evening, and then walked across the street to a small, intimate French restaurant. She was a flight attendant on British Airways and lived in Soho, London.

"So, I'm completely through with airline pilots. I never want to date another man in uniform. The last one I dated expected me to drop everything and go to Egypt with him. Can you believe he was obsessed with the pyramids and all the ancient stuff surrounding them? By day, he would search for their hidden secrets; and by night, if I was lucky, he would remember me. Each time I tried to leave, he would beg me not to, explaining how he was drawn to Egypt. How he couldn't stay away, how it was calling to him and trying to tell him something. Until, finally, I knew Egypt was the only thing calling to him. He was a man who seemed quite unable to feel any kind of passion for another human being. How distasteful is that? So, I'm through with anyone employed by the airlines or who has a love of Egypt," Loot concluded happily.

"Are you then through with love?" Potter asked as their drinks arrived.

"Through with love? Oh, good gracious, no! Why, wherever did you get that idea?" she said, laughing again.

"Well, you just said…," Potter began as she finished for him.

"I just said I was through with airline pilots and Egypt. To be through with love would be the same as being through with life, and that will never happen. I think we all search for that special someone, whether actively or passively. Why, surely you are also searching, if you are sitting alone outside a café on the Champs-Élysées in beautiful Paris. Surely you are also searching?" she inquired, her eyes alive and glowing as she looked deeply into his.

"Now you're surely challenging me?" Potter teased. As he listened to her he became very aware of his American accent. Like her, he was also born in England, but he now knew his English accent was long forgotten. He hung on her every look, every bubbly word, while her smooth English voice stroked his soul.

"And this is a bad thing...?" she challenged back. Potter was beginning to understand that this was a girl who could make him think about himself for the first time and the things he wanted from life. He had never thought he was worth enough for anyone to ask or care.

They talked on into the evening and then, at three a.m., together they returned to Potter's hotel and spent a crazy, happy, fun-filled night, laughing, teasing, and finally, as the sun began to rise, making love. Potter had never experienced anything like Loot. She was so joyful and sensuous and sexy all rolled into one. The next morning, she changed Potter's flight so he would be on her plane. Then they made love again, and afterwards Potter told her all about his plans; together they packed his things and prepared to return to her hotel to do the same. Some-time in the last twenty-four hours, Potter had fallen madly and deeply in love.

"Loot," Potter said, sounding very serious, as she turned and moved swiftly into his arms, "I love you." And just like that, he knew he really did. He also knew this was the first time in his life he'd ever been in love.

"Potter Moffit the Third, I love you, too."

With those three crazy words, Potter Moffit knew his life had changed forever...

Finally, Leaving Bankers Securities, Inc.

Three Months Later

A lot had happened at Banker's Securities, Inc. in the past three months. Most of it had gone unnoticed by many of the employees. Hugo held fast to his desire to distance the three of them from the company as soon as possible. At first, Al had fought him, telling him he was getting soft in his old age. But once the wire was placed in Saffron Moffit's office, it hadn't taken Al long to agree with him. The Grasshoppers had never been involved with drugs or any kind of illicit smuggling; it was something neither felt comfortable with. Hugo had seen firsthand the effects it had had on his brother Felix, and that was on a very small scale.

Somehow, Hugo and Al felt out of their depth with the many things happening inside Banker's Securities. They both knew it would be only a matter of time before the law became suspicious, and neither of them wanted to be around when the lid was blown off. Alastair had, so far, successfully siphoned five million dollars of interest each month from the investors' accounts. He then carefully changed the numbers for the report that was distributed. He knew he couldn't get away with showing poor performance for too long and remain unnoticed. It wasn't a big amount for the Grasshoppers, and never before had they taken small amounts on a regular basis. It was usually one large amount that disappeared hours before they did. However, fifteen million dollars was better than nothing. Their paycheck would be ten million and Neve's five million.

They were both worried about Neve, as she had been discharged as Brock Burke's secretary to become Saffron Moffit's secretary. Neither of them was pleased. Soon after the cocktail party, and due to her friendship with Siobhan, Brock decided he didn't enjoy playing head games with his wife, and Amanda was transferred before a new secretary was installed. Enid Shillington was everything Amanda Dolman was not. She had dark, smoldering good looks that had every man's heart aflutter. However, she was not at all efficient, and Amanda wasted many hours trying to show her around the files and the computer. She constantly got herself into trouble with Brock Burke's appointments, and never managed to get to work on time. Brock never noticed any of it and merely encouraged Amanda to help her settle in. In effect, Amanda Dolman was performing two jobs and became the highest paid secretary in the firm, much to Berry's annoyance.

Alastair continued to enjoy working with Brock, and over time they developed a comfortable friendship. However, Saffron Moffit continued to hammer Alastair with her fiery temper and easy tantrums. Usually, these attacks happened before or after working hours, but lately they seemed to happen any time. Alastair despised her like he had never despised anyone before, and spent many evenings telling Al the many horrid scenarios he imagined happening to her.

Neve continued spending all her free time with Siobhan Burke, and Al's nightly chats with her daughter now seemed a thing of the past. Al had already booked her trip to Switzerland to remove the money from the account they had created and transfer it safely into another account offshore. Hugo and Al were also booked to spend ten days in England with their son and his family before they were required to start work in San Diego. It was with a multi-million-dollar textile distribution company. They were seeking the services of a chief financial officer for a six-to-ten-month contract. The timing suited them perfectly, as they would be free in time to collect Felix from prison when he was released and make certain he enjoyed a better life from then on. Alberta was excited to be leaving. The big city of New York had fulfilled one of her lifelong dreams, but, like Hugo, it was not what they had expected and she never wanted to return. She was also feeling uneasy about the many things happening at Banker's Securities and knew Saffron would manage to take Alastair down with her should she get caught. Of that she was sure!

Tomorrow evening, Al was to fly to Switzerland while Alastair was going to make the last transfer the following day and then find a reason to leave. They had leased out there apartment and almost everything was packed. The movers were due to arrive Saturday morning, and Baxter was already getting their next rental accommodation organized in San Diego.

~

Baxter had worked for the Grasshoppers for nearly twenty years. He looked after their numerous homes around the world. He never spent any time with them when they were away and still had no idea where they went or why. Baxter was more than happy with his overly generous salary, his many bonuses and his current love life. When the Grasshoppers were away, Baxter would play. And play he did, all over the world in their luxury residences.

Three months ago, Baxter's conservative happy life had been turned upside down when he'd met Jon Riddly. Baxter's ten-year relationship with Lyle Boxer, the groundsman/gardener, had been over for several years, although they somehow remained friends. Unlike Lyle, Jon was a well-cared-for, pampered, middle-aged playboy with too much money and not enough sex. He'd played the field and had fun doing it, but now he yearned for a settled, committed relationship with a guy that didn't carry too much baggage or have a wild, ugly past.

He wanted someone who loved their own life but who also enjoyed being a part of his; someone who embraced being shown new things – and not only in the bedroom. Jon had recently discovered he enjoyed spending time alone and appreciated his own company and the life he had created. He was finding out new things about himself for the very first time. Baxter was proving to be the perfect boyfriend, and Jon never tired of him and never tired of spoiling him. At first, he'd hated it when Baxter told him they couldn't be together certain nights because he had to work. But now he felt it was these absences that added to his attraction and made him appreciate the times they spent together even more. Jon still had a desire to control Baxter, even though he knew it wasn't working, but controlling people was in his character and he hadn't learned how to turn it off. Jon Riddly thought Baxter was tailor-made for him and his needs. So far, this relationship was proving a perfect fit.

Baxter and Jon had been enjoying time in San Diego in the Grasshoppers' luxurious new condo overlooking the beautiful Pacific Ocean. But now it was time for Baxter to fly to Switzerland to prepare the small villa the Grasshoppers kept there, and Jon wasn't invited. Baxter said he would only be away a night or two, as Alberta would be arriving in two days' time and he had been instructed, as always, to leave before she arrived.

~

"Well, Hugo darling, here's cheers to another successful journey," Al said, raising her glass of Moët to Hugo. They were watching the sunset over the skyscrapers of Manhattan. They sat on their balcony enjoying sushi and drinking champagne.

"Here's to leaving the Big Apple, darling! Cheers!" Hugo added, as their glasses clinked.

"I'm not usually happy to move on so fast, but this time I can hardly wait. For me it can't be quick enough. Cheers, Mr. Rasnic!" Al said, laughing as she continued.

"You know it's only a matter of time before Ms. Moffit goes down, and believe me, she'll go down hard. She's not nearly as careful as she was several months ago, and she doesn't seem to care. She's a real loose cannon, and I think Brock Burke is finally on to her as well. I think he's hiring a private investigator."

"He always said he wanted to know who the mole is inside the company," Hugo added.

"But, Hugo, surely it's her. It has to be," Al replied, delicately placing a small sushi roll in her mouth.

"Of course, it is, darling, but I don't think he wants to believe it."

"Well, I think that somehow Brock's secretary – you remember, the one who was murdered was tied up in this mess. Brock might be opening a can of worms if he goes ahead with a P.I."

"I know, Al. I know. That's why I want us all to be thousands of miles away. This will prove to be the scandal to end all scandals. It only takes one spark to burn a forest," Hugo replied, feeling more uneasy than ever as he spoke.

The next morning, they were up at four a.m. Al was meticulous with Alastair's appearance, as always, but this morning she was openly worried that he wouldn't be able to escape Banker's Securities. After a fast breakfast, Hugo collected Al's bags and left the apartment. As usual, they didn't hear the soft click of the automatic camera in Apartment 7B as they passed. However, Fran Fillimoore was still sleeping, so no notes were taken. Hugo would drop Al at the airport before arriving at work. He had some things to purchase first. It was Berry's birthday and he was going to use it as the last catalyst to rile Saffron Moffit.

Hugo was always sad to say goodbye to Al. She was his strength, his security and his love. Hugo had never had a desire to be without Alberta. Each time they were apart, he hated it. He seldom slept or ate, and he felt a nervousness he was unable to control. As he passionately kissed her goodbye and watched her walk through the terminal gate, this time was no different. He tried telling himself he was a strong, confident, successful man, and sometimes it even worked. However, this morning it didn't work at all. As Al turned to give Hugo a final wave before disappearing from his sight, he felt hot tears threaten to escape his eyes. He took several deep breaths and tried to think of other things. After all, he would see her in just a few days' time, in England. As he drove into the city, he allowed the tears to roll freely down his face, although in his disguise he couldn't feel them.

Several strong cups of black coffee later, it was still only seven a.m. and way too early to go to the office. Saffron was an early starter, and that was enough for him to stay away until he felt stronger.

The moment Henri Bendels opened their doors, Hugo went in and purchased several items for Berry's birthday. He chose a red and gray fine silk scarf that would be from Sylvia Rasnic and a small bottle of Chanel Cristal from himself. He instructed the sales girls to gift wrap them before leaving the store.

It was almost eight o'clock when Hugo passed the flower stand outside the Fraser building. He chose two large bouquets of flowers. The biggest and brightest bunch was for Berry and the other supposedly for his wife, although it was actually part of his backup plan to get into Saffron's office. As he entered the office, he could hear Saffron's voice from her open door down the hall. Hugo noticed he was not the only one who could hear her.

"… I have already told you, Potter will train him; they can travel together until he knows the ropes. It's an advantage that he isn't too bright. I told you already…" Just then, she looked up from her desk and saw several early arrivals listening to her call, so she quickly moved toward the door and slammed it loudly.

That morning he was not the first to arrive, but no one saw him as he walked quietly down the hallway to his office. He quickly unlocked the door, placed his briefcase beside his desk and hid his purchases. Berry knew they were going out for lunch to celebrate her birthday, and even though she didn't show it, she had blushed deeply when he asked her to make the booking. Alastair had been asked more than once to have the end-of-month investors' reports on Saffron's desk first thing Friday morning, and he had repeatedly told her he would have them for her first thing Monday morning. He needed time to complete them, and recheck the figures before the report went into print. He preferred to do this at his leisure and with Al's help during the weekend. It had been the source of many ongoing arguments; Saffron said she liked to take them home so she could check them over the weekend herself. Alastair knew the reason she liked to have the numbers before the weekend; it was so the information could be passed on to her cohorts in Europe.

"Good morning, Mr. Rasnic," Berry said, putting her head around the door, before leaving to get his morning coffee from the kitchen. As she walked back into his office, he presented her with the bouquet of flowers.

"A very happy birthday to you, Berry," he said as she took the flowers. He was rewarded with her blushing deeply.

"Oh, Mr. Rasnic, I do declare you spoil me. Thank you, they're quite beautiful," she said, smelling the blooms.

"Well, Berry, I must say you do look attractive today," Alastair commented, looking at his usually drab secretary, who had carefully dressed herself in a smart charcoal gray suit and a red and blue blouse. The colors were very unlike Berry, and she had even done her hair with extra care. Her red heels were certainly higher than usual, and Alastair's nose told him she had used a little more perfume as well.

"Thank you, Mr. Rasnic. I haven't worn this for a while, so I thought it needed an airing," Berry said, turning to leave.

"Well, Berry, I suggest you remove the price tag from your new blouse then...," Alastair said, laughing, as she quickly fished around her neck to find the offending tag. Alastair couldn't see her, but he knew her cheeks would be bright red with embarrassment. Just then, Neve walked down the hallway on her way to her desk. As she walked past, she tried to give him a wink, but Berry stood outside his door glaring menacingly at her until she passed. Alastair felt he hadn't seen nearly enough of his baby girl and he missed her.

The morning flew by and before Alastair knew it, he was sitting in a small, cozy Italian restaurant opposite Berry.

"Happy birthday to you again, Berry. You're the best secretary a man could have."

"Oh really, Mr. Rasnic, you're much too kind," Berry said, tearing the paper from the two gifts he presented her with, and for the first time giving him a genuine smile. Alastair briefly got a glimpse of a very sad, lonely old lady who had somehow learned to hate the world.

"They're not both from me; one is from Sylvia, Berry."

"So, I see, Mr. Rasnic. What a charming card. I can't believe she remembered my birthday; you're a kind and considerate couple. May I borrow your cell phone? I must thank her immediately – the scarf is beautiful."

Hugo hadn't thought she would want to talk to Sylvia, so he needed to think fast. Instead, he put the call through to his home answering machine and handed it to Berry after the message had finished. She quickly left her thanks and never knew it wasn't Sylvia's phone. Hugo lingered over lunch. Between them, they managed to drink a bottle of rather expensive merlot. Considering Berry supposedly didn't drink, Alastair thought it was a gallant effort.

They arrived back at the office at three thirty p.m. Berry was completely shocked when she realized the time; however, she was drunk enough to say, giggling, that she should be allowed the occasional absence. Then she linked arms with Alastair and continued, "Anyway, I'm with my handsome boss, so how could it matter?"

However, the moment he entered his office he knew it mattered very much indeed. Sitting at his desk, tapping her long red nails on the wood, was none other than Saffron Moffit. Berry quickly sprang into secretarial mode and tried to defend her beloved boss.

"I don't recall you having an appointment, Ms. Moffit," Berry challenged, her words cold, her face tight.

"I don't recall needing one, Mrs. Pye. Now get out and leave us alone."

"I will not. I am responsible for every hour of Mr. Rasnic's day and you definitely weren't on his calendar."

Alastair couldn't believe Berry was standing her ground. He thought it courageous but foolish, considering just who she was dealing with.

"Berry, it's all right, thank you!"

"It's not all right. I take my job working for Mr. Rasnic very seriously, and all appointments must go through me," Berry responded, as red, blotchy circles appeared on her cheeks and her small eyes blazed.

"Get the hell out, you stupid old woman, and shut the door after you!" Saffron yelled, as Alastair saw several people farther down the hall leave their desks and walk towards his office once they heard the raised voices.

"I will go only when Mr. Rasnic tells me to and not before."

"You both work for me, and if either of you want a job next week, I suggest you leave now," she screamed as Berry glared at her from the doorway. A few seconds later, Saffron decided to forget Berry and focus her anger directly on Alastair.

"You went to lunch without leaving the reports on my desk. They were due this morning, as I instructed, you annoying little Jew!" she screeched.

Alastair kept his calm as he replied. "I have told you several times, Saffron, that you shall have them as you always do, first thing Monday morning," Alastair said calmly, smiling.

"Monday morning does not work for me!" she screamed, standing to her full five feet three-inch height, her cheeks red, her eyes cold as cracked ice and her words clipped.

"Well, Monday morning suits me; as it always has. If you'll kindly leave me now, I may manage to have them for you tonight," Alastair said, trying hard to remain cool.

"You unorganized little creep; do you know who you're talking to? I expect respect!" Saffron yelled as she darted to Berry's desk and grabbed the huge vase of flowers sitting there. Quickly, she hurled it across the room. Alastair ducked as it smashed heavily into the huge glass picture window behind him. For several seconds all was quiet, until they heard the loud cracking noise made by the enormous piece of tempered glass. Berry screamed at Saffron as she grabbed her hair, pulling her to the ground. Saffron hit Berry hard in the face, knocking her off balance. She fell backward into her desk with a crash, blood pouring from a large cut on her forehead as she lay where she fell.

Everyone crowded around. Alastair hurled Saffron to her feet and Brock appeared out of nowhere and lifted Berry off the floor. Saffron kicked and screamed all the way down the hall as Ross Moss held one arm and Alastair the other. It didn't take long before first the security officers arrived, followed shortly afterwards by the paramedics. Alastair instructed them to keep Saffron in her office. She was still screaming and yelling obscenities as Ross Moss held her arms behind her back and tried without success to put her into her chair. Alastair was concerned about Berry – her injuries had not been in his game plan, and he'd never expected such loyalty from her. He felt pride and guilt at the same time with her actions. He felt secretly relieved Al was no longer listening and watching.

Berry had her head bandaged; her clothes were covered in blood, as were her surroundings. As Alastair arrived back at his office, she was being taken away on a stretcher, although they said they probably wouldn't hold her in the hospital. Alastair walked beside the stretcher as they carried her toward the escalator. He apologized several times, but she kept saying there was no need and even smiled at him. He kissed her gently on the cheek as they entered the elevator. Berry blushed, smiled up at him and then she was gone. Alastair felt a deep sadness as he knew he would never see her again. Everyone was milling around when he returned. His plan had gone exactly as he'd thought it would, with the exception of Berry. Her desk looked like a disaster area, and all he could think to do was find a vase and a small area to place it. He then got the second bouquet of flowers and placed it in the vase with a note that wished her a speedy recovery and said again how sorry he was.

Alastair removed his company credit cards, his car keys and the office key and walked slowly into Brock Burke's office. Brock was sitting behind his desk with his head in his hands.

"Brock, I'm sorry about..." He didn't get time to finish his words. As Brock finished wiping Berry's blood from his hands, he interrupted Alastair.

"Alastair, no... I'm sorry. She has been getting more and more out of control. I have chosen to ignore it because I really didn't know what to do about her. I also hate confrontation with a woman, and Saffron can be a little spitfire at best. Are you hurt, Alastair?" Brock asked, genuinely concerned.

"No, Brock, no damage done, other than my male ego."

"Again, I can only apologize..." Brock stopped short as he saw the items Alastair laid on his desk. Alastair got to his feet as he held out his hand to Brock.

"What's this? What are you doing?"

"Leaving. I've had enough drama. Sorry, Brock, I've enjoyed working for your company and, you've been great," Alastair said as he took Brock's hand and shook it several times, before turning and leaving the room. Brock said nothing until Alastair was out of his office. He walked down the hallway toward Saffron's office. It was the same as when he had started at Banker's Securities: the NYPD were already arriving. Saffron sat quietly in her chair with a security guard on either side. She briefly looked up at Alastair as he entered.

"Are you going to press charges, sir?" one of the security guards asked as a uniform entered the room, also eager to hear Alastair's answer. Alastair shook his head as he asked for a moment alone with Saffron.

The moment they were alone, Alastair stood in front of her desk with one hand on the corner. He carefully removed the soft gummy stuff that had acted as a high-powered microphone, before he very quietly said, "Saffron, if you ever so much as touch a hair on Mrs. Berry Pye's head or say a cross word to her again, your many illicit activities will be made very public. You wouldn't want to end up like Brock's deceased secretary, now would you?" His voice was low and cool. She looked up at him with surprise and hatred in her eyes as she listened to his threats. He could tell she was barely hearing what he said, so he continued.

"Don't ever think of firing her. I also suggest you take my words seriously, because if you don't, there will be more than just your drug-trafficking friends wanting your head." He stood and looked at her for several more minutes, never blinking or taking his eyes from hers. Slowly, he saw the realization of his words sink in. Alastair was aware that she probably had listening devices still in her office, but he really didn't care. He was, after all, about to disappear.

Then he turned without saying another word. He held the door open for the security guards to re-enter. Without speaking to anyone, he walked down the hallway. He didn't respond to Brock as he called his name. He took nothing from his office, but carefully retrieved his briefcase from beside his desk – for the last time. At the end of the hallway, Neve was exiting the elevator. He discreetly winked at her. Before entering the second elevator, Alastair allowed Special Agent Bow Grismold to pass. He was about to speak to Alastair when one of the uniforms called his name. Moments later, the elevator doors softly closed.

Once in the lobby, he walked past the doorman, greeting him happily, and then out into the late afternoon New York sun. He took several deep breaths before swiftly walking the seven blocks to his apartment. Slowly, a small smile played on his lips. Yes, that had gone very well, very well indeed!

Instant Lover

Neve knew her parents were disappointed she wasn't leaving Banker's Securities, Inc. at the same time they were. She knew that by staying, she was changing the way they always worked. Neve had been spending all her free time with Siobhan; she was proving to be like the sister she never had. They enjoyed each other's company so much. They liked doing the same things, their sense of humor was very similar and they often knew what the other was thinking before it was said. Neve knew Siobhan was good for her; she felt like she was developing into a well-balanced and mature woman from her experiences with the older, worldly, Siobhan. Siobhan had often told her how she felt more confident and self-assured knowing she had someone watching her back, someone she could tell anything to and trust. The friendship was working well, and Neve wasn't about to let it go. Sure, she had school friends and girlfriends back home in Savannah, but never anything like the close bond she felt with Siobhan. It was like they had known one another forever. Siobhan felt she was strong in the areas Neve was not, and Siobhan also thought Neve strengthened her weaknesses. Both ladies were young, gorgeous, and strong individuals, but together they felt they could conquer anything.

Lately, Neve was thinking of revealing to Siobhan her true identity, but she must first discuss it with her parents. Neve knew this was one of the many things they dreaded about her being in disguise. Neve was getting to hate wearing her disguise every day and wanted to live a life without lies. The thought of telling Siobhan began niggling at her every time she was alone. But some-how she still had reservations about coming clean. So, she held back; after all, it was from Brock's company that the Grasshoppers had just taken fifteen million dollars, and Siobhan was a major shareholder.

Contrary to what her father thought of Saffron, Neve quite enjoyed working for her. Saffron was a hard, mean, cruel woman. As a boss she was precise, meticulous and expected everything done to perfection and on time. Even while helping Brock's new and hopelessly incompetent secretary with her work, Neve easily filled her role and met Saffron's requirements. She seldom spoke to Saffron for more than a few minutes each morning, but knew exactly what was expected of her. Once Saffron knew she was capable of being an efficient secretary, they seemed to achieve a healthy respect for one another and shared a comfortable working relationship. Saffron would often ask Amanda to spend the afternoon in her favorite designer stores. They were the same size, so she would instruct Amanda on what clothes she liked, and when Amanda found them, she would call her before making the purchase. Saffron was usually very pleased with her choices, and, so far, Amanda had only needed to return one outfit. Saffron was generous with her credit and often told Amanda to purchase for herself whatever she wanted. Amanda had taken her up on her offer several times, just to see her boss's reaction, but there had been none. It was during her shopping excursions that she often met Siobhan for lunch. They used Saffron's credit card and enjoyed a long lunch in some of the finest restaurants New York had to offer. Siobhan was educating Amanda on fine wines, and Amanda proved a fast learner.

Amanda was away on one of these lunches when Hugo exited the company. She knew it was to happen, but she was surprised to see Saffron's office crawling with police as she passed her dad in the hallway on her return to her desk.

"Amanda, call my lawyer and then Potter. When you have spoken to them both, you may leave for the day," Saffron instructed from where she was being detained behind her large semi-circular glass desk. Amanda was surprised to see her looking so disheveled. She didn't inquire as to what had happened, but merely did as she was asked, before collecting her coat and bag and exiting the 7th floor of Banker's Securities, Inc. The office was abuzz with whispers as she walked down the hallway, into the elevator and out of the Fraser building. The moment she was outside, she called Hugo.

"Dad, did everything go according to plan?"

"Baby Girl, absolutely it did; only a few very minor hitches, but when one is dealing with a bitch like your boss, it is to be expected."

"Anything I should be worrying about, Dad?" Neve asked in her usual happy voice.

"Nothing, Baby Girl. Everything went to plan. You fixed your part, I assume," Hugo asked, referring to Neve's removal of the wires and cameras.

"It all went according to plan, Dad."

"Let's meet for dinner, Honey. Can you? As Neve and Hugo…," he asked, and the thought of being themselves appealed to Neve more than she could say. Hugo knew a quiet café on the outskirts of Manhattan. Al had found it for him just in case. And quickly it was arranged. Neve wasn't seeing Siobhan tonight, and for the first time she didn't know what the older girl was doing or why they weren't meeting up. Neve felt sure she would call. Siobhan had been rather upset at lunch, as she was now completely sure Brock was having another affair with his new secretary. Neve had watched her try to sound strong and pretend she didn't care, but Neve already understood her friend too well. Finally, Neve had to admit to her friend that she knew her suspicions were right. She felt just awful telling her what she knew. They had promised to always tell each other the truth.

Neve knew she was living a lie being Amanda, and she didn't want to keep any further secrets from her friend. Siobhan had sobbed as she listened to what Amanda had heard. For the hundredth time, she said she intended to leave Brock, but then several minutes later she told Neve how she still loved her husband in spite of the way he treated her. Neve knew Siobhan was partly serious, as she often discussed becoming roommates. Neve didn't encourage sharing her apartment with Siobhan. This was another of her secrets she must keep from her friend.

Neve was enjoying the sunshine and window shopping as she strolled towards her apartment. She had several shopping bags that displayed designer logos, but this time she had made the purchases herself.

The long afternoon shadows rolled across the street as Neve decided to cross to the other side so she could continue walking in the sunshine. She was thinking of dinner with her dad and deciding what to wear. She then began thinking of Siobhan and hoped she was okay; things had been very rough between her and Brock lately and she hated seeing her friend so tormented. How things had changed in Siobhan's life in the past three months. Amanda had become very aware of just how life could change in a heartbeat and felt very thankful for everything she had.

She walked past a small café; it was long and narrow, with tables and chairs down one side. It was small, dimly lit and intimate; Neve had never noticed it before, even though she often walked this way. It was the flash of red that caught her eye. Neve stopped and looked more closely into the gloom of the interior. Siobhan had been wearing a slinky black outfit for lunch and a bright red silk scarf around her throat. Just then, a flash of red drew Neve's eye past several tables inside the front window. Neve cupped her hand to shut out the sunshine so she could look deeper inside the café.

She instantly recognized Siobhan's blonde hair. Quickly, Neve opened the glass door and moved inside. Siobhan looked up as she approached. Was it annoyance or guilt that registered on her face as she saw her friend? Seconds later, she concealed what she was feeling and her usual huge smile filled her face as she got to her feet, before giving Neve a warm, welcoming hug.

It was then Neve became aware that Siobhan was not alone. Sitting with his back to her was a man. As he turned towards her, their eyes met. He stared intently into her eyes and for several seconds their gaze locked. Her world stood still. Their worlds had collided. Then she became aware of Siobhan's faraway voice saying, "... and Chuck Hollingsworth is my P.I. I don't need to tell you why I have hired him..."

Amanda seemed unable to take her eyes from this devastatingly good-looking man in front of her. He was still holding her hand and looking down at her as he stood just inches away. Amanda was so aware of his closeness, she couldn't take her hand from his or look away. She vaguely knew Siobhan was still speaking.

"… as we are nearly done. Amanda, can you join us, if you have time for another coffee, Chuck…?"

"Yes… oh yes, Mrs. Burke. Amanda, you said…?" he replied, still unable to remove his hand as Siobhan continued.

"… so can you bring another chair, Chuck? That one over there will do." Siobhan realized no one was listening. She wondered what was happening as she looked from Amanda's face to Chuck's and then back again.

"Yes, oh yes. I am pleased to meet you also…," Chuck said in a whisper as he finally took his hand from hers. Amanda felt a deep feeling of loss as he removed his hand, but was not sure why. Somehow, it seemed to break the spell and he fetched her chair, placing it very close to his own. More coffee arrived as Siobhan continued talking.

"I very nearly hired Chuck before and then cancelled. But I know I really should have. He is supposed to be the best, after all."

"Yes, yes, I am the best, Mrs. Burke," Chuck replied, never taking his eyes from Amanda. Neither Chuck nor Amanda listened to Siobhan, and ten minutes later she left. She felt perplexed and confused by both Amanda's behavior and also the change in Chuck's behavior at meeting her friend. The last thing on her mind was romance, and Siobhan felt romance was strongly in the air. Siobhan hugged Amanda and told her to call her soon, and left. As she walked out of the café, she turned and stared for several minutes at the couple sitting closely at the small table, until another customer tried to move past her. Siobhan couldn't believe what was happening, although she had always thought Chuck very attractive, sexy and ruggedly handsome in a down-to-earth kind of way. Had things been different when they'd met, she may just have been interested in him herself. Chuck couldn't be more different from Brock.

Amanda sat looking at this stranger. She was very aware of his nearness and how very handsome he was. She was drawn to his magnetism and strong sexual energy. She felt oddly alive, like he'd woken her from a dream. In fact, until this very minute she felt like she'd been asleep her whole life. The chemistry between them was undeniable. Amanda was ashamed of her feelings of lust for a stranger. All she wanted to do was rip his clothes from his body and get as close to his nakedness as she could. She blushed deeply at her fantasy, as he said, "A penny for your thoughts, although I know they must be worth millions."

"No, not even a penny. I think they are thoughts I shouldn't be thinking."

"I've had the same thoughts for the last however long it is since you walked into my life," Chuck said, laughing partly from embarrassment. Amanda knew somehow that he must be thinking the same as her.

"You are the most extraordinary, beautiful, enchanting creature I have ever seen. It feels like I've known you forever. You must be that special something that's missing in my life," he said, feeling very foolish at his own words, but meaning them anyway. However, Amanda understood him completely.

"You're right, I feel the same way, but I don't understand these feelings at all…"

"I can't begin to understand mine either. You have totally enchanted me," he whispered, moving closer now.

"I think you have put a spell on me with your good looks and charisma," Amanda responded, moving still closer.

"Oh my. Where's Mrs. Burke? Why, I thought we were having coffee…," he said without thinking?

"I know. I know you were. She must have gone…"

"Oh yeah, I guess she must have…," Chuck said as his lips lightly brushed hers. It was the merest whisper of a kiss, like stardust from heaven. You could barely see it or feel it, but you sure knew it was there! The second their lips touched, they drew quickly apart. They both felt it. They felt it immediately and together; it was like a luscious electric shock. It took only minutes before they needed to try again. This time it lasted longer. It began as a soft butterfly kiss and quickly changed to hungry passion, then lust, then longing, until it finally became an all-consuming, burning desire. Everyone in the small café stopped to look. It seemed like their worlds had stopped turning when finally, they drew slightly apart. Opening her eyes, Amanda looked deeply into Chuck's blue ones. What had just happened? Was it some kind of magic? Had there been something in the coffee? Neither of them knew! It took some time for them to come back to Earth, and Amanda was the first to speak, although she didn't have a clue where the words came from or why she spoke them.

"Truly, madly, deeply…," she whispered, surprising herself, as again she began kissing him longer and deeper than before. Some minutes passed before they finally drew apart. Chuck's voice was little more than a raspy whisper when he spoke, also astounding himself with his words.

"You must marry me! Will you…?" he asked, before again kissing her.

Amanda's cell phone had been ringing for several minutes before she actually heard it and answered it. She was tingling all over and could barely speak.

"Hello," she said quietly.

"Baby Girl, I've just ordered you a martini; it's no fun drinking on my own. Just how long will you be?" Hugo asked.

It took Neve several seconds to realize it was her dad and that she was supposed to be dining with him; but finally she said, "Dad, I won't be having dinner with you tonight. Can I call you later?"

"But, Honey, why ever not? Are you all right?"

"Oh yes, Dad. I'm more than all right!"

"Baby Girl, talk to me. What's going on? Are you with someone?" Hugo asked, a little concerned, but more confused.

"Yes, Dad, I'm sitting here with the man I'm going to marry. Love you, Dad. I'll call you later," Neve said and closed her phone. The whole time she was talking they hadn't broken eye contact.

They sat for a very long time, closely staring at each other, until, finally, Chuck said, "I think I love you, …"

Loot Honor Whimsy-Sparrow

"Saffron, I'm not doing it," Potter yelled, his temper beginning to boil over and match that of his wife's.

"You will. It is not open for discussion."

"The hell it's not. Do you think I do everything you say?" Potter challenged.

"You do what's best for this family, and I know what's best!" Saffron screamed, her cheeks blazing.

"What's best for the family? Don't even go there."

"And just what is that supposed to mean?"

"Don't go there, Saffron. I mean it," Potter yelled, until his voice suddenly dropped to a whisper, and for the first time Saffron stopped and actually looked at her husband. But only for a moment, then she continued.

"All right, I won't. This is his address. He's a very short old man. His name is Gus and you are to pick him up at seven a.m. Monday morning on your way to the airport. His phone may be disconnected, so don't let him or me down," she ranted.

"Saffron, I work alone or not at all."

"You work for me. Don't you think it's a little late to get all self-righteous on me!" she screamed, her Brooklyn accent no longer hidden.

Potter had had enough; he didn't want this to continue. He couldn't believe she was springing this on him now. He had planned for this to be his last trip. He had transferred several million to his bank account in London under his Aunt Adele's name. Last week, Aunt Adele and Loot viewed the perfect house for him. He had seen it on the webcam and together they'd put in an offer that was quickly accepted. Potter decided to put it in both Loot and Aunt Adele's names, leaving his name off the contract at this stage.

He spoke to Loot several times a day. They missed each other terribly. She had just put her small flat on the market and would immediately start moving into their new home once the sale was complete. Aunt Adele told Potter she was a wonderful girl and everything Saffron wasn't. When they were first married, Aunt Adele would travel to New York and stay for a few weeks so she could help Potter with his young son. However, Aunt Adele soon tired of Saffron's moods and tantrums. Her visits had become less and less frequent, until finally they ceased altogether. She was again looking forward to having family close. Loot and Aunt Adele quickly became firm friends and had begun planning the wedding. Neither of them spoke of the divorce. They both understood it must happen first, but they preferred to focus only on the happy things.

It was Thursday evening when Potter's cell rang. He was surprised to see a New York number that he didn't recognize. Still getting himself together from his fight with Saffron, he wasn't ready to hear the voice on the other end of the phone.

"Oh, Potter darling, I wanted to surprise you, but…" It was Loot, and Potter had never heard her so distressed.

"Are you all right? Where are you?" he asked, his heart racing.

"I'm in New York. I was going to surprise you, but I also came here for another reason, and …" She couldn't continue as she started sobbing.

"Where are you?" he asked again, also distraught now. Through the sobs, she gave him her hotel and room number. Potter grabbed his keys and in less than thirty minutes he was knocking on her door. The moment he was inside, she crumbled into his arms, sobbing uncontrollably. As he held her close and tried to calm her, he looked over her shoulder and saw scattered on the bed many newspaper cuttings and legal papers. Potter had no idea what was going on.

"Loot, darling, please tell me what has happened?"

"Oh, Potter, I really don't think I can," she said as they moved toward the bed and pushed the papers to make a space in which to sit her down. As he did, he noticed an old yellowed newspaper cutting. He grabbed it before looking more closely, although he didn't need to; he already knew by heart everything the cutting said. He stared at the old yellowed black and white photo. Staring back at him was the face of his little three-year-old sister. Several of the newspaper cuttings were about her abduction. Potter didn't understand.

"Loot, darling, whatever is going on? Why do you have cuttings of my sister? Are you this upset because I hadn't told you? I'm sorry; I wasn't hiding anything, I just…"

"No, darling, no, I'm not upset at you at all," Loot said, pulling herself together slightly as she grabbed the cuttings and placed them back in the brown folder that lay open on the bed.

"Loot, there isn't anything that should make you this upset. Now just start at the beginning. Please, Loot, look at me. I'm in this for the long haul; we are forever, darling." At his words, another flood of tears began, and Potter held her close until the sobbing subsided. He had no idea what the matter was.

"Well," she began, feeling a little stronger now. Then her sobbing increased and she added, "Oh, Potter, I just can't. I'm not even sure."

"Sure, of what, darling?" he asked, feeling very confused.

"I'm not sure of several things," Loot said, sobbing again.

"I'm not going anywhere, so take your time. I'm a good listener, but I would really like to know why you have a file on my sister?"

"Potter, don't you see? That's where I've heard the name before. The name Moffit. Remember when you introduced yourself in the café in Paris?" she said, looking at him intently.

"Of course I do. What about it?"

"I'm still not a hundred percent sure."

"It's all right."

"One thing I'm sure about is that I'm pregnant!" she said in a soft whisper. Potter didn't say anything, he couldn't. He hadn't been expecting it. It was so out of the blue, he was stunned. He continued looking at her. Her face was so close to his, he could feel the heat from her tears. Suddenly, he realized he wasn't giving her the response she required, so he quickly drew her into his arms and held her tightly as she sobbed again. Potter knew there was no one else he would rather have a baby with than Loot, and he knew he was going to be overjoyed once he had time to think about it. He still didn't know just why she was so upset. Was she opposed to babies and children?

"Loot, don't you like babies? I know we have never really spoken about it. I thought you were on the pill or something. It doesn't matter, darling, we'll make great parents. I'll just have to get my divorce through a little sooner. Please stop crying. It will be fine, I promise you, sweetheart, you'll see." He comforted her, holding her close as her body shook.

"That's not all," she whispered.

"It's okay, you can tell me the rest later."

"I'll tell you now. I must, or I won't, and I'm not really sure…," she said, as Potter listened. He had no idea what she was talking about, but as she continued on he was not prepared to hear what she was about to tell him.

"Potter, when I was packing I found a letter tucked away down the bottom of a box. I think my parents were working with a guy from the FBI or something. His name was Sheffield Hollingsworth. Anyway, the moment I arrived in New York, I went straight to the office of his son, Chuck Hollingsworth, because his father, Sheffield, is now deceased. Well, his son presented me with this old file. It seems Sheffield Hollingsworth kept everything, every file, every letter and every note. I believe my parents think I'm the child that was kidnapped all those years ago. I think maybe I'm your sister… the one who was kidnapped!" Loot said, falling into his arms and sobbing loudly again. He held her shaking body close to his. Potter couldn't believe what she had just said; at that moment he prayed she was wrong.

He stayed with her until late that night, although for the first time they didn't make love. He lay beside her, holding her in his arms until she fell asleep, and then he continued to stare into the darkness. By that time it was almost three a.m. He tucked her into bed and gently kissed her as she slept. All was quiet when he arrived home. Saffron was leaving in the morning for a business trip, so he could spend the whole weekend with Loot. He was thinking of introducing her to Cox, but so much had changed, he wasn't sure any more. He wasn't sure about so much at the moment.

They enjoyed a wonderful weekend, and Potter even sneaked her into his home and showed her around. He knew Cox was not home, so he felt it was safe. He showed her all the photos of his family, and she commented several times on what a handsome boy Cox was. She said she couldn't wait to meet him. Potter could easily arrange it, but something held him back. Neither of them spoke about the previous evening, but concentrated instead on enjoying each other and the sights of New York. It was late that evening when they headed back to her hotel. On the way, she stopped to purchase a pregnancy test kit. Potter felt very nervous – he didn't know what result he was hoping for. Loot said it was the third kit she had purchased in the last ten days, and again it showed positive. The weekend flew by; they laughed and made love and went for walks. Somehow, when he was with her everything seemed brighter and more perfect than ever before.

Potter bought her flowers and perfume and then took her to Tavern on the Green. After the main course was finished, he got down on one knee and presented her with a three-carat single diamond ring. As she accepted and cried, neither of them was aware they had an audience due to the many mirrors around the room. As he put the ring on her finger, everyone clapped, and the happy couple responded with a long, passionate kiss as a cheer rose around the room. Potter knew the restaurant had just filed for bankruptcy, but he could not think of another place magical enough for his proposal to Loot. The night couldn't have been more perfect. Together they called Aunt Adele and told her the news; it felt great being able to discuss their future together with someone. As Sunday drew to a close and Loot prepared to fly out, they talked of more serious things. Potter assured her he would handle everything and look further into the matter of her birth. He knew Loot was growing more suspicious each time he went to Europe, but at this stage he didn't want to tell her the truth and place her in any kind of danger. She was much too special.

It was late when Potter arrived home and began packing for his departure early the next morning. He noticed several messages from Saffron, and for the first time he chose to ignore them – why ruin a wonderful weekend? He had written the note he intended to leave for

Saffron several times during the last month. Now he placed it downstairs on the hall table in a small white envelope with her name on the front. He placed it on top of the large yellow envelope that held the divorce papers he hoped she would sign. He then took a single rose from the display on the dining room table and placed it on top of the envelopes. He'd often done that when they were first married, and he knew she liked it. He realized the rose would possibly wilt in the next twenty-four hours, but he didn't care.

By the time Potter had everything ready and had left a text message for Cox saying he was finally going through with his plan, the sun was beginning its ascent. Potter left several loving messages for Loot on her cell, so, as always, they would be waiting for her when she landed. Finally, he fell into bed, exhausted. He hadn't thought he would get emotional as he was about to finally leave, but he couldn't help thinking of all the nights they'd slept side by side. The times they'd made love and the many times they hadn't. He could hear every one of her excuses running through his head: too tired, sore back, sore feet, headache, not in the mood, were just a few.

He clearly remembered the hundreds of times he'd rubbed her back, her shoulders, or her feet, and all he got in return was the sound of her voice yelling at him. Her voice was loud and threatening, telling him that she was still not happy with life, with work, with him. When had he allowed her to become such a bitch? Why had it happened? He didn't know the answers, and as he thought of his future with Loot, he didn't care. He was still in shock at the thought of her being his sister, and he quietly prayed she wasn't. How could God be so unkind? Then he thought of all their options, and there were some, but Potter knew that whatever they decided it would surely kill his parents if they found out.

It was coming up to five thirty a.m. when Potter had a quick shower before putting on clean clothes. He had placed several large boxes by the front door for Cox to send to Aunt Adele before Saffron arrived home on Tuesday night. He knew he could count on his son. Quietly, he crept in to Cox's room and gently called his name until he stirred and opened his eyes.

"Yo, Dad. You leaving?"

"Yes, son. I wish you were coming, too."

"Hey, Dad, you know I'll soon follow. I don't want to be here either, but you know I have to finish the school year before I transfer."

"I'll miss you, son, and worry about you every day."

"Hey, Dad, come on, I'll be fine. Just send me a text when you're safely in the UK."

"Okay, son. No need to worry about your old man. I'm just going on another trip, that's all," Potter replied, looking hard at his son and wondering, not for the first time, if he knew why he went away every month.

"Dad, it's okay, I understand. I promise I'll join you for Christmas, if not before." Cox got out of bed and hugged his dad tightly for several long minutes. They both had tears in their eyes, but neither wanted the other to know.

"My boxes are by the front door; be sure not to leave a paper trail."

"Dad, stop worrying. Have I ever let you down?" Cox said, getting back into bed, even though he was wide awake now.

"No, son, never. Love you, Cox…," Potter said as he walked down the stairs. He threw his carryall over his shoulder and picked up his two large suitcases. He placed his keys on the table by the rose and the handwritten letter to Saffron and closed the front door for the last time. As he walked toward the waiting cab, Cox called down to him from his bedroom window.

"Yo, Dad, love you, too; travel safe!"

Potter waved briefly and the cab drove off. Without turning around, he knew instinctively Cox was crying. He also knew his son would be watching until the cab turned out of sight.

"Is it to the airport like, bud?" the cabby asked him.

"Yeah, just one stop first – here's the address," Potter said, handing the cabby the address Saffron had written for him.

"Sorry, dude, I don't go to those areas; I'm a respectable cabby, like. I got a wife and kids, ya know," he said as Potter listened, shocked. He couldn't remember ever being in a cab that wouldn't take him to where he wanted to go.

"I just gotta pick up another guy, then we're off to the airport."

"I can't imagine what sort of guy ya going to pick up from that address. You been there before?"

"No," Potter replied, and then, as an afterthought, he added, "There's a hundred-dollar bill for you if you'll take me to that address."

"No, sir, not for a thousand dollars. I got a wife and kids at home who depend on me. I'd like to think they like me alive, too."

"Well, I have to pick him up and he doesn't have a phone…"

"Okay, bud, I'll tell you what I'll do then, but this is strictly between you and me, like. You look like a nice guy, live in a real nice neighborhood, too."

"Yeah, okay, what can you do?" Potter asked, beginning to get annoyed at Saffron for putting him in yet another difficult situation.

"Well, you tip me five hundred dollars and I'll park around the block, so long as no one approaches me, like. I'll wait for you for, like, fifteen minutes, then I'm outta there. I wouldn't want the word to get out, like. I wouldn't want to get noticed in that kinda neighborhood."

"Yeah, okay; you drive a hard bargain," Potter said, hoping he would have enough cash to give to Gus so he could make it back to the USA. Potter decided to make another stop at the bank.

"I need the cash up front, like now. I still expect you to pay the normal fare when I drop you at the airport, like," the cabby said, counting the money in one hand that Potter handed to him as he held the steering wheel loosely with the other. They said no more as Potter watched the scenery change from upper class suburbia to middle class and then, as they continued on, he witnessed the despair of the filthy slums. Potter had never seen anything like the fallen-down dwellings and broken faces as they passed. Soon, the surroundings became even worse, and Potter felt glad he was in the safety of the cab. By the time the cab pulled to a stop, Potter was feeling decidedly uncomfortable and an involuntary shiver rippled over his skin.

"Here ya go then, bud. Just walk around that corner and the second block should be the building you wanting. It's only three stories high, like, so it shouldn't take you too long. I'll wait for you, like, for fifteen minutes. Watch your bags; I will also," the cabby said, laughing as he got out a cigarette and lit it. Potter was not feeling at all comfortable as he carefully looked around before quickly getting out of the cab. He ran the two blocks to the apartment building. At first, he thought it must be condemned, as many of the windows on the bottom floor were boarded up, while the ones that still had glass were covered with bars. He found what he thought must be the entrance. Pulling it open and looking into the gloom, Potter almost threw up as the smell of stale urine and booze hit him hard. The hallway was filthy with old cans, bottles, hypodermic syringes and rotting garbage everywhere. Potter knew he wouldn't find an elevator, so the moment he saw the stairs he ran up them, hoping the air might be a little cleaner on the next level. It wasn't, and Potter had to swallow hard to stop himself from vomiting. Most of the doors didn't have numbers or only part of them remained; Potter thought it was hopeless as he searched each door in the gloom for the one he was looking for.

The only door with a complete number was the one he sought, and he quickly knocked.

"Yeah, who's there?"

"It's Potter… I'm looking for Gus Boozeman," Potter called. The next minute the door opened a crack and then a little more.

"Come in, I'm Gus."

Potter stared down in disbelief at the short man with long, greasy, grayish-red hair, broad shoulders, thin lips and chipped yellow teeth. The room stank and badly needed cleaning. It was small and dark, with the exception of a small, clean, two-door purple refrigerator which looked totally out of place. Potter desperately wanted to get out of this room, this apartment block and this neighborhood and never return.

"Me Pa's in the hospital," Gus said, grabbing an old used garbage bag.

"You ready? I've got a cab waiting," Potter said, eyeing the little man and wondering just what he was going to do with him. He knew he couldn't possibly take him into first class like this.

"You get a cab to come here?" Gus asked, obviously impressed, as he let out a low whistle. Potter nodded as the little guy continued.

"That must have cost ya big bucks," he said, grinning a half smile that showed his chipped, yellowed teeth. Potter knew those teeth had never seen a toothbrush.

"Where's your luggage?" Potter asked.

"Right here, you're lookin' at it – nearly all I own," Gus said, holding up a used garbage bag.

"Well, just leave it. I'll get you new stuff. Now let's go," Potter said, swallowing hard as another wave of nausea hit him.

"But I can't just leave…," Gus began, as Potter cut him off.

"I'm leaving; you can follow or not, but leave the garbage bag here. I'll take you shopping, we've got time. Now, you coming or not?" Potter asked. He was trying to hold down the nausea that was threatening to embarrass him. Potter pulled on the door as he tried to open it – he was not having much luck.

"Yeah, okay. You gotta push the bottom and pull the top; it's a tricky door, that one," Gus said, amused at the other man's discomfort.

Potter almost ran out of the building, and Gus literally ran to keep up. Potter paused briefly when he hit the fresh air and took several gulps, before hurrying towards the cab that he hoped would be waiting. As he turned the corner, he saw the driver about to pull away from the curb. He yelled and waved his hands and the cab stopped.

"Hey, bud, ya cut it a bit close, like. I was just leaving; your fifteen minutes were, like, more than up," the cabby said as he gunned the motor and headed out. Thirty minutes later they were en route to the airport and Potter instructed the driver to stop at the large shopping mall at the east end of the airport. Potter had to put down the window to enjoy the fresh air as Gus didn't smell too good up close.

Once inside Sears, Potter instructed the salesman to fit Gus with two pairs of new jeans, casual pants, a sports jacket, a casual jacket, several pairs of socks, shoes and briefs, a sweater and several t-shirts. Potter saw the salesman stay as far from Gus as he possibly could while taking his measurements. While Gus was being fitted out, Potter visited the bank. Once Potter returned to the department store, he purchased a small suitcase, deodorant, shaving cream and a razor, shampoo, a comb, nail cutters and a large tube of toothpaste and a toothbrush. Lastly, a wallet, as he didn't think Gus would have one, but he hoped he had a passport! When Potter returned, he saw all Gus' purchases piled on the counter. Potter paid the bill and instructed the salesman to remove the tags before placing them in the new suitcase.

Gus had to run to keep up with Potter, but the little man did his best. After several minutes trying to convince Potter he didn't need a haircut and that he liked his hair just the way it was, he was securely in the barber's chair. His hair was washed and cut, and when Potter offered to pay extra, Gus was given a shave. The difference was immediate and they headed to the cab.

Potter instructed Gus to shower and be sure to use plenty of soap, then brush his teeth in the first class lounge bathroom, and, lastly, to leave his old clothes in the bin. By this time Gus knew it was pointless to argue. When Gus finally arrived back at the table thirty minutes later, the little man looked almost human. He no longer got stares as they headed for the plane, and he didn't smell. Potter was very grateful. Gus couldn't stop talking about how great the shower was, how good the soap smelled, his new clothes, and he said the wallet was the first he'd ever owned. When he noticed the cash inside, he was elated! During their time on the plane, Gus talked. It became clear to Potter that Gus was very fond of his old Pa and he explained that he was doing this so they could have a better life. By the time they arrived at their destination, Potter almost liked him. He was uneducated and rough, but he seemed to have his heart in the right place. He didn't drink, smoke or gamble, and he cared a great deal for his aged Pa. Potter felt this little man couldn't have come into his life at a worst time. Potter actually wondered why he had come into his life at all.

They were to go straight to the pre-arranged drop-off place and supposedly receive the next pickup. Potter started instructing Gus about making the return trip. He gave him the address of the hotel where he would stay the night before flying out. As they arrived at the old deserted warehouse where they were to make the drop, Potter felt uneasy. Usually, they met in an upscale hotel bar. He pushed open the heavy wooden door and entered the gloom. Looking up, Potter saw two men on the second balcony. As they spotted Potter and Gus, they waved them up.

"Ya got the stuff?"

"Yeah," said Potter, handing over a large black leather bag. Both men wore black leather jackets and jeans; one was dressed in a white linen shirt, the other a black t-shirt. Their clothes were obviously designer and very expensive.

"I'm not taking a return. This is Gus, he'll be taking it. He'll be your contact from now on," Potter said.

"But, Potter, I'm only supposed to be meeting the guys on this trip," Gus said, looking from one to the other of them.

"What ya doing, memorizing our faces or something?" one of the guys said as he moved closer to Gus.

Gus shook his head and took several steps closer to Potter, as the other guy said, "You'll make a return as long as we tell you to; this isn't like a regular job."

"It's more like a regular job than anything I've had before and it pays," Gus said as Potter gave him a look to stop talking. Potter decided to not complicate things any further – he still had a feeling of uneasiness. So, he decided to take the stuff and give it to Gus at the hotel. It would only delay him by several hours.

The guy weighing the parcels suddenly turned and yelled at Potter, "You're short again. Where's the stuff? You double-dealing on us or something?" Potter couldn't believe it. How could it have happened again? Potter just didn't believe it.

"Weigh them again and show me," he said, moving toward the guy at the scales.

"You don't believe me? Who the hell do you think you are?"

"Boys, now let's keep it clean. Give him the package and let's get the hell out of here," the second guy said. At that moment, they heard sirens in the distance. Everyone froze! The sirens were rapidly getting closer.

"You set us up...," one of the guys said as he drew a pistol from under his jacket. It all happened so quickly that Potter never knew a thing. Four shots rang out loud and clear.

"You fool, you shouldn't have—"

"Why the hell not? They were short and they set us up. What you expect me to do, feed them wedding cake? Let's get the hell out of here…"

The sirens were almost on them. The two guys quickly grabbed the gear and raced down the back stairs, where their driver waited. Tires squealed, and in seconds they were gone.

Gus and Potter lay on the floor in a pool of blood. They died instantly.

~

Tuesday night in New York City, Saffron entered the house at almost eleven p.m. It had been a long flight and an even longer day. She grabbed the two thick newspapers that blocked the doorway, and without switching on the light, she threw the newspapers on the small hall table. The red rose had wilted as she picked it up. With the rose still in one hand, she immediately swept the newspapers off the hall table and into the conveniently placed garbage bin below. The newspapers took with them Potter's two letters. Still in the darkness, Saffron briefly held the wilted rose to her nose, before also throwing it into the garbage. She didn't turn the light on until she was in her bedroom. After a long and luxurious bubble bath, Saffron Moffit went to bed and slept soundly all night.

Eternity Happens

It was eight a.m. Chuck sat behind his clean, orderly desk in his almost new and still neat office. Blue managed to keep it organized and made being efficient appear almost effortless. Unlike her own often disheveled appearance, at work she kept everything in its place so each morning the office looked as it had before Chuck's first client.

Chuck sat with a big smile on his face. He didn't realize he was smiling, but lately he usually was. Chuck thought about Siobhan Burke and how she had accidently been his first client, and he thought about the chain of events which followed. He thought about her being the catalyst for changing his life. He thought about all the things he'd discovered about Brock Burke, and also about Siobhan Burke, and he felt sorry for the beautiful, pampered, wealthy lady who had so recently re-entered his life.

He'd thought she would cry when he gave her the address of the apartment her husband owned without her knowledge, but she hadn't. He thought she'd surely cry when he told her that he had reason to believe she was adopted, but she hadn't. When he had shown her photos of several of her husband's mistresses, he was amazed to see her composure never faltered. Then he had told her about some of the things under investigation at Banker's Securities, Inc. And she just moved her head from side to side and bit down on her bottom lip. He had given her the name of Special Agent Bow Grismold, who was handling the investigation.

He then asked her if she wished him to check through the adoption files and locate her birth parents. He found it hard to believe she hadn't known of her adoption, as both her parents were dark-haired with brown eyes. Her mother in particular looked slightly Asian. Chuck wondered why he hadn't heard from Mrs. Burke since their last meeting. She said she'd call him with further instructions telling him how to proceed. But it had been nearly two weeks since he'd last met with Mrs. Burke. Perhaps he'd given her too much information and she was unable to handle learning so many bad things all at once. Chuck could certainly understand it, if that was the case. He tried again the cell number she had given him and left another message. Chuck was perplexed as to what he should be doing for Mrs. Burke. It was not the first time he heard his father's voice telling him that the human mind is far too diverse and complex to ever understand, so he was not to waste time trying.

Chuck was no longer thinking of his caseload, but again, it was Amanda who filled his mind. The way her long blonde hair fell over her shoulders, the way she looked up at him with her eyes twinkling and the laughter in her voice. The way she kissed him… he had to stop there, otherwise he would never get through the day. This morning he'd left her asleep. He'd stroked her long blonde hair as it cascaded over the pillow, he softly touched her cheek with his lips; he left a short love note on his pillow, before leaving quietly so he could arrive early at work.

Although they had only been together a very short time, Amanda and Chuck recently purchased a small house, and Chuck was eagerly waiting for the phone call to say it was officially theirs. He wanted to know when he could pick up the keys. Almost on cue, the call came through, and his smile broadened. He quickly called Amanda to tell her the good news just as Blue entered the office. This morning she was wearing bright pink tights, a cobalt blue miniskirt covered with silver diamonds and a smart black blazer over a navy-blue blouse. Blue said her personality could shine through in the way she dressed. She said she would compromise and only dress for the office above the waist. She had long since stopped wearing all black, and Chuck was pleased to see her black nail polish was no longer present. Today it was a soft lilac and he commented.

"Blue, you sure have a way with clothes; you look good out of black," he said, wishing she could somehow control her unruly, frizzy hair. It was usually controlled by several combs in various colors when she arrived, but the first time she bent over, the combs would move or fall out completely. Chuck knew she must own dozens of them, as he was always picking them off the floor or out of the filing cabinet. Today he had found one on his desk and another bright green one in his garbage bin.

"Well, the way I dress tells you how my soul is feeling. Black is for depression or if you're overweight. I'm neither, as you can see. I'm a skinny, happy, well-balanced individual. I'm actually a skinny, well-balanced individual who hasn't had breakfast. How about I get us all one of those nice ham and cheese croissants from the little bakery on the corner? I could smell them all the way down the street. Surely you could eat, too, unless you have other things on your mind," she said, giggling infectiously. She winked at Chuck and helped herself to the petty cash, and then she was gone, leaving Chuck alone and giggling like a schoolboy. Just as Chuck sat back in his chair and began thinking of Amanda again, Blue popped her head around the door.

"Stop day-dreaming and put the coffee on."

Chuck did as she instructed, wondering how anyone could think food was so important. Amanda would be in her office by now; he sent her a happy face and a good morning e-mail signed with hugs and kisses. He then ordered a dozen roses to be sent to her with a note.

"Come and get 'em while they're hot," Blue said, interrupting Chuck's thoughts of Amanda. She was already placing the croissants on a plate and had begun to pour the coffee. Just then, Walter Dense entered the office; he was Chuck's newest employee and came with years of experience. Walter was five years away from retirement and had worked on the force as a youngster under Sheffield Hollingsworth, Chuck's late father. He was a lucky find and his experience proved invaluable.

"Morning, all," he said.

"Got you and Fred a croissant, and I'm just pouring the coffee," Blue said, handing him a plate.

"I really shouldn't – if my wife finds out…"

"She won't, Walter, because we won't tell her. How long did you spend at the gym last night?"

"Two hours, as always."

"Well, here, you've earned it. You really must be amazingly fit by now, Walter," Blue added.

"And thank you for not adding 'for a man of my age'," Walter said, tucking into the warm croissant.

"Well, boss, we should have him today. I'd bet me pension we will…," Walter said to Chuck.

"I think you're right, Walter; he's none too smart." They were, of course, discussing their latest case.

"I'll be glad to wrap this one up, boss. Let's stick to the rich and famous from now on; some of the places we've been with this one…" Walter stopped, not wanting to discuss it further in front of Blue. He enjoyed the last mouthfuls of his croissant and drained the last of his coffee.

"Thanks, Blue. Must be on my way; wouldn't want to keep Freddy boy waiting. See you at one o'clock, boss," Walter said as he quickly retrieved his gun from the locked safe in the back room and left. Blue told Chuck that Amanda was on the phone. The two chatted for thirty minutes, all the while Chuck had a huge smile on his face. However, the moment he saw Fred Block enter the office, he gave Amanda lots of kisses and hung up. Fred looked worn out.

"Long night, Fred?" Chuck asked as Fred removed his gun and locked it away before sitting with his legs up on the couch.

"Long and busy night," he said, taking the coffee and croissant Blue offered him.

"You look like eight miles of bad road," Blue added, giggling.

"When are you going to stop sitting behind that desk and help out in the real world, Baby Blue?" Fred replied.

"When Chuck allows me to," Blue answered, looking at Chuck, who merely shook his head and finished his cooling croissant.

"Oh here, Chuck, almost forgot. I checked out that jewelery store over the last week. His reputation is solid. Here's my report on the case," Fred said, handing over the wrinkled papers to Chuck.

"Great work, Fred. Walter seems to think we'll wrap it up tonight. What's your feeling?"

"Well, I'm too tired for feeling anything right now, but I sure hope he's right."

"Oh, Fred, I almost forgot, your wife called. You'll be pleased to know your mother-in-law has the baby. She said you're free to sleep all day. Said she'll see you about five tonight if you're still home."

"Wow, that's about the best news a guy can have. Why did it take you so long to tell me?"

"It didn't, you've only been here ten minutes," Blue said, giggling.

"Okay, I'm signing off. I'll be at the gym for an hour and then home asleep until five o'clock, so try not to disturb me," he said, playfully slapping Blue on the shoulder. He waved at Chuck, yawned widely and left the office.

"He really looks crazy tired," Blue commented.

"Well, Blue, he's got a baby he usually looks after all day and then he works all night; the man has responsibilities," Chuck muttered, thinking hard as he began reading the report Fred had just given him. Then he stopped as he wondered if Amanda had started packing for the move into their new home. The moment he finished reading the report, he placed it neatly in his top drawer, where he kept his active files. He placed it on top of Siobhan Burke's file and, as he did so, he saw the corner of the old, dirty Grasshopper file protruding from the bottom of the pile. Chuck had every intention of looking closely at the Grasshopper file, but not today. One day he hoped to close the file satisfactorily in remembrance of his late dad. He touched the corner of the file and for several seconds sadness engulfed him. Then he quickly closed the drawer.

Chuck had already started going through the many old files that once belonged to his father. Blue seemed to leave several on his desk each week; she said they made the office look cluttered. Chuck briefly thought of the young lady who'd visited him last Friday. He tried to remember her name, and it was a strange one. Yes, it was Honor or Loot or something weird like that, and she was from England. He had urged her to get back to him as soon as possible, but as yet he hadn't heard a word. He knew she had flown in from London and he also knew it had been a huge case when it happened many years ago. He wasn't sure he was capable of solving an old case of his father's, but Walter had urged him to pursue it, saying he would gladly help.

He'd asked for her contact information before handing over the file. However, all she showed him was the old letter she had found and her driver's license. He'd copied down her strange name before she quickly placed her driver's license back in her purse; he was unable to get her address. If she'd arrived during working hours, Blue would have her contact details in full. What strange creatures' humans are, he thought again. Surely, the young woman would want her kidnappers brought to justice and surely, she would want to find her real parents. He felt sure they would want to find her. It must have ruined their lives losing a young daughter to a kidnapper and never having closure. Chuck then read the information on the jeweler Fred had given him.

"Blue, I'll be back in a few hours; I'm off to see the jeweler. I'm sure you can handle everything here."

"Sure, of course I can. There's always lots of filing to do. Have you given any thought as to what you want to do with your father's old files?"

"I have given them a lot of thought, but no decision has yet been made. Everything you're sorting is great, even though it may take a while. I'm not even halfway through any of them. Be patient with me, Blue."

"Okay, I'll be patient, but they take up a lot of room and I could easily file them all if I had two more filing cabinets."

"I know you can, but I owe it to my dad to go through each one first. It's what he'd expect of me."

"Did you hear back from that girl who came to inquire about her old file? Do you know if she wants us to pursue her adoption or kidnapping?"

"No, nothing. See ya in a bit," Chuck said, whistling as he walked down the street to the jeweler's store.

Chuck stopped outside and looked in the window for some time. He could have taken half a day off and gone into New York, but he intended to make this little village his main shopping area because this was where his office was located. He would buy locally if he saw something he liked. Their new home was closer to New York; in fact, it was located in a suburb that was almost halfway between where he worked and the city. He knew he had only known Amanda for four weeks, but it was love at first sight and he knew this was the real thing. Chuck was sure Amanda felt the same. The bell attached to the door rang as he entered the small jewelry store, and a moment later the old jeweler had him comfortably seated on the other side of the counter.

~

Meanwhile, in the Fraser building on the 7th floor, Amanda Dolman was getting ready to leave for the day. Saffron had shopping for her to do and she hoped to meet Siobhan for lunch. Amanda couldn't believe how perfectly everything was working out. Siobhan was to take over the lease of her apartment once she moved in with Chuck, so she could keep her identity a secret a little longer.

But now she had the problem of keeping it from Chuck. She really needed to talk to her mom about gradually changing her looks. She knew this was exactly what they had been worried about. This was the reason they tried to discourage her from working undercover. It seemed impossible that anyone could instantly know when they had met their husband, soul mate and the person they wanted to spend the rest of their life with... but it had happened. It hit her like a freight train at a high speed and she knew it was impossible to stop it happening even if she wanted to, which she didn't.

Chuck was already part of her like the air she breathed and as dear to her as her beloved parents. It was inconsolable to think of life without him. As she walked up the hallway, the florist delivery boy was entering the 7th floor. She knew instantly they were from Chuck, so she stopped the delivery boy and took the long-stemmed roses. They were, as always, beautiful. '***The roses are beautiful but pale in comparison to you, love forever, C.***'

Amanda was finding it harder and harder to get through the day without Chuck; she missed him the moment they were apart. She intended to surprise him tonight at his office; she had never been there. It was a long cab ride out of the city. But first she wanted to share her news with Siobhan. She knew her friend would be shocked but happy for her. Amanda was in shock herself; she hadn't realized it could happen this fast or this easily. It certainly hadn't been in her short-term plans.

Siobhan and Amanda had a long lunch together; however, Amanda didn't get a chance to tell Siobhan her news. Instead, she listened to Siobhan as she tried not to cry over the many things she had learned about Brock and how hard she was finding it to come to terms with leaving him.

"Siobhan, he will probably never change," Amanda said, rubbing Siobhan's back as she continued to sob and wiping her tears away.

"I know you're right and I hate him for it. It's just that…" Siobhan sobbed harder again before she could continue. "It's just that I may never find another man I love. It's the way Brock smiles and the way his eyes crinkle when he's genuinely happy. It's the way he looks at me like no one else exists in the world, and it's the way he kisses me and tells me he loves me. The way we make love is like nothing I've ever known. It's always good, every time!"

"Oh, Siobhan, I understand and I will support any decision you make. You know Chuck is still wanting instructions from you as to how to proceed…" Amanda added kindly, trying to take Siobhan's mind off Brock.

"I don't know myself what I want to do. I don't want anyone to know how upset I am. I really didn't expect to feel this bad once I'd made up my mind. But, Amanda, I really don't know if I'm doing the right thing. I don't want to be divorced."

"I know you don't, and you don't have to move into the apartment."

"I know, but I will. I just don't know whether it will be permanent or just until I can clear my head. I have never actually left Brock before and I don't know how he will react. I hope it will be a wakeup call for him and us before it's too late. I'm not going to rush into anything." The two friends talked on until Amanda saw it was almost four o'clock. She told Siobhan she was going to surprise Chuck at his office and that she had some news to tell him. Amanda realized

Siobhan was only half listening as she replied, "You can't go all that way in a cab. Take the Porsche. I will cab it back to the house. I'll set the navigation for you."

"No, really, it's okay, Siobhan."

"I insist. Let's go, you better get moving so you miss rush hour; it can be hell at this time of day getting out of the city." And it was settled. Amanda hadn't driven a car since arriving in New York and she missed it. Amanda Dolman didn't have a driver's license, but it felt good to be driving and even better to be on her way to see Chucky; she called him on the car phone.

Chuck had just arrived back from relieving Walter for his lunch break. Unfortunately, that was the time their target had decided to move, and move he had. By the time Walter caught up to Chuck, their suspect was almost a hundred miles from where Walter had left him. It was almost four thirty p.m. when Chuck arrived back at the office. He stopped on the way to purchase candles, long-stemmed glasses and champagne. Finally, some giant Indian cushions and a rug. He was going to meet Amanda at their new home and he intended to take her out the back and sit under the tiny gazebo in the moonlight. The moment he arrived back in the office, Blue said Amanda was on the phone.

"Mandy, darling. Missing you terribly."

"Miss you more, Chucky. I'm on my way to your office; thought it was time I saw where you work – so stay put, darling, if you can," she instructed, giddy at the thought of seeing him soon.

"Mandy, I was just about to call you. Can you make a detour and meet me at our new home? I have the keys and I think we should christen it tonight," Chuck said with a naughty chuckle in his voice.

"Okay, I think I can. I'll just have to find the way."

"Aren't you in a cab, honey?"

"No, I'm in Siobhan's Porsche, and fortunately it's got navigation."

Chuck was thinking hard; he needed time to set up the gazebo before she arrived, and he hadn't yet got the rose petals he wanted to scatter on the pathway from the house to the gazebo. Chuck told her to stop at the next shopping center, otherwise she will have gone too far. He said he would call her in about an hour and then come and get her. Amanda thought this rather strange, but she knew he was going to surprise her by the laughter in his voice. She easily passed an hour in what would soon be their local shopping mall.

When Chuck finally called, she couldn't believe how the time had flown by. She had six shopping bags and she hurried to the car. Chuck didn't come to meet her, but told her how to use the navigation in the car. In no time at all she was pulling into the double driveway of their neat yellow suburban house. She stopped and smelled the freshly mowed front lawn; she looked up at the red magnolia tree in full bloom, it had daffodils and tulips at its base and squirrels running over its branches. In the early dusk the tall, graceful tree stood proudly in the center of the small lawn, brightly colored flowers making a brilliant contrast against the dark green of the lawn and the black wrought-iron fence. The double front doors were a dark reddish brown, but mainly frosted leadlight glass. Amanda saw the doorbell to one side and pushed it to see if it worked. It was exciting to hear the deep chime that sounded somewhere far away inside.

The moment the sound of the chimes faded, Chuck threw open the door and scooped her into his arms. They kissed deeply like two people lost in the desert as he twirled her around and around.

"Oh, but I needed that, darling. It seems like a long day without you," Chuck said, still holding her tightly in his arms.

"Chucky, I missed you the moment you closed the door this morning. Oh, the roses were gorgeous; you spoil me."

"Well, lady, you ain't seen nothing yet," he said, carrying her through the house. They checked out every room. It was almost dark by the time he carried her, still safely in his arms, outside. Finally, he put her down on the short pathway that he'd earlier covered in rose petals.

"Oh, how beautiful. Where do they go?" Amanda asked, looking ahead and seeing the candles twinkling in the dusk all the way around the gazebo. She took his hand and together they slowly walked the path of rose petals until they entered the gazebo and Chuck poured the chilled champagne.

"Will you be warm enough, darling?" Chuck asked, feeling the slight chill in the air.

"Just being with you warms me," Amanda replied, taking the glass as they linked arms and toasted their new home. As the bubbles tickled their noses, they drank champagne and stared into each other's eyes.

"Chucky, I have something to tell you. I don't know what you are going to think—"

Before she could continue, Chuck kissed her and then said, "Darling Mandy, I am a true gentleman, or I try to be, and I always let you go first; but tonight, I have something to ask you. It simply can't wait or I will burst. I must go first tonight! Do you mind awfully?" He was already on bended knee in front of Amanda, who was sitting in the center of the rug, resting on several brightly colored cushions. She shook her head and waited as he refilled their glasses. It felt magical as the candles glowed warmly in the darkness and the subtle scent from the two large blooming cherry trees filled the air. All around them the night was still and the world silent. Overhead, the stars twinkled brightly in the night sky. She noticed Chuck seemed a little nervous as he knelt in front of her. She expected him to move closer and wrap his arms about her as he always did. But he stayed where he was and fumbled in his pocket for something. Amanda was not expecting him to grab her hand and look deeply into her eyes as he muttered, "Darling, I love you and I have from the first moment I laid eyes on you. You are my waking breath, my night-time dream. You have become the last thing I see at night and the first thing I see in the morning. You are, and will always be, my everything. Amanda Dolman, I love you madly, truly, deeply. Will you do me the honor of becoming my wife? Will you please marry me?" Chuck asked, his voice no more than a whisper.

Slowly, he opened the black velvet box and a large diamond shone in the soft candlelight. It was a square diamond with two smaller diamonds on each side. Amanda thought it was the most beautiful thing she had ever seen. She continued to stare at the diamond in the black velvet box. Chuck let her right hand go as he took her left hand in his and began removing the ring from the box.

Amanda knew she would say yes, but she had to do the right thing and tell him her news; somehow, she didn't know how to start.

"Darling, you are just sitting there looking incredibly beautiful and saying nothing; you really know how to tease a guy. I've been so nervous all week and now you haven't answered me." Chuck stopped as he looked into her eyes and saw the seriousness there.

"Chucky, before I answer you, I must tell you something and then you can ask me again."

"You're scaring me, Mandy. Are you already married or dating someone else or something?"

Amanda laughed at his fears and it lightened the moment enough for her to continue. "Chucky darling, it's nothing like that. I just wanted to ask you how you feel about having children," Amanda said, holding her breath.

"So long as they're with you, I think that would be great. But we have plenty of time to think about children; after all, you're only twenty-four. However, you're right as always, darling, we really should have discussed this before now. I want at least one of each – and you?" He laughed, his relief openly apparent. As Chuck started to open the box again, Amanda knew she couldn't keep her secret any longer.

"Darling, I know we have plenty of time to think about children. About eight months, to be exact," Amanda said quietly as he reached for her hand. As she watched him, she saw the impact of her words finally sink in. He stopped holding her hand and sat back on the pillows, his mouth falling open as he just stared at her. Just then, his cell phone rang; he didn't seem to hear it until Amanda pointed toward the origin of the persistent noise.

"Yes, Chuck Hollingsworth," then a pause.

"Mom, you've called too soon – she hasn't given me her answer yet," then another pause.

"No, she's not hesitating, Mom." Another pause.

"We're at the house. Yes, it's great. Just give us another hour." A brief pause.

"Yeah, okay, Mom, talk to you then," Chuck said, closing his cell. "Sorry, Mandy, am I to believe we're going to have a baby, you and I?" he asked in disbelief.

"Yes, I'm pretty sure we are."

"But, Mandy, how can it happen so fast?"

"Well, how do you think, silly? Maybe it's because you are such a great lover."

"But it's only been a little over a month, darling," Chuck replied as a huge smile lit up his face.

"I don't think Mother Nature counts the days like we do. Anyway, it only takes once, Chucky," Amanda teased, smiling. She said no more as he pulled her into his arms and kissed her long and deeply until their desire overcame their need to speak. Thirty minutes later, his cell rang again. This time it was Blue, and he had much the same conversation he'd just had with his mom. Amanda realized everyone knew what was happening tonight except her.

As the third phone call came through, Amanda was beginning to think the whole world already knew.

"Chuck Hollingsworth." Pause.

"Fred." Another long pause.

"Oh, really? Great work," he said, pausing. "They have, already? Great! Good job, Fred." Another pause.

"It's great news, although the timing for me is not good right now."

"I'll let you know," Chuck said, ending the call. The magic of the evening was rapidly disappearing as Amanda sat and listened to Chuck speaking on his cell.

"Honey, the case is all wrapped up and tied with string. Cheers," Chuck said, elated, as he raised his glass in a toast.

"You sound relieved and I'm glad it's over. This case has caused you way too much stress, Chucky," Amanda said, moving back into his arms.

"Yes, he was a mean devil and armed also. I don't like putting the guys in that sort of danger. We're only P.I.s, not the FBI!"

It was after midnight when Chuck finally proposed again, and this time Amanda said yes. She was so delighted she said yes, several times, over and over as he slipped the ring on her finger. Then he called his mom. Amanda had previously explained her parents were traveling, but she could still see that Chuck was a little confused when she didn't even try to contact them. Amanda drove back and waited for Chuck at his place while he went to wrap the case up with the police. They made love again and again, then talked and didn't sleep at all. As Amanda drove to work the next morning, she knew she needed to find a house for Mr .and Mrs. Dolman in L.A. She placed a call to Baxter, telling him exactly what she wanted and fast. She needed a plan before she called her parents in England and told them her news.

It was later that same day when Baxter called her back it was while she was in the coffee shop. He told her he'd found the perfect house for the Dolmans. It was a deceased estate and they needed a quick sale. Apparently, the parents had recently died in a car accident, leaving two young children in the care of relatives. The relatives just wanted cash and were selling the house complete with everything; apparently, they wanted no memories of the deceased couple, so they were selling the property, car and all. Baxter further explained, that if they move quickly they could buy the house, the car and the furniture. Amanda deemed it perfect. As she sat and enjoyed her coffee, he sent her photos on her phone of the inside and outside of the house. She instructed him to purchase it under the names Sam and Ruth Dolman. Next, she called her parents.

"Sis, why are you calling at this hour?' Zax's sleepy voice asked as he rubbed his eyes before questioning her further. "Everything all right?"

"Yeah; in fact, everything's great."

"Why aren't you here? It's been way too long; we really were expecting you. Molly has things planned for her sister-in-law."

"Yeah, I'll visit soon, bro. Can you wake Mom and Dad? I really need to speak to them," Neve asked.

~

Neve's call came through in the middle of the night. Al and Hugo were naturally delighted to hear from her, even if it took a while for them to wake up. They had her on speaker phone so they could both talk and listen to her; just hearing her upbeat, happy voice cheered them. However, as they listened, they instantly became alert. First, she told them she was getting married to a private investigator. That alone scared Hugo half to death.

"Baby Girl, are you sure he's not tracking us or something and using you as bait?" Hugo asked, and instantly knew it sounded foolish.

"Dad, we're not like international fugitives or anything. Don't be silly. You'll both love him – I know you will. I have made a great choice and I know we will have a wonderful life together, just like you two. I'm stuck in this disguise and don't know how to get around the problem. I really don't want Amanda to marry Chuck; I want Neve to," Neve finished as they heard the concern in her voice.

"Honey, let me think about this some. But stay as you are until I have made-a-plan," Al said, already beginning to think the problem through.

"You promise not to do anything until we discuss it further," Al added again, worried.

Hugo quickly interrupted, "Baby Girl, this is just what we've always feared might happen. The thought of you getting stuck in disguise is frightening. Does he suspect?"

"No, Daddy, of course not," Neve said, laughing.

Al added, "Make sure you always enjoy your night-time activities in the dark; pretend you're shy or something, at least until we can work this out."

"Oh, Mom, how boring, but that's pretty much what I've been doing up until now." They could hear the laughter in Neve's voice, but Al and Hugo couldn't help exchanging concerned looks.

"Neve, we must be able to rely on you to never blow our cover," Hugo said, serious now.

"Yes, Dad, I know your rules and I will play by them. I guarantee my loyalty. I haven't even told Siobhan, and she's my BFF. I have thought about it, though."

"Neve," both her parents said together, slightly scared now.

"I won't, I promise," she said, still with laughter in her voice.

"Baby Girl, it's no laughing matter. Probably after all these years we may indeed be international fugitives," Hugo said.

His wife said, "Oh, Hugo, no one even suspects; we would have known by now if someone was onto us."

"Maybe we would and maybe we wouldn't; don't be so sure of yourselves, ladies. And, Neve, be careful with Siobhan; you haven't known her long and she may be more like you than you know."

"What is that supposed to mean, Dad?"

"Honey, she's your BFF and you're hiding many secrets from her, so maybe she is doing the same with you."

Both women objected strongly to his opinion, until, laughing, Neve changed the subject. "So, how's all the grand parenting stuff going?"

"Honey, it's great! You should be here; after all, you have one adorable niece and a very cute nephew – remember, you are their aunt. Bobby is quite the little man and follows Zax and now Hugo everywhere, imitating them both; he races around this huge old house at high speed and he's only been on his feet a month or so," Al said, laughing, before Hugo continued.

"Beth is the sweetest, most adorable baby; she has blonde hair and big blue eyes, she's always happy – definitely a Grasshopper, that one."

"I'm so glad you like being grandparents and I'm sure you're very good at it. Anyway, in about eight months' time or so you will be grandparents again. Yes, Mom, Dad, you'll be having another grandchild," Neve said, and waited for the scream of delight from her mother. But all she heard was silence for a very long time, so she waited, until finally she heard the scream of joy that she'd so eagerly been wanting and knew so well.

"Congrats, darling, I think that must have happened even faster than it did with your dad and me when Zax was conceived. So now you hold the Grasshopper record and not us," Al said, chuckling.

"Baby Girl, you almost gave your old dad a heart attack. That really came from left field, whacked a guy right over the head. I don't know what to say!"

"Anyway, Dad, Chucky wants to meet you, of course, and Baxter and I have made all the arrangements. All you'll need to do is maybe start your next job a few days later and wear yet another disguise. Hello, Sam and Ruth Dolman."

They talked on for another hour as the arrangements were fine-tuned. Al and Hugo didn't get any more sleep that night. Their emotions ran from elation and excitement to worry and dread. As is customary with the English aristocracy, their breakfast tray arrived at nine thirty a.m., along with little Bob, who had been waiting patiently outside their door for the maid to enter. Each morning he bounded into the room and tried to leap onto the bed with no success; however, they both admired him for constantly trying. The first two mornings he'd fallen and cried, but now Hugo was waiting for him and caught him in mid-air and lowered him gently into the bed between them. Bobby is only fourteen months old and already a pint-size ball of energy. He has all his front teeth and unlike the Grasshoppers, he has a mop of curly red hair, a round happy face, rosy cheeks and the very same smile as his mother, Molly. He sat quietly between them, looking from one to the other as he chewed loudly on a small piece of toast. Al watched as the crumbs dropped into the sheets around him.

"Ball," Bobby said, pointing to an old ancestral painting on the wall. It showed several old-fashioned and over-dressed men on a playing field holding a soccer ball.

"Yes, Bobby, that's a soccer ball," Hugo said.

"Occer ball for Bobby." Just then, there was a knock on the door and before it opened, Bobby called, "Dadda, Dadda," holding his arms out to Zax. Zax was already up and dressed in a suit as he entered the room. He was a tall, good-looking man, with a mop of curly light brown hair, dark bluish violet eyes and a large, happy mouth. He looked more like Felix than Hugo, although he definitely looked like a Grasshopper, even if he did act like Alberta's side of the family.

"You guys will be getting soft with all these breakfasts in bed," Zax commented, kissing his mom on the cheek as he scooped Bobby up in his arms, before placing him high on his shoulders.

"I must break the habit before I start work; much too cozy." The moment the words were spoken, Hugo regretted it. Zax had lectured them more than once about retiring from their dangerous and illicit lifestyle. Alberta and Hugo expected another lecture when they saw the look on Zax's face.

After a few awkward moments, Zax said, "I haven't asked you if you're comfortable here, or if you need anything. Already your ten days are up and you'll be leaving in the morning."

Alberta surveyed the large room with the high ceiling and the dark red walls, the plush carpets and ornate red and gold drapes. The many pictures on the walls of no one they knew; the overstuffed armchairs and writing table with its gold-leaf edging. Even though it was grand by any standards, like the rest of the mansion, it had a worn, shabby air lurking just below the surface. Al and Hugo felt very proud of Zax and the way he was turning the estate into a going concern and taking it out of the red.

"Thank you, darling, how could we not be comfortable here? We are so pampered and spoilt. What plans do you have for our last day?"

"Molly and I want to take you around the building project again; it's really advanced since you saw it on your arrival. Then we'll meet up with the Win-Stanleys at a little pub called the Drake and Slipper – it has a restaurant they both adore. It's located not far from here in the next village."

"Sounds wonderful. I'll just need some time to use the phone before we leave. I'll be as brief as possible, son," Hugo said. He had to cancel the next leg of their vacation so they could return to Los Angeles and organize everything for Chuck's visit the following weekend.

"I hope it's not work, Dad. I'd appreciate nothing illegal being organized under my roof," Zax instructed seriously, before telling them to meet him downstairs as he turned and left the room.

Al immediately said, "How can he come to the wedding knowing Neve cannot be herself? He'll hit the roof when we tell him, and she'll be miserable without him there. I think he'll be asked to be a groomsman."

"I don't know all the answers to this mess yet, Al, I only wish I did. What Neve's doing is really going to tear them apart, and they've always been so close. He was upset enough when she didn't arrive with us, and it didn't take him long to work out she was, again, under cover. I don't think he's quite forgiven us yet for placing his little sister in possible danger."

"Oh, Hugo, what have we done?" Al said, as she wiped several stray tears from her cheeks and walked into Hugo's loving embrace.

Zax had created a twenty-acre subdivision using land on the far corner of the estate, and he planned to lease the houses to the owners on a ninety-nine-year lease. Al and Hugo were extremely proud of him, as was his wife, Molly, and his in-laws, Lord and Lady Win-Stanley. Neither Hugo nor Al could imagine how two such overbearing and pompous fuddy-duddies could have such a down-to-earth, amazing daughter. They not only expected Al and Hugo to address them by their titles, but also their grandchildren. Neither Al nor Hugo had ever known what their first names were, nor had they heard anyone use them. Zax called them Your Lordship and My Lady. Molly called them Mother and Father, and everyone else called them by their full title. Al wondered whether they liked it that way or were just too pompous to realize how outdated they were behaving.

Al and Hugo were most impressed with the progress of the estate and that thirty-two of the fifty houses were now almost complete. In the last several weeks the land had turned from a work site to a potential suburb; the lanes and roads were now laid out, making it appear a lot more real than it previously had. Each house design was slightly different and the colors unique. Molly was in charge of the colors and interior design. She had chosen fresh, subtle lemons in one house, pale ocean blues in another, warm earthy browns, and so on. Zax and Molly had asked his parents to choose the home they liked the best, promising they would reserve it for them when next they visited. Next, Molly said she'd be sure to pick elegant modern furnishings that were nothing like the stuffy mansion, and they'd also oversee the upkeep of the garden. Molly's eyes were shining as she told them about each house, and she was most excited to see which one they would select.

Then, Molly showed them the house they designed especially for Al and Hugo. They assured them they didn't have to choose it, but it had four bedrooms while the others had three, and it had an entrance hall and large deck, which none of the others had. The colors were fresh and clean, and the interior spacious. In their mind there was no choice: it was by far the best house of them all. Molly was delighted, but kept telling them they could still choose a different one if they preferred. There was really no decision; the one Molly and Zax had so carefully designed for them was elegantly appointed and beautifully designed. Al and Hugo had not been expecting such a gift. Hugo quickly estimated the cost of a ninety-nine-year lease and wrote Zax and Molly a large check. They knew how the estate was struggling and they also knew that only twenty of the fifty houses were, so far, under lease.

"Dad, really, there's no need; this is our gift to you both. We want you to be active grandparents and visit us often!" Zax insisted.

Molly added, "We know how stuffy it is living in the mansion, and you must also find it very structured and pompous after your life in America."

"Once the estate is financially sound, we will be building our own small mansion on the west corner," Zax added, before Molly again took over.

"We can't wait. We're taking you there now to show you the land. We want to keep the building crew working – so if all goes well, we can break ground there in the next three to four months," Molly finished proudly as they headed to the waiting Land Rover.

"We'll have twenty very private acres for our children to grow up on," Zax added as they all bundled out of the Land Rover. They were on the top of a small hill. At the bottom, a clear stream meandered through the meadow. The surrounding meadows were lush and green, with many wonderful old trees and a superb view. They inhaled deeply the crisp, clean air that blew on the gentle breeze. Al and Hugo said it took their breath away, it was so beautiful. Hugo and Al wanted to stay and walk around the land that would soon house their offspring; however, Molly informed them that it must be a brief stop as they were already late for lunch. She reminded them how her parents were sticklers for punctuality and it was considered enormously bad manners to be even a minute late.

Zax drove a little too fast to get to the next village on time. They made it with seconds to spare, and Al and Hugo were both quite ruffled after sitting in the back of the Land Rover, which not only drove on the opposite side of the road than they did, but seemed to do amazing speeds through the narrow country lanes.

"Jolly good. Here they are then, Me Lady," Lord Win-Stanley said, addressing his wife.

"Oh yes, here they are, not a minute too early either," she added as Lord Win-Stanley checked his pocket watch and continued.

"Took the liberty of ordering us all a pre-luncheon sherry. No objections, I hope," said the small, rotund Lord with his balding gray hair, weathered and wrinkled face from too much indulgence in the good life rather than working outside. His fingernails were thick, long, yellow and unkempt. His teeth were also yellow, chipped and uneven. He was in total contrast to Hugo, who was about the same age, but his overall appearance was immeasurably better.

As usual, Lord and Lady Win-Stanley controlled the conversation, and today he seemed bursting with untold news. As the sticky treacle pudding was served, he seemed unable to contain himself any longer.

"I have an announcement… today we successfully managed to enroll Bobby into my old school, Eton." He beamed at his shocked audience. When no one said anything, he continued, "Also, I had to pull a few strings, but I have taken the liberty of getting Bobby a placement at the Sandhurst Academy for excellence in officers." He beamed afresh as he raised his glass.

"Fine job indeed, Me Lord, well done," Lady Win-Stanley said. Hugo knew Al was not known for holding her tongue, so after a few minutes of silence in which Molly and Zax exchanged looks of total disgust, Hugo spoke.

"But surely, Your Lordship, the parents should show their own children guidance in these matters."

"Guidance, be damned. Zax has no contacts at Sandhurst, and neither of them has even considered their son's long-term future. Molly's just our baby and always will be, and I'm sure she expects us to execute matters of family honor."

"Father, really, you have no right"—

But before she could finish, Lord Win-Stanley boomed, "No need to thank us at all. Just doing our job as grandparents – a job we take very seriously, very seriously indeed," he finished, as dribble escaped the side of his mouth. He smiled broadly at his daughter and son-in-law. Turning to Zax, he slapped him soundly on the back. Al had to speak – Hugo knew she was bursting to say something; he just hoped she would be subtle.

"Your Lordship, surely you see it as one of the enjoyments of parenting to make life choices for one's own children."

"Indeed, I do, fair lady. Molly will always be our child and we shall always be the parent; don't you agree, Me Lady?"

"Oh, quite so, Me Lord, quite so. We are thoroughly modern grandparents and we have selected not to meddle in Molly and Zax's parenting of their children, although there are certain things I would surely do differently if they were my own. However, His Lordship and I have chosen to stay out of the direct child-raising, unless asked, and therefore we have not organized Robert and Elizabeth's early years. The very last thing we wish is to appear pushy. My good friend Lady Mac-Willington Smyth recently saw her daughter attend Duke University in the United States, and we are seriously thinking of enrolling Elizabeth there as well. Naturally, you could both oversee her welfare while she's in the States, could you not?" Lady Win-Stanley finished arrogantly as she nodded at the Grasshoppers ,,

"You are referring to young Beth and Bobby, are you not?" Hugo added. However, she appeared not to hear him and continued on,

"I do believe you do not yet understand the English etiquette. But I would like to remind you next time you see the children you are to address them as Lady Elizabeth and Lord Robert. Their titles are their birthright and as so should be respected in line with their heritage and our customs," Al and Hugo were speechless at her rudeness and Hugo discreetly grabbed Al's hand to stop her from saying anything she may regret. He could feel her body trembling with anger. Molly was next to speak, although Al and Hugo could tell their son was not pleased with the discussion happening at the table either.

"Mother, Father, I think Zax and I will discuss this later. It is the Grasshoppers' last day here with us and I for one would like it to be a happy occasion." The mood around the table was strained, with the exception of Lord and Lady Win-Stanley, who seemed quite elated at their supposed good deed. It was later that night and after a very uncomfortable last supper with Lord and Lady Win-Stanley that Hugo asked Molly and Zax to share some private time. As they said goodbye to the older Win-Stanleys, Hugo and Al were again appalled by their coolness to their own family.

"Farewell, Lord Win-Stanley. Thank you for your hospitality," Hugo said, extending his hand to His Lordship.

"Farewell indeed, Hoppers, or Grass, until next time, I'm sure. You may not know our customs here in England, but it is customary to bow your head if you are a man or do a small dip if you are a female when addressing members of the aristocracy."

"Father, really, these are Zax's parents," Molly said, coming to the Grasshoppers' defense. Immediately, His Lordship backed down.

"My dear child, I am quite aware of that. I am in no way asking them to curtsy, but merely wanted to make them aware of the correct customary etiquette for the future."

"Father... really," Molly said, annoyed.

It appeared Lady Win-Stanley obviously had not picked up on the subtlety of the situation at all when she added, "As we're on the subject, I do think it's time for young Bobby to stop all his huggy, kissy carryings on. A simple handshake at bedtime or as a greeting would be quite acceptable. He is, after all, growing up fast."

"He's one, one year and four months old, Your Ladyship," Al said, appalled. She was about to say much more, when her son shot her a look telling her to stay quiet.

"Why, my dear Mrs Hopper-Grass, or whatever you call yourself—"

Al interrupted Lady Win-Stanley, she had had enough. "My name is Alberta Grasshopper."

"Yes, quite... always thought it sounds rather like a railway station. Anyway, if I may be permitted to continue, I was about to say how little you know your own grandson Bobby. He is, in fact, about to be fifteen months old. Jolly poor show, I would say, not even getting his age right, Mrs Whatever...," Lady Win-Stanley finished, holding her nose high.

Al had heard enough; she wasn't about to listen any more. She turned, and without another word, headed out the door of the grand dining room and up the stairs to their suite. Hugo followed close behind.

As they were leaving, they heard Molly chastise her parents. "Mother, that was quite rude and most uncalled for."

"Molly, I was merely setting your uncultured mother-in-law straight on a few things. She will surely appreciate it when she has time to think it through, and even thank me the next time we meet. Indeed, I am quite sure she will."

"Mother, really, you're incorrigible," Molly said as she also left the room, followed closely by Zax.

Hugo was trying desperately to calm Al as he sat on the love seat listening to her curse the Win-Stanleys.

"Darling, you said the very same things last time we were here, and the time before, if my memory serves me correctly. Remember, we agreed that we are here to visit Zax, Molly and the children. It is the only reason we are here, so let's focus on them, shall we?" Hugo concluded.

"But, Hugo, they're just beyond the..." She stopped when they heard a gentle tap, followed by Zax opening the door and peeking inside. He was holding Molly's hand and together they timidly walked into the room. Molly immediately put her arms around Al.

"Alberta, I'm so truly sorry for my ignorant, pompous parents. I know it's ruined your stay and I'm truly sorry."

Immediately, Al's expression softened as her daughter-in-law hugged her.

"Honey, it's okay, and certainly not *your* fault. Sadly, you were blessed with overbearing and pompously rude parents. Hugo and I came to see you both and spend time with our adorable grandchildren, and that's just what we've done, and enjoyed every minute of it."

"How ever did you manage to grow up so well-adjusted?" Hugo ventured, changing the subject, before thinking it sounded arrogant and knowing he shouldn't have asked. Molly and Zax laughed as he put his arm around his young wife and kissed her before she replied.

"Didn't Zax ever explain to you that I was reared by my Grandma? We lived in one of the small cottages on the estate. I wasn't allowed near the 'big house' until I was ten years old, and even then, only on special occasions, like my parents' birthdays or Christmas, and always with my grandmother present. My parents thought children much too bothersome and unruly to have around.

"My grandmother would take me on long walks around the estate; as we walked, she'd explain to me how it should all work. She often called her son a financial idiot and a waste of time. She said I was the only good thing that ever came from the marriage of two upper class ignorant snobs. Even though I had never been inside the mansion, grandmother explained each room in detail, where each was situated, who had occupied them and what they overlooked. She had a wonderful way with words and a magical sense of life and humor. When her husband, Lord Win-Stanley the 7th, died and her only son took over the title and property, the first thing he did was move her out of the mansion and into one of several dilapidated cottages on the grounds. Hers, like most of them, hadn't been occupied in years, so she spent a considerable amount of time and money renovating and redecorating. It's quite charming; I still keep it just as she did.

"The moment she was enjoying her newly redecorated little cottage, she was handed a note saying they didn't want me and that if she didn't care to look after me, then I was to be left at the orphanage. My grandmother was appalled, but she said it was one of the happiest days of her life. She always said I brought sunshine to her cloudy days. When she died, I moved into the mansion. I had a huge ache in my heart for a very long time. She died just before I left for university and met Zax.

"Grandmother always told me I was blessed and would have a wonderful life. She said my first blessing was being born at all. And my second was being left in her care. She knew I'd meet a wonderful man, and just as she predicted – I did. Neither of my parents could stomach children; they found them much too noisy and messy and too demanding also. So, the sooner we move into our new home, the better. Have I told you how proud I am of all the hard work your son's done? My parents are grateful, too; they just don't know how to show it. But Zax is their hero and he can do no wrong in their eyes," Molly said, looking lovingly up at Zax as he bent over and kissed her leisurely on the lips. By this time, Al and Hugo had forgotten why they were upset; just seeing their son so loved and appreciated was enough for them to endure hell, and Zax was loved and adored.

"So, Mom and Dad, did you actually have something to tell us, or did you just need to escape?" Zax asked as he cuddled Molly close on the window seat. Al and Hugo exchanged glances, not wanting to tell him about Neve and not knowing if they should do so in front of Molly. They hoped he hadn't told her anything, but they also knew how close they were and often wondered if he had.

"We did need to escape, obviously," Al began.

"But, yes, we have something to tell you," Hugo said.

"And we don't want you to get angry," Al added.

"Should I leave the room?" Molly asked. Al and Hugo wished she would, although Zax answered for them.

"Honey, you're part of this family. You never need to leave the room. Whatever my parents have to say, they can share it with you also."

Hugo and Al exchanged concerned looks at his words, but knew there was no turning back now.

"Well, darling," Al began, "your sister Neve is getting married soon; she has supposedly met the man of her dreams. She hasn't known him long, but she seems sure. You know Neve – when she makes up her mind about something."

"Oh, how perfect… a wedding! Can we afford a trip to America right now, honey?" Molly asked, clapping her hands together.

"Molly, just listen… I have a feeling in my gut there's way more to it than this," Zax said, looking worried rather than happy like his wife.

"Well, yes, there is, actually," Hugo said.

"Nothing I'm going to want to hear, I'll bet." Zax got to his feet and started pacing the floor as he waited for his parents to continue.

"Well, darling, there is more. Neve's just informed us – she's pregnant. So, the wedding will be very soon. We're to meet him next weekend."

"Oh, how super!" squealed Molly, again clapping her hands.

"There's still more, honey. I can feel it," Zax said.

Molly inquired, "Where do you think she'll get married?"

"New York, I think. That's where Chuck was born and raised," Al said, sharing Molly's excitement, until her son spoke up.

"That's where you've been working up until now, isn't it? And what was Neve doing in New York?" Zax was still pacing as he spoke. No one answered. Al and Hugo exchanged scared looks. Seconds passed as Zax saw the answer in their faces and exploded.

"So, Neve Grasshopper's not getting married, is she? How could you, how could you both let this happen? You pretend to be loving parents, and you involved her in danger like this and now I guess she's stuck there. Who the hell is she anyway?" he screamed. Al and Hugo had never seen him so upset, but they also knew everything he said was true.

Finally, Al said, "Amanda Dolman, and it was her idea…"

"But *you* let it happen. You didn't talk her out of it. How the hell could you?" Zax's face was crimson and he had tears streaking down his cheeks.

"Well, what does he do?" This was the second question they had dreaded, and silence again filled the room. Some time passed as Al tried to wipe the tears from her face before she replied in a whisper, "He's a private investigator."

The moment her words were out, Zax exploded again, as they knew he would.

"What the hell? What game is she playing? What the hell is going on here? How could she possibly meet a private investigator?" Zax fumed, and then added, "Oh, I guess he's a friend of yours?" His sarcasm did not go unnoticed as he continued, "Don't even bother to answer, 'cause I sure as hell don't want to hear it. And you have the nerve to judge the Win-Stanleys. I suggest she hasn't even mentioned she has a brother, 'cause my sister is Neve Grasshopper, not Amanda whatever. I want no part of it, none at all!" he yelled.

"Zax, surely you'll attend the wedding?" Al asked in a small voice.

"When hell freezes over! That's not going to happen. I want nothing to do with this charade! I don't want to know about it or hear about it. I just want to be a member of the Grasshopper family. In fact, don't even bother to call me again until I am! Tell Neve congrats. We'll send her a present, but don't expect us at the wedding. Good night!" Zax yelled as he walked out the door, slamming it loudly behind him. Alberta and Hugo had not ever seen him this upset, ever.

They sat and looked at Molly, whose face was as white as Al's.

Finally, she said, "He'll be all right in the morning, you'll see. If he's not, I'll take you to the airport. See you at nine." She got up and hugged then both tightly. It was enough for Al to release the sobs she'd managed to hold inside. Molly held her close for several minutes.

"I'm so sorry, Molly," Al said. "I'm sorry we are who we are. And I'm sorry we upset our precious son so much. I hope you'll find it in your heart to forgive us."

"No need, I already have," she replied, hugging Hugo briefly, who was also shaken to the core.

As she left the room, she turned and said, "Sleep tight – love you both."

Together, they replied in tiny voices, "Love you, too, Molly." She closed the door and was gone.

She was as good as her word and was waiting outside with the car at nine o'clock. Al and Hugo had hardly slept all night and Al wanted to go to her son. Hugo suggested she wait until he cooled off and came to them. However, that hadn't happened, and although they hoped he would join them on the drive to the airport, he didn't appear.

Molly was as sweet as always and apologized on Zax's behalf, saying he had urgent estate business to attend to and he wished them a safe trip. However, neither of them believed her, and it was a very silent trip to the airport, in spite of Molly's efforts to cheer them.

Molly had a gift for Amanda and Chuck. It was already wrapped in wedding paper and she asked them to purchase and sign a card to accompany it. She said it was a silver-framed photo of them all and was taken just the week before they arrived. Al kept hoping, until the last minute when they boarded the plane, that Zax would call. But he didn't, and it was to be a very long time before they heard his voice again.

Baggage of the Dead

It was late when they touched down in LAX. Baxter had ordered a car for them; they were very tired. Finding a house they had never seen was an unnecessary diversion. In the morning they knew they needed to transform themselves into people they didn't know. Al was still upset, and when their plane was delayed at Heathrow for two hours, she had understandably started to get grumpy.

The sunlight streamed in the unfamiliar window early the next morning. It warmed their faces and blinded their sleepy eyes as they first opened. They were both tired and disoriented, and it took several seconds for them to realize the amount of work they had ahead of them. Baxter had done a wonderful job washing and cleaning the house. He had started to remove many of the personal items belonging to the previous owners into black garbage bags. Hugo would complete the job and then take the bags many miles away and dump them. He hoped the car still worked, but felt sure Baxter would have had it checked. It brought tears to Hugo's eyes throwing out all the toys and baby photos of the deceased owners, and he wondered how the relatives could be so cruel as to leave all these memories behind. He saw no evidence that they were anything but great parents and a loving couple.

Meanwhile, Al worked tirelessly on their disguises. First, she composed them on the computer and then created photos of them with Amanda at different ages. Hugo carefully filled the frames around the house with their photos as he meticulously took away all traces of the previous owners. He then took all the bags to the car that he's previously placed in the garage. Looking around the garage, he saw he also needed to remove more items there. Once the car was filled with garbage bags, he would leave under cover of darkness.

It was later that night, after Al and Hugo returned from the supermarket and in their new disguises as Sam and Ruth Dolman, that the doorbell rang. Hugo had just unloaded the groceries and Al was putting them in the fridge and cupboards. He was just loading the last of the many black garbage bags into the small car when he heard a knock on the garage door. There were no windows in the old door and Hugo was not about to expose himself with the garbage bags half-loaded into the car. He stood where he was, thinking he may have been mistaken and maybe it was just the wind rattling the door. It was a place they didn't know and therefore all the noises were new. It was nine o'clock at night and Hugo stood still and listened.

"I know you're in there. I can see the light under the door. Open up!" came a raspy woman's voice as she knocked again none too softly on the door.

"Who are you and what do you want?"

"Me name's Carman Finnick, I'm ya neighbor across the road. Open up!"

"Hold on," Hugo said, racing into the kitchen where Al was putting away the groceries.

"Al, someone's at the door and I've forgotten our names," Hugo said.

"Oh, darling Sam, I am your wife, Ruth Dolman. Who is at the door at this time of the evening? I didn't hear a knock."

"I know, Ruth; she knocked on the garage door."

"How strange," Ruth replied.

"Yes, that's what I thought." The moment Sam spoke the words, the front doorbell chimed several times.

"I'll handle this, Hugo, I mean Sam. You get those bags out of here."

"Hello," Ruth said, opening the door wide and coming face to face with a rather unpleasant-looking old woman.

"Well, it's about time. Where's the boy?"

"Who are you?"

"Just told him, I'm Carman; Carman Finnick. I live across the road. Been watchin' ya all day from me livin' room window. I look straight across, ya know. Here, I baked ya a pie. Sort of welcome to the neighborhood, like."

"Thank you, how very kind," Ruth said, taking the pie that was wrapped in a dirty tea towel and thrust into her hands.

"Well, ya askin' me in?"

"Yes, yes, of course," Ruth said, instinctively not liking this intrusive woman.

"Where's ya boy? He was in the garage."

"He's gone out for a while, and he's my husband."

"Whatever. Ya haven't done much to the place, have ya?"

"This is only our second day here," Ruth responded, and then wished she hadn't felt as if she must defend herself.

"So, where's he gone? Thought we'd have a whisky – like a kind of welcome drink."

Ruth was beginning to feel very uncomfortable in the fat little woman's presence. She was obviously a busybody, and not a nice one at that. She had greasy gray hair combed roughly back from her face. Her cheeks were rosy, and not from good health – Ruth guessed it was from whisky. The intruder's eyes positively darted around the room, over Ruth and then back around the room, as if searching for something.

"Well, you wasted no time gettin' ya photos up," Carman said as the phone rang. Ruth assumed it must be a wrong number, as only Baxter, Hugo and Amanda knew the new number. She'd emailed it to them just a few hours ago.

"Ya young ones are all alike, all ya want to do is talk, talk talk…," Carman said as Ruth ignored her and answered the phone.

"Mom, I'm so glad you're there. You'll never guess what's happened today at work. I couldn't get hold of Chuck; he's already out on a stakeout." Amanda sounded very upset and Ruth immediately thought of the baby.

"Honey, I'll have to call you back; just give me five minutes. Sorry!"

"But, Mom, I need to tell you about my day. I don't know what to do. Chuck says I should leave…"

"Honey, I'm sorry, but I'll have to call you straight back," Ruth said as she hung up the phone. "Look, Mrs errr…"

"Carman, me name's Carman, and ya haven't even told me yours."

"Oh, I'm Ruth, Ruth Dolman. I'm sorry, Carman, but I'll have to ask you to leave. A family problem, you understand. We'll have that whisky another time perhaps," Ruth said, standing over the old lady, who was still comfortably seated and seemed to want to stay that way.

"Kids always have problems. Same with me own, always getting into trouble. Just do what I do and leave them alone, don't answer their calls when they need you. Let them sort themselves out, like. They need to realize ya got ya own life and don't need 'em either. It works, trust me. Why, I haven't spoken to mine in over five years and guess I never will now. That's not easy when they live right across the road, always wantin' things and expectin' ya to do things for them, like."

"I'm sorry, Carmen, but I must ask you to leave. Again, thank you for dropping by."

"Ya make ya call. I'll stay right here and wait," Carmen announced, her eyes still darting around the room as she spoke.

"No, Carmen, that just won't do. I need you to leave now," Ruth said, getting really annoyed at the old lady, who continued to sit. Ruth was prepared to lift her from the chair if she didn't move. Ruth was getting very worried about Amanda. She didn't like to hear her daughter upset, and she seldom was.

"I'll bet ya haven't even got no whisky, like, that's why ya want me out. Ya embarrassed; yeah, that's what it is. I knew it. Why, I know all about types like ya. They invite their neighbor over, like, and then don't even have any whisky. Cheap freaks, is what I call ya. Yeah, I'll be going; thanks for ruining me night. I would have stayed and had a nice little chat, like, but you're rude and a lousy hostess. Here, give me me pie and I'll get out so ya can make ya precious phone call. Your daughter don't care about you, she'll leave ya soon as a horny guy winks at her, you'll see, ya freakin' cheapskate."

Ruth was beginning to get worried about Carmen; she was certainly more than a little weird. Finally, she managed to get herself up off the chair, and quick as a flash she retrieved her pie from the counter where Ruth had left it.

"Just don't come a callin' on me when ya lonely and need a friend, like."

"Thanks for all your advice," Ruth called, slamming the door the moment she was out. Carmen had just turned to say something more, but instead she heard the deadbolt lock into place. Ruth peeked around the blinds to make sure she went straight home. As she spied on Carmen, she was pretty sure it was Sam's car she saw turn into the quiet tree-lined street. Ruth raced to the garage and opened the roller door so he could drive straight in. The moment the car was inside, she quickly closed the door, but not before she saw Carmen hurrying back across the road toward them. The old lady banged on the door as Ruth signaled Sam to stay quiet. Moments later, they turned off the garage light and locked the adjoining door.

"Darling, you look a little ruffled. Good thing she didn't stay long," Sam said.

"No, she's a weird old creep and I never want her here again."

"I thought she sounded a little crazy through the door. Do you think she's dangerous?"

"Probably, and I don't want to find out. Anyway, we need to call Neve – something's happened." Together, they made the phone call and spoke to their daughter on speaker.

"Baby Girl, is everything all right?" Sam asked.

"Oh, Daddy, no. You were both right and Chucky told me the same as you. I should have left Banker's Securities when you did," Amanda said as she began sobbing.

"Honey, we're here now, so tell us everything."

"Well, I only just got home. I missed seeing Chucky 'cause he had to stand in for Fred. Fred's baby is sick and his wife might be pregnant again. And I know just how she feels, 'cause every morning I feel sick when I get out of bed and then the thought of food makes me feel worse. Chucky's been amazingly helpful and supportive, but he must be getting tired of my complaints," Amanda said without taking a breath. Neither Sam nor Ruth knew what she was talking about, other than her morning sickness.

"Honey, calm down. Is this just about you having morning sickness? 'Cause if it is, I promise you, it will pass."

"No, Mom, it's not," she said, calmer now.

"Okay, Baby Girl, how about you start from the beginning?"

"Yeah, sorry, Dad, you're right. I shall start at the beginning. Well, this morning I went into work as usual. At about eleven o'clock, Saffron asked me to do some chores for her and pick up her cocktail dress for a function tomorrow night. She said I didn't need to come back to work and just to bring it in with me in the morning. Anyway, my work was up to date and I was looking forward to a leisurely day shopping, and planned to meet Siobhan for lunch. Well, the next thing I know, Saffron's halfway down the hall, screaming at Brock's secretary, Enid Shillington. Enid's a quiet girl and really all she has going for her are her stunning looks; but Saffron lays into her in front of everyone. Calls her a slut and warns her to stop sleeping with Brock.

"Enid says nothing; she just looks at the floor as everyone gathers around but keeps at a distance. Well, when Enid doesn't answer, Saffron really loses it and picks up Enid's computer screen and hurls it at her. Then she tells her to collect her things and pick up her paycheck and get out. 'You're fired!' she yells, then storms back to her office and slams the door. Everyone gathers around Enid and helps her clear out her desk and call maintenance to clean up the glass and computer parts that are scattered everywhere. Still, Brock's nowhere to be seen and I'm feeling a wave of nausea. So, I spent a while in the washroom and waited for it to pass. Several of the girls came in and chatted, so I must have been away almost an hour. Anyway, when I came out, everything's back to normal, except Enid's gone. I thought I'd sit at her desk until everyone was back from lunch. I called Siobhan and cancelled our lunch. Well, I'd only been there half an hour when the computer guys delivered a new screen. Shortly after that, a very tall, slim, attractive blonde girl of about thirty-five walks in with her briefcase. Two guys followed her, carrying several large cardboard boxes. She introduces herself as Floris McKrill, Brock's new personal secretary. She then dismisses me by saying, 'That will be all.'"

Sam needed to interrupt at this stage, so he quickly jumped in. "Baby Girl, none of this sounds much fun, but why are you so upset and so late home from work?"

"Dad, I'm just getting to that. Anyway, I really wished I'd left earlier, when Saffron said I could. I was just gathering my bag when down the hallway walks Special Agent Bow Grismold, flanked by two uniforms. He sees that I'm about to leave and advises me not to. He walks straight into Saffron's office. Well, I assumed Enid has made a complaint, and I wouldn't have blamed her either. Well, he's in there for ages; meanwhile, the two uniforms guard the door. So, I wait. Anyway, he didn't come out for over an hour and when he did we were all interviewed."

"Honey, why?" Al asked.

"Mom, Dad, Saffron's husband Potter was found shot to death in Europe. They say it has all the markings of a drug heist gone wrong and a mobster shooting." Amanda sobbed briefly, although she was almost composed by now. It was Sam and Ruth that gasped as Sam placed his arm around Ruth's shoulders and they continued to listen.

"Amanda, you've got to leave your job."

"I know, Dad. Chucky said the same thing. He said the roof will soon fall in on their little operation and he doesn't want me involved."

"He sounds like a good man, honey, take his advice."

"I'm going to, Mom. He makes good money, and it really scared me. Tomorrow, the auditors arrive, because they think Saffron's been taking money from the company and there's apparently a lot missing, much more than ours. Saffron is trying to blame Berry. Dad, I'm scared. Do you think they'll find out?"

"I don't know, honey, but Saffron won't go down alone, that's for certain."

"She wasn't even upset at losing her husband. Even when her son was crying on the phone, she didn't seem to care. You were right about her, Dad. Siobhan said I should hand my letter of resignation to Brock; she's prepared to call him up for me. Do you think I should, Dad?"

"Yes, Baby Girl, I think you should do it as soon as possible; tomorrow if you can, without raising suspicion."

"Okay, I thought you might say that. I could do with some time to help with the wedding. Chuck's mom, Rita, is doing a great job and so are the wedding planners, even though it's only a small wedding. I still need to pick a dress and there are lots of things I want to do around the house. By the way, I've decided Siobhan will be wearing apricot. The flowers will all be a vibrant orange, so the color theme of the wedding will be apricot and warm white…" Amanda paused then, as they heard Chuck arrive home.

"Hey there, Sam, Ruth. Thank you for cheering up my girl; hated leaving her like that, but I really didn't have a choice. I know she tries to put on a brave face for me and I love her for it. How are you guys?" Chuck said.

"We're fine now. You've given Amanda some great advice, and we've told her also to leave Banker's Securities as soon as possible. Glad you're looking after her, Chuck, and we're looking forward to meeting you this weekend."

They chatted on for a while before saying goodbye. Amanda sounded a lot happier. Ruth and Sam couldn't believe what they'd just heard. They were more concerned for Amanda than ever, and again wondered what they had gotten her into.

The next couple of days proved hectic for them both. Sam was due at his new job on Monday morning and it was already Thursday. Chuck and Amanda were to arrive on Friday evening and leave late Sunday afternoon. Then, Sam and Ruth would immediately take a flight to San Diego so Sam could start his new job on Monday morning. The following weekend they were to fly to New York on Friday afternoon for the wedding on Saturday. Sam and Ruth's wedding present to the happy couple was a ten-day honeymoon in Hawaii.

Ruth desperately needed more supplies for their next job, as this extra change of identity had left her very short of resources.

Ruth waved to Amanda the moment they walked through the gate; they knew she had no other way of recognizing them and didn't want their meeting to look suspicious. Their first impression of Chuck was of a tall, good-looking man, handsome in a rugged kind of way. He stood over six feet tall. He had sparkling blue eyes and an easy smile. It didn't go unnoticed by all who saw them that they made a stunningly handsome couple. Ruth liked him immediately, but Sam was not so sure: he couldn't forget he was a private investigator and felt rather uncomfortable having him around. Chuck was a very intelligent, good-humored guy who immediately took in his surroundings, recording and processing everything in the blink of an eye.

Sam could see how they adored each other and he had to admit they seemed a perfect fit. But she was his baby girl, and seeing her engaged to be married made him very aware she was all grown up and he felt like he was losing her to another man. The moment Chuck had Sam alone, he asked formally for Amanda's hand in marriage. Sam was impressed, but somehow wished he could say no and keep his little girl forever.

The weekend flew by and Amanda enjoyed seeing Chuck without the stress of work. He did, however, constantly keep in touch with his guys, telling them what to do and how he wanted each situation handled. They went out to some wonderful little restaurants which Sam and Ruth had to pretend they'd enjoyed before. Amanda and Chuck certainly seemed in harmony on all things, and their parents enjoyed seeing them together and hoped they would stay this happy forever. A lot of the talk was about the wedding, and Ruth was amazed to see how calm they were, considering they were just days away from becoming husband and wife. By Saturday evening, they were more relaxed with each other and lingered in the intimate Italian restaurant long after enjoying their meal. As they arrived back at the house on Saturday night, Chuck immediately noticed a shadowy form lurking in the bushes. Ruth had previously told Chuck about Carmen. Chuck instructed them to pull into the garage and pretend they hadn't seen her. He advised Sam to leave the garage door open. The moment they set foot outside the car, she was upon them.

"Come for me whisky, no point in waitin' to be asked," Carmen said, holding onto the half-empty whisky bottle as she moved shakily towards them. Ruth noticed she was in even worse condition than when last they'd met.

"I'm Chuck."

"So, what, what ya want me to do about that? Guess ya one of those pesky children of hers who keeps bothering me friend and takin' her attention away from me. Yeah, that's who ya are. She told me ya were coming... Call the cavalry, that's what I did – call the cavalry! Only way to deal with pesky kids who bothers ya."

"Okay, Carmen, I'll take you home now," Chuck said, firmly grabbing her arm.

"Ya take your grubby mitts off me person, ya young scoundrel. You're probably the one who killed me daughter, that's who you are. Yeah, I can see ya face now and I know for sure. Don't come near me, you murdering filthy son of a bitch," she screamed. Chuck didn't reply, but to everyone's astonishment, he picked her up and threw her over his shoulder – her bottle of whisky fell to the ground. She yelled all the way across the road right up until he put her down in front of her doorway. Sam looked up and down the road to see who had come out to witness the disturbance. The short tree-lined road remained silent and Sam guessed no one cared.

They could hear her yelling at Chuck from across the road. She was accusing him of manhandling her, of stealing her whisky and of becoming an ally against the new folks who had taken her inheritance and more. Finally, Chuck got her inside, and the yelling continued. Ten minutes later, he calmly walked into their living room and all was quiet. Chuck told them about the inside of her house and how she didn't want him to enter. He said when he did, he quickly learned her secrets, and discovered it was a complete mess.

"However, she has a high-powered, state-of-the-art telescope trained directly on your house, along with several very outdated listening devices."

"I would never have thought...," Ruth said, astonished.

"She's a weird, scary, sophisticated snoop. Keep your blinds drawn and talk when you're inside with the windows closed. Who knows what she's capable of? How did she know we were coming this weekend anyway, if you've only spoken to her once?" Chuck asked, looking from one to the other. When he didn't get an answer, he got up and went outside. They all followed. Around the back of the house he found a listening device attached to the telephone wire.

"I gave her my card, so I'll just leave this here for a moment," he said, then went directly inside to the telephone, before saying several loud words into the receiver. "Call me, Carmen. I'm pressing charges." He then returned to the outside of the house and removed the device.

While he was gone, Amanda whispered, "Didn't you check, Mom? I thought you always did."

"I never thought to check here in this old suburban house; anyway, we're not set up here, honey – in a street like this, why would I have imagined there was any need? All my equipment's already in San Diego," Ruth whispered just as Chuck returned.

Sam and Ruth wondered just how much he'd believed of Carmen's ramblings and decided it was probably nothing. After all, most of it was the ranting of a crazy mind. The weekend flew by and Amanda and Ruth were both tearful at the airport, even though they would see each other the next weekend.

The moment Amanda and Chuck were on the plane, back to New York, Sam and Ruth quickly raced back to the house. They hadn't ordered a limo for fear that Carmen might see them. They had changed out of their disguises as Sam and Ruth Dolman and were again Hugo and Al Grasshopper. Al carefully packed the disguises in their small travel bag; she was sure Carmen would be snooping around in their absence. They made their flight with minutes to spare and tipped the cabby generously for speeding. They relaxed briefly on the short flight. Al went over everything that she needed to set up, along with all the necessary paperwork for their false identities. Hugo concentrated on his new job that he was starting in the morning. He reviewed in his head the background of the company and company directors, the financial reports, the half-yearly reports, along with the numerous companies and who they had as customers and their many suppliers that he knew of. All too soon they were landing.

You're Now in the Family

San Diego was a twinkling, welcoming wonderland as they touched down in their new home city. The air was warm and the drive to their condo was scenic. The condo sat high on a cliff overlooking the beautiful Pacific Ocean; it was located in Del Mar. Should you look over the balcony to the left, you could just see Black's Beach amongst the tundra and scrub that separated it from the highway.

After the tiny suburban home of the Dolmans, the condo was three thousand square feet of sleek modern luxury. It was finished in polished wood and muted taupes, golds and warm beiges. The furnishings were low, square and sleek, and as usual when Baxter visited, everything was left meticulously clean and shiny. Hugo often thought Baxter was maybe even more meticulous than they were themselves. The fact that he liked to achieve perfection in all he did was one of his best features. Baxter had stocked the fridge with all their favorite foods, although tonight Al was too busy to eat. She didn't sleep at all that night, but set up her electronics and prepared everything for Hugo's new employment at E.M. Distributors Pty. Then, as four a.m. arrived, Al was checking and rechecking to be sure everything worked. As Hugo sleepily entered the room, she was again going over her checklist of things he was to wear, carry and use, making sure they would work how they should.

By five a.m., the creation of Harrington and Millington Hoarders was in full swing. The fact that Al hadn't slept at all didn't seem to stop her from being particular to the point of obsessive with Hugo's appearance. By six a.m., she was showing him all his necessary ID cards and the corporate affiliated cards he should have.

"Darling, I don't have time to link into the security camera's at E M Distributors so I don't know what they all wear. I think a suit today, until we know what they're like as a company. Remember, they are family-owned, so you must look like them before you can begin to be accepted."

"I understand, Milly," Hugo said, winking lovingly at his wife, who was, as always, very serious about even the tiniest of details.

Then Hugo added seriously, "This is my last job, Al. I don't want Zax out of our lives any more than you do. If we must make a choice between him and our work, then I, for one, say it must be our son. Although he has no right." Hugo was expecting an argument from Al. He knew she had no intention of giving up their exciting international life of embezzlement. Although he knew the thought of not seeing Zax and their grandchildren must have helped make up her mind. Hugo thought his wife was too distracted with the finishing touches she was making to answer him, but after several minutes, she stood back to admire Hugo, who was now Harrington Hoarders.

"Yes, Hugo, I know it's our last job. I just hope it's nothing like New York."

"Really, darling? So, you do understand," Hugo said, delighted at the first sign of their retirement. Al nodded and kissed him lightly on the cheek, then she began to tell him about Harrington Hoarders' background.

"Darling, Harrington and Millington Hoarders used to own one of the biggest textile mills in North Carolina. They passed away ten years ago and the mills have since been sold and flattened to make way for a massive housing complex. I think you may find Colonel Wiggins or Sanders will know the name, so I suggest you say we are cousins and they are from a branch of the family we never got to know."

"Thank you, darling. Are you going to be able to get some sleep today?"

"I wouldn't want to sleep through Harry Hoarders' first day at work! Hardly," she replied with a chuckle in her voice.

"Anyway, after Banker's Securities, I have learned not to take anything for granted. I thought I was one of the best in the business. I have millions invested and I thought I had the very latest and greatest techniques and equipment. But New York tested me to the hilt. I'm glad we're out of there, and I hope they have no way of tracing Neve to the missing money."

"I'm sure it will all work out just fine," Hugo said, sounding more reassuring than he felt as he hugged his wife. He knew she was an amazing woman and worked harder than any of them. He would never let her take the fall if they were caught. He would go down alone.

They enjoyed a leisurely breakfast, followed by Al making a few last-minute adjustments to his face.

"Good luck today, Harry. I hope we hear from Neve soon and she is finally out of the Bankers Securities. I will feel so much happier knowing she's safe." she added, kissing him on the cheek before closing the door behind him. As Harry walked to the car, he realized his wife had been a lot more shaken than she'd led him to believe, by their time in New York. E.M. Distribution was on the outskirts of San Diego and, for Hugo, about a forty-five-minute drive, if he missed the main rush hour.

He drove into a large, well-kept outdoor car park. Around the edges and between the cars were well-tended gardens with happy shrubs and tall evergreen trees that gave much-needed shade in the summer. Only a few cars filled the spaces, so Hugo drove around the vast area several times before returning to the space in front of the building marked 'Lindsay Proctor, CFO'. It was the guy's name that he was replacing printed neatly on the plaque, so Hugo thought it was safe to park there. In the last week Hugo was finding it harder and harder to remember who he was; too many identities in too short a time – this game was definitely getting tiresome. He checked his look in the car mirror and wondered why he had to look like such an old man. Granted, he looked distinguished with his mop of curly salt and pepper hair, his full cheeks, square jaw, full, well-shaped lips and white false teeth, but who wanted to look aged? He had to admit that yet again Al had done a wonderful job on his appearance. She was extremely clever, and he had a face everyone would love and trust. He looked like everyone's handsome grandfather with his tall frame, padded shoulders and small belly.

Harry got out of the driver's door and opened the back door to retrieve his briefcase. He was just closing the back door when a smart black Cadillac pulled into the parking bay several spaces away. Seconds later, an elderly gentleman simply bounded out of the car. He was beaming from ear to ear, his cheeks rosy and his clear, sparkling blue eyes welcoming. He had a full head of whitish gray hair that he wore slightly too long, a tall frame and a spring in his step of a man twenty years his junior. He spotted Harry and immediately bounded towards him.

"Harrington Hoarders, I presume!. Well, I knew you'd be early on the job, and it looks like I was right. Welcome, welcome to E.M., glad to have you aboard." He still hadn't released Harry's hand; he held it firmly in his as he continued vigorously shaking it. Harry could only nod as the exuberant older man continued.

"Colonel Emmet Wiggins, President, CEO and member of the board. I just knew you'd be early; sign of a good man, I always say." He still hadn't released Harry's hand, so he jumped right into the conversation.

"Great to be here, Colonel Wiggins. I like your location very much."

"So, do I; chose it myself. It's a little out of the mainstream, but then so am I. It's Emmet, by the way, Harrington, nothing formal here," Emmett said, and Harry could almost hear Al's reaction as she watched. She would be clapping her hands with delight at this wonderful, full-bodied character. Harry quickly looked sideways at the other man as they walked toward the entrance. He was wearing a brightly colored floral shirt, which looked like it belonged to the seventies, tight white denims and leather sandals. He carried a small, black leather handbag over his left shoulder, and Harry wondered if maybe he was gay.

"You like the bag? My wife tells me it's the very latest fashion in Europe – she's just got back from a trip with her girlfriends. One of my gifts; very handy I must say, but I felt like a raving queen when I first wore it. You should see the looks I get. I am use to getting looks anyway having such a gorgeous blonde thirty-year-old beauty on my arm, but carrying a men's bag, I get even more. I find it all most amusing, Harrington."

"Harry please, Harrington sounds so formal" Harry added quickly as the other man barely took a breath before continuing, "You'll need to get out of that suit Harry; we don't do those around here. Men's bags we do, suits certainly not. We're a relaxed, happy bunch, one big happy family." They were walking through the reception area now and it presented beautifully in dark brown metal and chrome, with 'E.M. Distribution' in large neon purple lighting that matched the sign at the front of the building. Harry was most impressed.

However, the moment Emmett opened the door that led to the offices, everything changed. Piles of papers and overflowing garbage bins filled every desk and every office. Filing cabinets were opened, and files were stacked on the floor beside them, on top of them and on any vacant surface. Every single desk was cluttered to various degrees, not only in the main office, but in the side offices also.

"My office is upstairs in the executive area; great view from up there. Lindsay Proctor, the man you're replacing for a while as chief financial officer, had the choice of having his offices up there also, but he said he liked to be with his team. We're all team players here, Harry. Well, you've seen the tidy area of the building, now I'll show you the warehouse and then I know you'll be eager to see the accounts department," Emmett said, waving his arms in the air almost as fast as he talked and walked. Harry was in shock. He'd never seen anything like it. The warehouse was huge and already the morning's activities were beginning. About seventy guys were gathered in one corner enjoying McDonald's coffee and breakfast biscuits. A very loud and excited early morning meeting was in full swing as Harry passed, and he heard several

x-rated jokes being told as the guys all laughed loudly. Emmet stopped talking briefly. Then he moved through the crowd and the workers all greeted their leader with slaps on the back and smart retorts.

"Jethro, my boy, meet Harrington, or let's call him Harry; yes, this is Harry Hoarders. Harrington's much too formal here, and with a name like that no one will take you seriously. We're a very informal lot, Harry. Anyway, boys, he'll be taking over Lindsay's place while he's in the hospital. Jethro's my third cousin twice removed on my mother's side."

"Howde do," Jethro said, almost breaking Harry's hand as he shook it tightly. Then Emmet addressed the crowd, which had quieted somewhat since their arrival.

"I'm Storm, Storm Patricers – you look after me, Flower, 'cos I'm her old man, like," yelled a large, hairy man with tattoos on his neck. Harry nodded, still not really knowing what any of it meant.

"Boys, meet Harry, our temporary CFO." They called out their welcome in unison as Jethro told them they were five minutes late for their eight a.m. start. He said it would come off their lunch breaks. There were a few boos from the boys as they quickly dispersed. Harry didn't know whether Jethro was joking or not. Although the way they hurried off to start work, he guessed that maybe he wasn't joking after all.

Emmet then took Harry around a small part of the huge warehouse and explained the area where the different fabrics were kept. He began with the upholstery fabric and said the expensive stuff for high-end stores was on the higher shelves; while the cheaper stuff that went to covering readymade furniture must be within easy reach, as they sold much more of it, but made less profit. Then onto the area where they had marine items: fabric to make sails for yachts and coverings, waterproof fabric for the interiors of boats and ships. Then it was onto the outdoor fabric: fabric for furniture, tents, lean-tos, sleeping bags and awnings. Emmet explained again how they rated them in price order and placed the items they sold most on the bottom shelves and the ones they sold least on the top, where a cherry picker was needed to access them. Everything was marked precisely with a number and a name and also a code. It was very impressive and a lot to take in. Harry already felt exhausted.

"I'll show you the cafeteria and then I'll take you to meet your crew. They should all be here by now. Lindsay never ran a tight ship, so everyone arrives and leaves as they wish. Most of them have young families, including your Flower."

Harry didn't answer. He was having trouble keeping pace with Emmet, who moved swiftly around like a man half his age. He bubbled over with energy and vitality and almost ran instead of walking. Harry briefly wondered what his Flower was, but they were already climbing stairs two at a time and walking down the plush hallway of the second floor. On one side were the executive offices, large and elegant and very tidy. On the other side of the carpeted hallway were clear glass panels that went from floor to ceiling and showed a view of the workers below. Gurther down the hallway the offices changed to dark wood panels, red walls and navy accents made for a solid, manly atmosphere. Harry was introduced to anyone who was in his office. He noticed not their faces, but mainly their clothes: most were dressed casually in jeans and t-shirts.

The cafeteria was again another contradiction of space. It was bright, new and very modern. Everything was orderly and in its place. Each table was neatly set with a white tablecloth with several flowers in a silver vase in the center.

"Silver service, Harry," Emmet said, looking around proudly. Harry believed him.

"We like to look after our people, so everyone has an allowance to spend here every month. One of your girls' looks after it, so I know you won't find it a bother." Harry was only half-listening to Emmett's words, mesmerized as he was by the view. One side of the cafeteria was a full glass window, and the view was breathtaking.

Then, still at a very fast walk, they raced down the stairs and through the hugely messy area of desks, some with people already working in them. Most were writing on papers stacked on top of papers; some were on computers. Emmet didn't slow his pace as he navigated the desks, somehow finding a small area of uncluttered floor as he went. He called out introductions to several of his staff as he passed, but Harry was unable to see who he was addressing at the speed they walked.

Finally, in the far corner of the huge open area, Emmett took Harry through a door; inside he saw about a dozen or so desks, with even more clutter on them than the other part of the office. Harry's office was large and cornered-off from the desks with floor to ceiling glass partitions. It also had a glass door. Outside the door was a large L-shaped desk completely covered in paper that spilled onto the surrounding floor. The top of a computer screen was barely visible.

"Well, here we are. Guess the crew haven't arrived yet. Probably on purpose; I guess they're kindly giving you some time to get oriented. Enjoyed the tour, great showing you around; and again, welcome aboard," Emmett said, and in a flash, he'd left Harry's office and closed the door on the outer office. Harry's phone vibrated and he knew it was Al.

"What the hell was that?" she said, laughing.

"I'm not sure. Have you ever seen anything like it?" Harry asked, sitting down at his desk after removing a tall pile of paperwork from the seat.

"Well, darling, you did say you didn't want it to be anything like New York, and I think you have your wish," she giggled as she continued on. "Good work, getting the bug in Emmet's office. I was feeling tired just watching the speed he travels! Who needs the gym?"

"The man's exhausting." Just then, Harry and Al heard a voice.

"Hello?"

"Talk later, darling," Harry said and closed his phone. He was sure to place it carefully in his jacket pocket; he knew that if he put it down, he may never find it again. The very moment he slipped his phone into his pocket, a tall, slim girl burst into his office. Harry stared at her and she stared right back at him. Her long, straight brown hair was held in place by a brightly colored woven headband around her forehead. She wore a floor-length caftan with huge bell-shaped sleeves and a small slit down the front of her throat. There was embroidery around the neck that matched the brightly colored headband. It was colored with old-fashioned, large red and blue roses with curly green leaves intertwined through the pattern. The background was a pale blue. But more amazing was the way it hung off the slim body of the girl. The fabric was heavy and very stiff, and it almost looked like it was standing on the floor all on its own. He noticed she smelt like a furniture store as she entered. Unless she moved her arms, it looked like a head sitting on top of an A-shaped tent.

The girl herself was, at first glance, very plain, but in a wholesome sort of way. Her eyes were a soft brown, her skin looked pale but healthy, and her smile livened her up immediately and changed her look from plain to attractive, in an earthy, sexy kind of way. She had carefully removed a pile of papers from the chair across from him and placed them on the floor at her feet. She then let out a low whistle and sat down. Harry was instantly intrigued.

"It's been a long time since I've seen a man in a suit in these parts. Really long time, wow! But you look good. Always did like a man in uniform; why, there's just something 'bout them, you know, sexy as all hell. Wow, but you look good! I reckon the Colonel made a real good choice this time. You going to wear that every day or is it just to impress us girls today?" the girl asked talking with an accent Harry was unable to recognize. She again let out a low whistle. Harry couldn't take his eyes from her. As she sat, her caftan barely moved, and she appeared to shrink down inside it as it engulfed her in its fabric. As he watched, he noticed that once she was completely seated she seemed to almost disappear altogether.

"Well, you sure talk pretty."

"Thank you. I'm Harrington Hoarders."

"Wow, really fine name, too, real fine. Harrington, what a fine name. Wish I'd met you sooner, I would name one of me children after you. Always looking for new names, like."

"Thank you, but most people call me Harry."

"Well, Harry it will be. Me name's nothin' fancy like that. I'm Flower, Flower Patricers. I'm your secretary, and if you're anything like old cousin Lindsay you'll do nothing all day, 'cause I do it all for you. All I need is a bonus at Christmas, like. If you're still here, otherwise before you leave will be real fine, like." Harry was astonished at her words and only nodded.

"You see, I'm married for the first time, married to a big clod named Storm. Better off than I ever was, but I think he only married me 'cause I'm a landowner, like."

"Oh," was all Harry could manage at her words. She was a most intriguing young woman, and even though he could see a few of his staff arrive in the outer office, no one bothered them and she kept on talking. Harry noticed immediately that several of them were dressed just like Flower.

"Yeah, you bet I am. Why, I got meself a half acre of municipal land when they sold it off. I was right quick off the mark; the Colonel, you know, 'Fast-foot Wiggins', helped me a little, but we've paid him back now, so a few more payments to the bank and I'll be a landowner free and clear. Why, it even has a building on the land already! How lucky was that? We live there."

Harry thought it strange she said *building* and not *house*, so he asked, "What kind of a building?"

"Well, it's not like a regular house or nothing – couldn't afford that with all me kids. But it works okay, and one day we'll even get a shower and a real kitchen. I know what that sounds like, considering…"

"Not at all. I guess it was just a shed on the property?" Harry asked, as Flower giggled.

"No, sir, we've got solid double brick walls and almost ten small rooms."

"Wow," said Harry. "It sounds like a small mansion." Again, Flower giggled and the laughter lit up her face and her eyes sparkled.

"No, nothing like that; why, no Patricers have ever lived in one of them mansion things. No, me building is a washroom. Yeah, it had eight toilets and a urinal for four. Course, we've converted it some. Me and Storm, we sleep where the urinals used to be, and its way cozy. We still got two toilets; pure luxury, don't you think? It's just that I got meself a new sewing machine rather than putting in a shower. Got to get your priorities right, don't you think?"

"I guess you sew a lot then?" Harry asked. She had stopped talking and, instead, she stared wide-eyed directly at him with her liquid brown eyes.

"Well, of course. I made this new outfit especially for you," she said, jumping up and twirling around inside the huge tent-like thing that didn't move at all.

"Storm managed to lose a couple of yards of Sanderson linen. It's one of the finest upholstery fabrics we carry, and the nicest thing I've ever owned. Why, I made me son a waistcoat and me daughter a skirt.

We had enough for all of that. Sometimes, having Storm around comes in useful."

"So, your... outfit... is made of upholstery fabric and you live in a toilet block?"

"Yep, and right proud of it too. You see before you a real landowner. Bet you haven't known many families that live in municipal washrooms, now have you? So now you can see why I needed that sewing machine, can't you? I make clothes for lots of me relatives, see them outside. Why, tomorrow I've got another new outfit made from boat sail fabric. You should hear the sound it makes when I walk. It kind of crinkles, like. Very fashionable it is, too," she said, pointing to the outer room that was now half full of workers, many of which were wearing her creations. They didn't appear to be doing much work as most of them were drinking coffee and talking. The more she spoke, the more Harry was amazed at the things she said; he didn't ever recall meeting a more unusual person.

He had to ask the next question. "So, how do you bathe?"

"Easy, like, I bring Storm and all the kids here every Sunday and we use the showers in the executive bathroom. The cleaners come in last thing Friday night, so they are always stocked with new soap, some of which we take home. Shampoo for our hair; we've never used shampoo before, and it makes your hair feel real soft, like. Here, feel...," Flower said, holding out a handful of her long, brown hair toward Harry. He had to admit it was soft. Then she continued, "...and fluffy towels. Every so often we take one of them big fluffy towels home; already we've got nearly one each."

"Wow, doesn't Emmett mind?"

"Hell no! Mind? Why, he thinks the kids should go to school clean also, even if they get a bit messed up during the week. We wash our clothes in the shower while we wash our bodies, and then take them home to dry. Why, the Colonel is me third cousin twice removed on me dad's side; smart lot they always were, just like the Colonel. He's the father of me eldest, although he's left home now. The Colonel paid for Swift Wiggins to go through University and become a scientist. He lives and works in Florida now. I've never forgiven the

Colonel for that. The rest of them I keep close, now that I know what he's capable of, like."

"How many children do you have?"

"Well, I got five kids at home at last count, but probably a few more around the place." The moment Flower mentioned her children, she almost leapt over the desk at Harry, who was not expecting her sudden movement and jumped backward, almost falling out of his chair. She pulled out a wallet of photos from deep inside her caftan and watched as they concertinaed out in front of him. There must have been at least twenty photos.

"This here is Angel Wings, she's my daughter; love having girls, pretty as a picture and smart as a whip. Why, she can catch a pigeon with her bare hands, and does so often; more use than most of her brothers put together. No clue who her father is. Then there's Pet Arbry; he's an okay kid. He's Storm's favorite out of the boys; his dad's Peter Arbry, he sings some. Then, this here is Lamb Sonny, and yes, his dad was black. Lamb's the nicest boy you'd ever meet, a little slow, but real nice, heart of gold; he'd help anyone, unlike his dad; he was a real arse – raped me and left me for dead, he did. I'd kill the son of a bitch if I ever see him again. This little cutey is Trigg Smith; he has a waistcoat that matches me caftan – it was his turn. Trigg's a fighter, always in a scrap, given up trying to keep him clean. He's a good kid, so long as you don't challenge him, then he'll have you in the dust before you know what's hit you. He thinks he wants to be a professional wrestler when he grows up; I just want him to keep all his teeth, like; other than that, I don't care whatever he chooses to do. And last but not least, there's little Colt, cutest baby you ever saw, or maybe the only one I can remember. He belongs to Storm and me – can you imagine him wanting to marry me after all these years of me being on my own? I'm a child of the revolution, a flower child, peace man, peace," Flower said, leaping back to her chair as several piles of papers fell on to of the other papers already piled on the floor. She made a 'V' with her fingers as she sat down again. Harry was aghast; in fact, he was speechless, not that Flower would have any idea just why he felt this way. He knew, to her, her world seemed completely normal. He expected she may be about to leave and go to her own desk, but she just sat and stared at him with her huge liquid brown eyes.

So, finally he asked, "How long have you worked here?"

"I've worked for 'Fast-foot Wiggins' for over twenty years."

"Really? That's a long time," Harry answered.

"Bet you thought I wasn't that old; well, it's all the sex that keeps me young."

"Really?" Harry replied, still astonished at the things she said.

"Yep, always liked it. Would you believe that I wear nothing under this here caftan?"

"Really?" Harry said for the third time.

"Yep, it's true. The world is all about appearances, so we save on underwear. Although Angel's going through a stage where she wants to wear undergarments. She feels a need to fit in, so she wears it only because the other girls at school do. Expensive it is, like. She's wearing it 'cause she wants to be like the other girls, that's all. She'll soon grow out of it, you'll see, or else we won't be able to afford to buy her both fancy underwear and send her to school – one of the two, like."

Harry listened in amazement and was beginning to feel quite exhausted. "Flower, maybe you should show me the books and get me up to speed so we can do some work."

"Tomorrow I'll take you down to personnel, get you signed up proper, like. They'll have a credit card for your expense account and each month you can take us all out for lunch; keeps the team spirit going, like. Bet they'll have car keys for your car, like, also. No need to concern yourself with any paperwork, everything's up to date. I put that pile there in case you got bored or something," she said, pointing to the pile of paperwork he had earlier removed from his chair. Then Flower continued, "Yeah, we're just one big, happy family here, and we like to keep it that way. We're all nice here, like. Except…" Flower lowered her voice as she suddenly moved across his desk again. Again, Harry was not expecting it, but this time he moved slightly toward her as she spoke in a whisper.

"Except Handy Sandy. Or you'll know him as Colonel Tom Sanders, no relations to all them tasty chickens or nothing; pity that, like. Anyway, Handy Sandy's related to Jon Frisby in Sales, although he was actually adopted, so fortunately Handy Sandy's not really related to any of us. You gotta watch his hands – not me, but you guys. He'll have those hands all over ya like an octopus in no time. I'm told it's hard to get him off you once he starts; he gets real excited real fast, puffing and panting and making those gasping noises. Why, I heard him once with one of the temps. He didn't know I'd dropped me pen behind a pile of paperwork and while I was down, he appeared from nowhere and attacked the new temp. Guess he didn't know I was there; thinks he's discreet, like, he does. I think the temp was only working back 'cause he felt guilty because of all the paperwork around here."

"Really, Flower, why is there so much paperwork piled everywhere? Why don't you file it away?"

"We have some filing cabinets for current stuff just so we can find it, like, but after that we just pile it. What you got in mind, Harry?" she asked, her eyes wide and staring as she moved in closer again.

"Well, I would have thought you could have bigger filing cabinets, like four or six drawers, rather than those little two-drawer ones I see scattered around. All the papers that have been actioned should be stamped and filed in the archive room. The filing cabinets should then be labeled so you can find your old files should you ever need them. Maybe it would save even more room if you transferred everything onto microfiche or recorded it on a computer disk and destroy all the paperwork."

"Wow, Harry, wow, you really are good, very innovative, like. Do we need a separate room for all this and more staff to look after it?"

"I should think so."

"Wow, cool, man, you're real cool. I'll order the filing cabinets tomorrow, and tell 'Fast-foot Wiggins' your thoughts on the latest technology; like, he'll be most impressed, Harry, most impressed. We're always looking for ways to stay in front. Some of us may even be able to find our computers again. Cool, man. What was the name of that fish? My Angel, she can go catch some, like. Catch anything, she can," Flower said excitedly, jumping up from her chair and clapping her hands together. Harry was amazed at her response; to him it all seemed obvious, although he knew that some of his suggestions were a little too advanced for her.

Then he changed the subject and asked, "So, is Colonel Sanders gay?"

"Peace man, it's a gay world…"

To which Harry replied again, "Really."

Finally, Flower got to her feet and stopped, staring wide-eyed at him. "It's morning tea-time. I'll just get you a nice cup of rose petal and jasmine tea; back in a jiffy," she said, leaping from the chair she had again just sat back down in and heading quickly out the door. Everyone seemed to move so fast around here. Harry was astounded; in fact, he was quite bewildered at the whole operation. Soon, Flower returned with a large mug of pale pink tea. It smelled wonderful. Then, Flower quickly left his office and passed around huge cookies to everyone from out of an old rusty tin, before returning and placing two enormous cookies on his desk – they looked like they might be chocolate chip.

"Flower, really, thank you, but I can't eat two; maybe give one to someone else."

"But, Harry, you're the boss, you're entitled. You need two, help you through the day, like. Lindsay always kept one in his top drawer for later – he loved my cookies. He said they made the world a happier place. Anyway, any man in uniform that works here deserves two cookies, like. You might not believe this, Harry, me being a woman of the world and a landowner and all, but I'll let you in on a little secret – I've never been with a man in uniform. Hard to believe, but true, like," Flower said, giggling again as she sat down and bit into her cookie, before staring at him with her huge liquid brown eyes.

"Really?" was all Harry could manage to her last comment. He wasn't at all sure what she meant by it.

Harry only managed to eat half a cookie – he thought they tasted very strange. Somehow, the rest of the day drifted past in a haze. Around four thirty p.m., everyone seemed to disappear, and Harry sat staring at an empty office that was drowning in paper. It took him a while to recognize the vibration of his cell phone and when he answered it, he realized it was Al.

"Hugo, Hugo, listen to me."

"Hi, darling, where are you? I haven't got much done today, but who cares, I'm getting paid anyway."

"Hugo."

"I think the name's Harry. Who's this?"

"Harry, stay where you are. I'm just jumping into a cab. I don't want you to drive. Do you understand?"

"Yeah, sure. I don't want to move anyway. This place is great; everyone does everything for you."

The next thing Harry remembered was a strange woman dragging him to his feet and saying she was his wife. By this time the offices were completely empty.

"You're not my wife. Why, you don't even look like her."

"Harry, please, behave. I'm Milly, your wife, and I'm taking you home. Flower managed to get you completely stoned. Probably put LSD into her cookies or mixed it in the tea. I'm taking you home," Milly said, holding him up as she searched his pocket for his car keys.

"You feel nice, but I usually go for the younger ones. But it's okay, you're here now, so you can take me home; just keep touching me...," Harry muttered as Milly somehow managed to get him into the car.

Moments with Jon Riddley

Jon Riddley was not enjoying the long absences from his partner, Baxter. He couldn't believe Baxter's employers could be so demanding as to call him at a moment's notice and send him to Los Angeles to purchase a house. Why hadn't Baxter asked him to stay and join him, instead of sending him home after just three cozy days of enjoyment and adventure in San Diego? Jon was rapidly realizing he had more freedom away from his partner than he wanted. Had he done something wrong? Was he not playful enough? Or was he lacking as a lover?

Yes, Jon Riddley was having doubts; not so much about Baxter, but about himself. Baxter was proving more of an equal than any of his former younger partners. He was used to calling the shots and having total control; he thought he was ready for a change. Jon had just designed matching diamond pinky rings and was waiting for the right moment to present them to his lover. Jon hoped this would prove his total commitment to Baxter. But lately, he was having doubts; maybe being with his equal was just too challenging?

Baxter was about to board yet another plane to take him home to the Grasshopper Estate in Savannah, Georgia. Baxter told him it was the Grasshoppers' main residence, and informed him it was a masterpiece, in architecture, interior design and landscaping. Five acres of private land surrounded by high brick walls, complete with state-of-the-art security. Baxter had his own cottage on the estate; it was the largest of three. It stood surrounded by shrubs and tall trees that completely concealed it from the main house. It boasted three bedrooms, two bathrooms and a wonderfully private deck and entertainment area. Lyle also kept rooms, as did the housekeeper, who was away most of the time and called in once a week when the Grasshoppers were not in residence.

However, Baxter often spent his time in the main house; he enjoyed the luxury. And that is exactly where he intended to entertain Jon when he arrived. As Baxter walked toward the gate to catch his flight, he decided to call his boyfriend.

"Hey, Bunny Poo, I'm still thinking of you, if you know what I mean…," Baxter flirted discreetly into his cell as he walked.

"Hey, you," Jon replied, delighted to hear from his guy so soon.

"You in a funk, Jon?" Baxter asked. He was beginning to realize Jon often got depressed or annoyed when things didn't go exactly as he'd planned or, when he wasn't getting enough attention. Baxter was even-tempered and he usually enjoyed a happy disposition. He liked his job and his life. Over the years he had invested in real estate and owned several small apartment blocks around the world. His shrewd investments alone brought him enough income to live very comfortably, even if he never worked again.

Baxter didn't want or need a whining, spoilt millionaire who required his every whim pandered to. Jon appeared to be turning into the type of guy Baxter despised, although he decided to give him the benefit of the doubt a little longer. Clingy and needy he didn't want, and he hoped Jon wasn't falling into that unacceptable category. His past, however, indicated that he was. He had always been surrounded by pretty boys with no brains and too much brawn. They had nothing in their lives, so Jon easily held their total attention and kept them under his control.

"Missing you, lonely without you. Why can't I be with you when you're working? What am I supposed to do while you're away from me? I've left you three messages… where were you?"

"I'm here now and I thought you enjoy your own space," Baxter replied, ignoring the tone in his voice and his questions.

"I've had enough space. I want to be with my boy. When can I see you? I hate sitting around just waiting for your calls."

"Well, Bunny Poo, why don't you jump a flight to Savannah, Georgia, tomorrow and I'll get the big house all ready for your arrival," Baxter suggested, expecting Jon to be excited.

"Why can't I jump a flight right now, and we can hook up at the airport?" Jon still had that tone in his voice and it was beginning to annoy Baxter.

"I'll be working till after midnight as it is. I'm a working guy, not so much time to pamper myself as you have."

"Well, handsome, I just had my back waxed for you – oh, the pain of it all. What we gals have to go through to stay beautiful, honey. I miss you and I don't think I can wait until tomorrow."

"Look, Bunny Poo, I'm on the plane now. So, let me know in the morning when your flight lands. Kisses." Baxter didn't wait for an answer as the lady sitting beside him was giving him strange looks and it didn't suit him to hear Jon's voice the way it was.

"Your wife?" The woman beside him inquired, raising one well-tended eyebrow slightly higher than the other as she flirted outrageously.

"No, just a friend."

"You're awfully handsome to be single, aren't you?" she inquired, and Baxter looked at her for the first time. She was about his age and very attractive in a sensual, exotic sort of way. She had slinky emerald green eyes surrounded by long dark lashes. Her lips were full and simply dripping with a shiny, pale pink lip gloss. Her nose was straight and her cheekbones high. She had perfect skin and elegant, slender, beautifully manicured hands. Her nails were long and covered in pale pink nail polish and the ends were tipped in gold. Her clothes were, like her perfume, obviously expensive, and Baxter couldn't help noticing that she wasn't ashamed to show off her ample assets. Something stirred deep inside Baxter at that moment, something that had been sleeping for a very long time. Baxter had only ever been with one woman and that was in college, but he definitely swung both ways. He could feel the animal magnetism she radiated and he became intrigued. Maybe, it was time for a change.

His cell rang at seven a.m. and Baxter ignored it. He'd stayed up and attended to the accounts, then checked to make sure the staff had been paid. He'd instructed the housekeeper to clean the big house first thing in the morning and stock it with the list of items he had given her. It was after two a.m. when he'd finally enjoyed a leisurely bubble bath while he sipped on several glasses of champagne. Jon had been on his mind as he fell asleep, but it had been Chartreuse, the lady he'd just met on the plane, who filled his dreams.

His cell rang again at seven fifteen a.m. and then again at seven thirty a.m., followed shortly afterwards by his home line. Annoyed at having his beauty sleep interrupted, he answered it on the third ring.

"So, where the hell have you been? I've been ringing you for an hour and this was my last try." It was a very testy-sounding Jon, and it was easy to tell he wasn't happy. Baxter didn't care for the tone in his voice. It was the first time Jon would visit him at the Grasshopper Estate and he was already regretting his invitation.

"What's your problem, so early in the morning? Can't a gal get his beauty sleep? You do want me looking good for you, Bunny Poo."

"When you didn't answer, I thought maybe you had forgotten me and turned me over for another younger, slimmer, and more handsome guy, honey," Jon said, knowing he had gone too far as he cooed gently into the phone.

"I'm still sleeping, Bunny; can this wait another couple of hours or so?" Baxter asked, hoping to get him off the line.

"Well, it may have to, 'cause I'm just boarding my flight. Pick me up at ten, honey. Can't wait to see you... miss you! Bye, handsome," Jon said, blowing kisses into the phone.

Baxter pulled into the front entrance of domestic arrivals at three minutes past ten. There was no mistaking Jon; he was standing casually beside four large, matching, brown and burgundy plaid Louis Vuitton suitcases and waving a white silk scarf excitedly. Baxter drove up in his navy-blue Ferrari with the top down and sunglasses masking his eyes. Baxter's first impression was that Jon's luggage would never fit in the Ferrari; his second thought was of just how gay Jon looked. Jon stood just over five feet eleven inches tall; he had a round face with hazel eyes and full lips. His skin often appeared blotchy and his face red and puffy, and today was one of those days. His hair was thin and a light brown: it always appeared a little too long and wispy. Jon was dressed in a pink striped shirt, open to the waist; he wore numerous chains around his neck and a large diamond stud earring in one ear. Today his white leather pants were definitely too tight; Baxter could see they left nothing at all to the imagination. Just the sight of Jon waving madly from the curb made Baxter cringe inside. He had always acted with discretion in all things and he wondered if Jon was a little too out there for his taste. The moment Baxter drew up to the curb, Jon jumped in.

"Put the roof up, honey, my hair," Jon ordered, and the moment the roof was in place, Jon proceeded to hold Baxter in a tight embrace and kiss him passionately on the lips. Baxter tried to pull away – he was horrified with this show of affection in such an open and public space.

"Sorry, thought you'd be pleased to see me," Jon said coolly, sensing Baxter pulling away.

"I am, Bunny Poo, but just not here. We've got plenty of time for all that later."

"I'm a spontaneous sort of guy, and proud of it, what can I say?" Jon replied coolly.

"I can't fit all those bags in this car."

"Well, why didn't you bring one of the other cars then?" Jon asked.

"I only have one car."

"So, these are your wheels, your very own and paid for?" Jon asked sarcastically, and when Baxter nodded, Jon let out a low whistle and continued, "Just how much do they pay valets these days?"

Baxter chose to ignore his question; he had no intention of answering him when he used that tone. Instead, he addressed the amount of luggage Jon had brought with him.

"My Ferrari is built for speed, not cartage. I wouldn't want your bags to scratch the paintwork."

"Well, you're the valet, what are we going to do about it? I guess the bags can follow in a cab, 'cause I'm not leaving them here," Jon replied, and when Baxter didn't look like he was about to make a move, Jon quickly got out and hailed a cab, instructing him to load the luggage and follow.

As they roared to a stop in front of the two huge wrought-iron gates that were beginning to open onto the estate beyond, Baxter noticed Jon had become very quiet. It was a spectacular estate and it sat at the end of a short street aptly named 'Grasshopper Lane' on the top of a small hill. The main house was about a quarter of a mile from the gates and the driveway weaved in and out of lush, well-kept landscaped lawns and gardens. As they rounded the last bend and approached the house, the Atlantic Ocean twinkled in the distance, framed by tall, healthy green trees that swayed gently in the breeze. The moment the cabby was paid off and left, the gates closed and they were in their own secret paradise. Jon had still not spoken, but he stood looking up at the huge mansion in front of him with its towering white columns that stood fifty feet tall, its enormous granite entranceway and the long windows that seemed to go on forever. Jon had his head back, looking upwards, when Baxter said, "It's quite awesome, isn't it, Bunny?"

"I had no idea, no wonder they pay you so well – what is it you said they did?"

Baxter had no intentions of answering either of these questions, so he grabbed several of Jon's bags and headed towards the huge glass doors; sensing his approach, they softly opened. If Jon had thought the outside was inspiring, he hadn't seen anything yet. Baxter decided to take him on a tour of the house before they lugged his bags up to their room. The master suite was reserved for the Grasshoppers' sole use, but Baxter knew Jon would still be very impressed with the guest room he had chosen for them. Baxter had always thought it was the best of the nine, as it had the largest balcony and a perfect view over the Atlantic.

An hour later, they were almost at the end of the tour. They were just walking back down the east wing when Jon asked, "What's up there, up those narrow stairs?"

"Nothing, Jon, it's out of bounds, used only by Ms. Alberta. I've never been up there."

"Well, let's go up now. I love exploring new things."

"No, Jon, let's leave it." Baxter was too late: Jon was already halfway up the narrow staircase.

"There's nothing up here, just a window, I guess, behind this curtain," Jon said, grabbing the curtain to try and draw it open. However, what he found was a large, solid wooden door with several locks and a paddle barring his way.

"Come on, Jon, it's lunch time. I'll show you the kitchen – it's state of the art."

"No way, honey, this is way more interesting. Bet I could get in, given a little time."

"Leave it, Jon, let's go," Baxter said, still standing at the bottom of the stairs and beginning to get annoyed.

"Okay, I'll leave it, for now. It's a challenge; who knows what she has in there – it could hold corpses, jewels or almost anything. Haven't you ever been curious, honey?"

"It's something called respect, Jon, and valuing my job. Let's go, I'm starving."

"Show me our room first and I'll bet I can make you forget all about food," Jon replied.

Two hours later, Baxter stirred from a sleep he hadn't known he was enjoying. He slowly opened one eye; Jon was not on his left where he usually was, so he turned over and Jon was not there either. Just then, the security alarm went off and Baxter knew exactly where he was. Baxter couldn't believe Jon would be so foolish and disobey his wishes. The door to Alberta's sanctuary was firmly bolted when Baxter arrived, still doing up his trousers. However, somehow Jon had managed to unlock one of the three locks. Baxter stood at the bottom of the small staircase, shaking his head at Jon, when the security screens all around them began to close and create lockdown inside the house – it grew instantly dark. Baxter was about to voice his disgust and disappointment at Jon's actions when they heard the voice over the speaker; it was coming from directly outside.

"You're surrounded, come out with your hands up!"

"What the hell is this?" Jon asked, angry now, as Baxter raced up the stairs toward him. "I was just having a little fun. Why, I would have had these locks undone in another couple of minutes," Jon said, his anger subsiding as he looked bewildered.

"This is your final warning. You are surrounded; you are to come out with your hands in the air."

"Come on, Jon, hurry! Otherwise they'll break the door down to get in here." Baxter grabbed Jon by the arm and almost dragged him through the house, until finally he threw open the front doors. They stood side by side, catching their breath, with their hands in the air.

"Face down, spread it, spread it," yelled the cop with the baton. They obeyed.

"They're clean!" called the same cop.

"IDs first and then tell me what you're doing here," ordered the police officer in charge, as another guy in a nearby car called to him. Baxter could only hear some of their conversation.

"He's the valet; he's lived here for years." Then a pause when the other guy said something.

"It looks like that Jon Riddley character, but I thought he'd been clean for years. He must be onto something big, if he's here at the Grasshopper estate."

Baxter couldn't hear what else was said. As he watched, another ten officers appeared swiftly from each side of the mansion, all armed and ready for action.

"Let the butler go and take the other one down the station, fingerprint him and watch him like a hawk – he's a slippery character, been in and out of the system for years, thought he'd retired or something. But he was one of the best international jewel thieves of his time. I'll stay here and have a few words with the butler, or valet, or whatever he calls himself."

Several hours later, Baxter was sitting on one of the many large decks that held a magnificent view over the Atlantic Ocean. The blue, sparkling waters twinkled in the late afternoon sunshine as it lay flat and smooth far off in the distance. Baxter was enjoying a glass of vintage champagne that he had earlier put on ice to share with Jon. Baxter was deep in thought. Jon hadn't been who he thought he was; he'd lied and then gone behind his back and tried to get into Ms. Alberta's private room – but why? Did Jon really think it was just fun to betray someone else's trust, or was it more? Baxter remembered the policeman's comments, and now wondered himself if Jon had previously planned their meeting, and if he had, was it something more than it appeared?

Baxter had never brought anyone home to the Grasshopper Estate before; Jon was the first. He should have listened to his gut; he should have gotten to know him a whole lot better. Baxter was feeling betrayed and used, but, most of all, he was feeling very foolish.

After he poured himself another three glasses of champagne and ignored yet another call from Jon, his decision was made. Jon was not the one for him. He should learn a valuable lesson from this and move on. The moment his decision was made, he felt better. He listened to Jon's messages on his cell and then sat and felt sad briefly for love lost and love that never was, but mainly for love that wasn't what it promised to be. Just like love hurt, so did deception. Then he went to the Grasshoppers' garage and drove their Hummer to the front door. He opened the back of the vehicle before retrieving Jon's matching brown and burgundy plaid Louis Vuitton suitcases from where he had earlier left them. He gently carried them out of the house and closed the front door, before roughly throwing the expensive luggage into the back of the waiting Hummer. On his way to pick up Jon from the police station and take him to the airport, he decided to call Chartreuse. It was definitely time for a change…

Absolutely — I Do!

Harry had planned to leave work shortly after lunch on the Friday before the wedding. No one seemed to care; Flower had made her regular batch of huge cookies that contained heaven knows what. Harry had again managed to conceal them amongst the clutter in his drawers and decided to place them all in his briefcase to dispose of rather than risk leaving them for the mice to attack over the weekend. However, as Harry looked up from his desk shortly after one thirty p.m., he noticed most of the desks were vacant and outside in the main office the place was rapidly emptying out for the weekend.

Harry wondered yet again just how the place continued to run and make such an enormous profit each month. Al, or rather Milly, had offered to pick Hugo up after she had finished her shopping. They would then go home and change from Harry and Milly Hoarders to Sam and Ruth Dolman; these changes were proving too hard and too often for either of them. Milly had been trying to work on a foolproof plan to change Amanda back into Neve before the wedding, but everything she came up with she deemed too risky. She decided in the end that Amanda would have to stay as she was for a while longer, although Milly thought they could safely manage to change her out of her disguise next time she stayed with them. The simplest way would be a fake car accident. But Milly had to work on her plan a lot more before it was perfected.

Harry was just leaning over to close his briefcase with the offending cookies safely inside, when he felt a hand rub slowly up his back and then begin to move down his chest.

"You're early, Milly darling, do you really think we..." Turning around, he came face to face with a short, round little man with white wavy hair and beady brown eyes set deeply into his fat, round face. Sweat glistened from his forehead as he closed the space between them. Harry was surprised; he tried to get up from his chair, but the little guy was much too close. Harry was aware of his arid body odor and the wine he had drunk for lunch.

"So, we meet...," the little man said.

"Who—?" Harry began.

"No need to speak, I can read your thoughts," the little man said, his hands moving like greased lightning all over Harry's body. Harry was half standing as his chair rolled back and he almost escaped, but the little man was fast, and in seconds Harry was pinned up against the bookcase. The hands were running over his body, and Harry felt like his skin was crawling. As they moved toward his crutch, Harry tried with all his strength to move away. It was just as the horrid little man had Harry's arm twisted up his back and he was about to plant a wet kiss on Harry's lips that Milly arrived. Harry had no idea how long she had been there.

"So, darling, this is your office." At the first sound of the female voice, the horrid little man composed himself and turned to Milly.

"Well now, you must be the little lady. He has your photo on his desk. I'm Colonel Tom Sanders, and before you ask, no I'm not into chickens; I prefer a much larger prey, my dear," he said, panting heavily and extending his sweaty hand towards Milly as he winked at Harry.

"I'm Milly Hoarders, Colonel."

"Charmed, I'm sure. Always good to meet the woman behind the man, if you get my meaning," he answered, wiping the sweat from his red puffy face with a soiled napkin he took from his back pocket, before he again winked devilishly at Harry, who was now hurriedly gathering up his briefcase and heading for the door. However, the Colonel didn't let him pass, but continued on.

"I'm the chairman of the board, dear lady, and if your husband plays his cards correctly, I could make sure he is in our employ for a considerable length of time. We offer very generous pensions, you know; everyone wants to work at E.M.," he said, again eyeing Harry from the top of his head to his feet and then back again as his discretion rapidly disappeared.

"Well, you have a good weekend, Colonel Sanders, goodbye," Milly said as Harry squeezed past the Colonel, who was still blocking most of the doorway. As Harry moved past the chubby little man, the Colonel pinched him hard on the rear before quickly reaching for his crutch. Harry let out an involuntary yell and almost ran to the car.

"Well, you must be my guardian angel, Milly! The man's an octopus, no wonder they call him Handy Sandy – he's got hands everywhere," Harry said, shivering, before continuing, "Have I time to take a shower? I don't think I've ever felt more like one."

"I can imagine, although it will have to be quick. We can't afford to miss the flight; the airlines are booked solid. We both need to change our disguise, too," Milly said as she navigated her way through the traffic.

They made the flight with minutes to spare, and as they settled into first class, they gradually relaxed. The flight from LAX to La Guardia in New York seemed to last only minutes as they fell into a deep sleep. Ruth reapplied her lipstick before they left the plane, feeling and looking refreshed from their brief naps.

"Al, it feels wonderful to be away from the craziness of E.M., if only for the weekend."

"I know, darling, it certainly is an unusual place. It really is better than a soap opera. I laugh all day; Flower truly is like no other," Al said, giggling as she thought of Hugo's unusual secretary, before she continued, "I did tell you they have no security on their computers. Although, it makes our job almost too easy, like taking candy from a baby, Hugo. I kinda like them all in a strange and unique way. When you leave, I think they need to be better for having known you. Their bank balance shall be lighter, but money is all we take; allowing them to remain vulnerable is not something I would feel good about."

"I do agree, and what a healthy bank balance they carry. Fifty sounds like a nice figure to me, and I doubt they will ever miss it. I won't miss their wackiness, strange clothes and giant cookies, but some-how I'll miss their naiveté. In today's electronic world, it really is hard to believe how they survive. You do know that Flower and Storm asked us over for supper, as she put it, one night?"

"Yes, Hugo, I do. They probably sit around getting stoned. I don't know whether I would want to eat anything that was cooked in a municipal washroom, either."

"I know, Al, I know. Flower tells me her daughter Angel has found a stream where she can catch microfiche. So, we'll be having a fish bake," Hugo added, as they both laughed.

They were both aware of the different vibe in New York, the hurried pace and suspicious faces. They had only been away a short time but the comparison between New York and Los Angles felt plateable to them both. Soon, they were walking through the gates, searching the faces for Amanda and Chuck, but they were surprised to see Siobhan and Brock holding up a big sign with their names on it. They, of course, knew Brock and Siobhan, but knew Brock and Siobhan didn't know them.

"I thought Neve said they were divorcing?" Hugo whispered to his wife before they made their identities known to the loving couple.

Neither of them could believe what they saw; in fact, they were astonished to see them together after all they'd been through. They appeared to be very together as Siobhan held up the sign and Brock nuzzled her neck while they waited, and they were both giggling like a couple of newlyweds.

"Hello, we're the Dolmans, we were expecting our daughter Amanda," Al said, a large smile on her face as she greeted the two lovebirds.

"I know you were. I'm Brock Burke, and this is my wife, Siobhan. I guess your daughter has spoken of us?" Brock said as they both waited for the Dolmans' response.

"Only briefly; we're so pleased to meet you," Al said, again smiling broadly as they shook hands and hugged. Siobhan and Brock instantly looked relieved when they realized they were not going to be judged or questioned by the older couple.

"Do call us Sam and Ruth," Sam added.

"You know, you remind me of someone, just can't place it. Maybe you have a double," Brock said, thinking hard.

"Darling, we all have doubles somewhere," Siobhan said, as Brock continued.

"I'd like to find yours, my darling. Isn't she something?" Brock asked, placing his arm firmly around Siobhan's waist.

"Yes, she is. You and my daughter must certainly make a statement when you're out together," Ruth said, before she continued, "Yes, I do agree, we all have several doubles around the world, but we hardly ever see them. I remember my mom once met a girl everyone said was her double, but, when they met, she just couldn't see it at all."

"There really is something about the girls. The more time I spend with them both, the more similarities I see. It really is quite amazing, although there's only one girl for me. You do know that, don't you, darling?" Brock said, again nuzzling Siobhan's neck. There was an awkward silence for several seconds until they reached Brock's Mercedes.

"It's just as well we travel light; do you think we'll all fit?" Sam asked, eyeing the two-door convertible Brock had brought to the airport.

"Well, we certainly wouldn't have fitted everything in the Porsche; this baby is all space and speed with no junk in the trunk," Brock commented, opening the truck and sliding the Dolmans' suitcases easily inside. However, it was a slightly cozier fit for the Dolmans themselves. Siobhan offered to sit in the back with Ruth, but Ruth wouldn't hear of separating the lovebirds. She also didn't feel comfortable sitting so close to the younger woman.

"So where is our girl?" Ruth asked once they were successfully squeezed into the back seat and on their way.

"Last-minute alterations; can you believe her bust has expanded in the past two weeks?" Siobhan said, laughing.

"I bet Chuck's got no problems with that," Brock added, as Siobhan slapped him lovingly on the knee.

"Actually, Amanda wanted to wait until you arrived, Ruth. She said you'd be able to easily fix the problem. I guess you sew?" Siobhan asked, as Ruth wondered just why she hadn't waited. She could easily have reduced her skin suit without touching the dress.

"Well, I wish she had waited," Ruth said, winking at Sam, who totally understood what she meant and why.

"We all had a terrible job convincing her to get it fixed by the seamstress. We knew you'd want to rest as you are on such a hectic schedule. This morning when she tried it on after it arrived, she couldn't do the zipper up. It was at least an inch and a half too small. Everyone was laughing, but Amanda didn't seem to be at all concerned. With the wedding tomorrow, no one can believe how calm they both are. Have you met Chuck?"

"They met him last weekend, darling," Siobhan replied for them, before drastically changing the subject. "I hope you boys have your speeches ready? Brock's the emcee."

"I guess I'll stumble through," Sam said.

Ruth added without thinking, "Oh yes, my husband's a seasoned speaker."

Sam shot her a look, but there was no explanation necessary as they drove into the double concrete driveway of the neat yellow suburban house with the rustic-looking reddish-brown leadlight front door and the huge magnolia tree in the center of the front yard. Ruth and Sam thought it enchanting in a plain, homely kind of way, and said exactly that as they somehow managed to squeeze out of the back seat and gulp the fresh air.

Mazey Dook, the wedding planner, was the first one out the front door. Sam and Ruth thought her a very unusual choice; it was not the way she dressed so much as her overall appearance collectively. Mazey had thick, straight, deep purple hair; one side of her head was almost shaved to the scalp, while the hair on the other side was combed straight down beside her face; the top was combed straight up and sat in spikes tipped with silver on top of her head. She was a small, thin woman. She wore small, thin red-framed glasses over her thin brown eyes. Her eyes were heavily accented in fluorescent violet eye shadow. While her mouth also was long and her lips thin, they were painted in the brightest of reds and were very shiny. Her hands were long and very thin; due to her long thin nails that were painted in a peacock design and were mainly green and blue, her hands looked even longer. Mazey's skin glowed the color of dark ebony and she darted around, much like a bird trying to build its nest too late in the season. Mazey wore five-inch stilettos in fluorescent pink, while the rest of her clothes were all black.

"Hello, I'm Mazey Dook, the wedding planner. You must be the Dolmans. I was hoping you would arrive earlier, but never mind, you're here now. Mrs. Dolman, I need to see what you are going to wear as mother-of-the-bride. The theme colors are apricot and warm white; I believe you are aware of this. Mr. Dolman, as father-of-the-bride, you have responsibilities which I will discuss with you later, but right now let's get you inside and see your wardrobe choices." Mazey quickly herded them inside like a mother goose. They were ushered straight into the bedroom. On the way, it was a quick hug from Chuck, who was about to speak, but didn't get a chance. Then Rita Hollingsworth introduced herself. Ruth felt she liked her immediately, even though she had no time to respond.

The master bedroom was larger than the Dolmans had expected, but with all the people hovering around inside the closed doors, it was hard to tell what the décor was.

"Mom, Dad, I'm so glad you're here!" Amanda threw herself into their arms and they stayed locked in a warm embrace until Mazey tapped them both on the shoulder.

"All this affection is great, but time's getting away and we have rehearsals in less than an hour. Have you done with the bride yet?" Mazey asked a woman who was bent down on the floor with a mouthful of pins. The woman immediately got to her feet, nodded, gathered up her sewing things before leaving the room.

"Now, Dolmans, let's see your clothes, and also what you're wearing for the rehearsal dinner tonight. You sure travel light for a wedding," Mazey commented as they opened their suitcases. Neither of them had expected a rehearsal dinner, but Ruth had put in several nice outfits in case they went out for dinner or cocktails. They hadn't expected to need a sparkly cocktail dress, but the moment Mazey spotted the sapphire blue sequined dress it was deemed acceptable. Sam didn't fare nearly as well, and Mazey quickly borrowed a suitable tie and jacket from Chuck's closet. Sam was almost as tall as Chuck, although his frame was somewhat slimmer and his shoulders not so muscular. However, Mazey quickly congratulated herself on the choices she had made for Sam from Chuck's closet, and left the room. They were alone with Amanda, who was waiting to step out of her wedding dress the moment Mazey left.

"Darling, you look like a princess," Sam said with tears in his eyes.

"Honey, you take my breath away," Ruth said as they again hugged.

"There's just so much of it. Do you really like it? I would have liked you to have been with me when I chose it; instead, it was Mazey, and her tastes are rather more extravagant than mine. Although Siobhan was there also and they both said it looked perfect on me."

"Darling, you look amazing! Has Chuck seen it?" Sam asked, wiping his eyes.

"No, Dad, of course not. It's bad luck. He's staying with Rita. But Rita's seen it and, like you, she cried and said she wished her husband was alive to meet me."

"You are the perfect bride, Baby Girl," Sam added.

"Mom, I need to get out of my disguise. I can't stand it, and everyone thinks I'm such a prude and I'm not. Do you have a plan yet?"

"Honey, I'm still working on it, but I haven't forgotten. Enjoy your wedding, we'll work something out," Ruth said.

"I don't want to be Amanda Dolman either, I really don't. I left Banker's Securities on Wednesday. Siobhan contacted Brock for me and now they're back together. I didn't want any of that to happen. I'd already told her I would give them two weeks' notice, but instead Siobhan insisted on contacting Brock."

"Yes, we noticed. Thought it may have been something like that, honey," Ruth said as a light tap came from the door, followed by Siobhan poking her head inside.

"Are you guys ever coming out? We have champagne and I want your parents to meet my parents. My mom's driving me crazy," Siobhan said, closing the door again.

"We all need to get dressed for the rehearsal dinner and I wanted to show you how they've transformed the back garden for the ceremony before it gets dark. I'll take you to your bedroom and then when we've changed I'll introduce you around," Amanda finished, and that's just what they did, although with a house full of people and Mazey in charge it took longer than it should have. Ruth felt very overdressed in her sequined cocktail dress, until she entered the living room and everyone was dressed in formal attire, including Mazey, who wore a floor-length purple sequined tight-fitting dress that matched her hair and eyes. Ruth had to admit it made for a striking contrast against her skin. The moment they stepped out, they met Blue, Chuck's assistant, who was retrieving one of her hair combs from under a chair.

"I'm Blue Satine, Chuck's secretary, I'm not required to attend the rehearsal dinner so I'm leaving until tomorrow, just thought I could help, so much to do, all very exciting," Blue said still with her head under the armchair as she tried in vain to reach her hair comb that had tumbled out of her hair and bounced under the chair.

"Hello, Blue, pleased to meet you," Ruth and Sam said awkwardly, looking at her rear.

"Almost got it; there, I have it!" Blue said triumphantly as Sam and Ruth also bent down. She was just wiggling out from under the chair when her remaining hair comb got caught on the bottom of the chair and immediately fell out and went farther under the chair.

"Oh bother, I can never keep these things in place, but they still work better than anything else," she said, finally standing up and replacing both her combs in her unruly, brown hair. Giggling contagiously, she shook hands with the Dolmans, who by this stage were also giggling.

"Attention, everyone, the limousines are waiting, everyone outside. Family first, please – into the white one. Everyone else who is attending rehearsals, in the black," Mazey ordered, clapping her hands and standing up to her full five feet. With her tall, thin heels on, she looked like she might snap in half any second, she was so thin.

It was later that night when the Dolmans finally met Siobhan's parents.

"Well, we finally meet. I'm Esmeralda Ginzo and my husband Dr. Enoch Ginzo."

Ruth and Sam were amazed that these people could possibly be Siobhan's parents. Her mother was olive-skinned and looked oriental, while her father had lighter skin but also looked somewhat oriental. Ruth and Sam assumed Siobhan had been adopted. However, they smiled sweetly and said nothing.

"What line of work are you in, Enoch?" Sam asked, needing something to say. It was his wife who answered.

"He's not a GP or anything useful like a cosmetic surgeon," she said, laughing. Enoch was about to speak for himself when Esmeralda again jumped in for him.

"No, Enoch is an aeronautical scientist. Enoch is under contract with NASA, but works from home most of the time," she said, shooting her husband a contemptuous look.

Enoch obviously thought he needed to justify his working from home, and he added, "Thought I'd utilize my home office a little more; after all, why have these things if you never enjoy them? We certainly have enough space – ten thousand square feet and just the two of us plus some servants rattling around. Anyway, I decided to spend more time at home the moment Esmeralda told me our little princess would be moving back home. But like the diva she is, she was misinformed again, or maybe just didn't listen," he said, looking pointedly at his wife. Esmeralda's claws were out and sharpened as the Dolmans made an excuse to move away.

"Walter Dense. Glad to meet you; I work with Chuck. He's a great boss and a top-drawer P.I. His dad would have been so proud. Anyway, enough of that, my wife's somewhere around, you may as well meet the whole team while it's still small, but with the success we're having dealing with the rich and famous, I'm sure we'll soon be expanding."

"So, you don't work nights?" Sam inquired to make conversation.

"No, Fred Blook does night surveillance. Leave it to the young ones, unless he needs backup, of course."

It was after midnight when they arrived home after dropping off Chuck and Rita. Amanda didn't seem at all tired and wanted to talk all night, so Sam said goodnight. As he drifted off to sleep, he heard Ruth ask, "Does everyone know about the baby?"

"Oh no, Mom, we won't announce it until after we're back from our honeymoon. Thanks for spoiling us, by the way. You certainly booked us five stars all the way. I think we'll both be exhausted, and I'm looking forward to having Chuck all to myself, away from his work."

"Does he know you're a wealthy woman in your own right, honey?" Ruth asked, and as tired as Sam was, he just had to hear the answer to this one.

"No, Mom, not at all. We live entirely on his money. We share all his accounts and I have my own credit cards and checking account, and he has ordered me a new car. I thought it best like this so he wouldn't become suspicious..." Sam didn't need to listen any further: his baby girl was smart. He was glad she wasn't completely blinded by love.

The Saturday morning of the wedding dawned sunny and clear. A gentle wind blew in from the East and a few lazy clouds sedately held court in an otherwise perfectly clear sky.

Sam and Ruth had only just woken from their slumbers when a loud knock came from the door. It was followed by the unmistakably harsh accent of Mazey.

"Rise and shine, people! We're all leaving for brunch in one hour. Let my crew have time to pull this place into shape uninterrupted. One hour, everyone, see you out front," Mazey said again, banging on the next door and repeating herself.

"That girl should be in the Army," Sam said as he began to get out of bed.

"Yeah, darling, I agree, but she's so skinny they wouldn't have to shoot her, they could just blow her over," Ruth replied.

"I'm surprised she hasn't already been shot. She's more like a drill master than a wedding planner. I can't imagine where they found her," Sam said, pulling on his jeans and a pale blue linen shirt.

"Hope she approves of our clothes," Ruth said, observing Sam's choice.

"Well, she'll just have to; I don't have anything else apart from my tuxedo. Anyway, she always approves of yours," he said, making a face like Mazey.

The morning flew by. The restaurant Mazey had chosen for brunch was very quaint, and she'd booked out the whole place, although it only seated about fifteen at the most.

Before they knew where the time had gone, Ruth had completed her hair and makeup herself, much to Mazey's annoyance. Time seemed to pass in a flash and, all too soon, Sam was standing at the end of a small, pale green carpet; it loomed before him strewn with apricot and cream rose petals.

It was only a short walk to the gazebo, but for Sam it would be the longest of his life. Beside him stood Amanda, who looked like a princess and held a calmness and serenity about her that Sam wished he could share. With a huge smile permanently on her face and Sam's arm through hers, in her other hand she held her bouquet of apricot roses, lily of the valley and cream gardenias. Together they stood and waited while Mazey and Siobhan endlessly fussed with her dress.

Sam felt numb at the thought of losing his baby girl and was really trying to focus on keeping it all together. As he stared at the gazebo, he watched Chuck arrive on the arm of his mother, Rita; she kissed him tenderly before he took his position. He looked tall and handsome and ready to become Amanda's husband. In fact, they were both so calm, it made Sam and Ruth feel even more scared than they already were. The moment the dress was in place, the organ music started, Siobhan kissed Amanda on the cheek and took Hunter's arm in hers. Hunter was Chuck's cousin and best man. Siobhan looked radiant in a tight bodice of apricot chiffon; it was sewn with tiny scallops and had seed pearls and diamantes inserted into each fold. The skirt was flowing and cascaded from her small waist to where it fell on the ground in oceans of soft, wispy fabric.

Siobhan and Hunter slowly walked down the aisle to where Chuck waited under the gazebo. When they were halfway down, and just like they'd rehearsed last night, Sam and Amanda took their cue.

"Love you, Daddy, thanks for always being my rock," Amanda said, throwing her arms around him and hugging him tightly, before placing her arm through his again. Wiping away a stray tear, Sam was barely able to take the first step. Once he began moving forward, he felt Amanda pulling him onward. He struggled to hold back the tears. Once Sam passed Amanda over to Chuck, Ruth got up and stood beside him, just like they'd planned. It was decided they would both give her away. Both Chuck and Amanda had written their own vows. As their words tumbled forth it was obvious to everyone they were truly, madly and deeply in love and completely ready to commit to a caring and happy life together. There was barely a sound as everyone listened to Chuck and Amanda read tearfully about how they felt. No one could possibly have a doubt their vows came straight from the heart. Ruth and Sam watched the whole twenty-minute ceremony through bleary eyes as they continued to wipe away the tears. Ruth noticed Rita doing the same, and when she looked around, everyone had a tear in their eye. It was a beautiful ceremony and the backyard was perfectly transformed into a magical wonderland.

The place they'd chosen for the reception was equally as perfect. It was situated beside a small man-made lake. White swans swam around and the landscaping was breathtaking. One side of the reception area opened onto the lake. Ruth and Sam knew the wedding must have cost a pretty penny. They had no idea about Chuck's financial situation, but decided Chuck must not go short.

After the many toasts were complete, it was Sam's time to make his speech. He looked into the radiant faces of Amanda and Chuck, and behind their smiles he saw the promise of so much hope for the future. Then Sam took a deep breath and tapped his glass with his fork. The room fell silent while the champagne continued to flow.

"To those of you who don't know me, I am the proud father of Amanda, and beside me sits Amanda's equally proud mother, Ruth. Thank you all for sharing this special day with us. I know the band is itching to play, so I'm not going to be one of these fathers or fathers-in-law that hog the spotlight. What I am about to say comes from my heart and I'm sure also from Ruth and Chuck's mother, Rita.

To my beautiful daughter, Amanda, and my new son, Chuck… I speak for all of us… when I say… this has been a very fast and sudden adventure. Sometimes when you're just having fun – life happens! When life happens, you open the door to your heart so love can follow. However, in order for it to do so, you must be someone who has not allowed work or your surroundings to define who you are. Love can only enter an open heart – it shall avoid those who allow their daily burdens to weigh them down. If love was a nightingale, it would choose to fly in an open window and nest in a happy heart.

The two people I see before me have allowed this, and have, in fact, welcomed it. Patience is the gateway to understanding, patience is definitely a virtue. It goes hand in hand with trust, loyalty and respect, and nestled in there is the foundation of your commitment – love.

May your home be happy, your trust never be doubted, your loyalty never require forgiveness and your respect never be compromised. May the bluebird of happiness follow you wherever you go, and may your bed always be warm at night. As I said previously, when life happens, love follows. May the same love you see today in each other's eyes increase with every moment it is shared. Please raise your glasses in a toast to Amanda and Chuck Hollingsworth," finished Sam, taking a deep breath as he discreetly wiped away a stray tear. Everyone clapped, raising their glasses in a toast to the happy couple as the band started playing.

Sam and Amanda had the first dance, but Chuck quickly cut in. Ruth held Sam close as she whispered, "Darling, I'm proud of you. I don't know how you held it together – I couldn't." Sam took that as quite a compliment coming from his self-controlled wife.

The three-tiered coconut cake was decorated with swirls of cream icing and apricot roses. Amanda and Chuck cut the cake with an antique sword belonging to Hunter's father, who'd had a distinguished career in the Army. Everyone cheered loudly as the three-tiered confection was finally dished out. Siobhan brought their cake to the table and Ruth asked, "Where did they find Mazey? She's quite something."

"Yes, she is, isn't she? I think Blue, Chuck's secretary/assistant, was the one. I believe they went to school together or something," Siobhan finished, as they all watched the main source of the entertainment, Mazey. Then Chuck came and whisked Siobhan onto the dance floor.

"You've been great, Siobhan, the perfect bridesmaid or rather matron of honor, and also the best of friends to Amanda," Chuck said.

"It really was a beautiful wedding. Maybe Brock and I should renew our vows, although I doubt it would do much good; he is who he is," Siobhan said wistfully as Chuck twirled her around and waited for her to continue.

"Chuck, I know this is not the time or the place, but I've been thinking about finding my birth parents. Mom and Dad are still in denial and won't admit one way or another if I am their natural child. All they want to know is the source of the false information I'm receiving. Although I have always suspected, I mean, look at them and look at me. Why, I look more like Amanda than anyone else here."

"Okay, I shall begin the search. I'll be in touch when I know something." Chuck had only just got the words out when Brock cut in.

Shortly afterwards, the newlyweds left for their late-night flight to Hawaii, but not before Ruth had a moment alone with Amanda to adjust her skin-suit. With her rapidly expanding tummy, Ruth showed Amanda how to adjust it, as she knew she would have to do so often.

"Mom, you do know I want out of this, first the skin-suit and then the whole charade."

"Honey, I know that, I just need a little more time."

"I know, Mom. I do realize I got myself into this against your warnings. You both told me it was too dangerous, and now I guess this is my punishment. But you brought us up to not only follow the Grasshopper motto, but also to follow our hearts."

"Yes, Neve, I did."

"Mom, don't...," Amanda reprimanded her for using the wrong name. It was at that moment Chuck knocked on the door. Amanda shot Ruth a look that said it all, although they both knew there was too much noise for him to hear what they were talking about.

"Darling, we'll miss our flight!" Chuck called through the door. Amanda was dressed in a soft, flowing apricot sundress with small lace straps and a wide sash around her expanding waistline.

"Love you, Mom. Call me when you're home." And just like that, she was gone. On her way out, she hugged Sam tightly, not wanting to let him go, and they both had tears in their eyes, as did Siobhan and Rita, and then they left. The party continued, and it was another two hours before Ruth and Sam left, and at that time, only a few diehards remained. Sam and Ruth would be staying the night in Amanda and Chuck's little yellow house. Ruth had decided, unbeknownst to anyone, to place a wire in the living room. She had no intention of listening, but she had a niggling feeling it may just be required in the future.

Sunday was spent with Rita. Ruth liked her very much. They enjoyed a leisurely lunch and talked mainly of the wedding and their children's future, although Rita was obviously still missing her husband, and included him into most of the conversation. The moment Rita asked them what they did for a living that kept them so very busy, Sam produced a large yellow envelope full of hundred-dollar notes.

"Rita, we were going to leave this at the house. It will help cover expenses, but maybe you would give it to them or put it into their bank account. I know they won't want to take it as we have offered previously several times."

"Sam, I also gave them cash and a present, and they didn't want my money either, although Sheffield left me more than comfortable with his smart investments. I will see what I can do and let you know," Rita said, reluctantly taking the envelope, which was brimming over with crisp green one hundred-dollar bills.

Once Sam had left little love notes all over the house for the newlyweds to find on their return, they headed back to San Diego and another crazy week at E.M.

Remnants of a Life

Cox Moffit heard of his beloved father's death in a most unkind way. He was about to call his friend who had one of his study books and he'd picked up the phone by mistake. Saffron was on the line having a conversation with a detective, and Cox was unable to stop listening. Cox had known Potter was concerned about many of Saffron's business interests, although he hadn't known just what they were. The moment she hung up the phone, Cox debated whether to confront his mother or try and call Aunt Adele in England. He decided he would get more information from the latter. It was the middle of the night when he called, and it was not Aunt Adele who answered the phone at Potter's new residence, but his girlfriend.

Apparently, she hadn't seen Potter and was more worried than she could express. She sobbed openly on the phone and said she thought Potter had abandoned her and gone back to his wife. Cox couldn't sleep all night. He wanted to confront his mom, but something his dad once said about her being devious and dangerous, stopped him. At the back of his mind he knew his mom was responsible for everything. He couldn't sleep.

In the morning, he found the number of Saffron's secretary, Amanda, whom he had spoken to several times when she had dropped things off. She had given him her number at one time when he'd complained about just how hard it was to get a hold of his mother. Amanda had said to call her, as Saffron was indeed a busy person and hated being disturbed. He placed the call at eight a.m., thinking she would be on her way to work, but her voicemail picked up. He didn't want to leave a message; anyway, what could he say? After some thought, he decided to try Brock Burke; he had always gotten on well with him on the few occasions they'd met.

Brock was very sympathetic, and Cox could tell he felt just awful having to tell him the sad news. He then passed him over to his secretary, Floris McKrill. Cox was in shock as he spoke to her, and she was all business and didn't seem to understand just who he was. She gave him the contact details of Special Agent Bow Grismold and hung up.

The doorbell rung several times before Cox realized what it was. Finally, he got up and answered the door; it was his Asian friend returning his study book. Cox could barely speak – he was in deep shock. The other boy walked into the entrance hall and they stood silently for several minutes, until they became aware of the houseboy talking quietly into his cell phone in the kitchen. Cox's friend was born in America, but he held a fascination for all things oriental. He spoke fluent Chinese, Cantonese and Mandarin, so when he put his finger to his lips and told Cox to stay quiet, he moved silently closer to the kitchen door and listened. Cox sat on the stairs and waited until finally the houseboy finished his call. Cox's friend told him to follow him out to his car and then proceeded to tell him just what he'd heard.

"I didn't hear the beginning of the conversation, but it appears the houseboy thinks he may be responsible for your dad's death. By the way, where is your dad, Cox?" the boy asked, as Cox choked back the tears.

"I'm so sorry, man, when did you find out?"

"Just now; my mom never even bothered to tell me," Cox replied, crying openly now.

"I'm really sorry; I will go now. I just wanted to give you your book back. I'm sorry, Cox, I didn't know," the boy said, easily feeling his friend's pain. He was waiting for Cox to get out of the car, but Cox didn't move. He was trying to remember what he needed to hear from his friend before he left. Finally, his head cleared enough, and he asked to hear the rest of the conversation his friend had overheard. His friend didn't want to discuss it, seeing how upset Cox already was, but Cox persisted.

"No, I need to hear what you know; tell me what you heard," Cox asked, as the tears ran down his cheeks. His friend hesitated for several seconds, knowing it was not a good time to tell him, until finally he knew he must say what he'd overheard.

"Your houseboy says, no more drugs, he says he doesn't like stealing – Mr. Potter always good to him. He says he regrets taking them and wished he hadn't. Then he listened for a while and sounded very scared and said some kind of Mandarin curse word or some religious thing I didn't understand, and he hung up. Does this mean anything to you, Cox?"

Cox shook his head. "No, nothing; my dad wasn't into drugs – I would have known. He was the most grounded guy ever; after all, he managed to put up with my mom, somehow. Anyway, thanks for returning the book," Cox said, opening the car door.

"You going to be okay, man?" his friend asked, concerned. Cox merely nodded and headed inside.

Cox lay on his bed for several hours. During that time, he experienced a range of feelings, from grief to anger and then sheer disbelief. He expected his dad to walk through the door at any moment. He'd slept fitfully that night as his mind tried to put some order into the events that had happened. In the morning he knew he would call Bow Grismold. He waited until his mom left the house before placing his call. It was only six a.m. The call was not answered, so he waited for what seemed like an eternity until nine a.m. when he tried again. This time he made contact with the detective.

"Hi, my name's Cox Moffit and I'm the son of—"

He hadn't finished when Bow cut in. "Potter Moffit, of course. Why, we called around to your home several times, but there was no answer, so we visited your mom at her office…"

"Yeah, well, I've just found out about my dad—" Cox began, as again Bow cut him off in mid-sentence.

"You just found out? Sorry, kid, I thought you may have some information or a confession or something," Bow said.

"A confession…? What the hell are you talking about? I guess I made a mistake calling you. It's me who needs information; he was *my* dad!" Cox yelled, his voice shaking as he slammed down the phone and collapsed on his bed as another wave of tears engulfed him. He expected the phone to ring again the moment he'd hung up, but it didn't, so he was sure there would be no help from that direction. It was lunch-time when the doorbell sounded; it was his friend who often borrowed his books. He wanted to know if he was okay. He was far from okay, but he didn't want to talk, either. A few minutes after he closed the door, the bell rang again. Cox assumed his friend was concerned enough to have returned.

"I told you I'm fine," Cox said, his head hung low. It was the shoes he noticed first; they were not the sneakers of a school boy, but buffed black patent shoes. From there he looked up the tweed trousers and the neat white shirt under the gray trench coat.

"You must be Cox Moffitt. I'm Special Agent Bow Grismold. I apologize about sounding cold on the phone earlier; guess I sent the wrong message. It's easy to become suspicious of everyone in this game; it's just that I met your mom at her office and… well, anyway, there is no excuse."

"That's okay," Cox said, holding back the tears as he was about to close the door.

"Wait a minute, Cox; can I come in for a moment?" Bow asked, and when Cox shrugged his shoulders and walked away into the living room, Bow followed, shutting the door behind him. Bow gingerly sat on the edge of the couch as he observed the boy. Neither said anything, and after a while Bow could feel the boy's pain was genuine and he softened towards him. He was a good-looking boy in his late teens, tall, with probably a handsome face when he wasn't crying. Although he didn't look exactly like his father, Bow could easily see some resemblance from the photos he'd seen of Potter Moffitt.

"Son, when did you find out about your dad?" the detective asked, carefully softening his tone. As he waited for a response, he looked around the expensive home in the gated neighborhood. Detective Bow Grismold sat in an expensive chair in the beautifully decorated room. Someone here was not only a neat freak, but also a perfectionist, Bow thought at a glance.

"I just heard," Cox softly replied.

"When, last week, yesterday, when?" Bow asked, and for several seconds he thought the boy would start crying and not answer. He waited patiently until eventually he did get an answer.

"I just heard by accident yesterday. My dad was my best friend. He brought me up, he went to all my school plays and sports games, he was the one who attended the school outings with all the other kids' moms. Dad brought me up, not Mom," Cox said, crying again.

"Did your mom tell you about your dad? Did she tell you any details?" Bow asked.

"No, she didn't tell me about him. If she'd told me details, I wouldn't have contacted you. You've told me nothing anyway," Cox finished, sneaking a look at the man as his head remained downcast. Bow felt truly sorry for the boy now that he knew his mother hadn't even told him. Although, after meeting the emotionless Saffron Moffit, he could understand her being cruel; she was obviously no mother to the boy and never had been.

"Cox, the details are not pretty. I think it would be better if you waited a while before I tell you all I know," the detective said kindly.

"No, tell me what happened to my dad. I am a big boy and I need to know."

"How old are you, Cox?" Bow asked.

"Eighteen at the last count, why?" Cox said, composing himself slightly and raising his head to look at the other man for the first time.

"It's just that if you're a minor, I can't give you details. However, at eighteen you're considered an adult. Are you sure you want to hear what I know, Cox? 'Cause we can easily do this later; I'm not planning on going anywhere," Bow said kindly.

"I want to know and I have a right," Cox replied as a sob escaped. Bow debated whether he could trust the boy and take him into his confidence. He knew he was vulnerable right now, but he also felt the boy seldom saw or spoke to his mother and that was important if he was to be trusted.

"Do you want to hear what we know about your mother also?" Bow asked.

"Why, is she dead as well?... Pity she's not..." His last word was only a whisper, but Bow heard him and it was enough for him to know the boy could be trusted.

"Cox, we have been following your mother's movements for some time – years, actually – and we suspect she is linked to a worldwide drug organization. Now, sadly, we believe your father to be one of her runners. We think one of his packets weighed in short and that was the reason he was shot. It was certainly a gang shooting and it had all the markings of a drug deal gone wrong. We believe he was training another guy as well; sadly, he also lost his life." Bow hadn't finished when he saw Cox place both his hands over his ears.

"No, no! It's not true! My dad would never be involved! He always taught me how bad drugs, drink and cigarettes are. He would never take drugs, I know he wouldn't!" Cox yelled, as he started to leave the room.

"Cox, you said you were an adult, now please sit. I never said Mr. Moffit was taking drugs. I said he was a drug runner who probably worked for your mother…"

"I hate her," Cox said, as again the tears flowed.

"I'm sure you think you do right now."

"I've always hated her, and the way she treated my dad just wasn't fair."

"Cox, I'm sorry to have upset you. I know you're not involved; I just thought maybe you might know something…," Bow said, getting up to leave and now feeling truly sorry for the boy. He moved slowly out of the living room to the door as he hoped Cox might remember something he could tell him, but he seemed too upset. Bow was just walking down the pathway when the door flew open and Cox asked him to return.

"Look, I don't know if this means anything or not, but we have a houseboy who works Monday, Wednesday and Friday. Mom didn't trust Dad around a woman. Anyway, yesterday my friend was returning a book; he speaks Mandarin and he heard Mingh, our houseboy, talking in the kitchen on his cell phone. Whoever he was talking to, he was telling them about taking some drugs from Mr. Potter. The person on the other end of the phone said something and he got mad."

"Did your houseboy know that your dad was dead?"

"Yes, he did; he actually said he thought he may have caused it."

"Cox, thank you, you've been a big help. Would you mind if I returned later with a sniffer dog and go over your house?"

"No. In fact, I think you should. But not when my mom, the houseboy or gardener are home."

"When would be a good time? Aren't you supposed to be at school or something?" Bow asked.

"Yeah, but I can't go to school right now; I need a little time. I'll still pass my exams, but I just won't get honors; who cares anyway? What's the point? I only ever did good to make my Dad proud."

"Just let me make a call; if the guy's got his dog and he's not on another job, maybe he can come right over. I suggest you don't tell your mom," Bow said.

"You got no worries there. There's only one thing I'll be asking her," Cox said, and Bow waited for him to continue; when he didn't, he made his call. The guy with the drug dog was only half an hour away, so Bow asked for a cup of tea, mainly because he knew Cox needed one.

The officer with the sniffer dog arrived an hour and a half later. He quickly went through the house, and when he went into one of the five spare guest rooms the dog began scratching at the dressing table. Once they moved the dressing table away from the wall, the dog sniffed the baseboard several times and barked. As Bow knelt on the floor, he was able to remove a small strip of baseboard easily from the wall. Concealed behind it was a large plastic bag. When it was squeezed out through the hole, they saw several hundred tiny bags inside the larger one, all containing white powder. To Cox's astonishment, Bow Grismold didn't take them with him, but instead he carefully opened the larger bag and placed a tiny strip of what looked like cardboard amongst the packages. Then, he replaced the package in the wall and put the room back exactly as it was.

Bow thanked Cox and suggested he didn't discuss any of this with his mom, otherwise he would definitely become an accessory. Bow had twin daughters at home the same age as Cox, and he was very aware of how kids of his age needed their parents' guidance. He knew Cox had no support from his mother and realized his father had done a great job rearing the boy. Bow handed Cox another of his business cards and again urged him to call if he needed anything at all. On the back he wrote his home number and hoped the boy would use it.

Cox assumed he would never see the detective again, so it was a surprise to hear the doorbell ringing incessantly at seven a.m. on Friday morning. Cox opened one eye; he had slept fitfully all night, dreaming of his dad each time he closed his eyes. Finally, at five a.m., he'd fallen into a deep and exhausted sleep.

Cox thought he was dreaming, dreaming of his dad coming home; maybe he had forgotten his key. Cox dragged himself from his sleep, wandered into the bathroom and splashed cold water on his face and then went downstairs as the bell continued to ring. He moved swiftly to the front door. He peeked through the peephole before opening the door and saw the detective begin to turn away. Cox opened the door a crack, and as the detective turned, he opened it slightly wider.

"I need to come in. I must talk to you," Bow said, pushing his way through the door and into the living room.

"What's happened now? Have you found the guys that did it?" Cox asked, thinking it could be nothing else.

"What guys?" Bow replied, a blank expression on his face.

"The guys who shot my dad," Cox said, almost in tears.

"Oh, no, son, sorry, I haven't," Bow replied, seeing the sorrow in the boy's eyes.

"Well, what do you want then?"

"Is your mom home by any chance?" Bow asked.

"No, she leaves for work early. Why, are you going to arrest her or something?"

"No, son, not yet. I promise not to do anything without letting you know," Bow replied, almost hating being there.

"Well, what do you want? You leaned on that doorbell long enough. It must be something pretty important at this hour," Cox asked, now lying on the couch as the detective stood looking down at him.

"Well, son, it is. I'm sorry to wake you. I know you probably get little enough sleep these days. However, could you tell me if the man in this photo is your houseboy?" Bow said, proceeding to show Cox a large color photo. Cox stared at the photo and nodded. It seemed to Cox this was the photo of a dead man.

"I'm sorry to be the bearer of more sad news, but he was found shot to death in a back alley not far from where he lived. The shooting was similar to that of your father's. We suspected it was a gang shooting, and we suspect that drugs were the cause."

Cox sat and listened, but said nothing; he didn't know what he was supposed to say.

Finally, the detective asked, "Have you got anyone you can stay with, Cox?"

"Sure, but I got to finish my exams."

"Yeah, I understand. Do you know anyone outside the U.S. you could move in with, then?" the detective asked, looking very serious.

"Yeah, I guess I could stay with Aunt Adele in England."

"Okay, will you make the arrangements and promise me you'll leave the minute your last exam is completed?" Bow asked.

"Yeah, okay, if you think it's that important."

"It is. I think I can stop this going down until then. Call me before you leave, Cox. And if you want to be safe, tell no one, you'll only be putting yourself and them in further danger," Bow instructed, as Cox nodded. The detective turned and headed for the door, while Cox stayed where he was.

"Cox, I'm really sorry to have ruined your day with this," Bow added from the open doorway.

"It's okay; my days were forever ruined the moment I lost my dad."

Yonder Swims a Microfiche

Harry had done a lot of reorganizing within E.M. Distributions. He'd changed the small outer office of the accounts department around so the accounts payable staff was now situated on one side and the accounts receivable staff on the other. They all had nameboards on their desks, along with their title. He'd divided each area alphabetically so that each of his staff had equal duties. And now the office was cleared up and he'd explained the usage of the filing cabinets beside each desk and also the ones for storage that were located in another area. Things ran a lot smoother. There was more than enough staff for the job; and they no longer needed to draw straws to see who would do the day's work. Now everyone had a purpose and knew what was expected of them. They still didn't have a full day's work, but they all worked at least part of the day.

Harry was slowly teaching them how to use their computers correctly, although with so much clear space on each desk and walking space on the floor, the computer screens often crashed to the ground. This was due to his staff sitting on their desks and talking or sleeping on their desks if they were tired. Harry had casually mentioned to Flower how he thought the accounts area was way overstaffed; however, Flower quickly justified it by reminding him that all her relatives needed jobs, so it was indeed necessary to have so many people.

Everyone showed up for work on a regular basis now, although no one but Flower put in an eight-hour day. Where they had usually lazily drawn pictures in the dust on their blank screens, they now wiped them every morning and turned them on. This increased the workload for the IT department, who just happened to be three of Flower's cousins twice removed, but Flower said not to listen to their complaints as she thought Harry was doing an excellent job. The more changes Harry made, the more impressed Flower became. She showed Harry just how much she liked him by the size of the cookies she presented him with for morning tea each day – the cookies were getting noticeably bigger and bigger. The last ones she presented him with were almost the size of a small pizza.

Disposing of Flower's unwanted cookies was definitely posing a problem for Harry and Milly; they were worried that one day they'd get sprung. Not wanting to put the cookies in the trash, Harry and Milly often walked to the local park. Once there, they sat on the wooden benches and broke the cookies up into tiny pieces before feeding them to the ducks. Although, lately, the ducks had been acting rather strangely; no one had ever seen ducks swim backwards in circles or swim along fast with their heads under the water. It was a weird sight and usually began about thirty minutes after they ate the cookies. A crowd would gather, and lately folks had been arriving just to see how the ducks were behaving today. Harry and Milly knew another park was needed.

Harry and Milly also knew Flower had been sewing, and Milly was very worried she'd make something for her. Just in case, Milly had given Harry a pendant in the shape of a marigold. It was on a gold-plated chain inside Harry's briefcase. Harry arrived several minutes before Flower. He'd met up with Emmet Wiggins in the car park and Fast-foot Wiggins had proceeded to ask Harry to join him on his morning stroll around the warehouse. Well, Fast-foot Wiggins didn't stroll; Harry thought he wouldn't know the meaning of the word. For Harry, it proved to be more of an early morning and very exhausting sprint up and down many of the long aisles of the warehouse. Emmet talked continually, and Harry tried to put in the occasional grunt so the Colonel knew he was still there and listening. Finally, Emmett slapped Harry several times on the back, raced up the stairs two at a time to the executive offices and began another fast-paced day inside E.M. Distributors. By the time Flower arrived, Harry was exhausted.

"Morning, boss, thought I'd dress up for you today, seeing it's my birthday, like. Felt like adding a bit of elegance and class to the office – do you like it?" Flower said, twirling around several times in her latest creation. Harry was not sure what to say. It was the same design as all the rest. Harry had long since thought she only had one pattern. Flower's latest caftan was made of Army camouflage tent fabric. Harry thought it might be even stiffer than some of her others. It looked very heavy; in fact, as she twirled, she seemed to visibly sag under the weight of the thick Army canvas.

"This is a one-of-a-kind designer caftan; and my very own design; it's made of pure 18oz Army Duck canvas. Storm got it especially for me, like. I made me Angel Wings a cute little jacket, like, out of the leftover fabric, but would you believe she said it was too heavy and she couldn't bend her arms fast enough to catch pigeons! Harry, she's such a great kid! Why, she gave her new jacket to Lamb Sony, she did; now what a sweet girl she is to do that, like. Anyway, Lamb Sony is younger than my Angel Wings, and he said he doesn't care, like, if he can bend his arms or not. He says there can only be one pigeon-catcher per family; smart, that kid, real smart, like. So, he was real happy with his new jacket. Anyway, I had to shorten the sleeves for him and I had enough of this fine 18oz Army Duck canvas left over to make your lovely wife her own one-of-a-kind personally designed headband. Here, Harry, I wrapped it, too, like," Flower said proudly, handing him a small package wrapped up in a torn green garbage bag.

"Well, Flower, I don't know what to say," Harry said, eyeing the roughly wrapped headband as a strong smell of rotting food filled the office.

"I did tell you that it's made of genuine 18oz double-weave Army Duck camouflage canvas, didn't I? Why, there isn't nothin' finer. My Storm says only the best is good enough for his Flower. Mind you, he said that after the best sex he's had in a whole week and he'll say almost anything afterwards, like. He's real lucky to have me, Harry; you know, I'm not only a landowner, an accountant, a great cook and a clothes designer. I'm also a very experienced sexual partner. You know, I've probably hooked up with nearly every man I'm not directly related to, like, in these parts, and then some that I am directly related to, like."

Harry was feeling somewhat uncomfortable with the way the conversation was headed. He now realized he often felt this way around Flower – she said whatever was on her mind. Harry decided to jump right in and short circuit her before it became too racy for his ears.

"Flower, I almost forgot, my wife has a gift for you, seeing it's your birthday. It's actually from both of us," Harry said, retrieving the necklace that was wrapped up in pretty paper from his briefcase.

"Happy birthday, Flower," Harry said, handing it to her.

"Why, Harry, I feel like I know you so well. Now isn't there no kiss to go with your pretty present?"

"Ah, well, actually…" That was all he had time to say, as Flower came flying across his desk, the smell of dusty canvas filling his nostrils. She grabbed his face between her two hands and kissed him deeply with a tongue that moved almost as fast as Colonel Wiggins' feet, but not quite as fast as Colonel Sanders' hands.

It was hard to get away, but once he did, all she said was, "Harry, you taste about as good as the fish bake you're coming to tomorrow night, I swear you do. I don't know what you ate for breakfast, but it sure tastes good, Harry. It's my birthday and I think I want more, like."

This time, Harry was too fast for her; as she was about to dive across his desk, for the second time he pretended to search in his briefcase for something he'd forgotten.

"Why, Flower, you haven't opened your present."

"Harry, it looks just great, I love it. I really do. It's, like, the prettiest thing I've ever seen. So, do you want to taste me again?" Flower asked eagerly, her large eyes wide as she stared hard into his. When she did this she always made him feel most uncomfortable, but he stared right back as he didn't want to kiss her again. She tasted like a dusty doormat, complete with fluff balls. He had no idea just why she tasted like that, but he knew for sure one kiss was enough.

"You know, Flower, it's your birthday and I think you should spend some time walking around the whole office building and the warehouse, too, so all your relatives can wish you a happy birthday."

"Well, Harry, I swear if ya ain't just the sweetest, kindest, cutest boss a gal could ever ask for. You know, I could just eat you alive I could, like. I swear I could lick you all over and eat you up for me breakfast, like." Flower was again eyeing him up with her large liquid brown eyes, and he felt sure that she was about to pounce at any moment.

"Flower, if you don't open your present, I won't be able to tell my wife what you think of it," Harry quickly added.

"But, Harry, why, I just said how I like it – I do declare your wife has a way with paper; prettiest darn thing I ever seen, like," Flower said, turning it lovingly over and over.

"Flower, the pretty paper is not the gift, there's more inside," Harry said, laughing as he realized Flower didn't know she had to open it.

"More inside? What do you mean, Harry?" Flower asked, wide-eyed.

"Well, you open the paper and find what's inside."

"What, you want me to mess with the pretty paper thing your sweet wife made for me? I don't think she'd like that, Harry. Why, I could never put it back the way it was," Flower replied, sounding shocked at his words, with her eyes still firmly on Harry.

"Flower, you don't need to. Please undo the wrapping carefully and look inside."

"Well, if you insist, but I don't want to get you into trouble with your dear wife, like," Flower said, as Harry assured her it was okay. So, very slowly, she turned the gift around and around on the desk as she looked for a way inside. Harry showed her how to remove the tape so she could rewrap it if she wanted to. Finally, she was able to slide the box carefully out.

"Why, Harry… it's perfect, a red velvet box; oh, thank you!" she began, about to leap over his desk again.

"Flower, the box opens…"

"No, it never does, Harry. Now I know you're playing with me, like," Flower said, just happy to own such a pretty box.

"Open it, Flower," Harry instructed, as she pulled this way and that before the box opened to reveal the necklace inside. Flower let out a little scream of pleasure as she saw the small orange marigold with the black center and the gold chain. Flower was ecstatic. She said she had never had anything so beautiful; in fact, she said it was the only piece of jewelry she had ever had.

"Wow, Harry! Even when Storm and I got married, all we had was a tattoo of a wedding ring; you see, his cousin did it for us. It hurt bad, too," Flower said, showing him her ring finger. It looked more like a child had scribbled around her fingers, but Harry lied and said it looked great.

"Harry, I'm off to show everyone your gift, but I'll be back in time to blow out the candles on my cake. I think it's the best cake I've ever made; I put a little bit extra of everything in, like, seeing it was my birthday. I can't wait for you to try it, Harry, it will really brighten your day...," Flower said eagerly, her eyes sparkling and her cheeks flushed a soft pink as she twirled around to show him her new pendant. Harry had never seen anyone so excited to receive such a small gift.

"I'm going to show Storm first. We might even sneak in a quick one up on the shelves, like. We have our places; why, a gal can't be expected to last all day with no lovin' from her man, like," Flower said, racing out of the office.

Harry wondered again why everyone moved so fast. Fifteen minutes later, he looked up to see Storm. He had a face to match his name and he was hurrying toward Harry. For such a large guy, he was moving fast through the offices, crashing doors as he moved. Harry did not like the look of him at all, and he was headed toward Harry's office. Harry quickly stood up from behind his desk.

"Well now, Mr. Harry, suppose ya explain," Storm said, his anger barely in check.

"Explain?" Harry asked.

"No good lookin' miffed at me, Mr. Harry. We both know what I'm a talkin' 'bout."

"Storm, do sit down and explain just what you are talking about."

"No, there won't be no sittin'. I know 'bout your tricks; the moment I sit, like, my anger will diminish. And Storm likes all his here anger boiling over inside of him, like."

"Storm, why are you angry?"

"I see you're a tricky one, all innocent, like," Storm said, cracking his knuckles as he looked down at Harry. Harry could feel the perspiration on his forehead now and his palms began sweating.

"Storm," Harry began, sounding more in control than he felt, "you tell me right now what brings you in here all hot under the collar!"

"I don't wear no collar, this here is a t-shirt. Maybe you really are innocent, like."

"Storm, I want you to tell me why you're so upset," Harry ordered, still keeping his distance.

"You know exactly what I'm angry about; why, she's my Flower. My Flower!" Storm yelled, his face flushed and cracking his knuckles loudly.

"I know she is, and you're made for each other."

At Harry's words, Storm's face immediately softened. "Ya mean it, you really think so? You really mean it?" Storm asked, looking very relieved.

"Well of course I do. Why, everyone knows she's your Flower," Harry replied smoothly, thinking Storm might be about to cry.

Then his expression changed again as he straightened up and yelled, "But you gave my Flower a gift. And you know what that means when a man gives a woman, especially one as attractive as my Flower, a gift, like, Mr. Harry?"

"The gift was from my wife and me for her birthday, Storm, nothing more. It's what a good boss does for his secretaries."

"It is? Then you'll not be wantin' to fight me for her or nothin'?" Storm asked, baffled, but the relief was evident in his voice.

"Storm, I have a perfectly wonderful wife of my own, and I am very happy with her!"

"Yeah, really? I bet she's no landowner or clothes designer or cook; I bet she doesn't know the numbers, like."

"Storm, you've got a real good deal there. I just want Flower to be my secretary and enjoy her work; nothing more."

"Really? Why, she can sure do her work and she's real good at it, too. I best be leavin' ya before me Flower finds me here and beats me up. This is her area and out of bounds to me, like, and the rest of us workers. Bye, Mr. Harry," Storm said, his eyes downcast as he quickly left the office and almost ran through the outer offices until he reached the safety of the warehouse door.

Harry exhaled a long breath as he sat behind his desk again; he thought working at E.M. was like living in a soap opera. An hour later, Harry looked up to see three guys carrying the biggest cake he had ever seen. It was also the strangest cake he had ever seen. The icing was a dusty brown and the tall yellow candles looked like they belonged on a church altar.

Of course, Flower wanted to give Harry the biggest piece, and she was not about to be talked out of it. Finally, he showed her how much he wanted as everyone laughed – he had to say he was on a diet on account of all the good cookies he ate for morning tea. Flower personally spoon-fed him the first few mouthfuls; it tasted like sweet dust, although it really did melt in his mouth. Harry could only wonder what it was made of. After several mouthfuls, everyone looked a whole lot better, and Harry knew he wouldn't be eating anything more. He washed it down with some rose petal tea and felt only a little more awake. It was long after his staff had finished dancing the jig on the desks and Flower had disappeared to make out with Storm for the second time that day, that everyone seemed to leave for the day. Harry's cell soon vibrated and Milly told him she couldn't believe the mess he allowed himself to get into, yet again. She was coming to get him. She told him to lock the door to his office and sit tight in case Handy Sandy was around.

However, Harry couldn't find a lock on his office door and he didn't really know who the woman on the phone was. When Milly arrived about an hour later, Harry told her she wasn't his wife, and he protested all the way to the car. He was asleep before they arrived at the condo. With help from the doorman, they managed to get him inside and to bed. He didn't wake until the next morning. He had slept in his disguise, so Al awake next to Harry Hoarders on Saturday morning.

Milly was concerned about the pending visit to Flowers home. She spent most of the day anxiously trying to decide what they should wear. In the end, she purchased some secondhand jeans with several well-placed holes and embroidery around the legs and hemline. Milly found a peasant blouse in white muslin and Harry an old lilac t-shirt with 'Peace to the World' written across the back. Milly needed to wash them before tonight, as these were secondhand clothes and some of the few they had ever purchased. At the same secondhand store, they purchased a tambourine. It had caught their eye because it was brightly colored and had long ribbons hanging from the edges. Neither of them wanted to go to the fish bake at Flower's place, but they couldn't say 'no' any longer. They didn't know what to expect, but what they did know was that Flower was very excited about them meeting her family.

Milly and Harry drove slowly to the address Flower had given him. Milly followed the hand-drawn map as they went deeper into the wild semi-rural countryside. Occasionally, tiny shacks were just visible through the trees. They had no gardens, and both Harry and Milly suspected what they were growing on their properties wasn't vegetables. The road now narrowed and was no more than a dirt track; trees bent low over the car, often hitting the windshield as they drove.

"Milly, surely we're lost! She can't live out here?" Harry commented, slowing down even more.

"Well, according to her map, we should be nearly there. It used to be a town some years ago, until they closed off the main road and flattened all the buildings. I checked it out on the internet. Most of the farmers were growing acres of weed and not much else. So, the authorities came in and flattened the lot, burnt most of it and told the famers who had owned the land for hundreds of years to move on. I believe a lot of them now live in trailers about five miles up the road, and some also work at E.M. Interbreeding is very normal in these parts as they are so cut off from the rest of the world."

"It's hard to believe in this day and age, isn't it?' Harry commented as he dodged another low branch.

"It's even harder to believe that people like Flower still exist and know so little about the rest of the world. Oh, here's the old railway line, that's on the map, and a little way up there should be a stream.

Flower says not to go over the wooden bridge with your car as it will collapse. We are to walk the remainder of the way, Harry."

"Milly, I'm liking this less and less."

"I know, me, too; we won't stay long," Milly said, as, rounding a slight curve, they almost landed in the stream. The old bridge was partly broken, but looked strong enough to hold them. Milly had presents for the children, so they had several large sacks to carry. The moment they were outside the car, they knew they were in the right place. They could hear hooting and hollering, and children singing, yelling and laughing. They looked further into the trees and there they saw a thin trail of smoke.

"That must be it," Harry said, as they set off in that direction. Suddenly, two young boys tumbled out in front of them; they were locked in battle as the bigger boy yelled, "You take it back!"

"I will not!"

"You take it back or—"

Just then, they noticed the newcomers and broke apart, before running into the trees.

Soon, Milly and Harry were greeted by several children yelling, "They're here, they're finally here!"

"Can we eat now?" said another.

"Harry! Finally, I was just about to send out a search party," Flower said as she ran straight for Harry. Harry had to catch her as she leapt into his arms and kissed him passionately on the lips. Harry was taken aback, but some-how he knew he should have expected it from Flower. Harry hadn't known they were late, so he didn't reply, but merely let her slide to the ground.

"Hey, Mr. Harry – what ya carryin'?" Storm asked, walking quickly towards him and eyeing up the huge bags and the camera Flower had instructed him to bring.

"I brought something for each of your children, if that's all right, Storm? This is my wife, Milly," Harry said.

"Sure, it's all right; why, the kids never say no to nothin' we don't need to pay for," Storm said, before looking at Milly. "Wow, Harry, you sure were right, she sure is a pretty one. You got all dressed up, too," Storm said, letting out a low whistle as he walked around and around them. Quickly, the children joined in the game as they became quiet and also gathered around. Storm looked even worse than he did at work, and he didn't smell too great either. Harry knew Milly had noticed; she hated bad smells and Storms smell was one of the worst. He wore no shirt and he displayed the word 'Peace' tattooed across his back, and across his chest he had a large rose with Flower's face in the center, and over his large belly, the words 'My Flower'. The tattoo was in color and was very large.

"Hi, Milly, I'm Flower. Why, you sure got a cute husband; he's kinda shy, but that just makes him all the cuter," Flower said, hugging Milly tightly. Harry could tell they had already been enjoying cookies or something similar; even the children seemed happy.

"Now, I want you to meet my wonderful children. I'll introduce them in age order just so you can get it right, like. This here is my daughter, Angel Wings. She's almost twelve years old; say hello now." A young girl came forward, she had long blonde hair that was uncombed and knotted, her complexion was clear and she had big blue eyes similar to Flower's brown ones. Her skin was tanned a soft golden color; she was very pretty. Harry noticed that Flower had been right in her description of Angel Wings, right down to the underwear, which was the only thing the young girl was wearing. She had a fabulous young body with curves in all the right places and long, shapely legs. She wore a black lacy bra and matching panties with a black lace camisole.

"Angel Wings got all dressed up for you, like. Her best underwear, like, and that stuff costs a fortune," Flower said. Even though the girl was very pretty, she was none too clean and badly needed a bath and her hair washed. Harry remembered that bath day was Sunday and wished they'd arrived after they'd all bathed. Milly gave the girl a gift and Flower instructed her that it was okay to unwrap the pretty paper. Angel Wings was thrilled with her hair brush and lip gloss, but moments later she complained that you couldn't see it when she drew on her leg. Milly quickly explained it was for her lips and showed her how to use it. Everyone crowded around and watched closely.

"Thank you, Mrs. Milly, but I'd rather have a fishin' net. It's real hard work catching all those little itty bitty fish you like so much, with your hands. Why, they're so small, they swim right on through your fingers, like," the girl said in a rather deep voice that astounded them both.

"This here is Pet Arbry. He's the one who likes to clean up; none of us mind, like. Both Storm and I like the lived-in look, but Pet Arbry likes things neat, don't ya, Pet Arbry? And that there is his Pa, Peter Arbry; as ya can see, he plays guitar and sings, like. We hired him special, like, 'cause you were coming to our home," Flower said, proudly holding the young boy who was tugging at her arm to escape. He was a dirty looking boy with a mop of curly brown hair that hung over his face and in his eyes. Harry produced a small two-wheeler bike from his large bag.

"Wow, thanks, but what am I to do with it? Ya can't carry much in this, like," the boy inquired, holding it above his head by the wheels that kept moving. Harry and Milly were amazed the boy didn't know what to do with the bike. When Harry showed him how to ride it, they were all in awe of the thing and said they had never seen anything like it in these parts before. Although, when Pet tried to ride it, he quickly fell off and realized it took some practice.

"This here is Lamb Sonny," Flower said, as a gentle-looking boy with dark skin and his mother's limpid eyes stared up at them, before moving closer to his mom. He gently wrapped his arms around her, trying to hide his face in her billowing caftan. Harry gave the boy a large ball; it had a red and black picture of Superman on it. Harry knew Lamb Sonny would not recognize Superman, so he didn't bother explaining who he was. Lamb Sonny turned the ball around and around until Harry showed him how to throw and catch. Lamb Sonny was unable to catch it at all at first, but Harry assured him he just needed some practice. Then they met Trig Smith, a rough-looking kid who seemed to have an enormous chip on his shoulder. He was also dressed a little strangely, as all he wore was an old pair of jockey underpants. Harry gave him a Dr Seuss book, *The Cat in the Hat*.

"I don't want no girls' book," he said, racing back into the trees.

"Sorry about him, he's always fighting, but I'm sure Angel Wings will like the book; she's a good reader. She knows about twenty words by sight and can count up to fifty; we're real proud. This little guy is our baby, Colt," Flower said, lifting up her billowing caftan and producing a rather large child who was cradled on her breast in a ragged sling. She had draped the sling around one shoulder under her caftan, and both the sling and the boy were completely concealed. Milly and Harry noticed immediately Flower wore no underwear and looked quite pregnant. The little boy, who looked about two years old, resented loudly being taken from the comfort of his hiding place. Milly and Harry were amazed to see the little boy wore no clothes at all.

"These are some crayons, coloring pencils and some coloring books also," Milly said, digging deep inside her large bag.

"And what you supposed to do with them there colored sticks? It's not much to light a fire with, Mr. Harry," Storm said, as the little boy wobbled over and hugged Harry's legs.

"Thank you, Mr. and Mrs. Harry," he said, then put his thumb into his mouth as Angel Wings scooped him into her arms. Milly opened the large book and began to draw a cat; everyone soon crowded around and watched in silence.

"Wow!" said most of the kids together as Milly drew the cat.

"It's girl stuff; I just want to fight," Trig Smith said, disappearing again into the trees. Peter Arbry continued softly playing his guitar.

"These last two things are for you and Storm," Milly said, handing the tambourine and a bottle of white wine to Storm.

"Why, Harry, Milly, this is real kind, you been real kind to us both and our family. The tambourine we will enjoy, but we don't drink no liquor, like. We don't smoke or take no drugs either, like, so ya best be takin' it home. Come, I'll show you our home."

Harry and Milly were amazed at her words, but quickly put the bottle back into the large sack they were carting around. The inside of the washroom was much like the outside: it was total chaos. Someone had taken several walls down and blocked off some of the toilets. They had old carpet partially spread over the floor, and several dirty sleeping bags lay in the corners. In the far corner sat a large table with a new Singer sewing machine on it and scraps of fabric that Harry recognized immediately. Both the table and chair, like the sewing machine, looked almost new. In the other corner stood a small table with four chairs; this appeared to be where the children did their homework. Two broken wooden chairs scattered in the central area were the only other furnishings, and the old stove and sink made up the kitchen. The stove had one large burner and a very large oven. Milly could never remember seeing anything quite so old. Some of the walls had been roughly painted white, while others still had the original graffiti showing through. Flower asked if Harry would mind taking some photos of her home, and he happily obliged.

"It's quite somethin', ain't it? This was the only municipal toilet block in the whole town and I got it. I almost own it all, too. Why, it's the only thing left that has running water. This is where we're going to put in a shower when we can afford it," Flower said as proudly as if she was showing them Buckingham Palace.

Harry remembered just how shocked he'd been when he first saw the wages the staff earned. He knew his was lower than he could have imagined, but what they paid the workers would only keep them just above the poverty line. He now understood no one knew the difference, so he decided to say nothing; he guessed it was better to keep them all in work than have them and their families go hungry. Flower took them into the far corner of the toilet block and showed them the master suite. Storm had roughly constructed several wooden packing pallets on the ground and Flower had made them the largest sleeping bag Harry and Milly had ever seen. It was made from many scraps of fabric all sewn together, and she had padded the underside, which sat on the pallets and was now at least ten inches from the ground.

"Would you believe we just keep on breaking them wooden pallets? Flower and I have such a passion for each other...," Storm said, laughing as he wrapped his arms around his wife. Milly and Harry didn't reply as they were not sure what to say.

Soon, Flower continued, "We made our darling Colt right there in that there sleeping bag; why, I remember it well. It was the first time we slept in the new bag. These were the first fabric scraps Storm got for me. I knew it was love right there; what other man would put his job on the line to get me the biggest scraps of fabric, unless he loved me?" Flower finished, gazing lovingly at Storm.

Finally, Milly found her tongue. "Just how many children do you have, Flower?" she asked. Harry had only been told about five, so he eagerly awaited the answer as he had often wanted to know himself, but didn't think he could ask the question without Flower trying to get close to him.

"Well, I'm not rightly sure. Why, it's not the type of thing you really count now, is it? I have five at home here with us at present." She paused to think.

"Well, you said the eldest is living away from home, didn't you? Are there any more?" Harry asked.

"Well, I should say so. Why, my Flower was a wild child in her day. One of the wildest; why, there was no one who escaped her charms. I'm one lucky guy!" Storm said with a wide smile on his lips as he enjoyed remembering his good fortune.

"Why, I think there is another four or maybe five that live with their fathers. I didn't want to be burdened with kids in them days, too much going down, like. I was a child of the revolution, Milly, a Flower child – that's where my name comes from. Peace, man," Flower said, making a 'V' with her fingers. They moved slowly outside to the sound of Peter Arbry playing a fast tune on his guitar, while Angel Wings played the tambourine equally as fast and danced around the large fire in the middle of the yard. She was quite a sight with her cheeks flushed and her hair flying out behind her. Harry and Milly noticed that Peter Arbry couldn't take his eyes from the young girl.

"The fish fry's a-ready and the pigeon pie is cooked! Everyone, get ya plates!" Angel Wings ordered in her strange deep voice that sounded more like a man than a young girl.

"Ya brought ya own plate, I hope," Flower asked, eyeing the large bags that lay empty on the floor.

"Well, no, I didn't know…," Harry began.

"It's okay, Pet Arbry and Trig Smith can wait their turn."

"I'm starving, Ma. I been fightin' them Huskin boys all afternoon, yonder down by the creek," Trig whined.

"Hush now, Trig, ya moms made her mind up. Our guests will eat first, and there's plenty to go 'round," Storm said, handing Milly and Harry a dirty tin plate each and an old bent fork and spoon.

"Well, we're right glad you put us onto them Microfiche. Why, they must be the smallest fish I ever did see," Flower said, as she took a huge spoon and stirred the vat of oil cooking over the fire. She then scooped out several large deep-fried balls of batter, while Angel Wings dished up her pigeon pie. Harry and Milly had never tasted anything quite like it. The fish must have been incredibly small, as they could only taste the batter, although they did retrieve several tiny bones.

The pigeon pie was quite tasty, once the occasional feather was removed from your mouth. Harry snapped photos of Angel Wings dancing around the fire and managed somehow to get all the other children without them knowing. After the meal, Harry asked Flower to gather around her family so he could take some shots of them all. She assured Harry again this was the reason they were all dressed up in their best. Everyone was rather shy in front of the camera. Trig wouldn't come out of the trees for some time. He then raced through several of the shots, before Storm grabbed him by the arm and held him fast. Once the photos were taken, the mood again lightened, and the kids all began to dance and Flower served herb tea. Milly noticed how Peter's guitar playing and singing drastically changed after his first cup. The tempo quickened and everyone danced, hooted and hollered. Milly passed on the herb tea Flower had made especially for the occasion. After Harry's first cup was partly drained, he realized why.

Harry didn't know how they made it home, but he awoke the next morning with a fierce hangover and a very dry mouth. He was glad to be safely in his own bed.

Baby Charlie

Seven Months Later

"Sam, Sam darling, it's a boy! Chuck and I were both with her. Mother and son are doing fine. His name is Charles Sheffield Hollingsworth. He's the most handsome baby ever!" Ruth Dolman yelled into the phone in the corridor of the hospital. She was dressed in her hospital gown and had a mask covering her face.

"Oh, my baby girl's a mother," Sam cried into the phone as he sat in the condo in San Diego. Just then, another call sounded on Chuck's cell, so Ruth handed him the phone and returned to her daughter's side. It had been a long and stressful thirty-six hours for Ruth, and all the emotions were taking their toll. The moment Rita returned to the hospital, Ruth said goodbye and promised to return first thing in the morning.

The previous day was Harry's last at E.M. Distributions. They had planned to fly out that night and allow Baxter to pay out the lease and pack the condo. However, Flower organized several parties, and Harry had made the mistake of eating and drinking what she had so lovingly prepared. As a result, he suffered heavily. He presented Flower with the photos he had taken at her home, some of which Milly had carefully framed. Harry had to show her, in detail, how she could hang them on the wall in her home, and once she understood the procedure, she was thrilled. She was so grateful, she stared at Harry for several minutes with tears in her big, soft brown eyes. He knew she would always have his back. The last thing he remembered was Flower holding both her hands on each side of his face and telling him how much she'd miss him, before kissing him deeply. He could still feel that dusty taste he had experienced before.

Milly needed to rescue him, although by that time he didn't recognize her. She just took him home and deposited him safely into bed. She was booked on a flight to Switzerland in a few hours' time, where she would organize the fifty-seven million dollars they had so easily skimmed from the large bank balance of E.M. Distribution. Baxter was to leave Switzerland and arrive in San Diego. However, the surprise parties had caught Harry off guard; as he didn't want to raise suspicion, it was agreed he must attend. Everyone wanted him to meet Lindsay Proctor, the guy he had replaced. Lindsay Proctor was now out of the hospital and well enough to return to work, and he very much wanted to meet Harry.

~

Harry planned to leave San Diego that night, or at least be home in Savannah, Georgia, tomorrow. Felix was soon due for release from prison, and certain arrangements must be made to ensure he never returned. He was to stay at the Grasshopper mansion until he was set up in the outside world again. Harry also knew he could use some help setting up Alberta's fiftieth birthday party. It was to be a huge affair and held at the mansion. Only close and trusted friends would be invited, but the Grasshoppers had no shortage of those.

Then the call had come through. It was diverted from the Dolmans' home to their San Diego condo. They hadn't expected the call for at least another three weeks. It was Chuck; he was on his way to the hospital. Chuck said everything was happening so fast. So, Switzerland was momentarily forgotten and Baxter was allowed a two-day holiday somewhere in Europe. Ruth was on the first flight to New York. She was completely unable to wake Harry, so she left a note pinned to her pillow.

Chuck Hollingsworth gazed lovingly into the sleeping face of his wife, and then looked at his son, who was also sleeping peacefully. Charles Sheffield Hollingsworth the Third looked just like his mom, although he had his dad's jaw and nose, or, thought Chuck, it was actually more like Sheffield's jaw and nose. As he sat peacefully watching over his family, a tear escaped his eye; he wiped it away. Was it a tear of happiness, of new beginnings, because he was so proud of Amanda, or was it for times passed and precious people lost?

He wanted to name his son, not only after his father, but also after Sam Dolman, but Amanda wouldn't hear of it. Chuck now realized why he was crying. It was still too soon for him to have another Sheffield in the family. He wished more than anything his dad could have been here.

"Here, Chuck, thought you might appreciate this. It's going to be a long night if you sit here and watch them sleep," Rita Hollingsworth said, handing her son a Styrofoam cup of steaming coffee as she pulled up a chair.

"Mom, I know for sure I am truly blessed. I can't believe how my life has changed in the past year," Chuck said, full of emotion, as he stroked Amanda's forehead gently while she slept.

"I know, Chuck. I just wish Sheffield was here to be part of all this," Rita replied, a little teary-eyed, as she watched her new grandson sleep.

"Me, too, Mom... me, too."

"I think he has your dad's jaw and nose, son," Rita said, gazing down at the newborn.

"I thought so, too, Mom," Chuck said, yawning widely.

"Did you tell Amanda what happened to your father?" Rita asked, sitting down again beside her son.

"No, Mom, but I shall when the time's right – it's still too painful."

"Yes, Chuck, it seems like just yesterday," Rita said, hiding a stray tear that escaped her eye.

"Mom, I'm going to find the creep that did that to Dad. I have already started the search. He was fired from the trucking company where he worked, but we did locate the truck."

"Oh, Chuck, really?" Rita was unable to conceal her sobbing at his words. Chuck gathered her into his arms and held her tightly for several minutes.

"Mom, if you're not ready, I can leave it for a while. I meant to tell you yesterday, but so much happened," Chuck said, as Rita pulled away and tried to compose herself while she sipped her coffee, got to her feet and paced the floor.

"Yesterday was a blessing, just like Amanda and baby Charlie. I guess I'm just tired, like you, son. Of - course I want you to find the son of a bitch who did this to the man we loved," Rita said angrily. Chuck was shocked to hear his mom talk like that; he always thought of her as a gentle, softly spoken lady. Several minutes' silence followed, before Rita sounded like her usual self again.

"Nanny Bates is installed in your home; I spent some time with her this morning. She seems fine, knows her stuff, I think. She will arrive at six p.m. every evening and stay until ten a.m. every morning. When Amanda first arrives home she will be with you twenty-four hours a day for the next five days. If you want her to stay longer hours, just say the word, son. There's nothing more important than family," Rita said, touching his shoulder as she paced the floor.

"Mom, you've been more than generous. You know I have more work than I can handle at the agency. I have great staff, and the new guy, Tom, is also working out well. He fits right in. There is really no need for you to pay for our nanny," Chuck said, voicing how he knew Amanda and he felt at his mom's generosity.

"I know you're doing well, but I want to do this for you both. It makes me feel needed," Rita finished, as a soft tap came from the door. They turned together to see Blue peek around the door. Chuck beckoned her to enter. She was holding a giant teddy bear with a huge blue ribbon tied around its neck. As she greeted Rita and peeked at Baby Charlie peacefully sleeping, she, too, had a tear in her eye.

"He's just so perfect," Blue whispered.

"Everything all right at the office?" Chuck asked, thinking this a very strange hour for her to visit.

"Yes, everything's fine, but we are very busy at the office. The guys are coping well. Walters is proving a true leader. I just need to talk to you about a few things, Chuck," Blue said, giggling as she always did. Just having her in the room lightened Rita's mood.

"Do you need to talk to me now, Blue?" Chuck asked, thinking it could surely wait until the morning, and then realizing he would probably still be here in the morning.

"It could, but I really think…," Blue began, as Chuck interrupted her.

"Okay, Blue, outside."

They both quietly left the room. Blue was still carrying the huge teddy bear – so she quickly returned to the room and left it in the chair Chuck had just vacated.

"I didn't really want to bother you, boss. It's just that you've been trying to contact her for so long."

"Who, Blue?" Chuck asked, wanting to get back to Amanda.

"Well, Holly Bond called all the way from the U.K. You were right. She is a pilot with British Airways. She holds residences in both London and L.A."

"Finally, she called. Did she say why she has called now, after all these months?" Chuck asked, now totally focused on Blue.

"Yes, she has teenage and adult children. So, she needed to find the right time, as she knew you'd want to meet and speak to her. She had an idea what you wanted, but said she requires total confidentiality before you meet. Of course, I promised her that. She said you can meet her at her home in L.A. this weekend. It is the only time she will be on her own. I did ask her if there could be another time, as things were busy for you right now. And she said it may be months before she can meet with you again. She is flying the long haul from U.K. to Sydney, Australia, for three months, so she won't be in the States for some time. She said it took her a lot of nerve to call and that if you are too busy to see her, she really doesn't care," Blue finished.

"Did you mention her meeting her birth daughter, Siobhan Burke?" Chuck asked.

"Yes, boss, I did. She made it quite clear she doesn't want to have her daughter in her life. She also made it clear that she doesn't want her husband or family to know about her 'mistake', as she puts it. But she said she will meet with her if it is important to the girl," Blue concluded.

"She sounds very uncaring, Blue," Chuck commented.

"I don't think she's uncaring, just scared. But she's definitely a career woman. She knew the baby was placed with a wealthy family and she knows all about their background," Blue said.

"How does she know all this, Blue? I thought adoptions were kept confidential."

"Apparently, not this one; she claims to have had access to the adoption files. She received big bucks from the family her daughter was placed with. She said they got a good deal, they got the baby they wanted and she got the cash she needed. It put her through college and then she went into the Navy, where she got her wings and met her husband," Blue finished, looking pleased.

"Blue, you've certainly been busy in my absence. I can't imagine how you found out so much, and frankly right now I don't want to know any more," Chuck said as he saw she was bursting to tell him everything. Chuck heard the baby begin to cry inside the room as a nurse hurried in. Chuck quickly asked, "Blue, is there anything else that's really important?"

"Yes, boss, I also have the name of the truck driver you were chasing."

"Amazing! Blue, you're turning into quite the little private investigator yourself, aren't you?" Chuck said, now urgently wanting to get back to Amanda.

"His name's Ali Singh, and he works at—" Blue said, as Chuck cut her off.

"Blue, you've done a great job. I'm really proud of all the information you've discovered and everything you've found. You must have been working really hard, but right now I need to get back to Charlie and Amanda. I'll call you and look in on the office tomorrow once Amanda and Charlie are safely home. Nanny Bates will be with us twenty-four hours a day for the next five days, so I promise I'll call into the office. Thanks for dropping by and for bringing the large teddy bear," Chuck said, and he was gone.

Chuck was thrilled with all Blue's findings, although the timing was not great for him. He had been tracking Siobhan's birth mother for months. However, each time he tried to contact her, she was not available; she appeared to move around a lot. He didn't leave any messages, as he didn't want to compromise her privacy. He had no way of judging her reaction until he spoke to her, and he was beginning to think that may never happen. Siobhan had not been pleased with the time it was taking. Over the last months she had almost divorced Brock and then just last week they again reunited. Chuck had given up counting how many times this had happened, but the Burkes were proving for him the source of a reliable and consistent income.

Just before Brock and Siobhan reconciled again, Chuck was shocked to learn of the murder of Brock Burke's secretary, Floris McKrill. Like Brock's previous secretary, Marlene Brice, she had been murdered in her office and her left hand had been removed and left in the dumpster downstairs. When it was found, she still wore on her waist a valuable diamond bracelet. If Siobhan hadn't been Amanda's best friend, Chuck would have distanced himself from the Burkes long ago. He was also aware that Amanda had been one of Brock's numerous secretaries, and he'd often wondered just what had transpired between them. However, discretion would never allow him to ask. It was like discussing his cases with either Amanda or Rita – that would never happen either. He had been taught by his dad to be the soul of discretion in all things.

Chuck slept in the chair beside Amanda's bed that night in the hospital, and he was surprised to find it was morning when Ruth gently nudged him awake with a cup of coffee. Several hours later, they were bringing baby Charlie home to his newly painted pale-yellow nursery decorated with all the exciting baby mobiles and toys they had been given in the previous months. While Amanda and Chuck got acquainted with Nanny Bates, Ruth made lunch. Ruth's flight was at three p.m. and already she knew she would hate leaving her little girl and new grandson. However, the importance of her trip to Switzerland overruled her staying. Amanda totally understood, although Ruth knew Chuck didn't. He'd asked her several times to stay at least another few days, but she just couldn't. This was their last job, and the thought of them getting caught was too great to postpone her departure any longer. Hugo would already be home in Savannah and enjoying a much-deserved rest. Once Al returned, they would start preparing for Felix's arrival home. This time they would be picking him up at the gates of the jail the moment he was released.

Charlie proved the perfect baby; he quickly managed to charm everyone he saw. When he was awake, he'd gaze up into Amanda's eyes and it took her breath away. Neither Amanda nor Chuck had ever thought they could feel such love for something so small, so quickly. The moment lunch was over, Amanda said she would drive her mom to the airport, leaving Chuck to get acquainted with his new son. The moment they were driving, Amanda told Ruth how she was no longer wearing her skin-suit, explaining that it was too difficult once her belly expanded. Ruth had been concerned about just that, but Amanda assured her that Chuck had seen so many changes in her body, he would accept anything at present. Amanda voiced her desire to change her looks back; she hated her disguise and her long blonde hair and the time it took to look good each morning. Ruth promised to work it out soon.

"Amanda, are you happy? You have been through so much in the past year," Ruth asked, her concern for her daughter's happiness evident.

"Oh, Mom, Chuck is the most perfect husband. He's caring, considerate, loving, charming, funny, and always the chivalrous gentleman. He's also eye candy, in case you haven't noticed. So, what more could a girl want? He does everything for me, everything I allow him to do and then some. I want for nothing, Mom. I really think we should tell him our secret. He's very discreet and I know we can trust him," Amanda said, sneaking a sideways look at her mom as she drove.

"Amanda... or should I say... Neve, Chuck is also a P.I., and he was a private investigator before he met you, and before that he was in the FBI. His father was also an FBI agent. Don't you think that's all rather too close to the law? You do realize we're wanted criminals, Neve? You can only imagine the millions of dollars we have defrauded from numerous companies over the years. Why, there's been so many, I couldn't even name all of them. But the one your dads just finished working for will be our last. It was also, by far, the most unusual."

"I know the timing was impossible. I'm glad Dad saw it through. I know how it must have tugged at his heart strings not being here for Charlie's birth," Amanda said.

"Yes, it did; he's such a big teddy bear with his kids and his grandchildren," Alberta said, knowing how upset Hugo was at missing the big event. Al felt really bad sneaking out and leaving a note on the pillow, but she also knew if she hadn't made that flight, she wouldn't have been at her daughter's side in time for the birth.

"So, tell me about Dad's last job?" Neve asked. Al told her everything. They laughed all the way to the airport. Neve was shocked at things she heard and couldn't imagine how people could still exist like Flower and her family did.

The rest of the week flew by. Charlie captivated everyone who visited, and Chuck and Amanda spent hours just watching him sleep. They both appreciated having Nanny Bates with them at night, as Charlie enjoyed a regular three a.m. bottle feeding by Nanny Bates. Chuck had intended to go into the office for a complete day, but instead he seemed to only briefly call in and relieve his staff when they were on a stakeout and needed a lunch break.

"Chuck, are you and Mrs. Burke flying to L.A. to have a meeting with Holly Bond? Mrs. Burke called five times and needs an answer; she says she has arrangements to make," Blue asked.

"I know, Blue, she's called the house and even mentioned it yesterday when she stayed for dinner."

"Well, boss, you have to go."

"Yes, I know, Blue, make the arrangements. First class all the way. It'll be hard leaving Charlie and Amanda, but we've been chasing this woman for so long now."

"Consider it done, boss. The itinerary will be in your top drawer, as always. Mrs. Burke suggests you leave Friday night."

"Friday night? Why not Saturday morning?"

"I'm just telling you her preference, boss," Blue said as she continued with her filing.

"Blue, I know I've been absent from the office too much lately, but next week will be different."

"Sure, it will. You're the one who always says how quickly things get away from you if they're not managed constantly; wouldn't want you to fall out of the loop. Hate to remind you, boss, but...," Blue said, giggling.

However, it was enough for Chuck to know he must get back to work, and as of next week, he decided to do just that.

"Blue, do you still have the information about the truck driver?"

"Sure, boss. His name's Ali Singh, and he drives a courier van now for Faster Courier Service. The head office is only fifteen minutes away. Here's all the info," Blue said, placing a file in front of Chuck. Chuck had been thinking of taking over from Tom on the stakeout and then going home for the afternoon, but somehow the sight of the file containing the name of the man who killed his father shook him to the core, and Chuck sat looking at it for several minutes, unable to open it and read the contents.

"Here's your itinerary, boss. Shouldn't you be making a move? Tom's been on the job since six a.m.," Blue said, seeing the blank look on Chuck's face.

"I'm outta here, Blue – hold the fort," Chuck said, grabbing his coat and his Thermos of coffee, before quickly returning to his desk and dropping the file on Ali Singh into his second drawer, where it landed on top of the Grasshopper file.

~

Amanda and Chuck had an active love life, even while she was pregnant. It hadn't changed, and now that she wasn't pregnant, it was better than ever. However, with Charlie in the house, their love had changed. It was deeper and more fulfilling somehow. They both decided life held more meaning now they were a real family.

Chuck said, "Darling, why don't we get Mom over for the weekend and you can come with Siobhan and me to L.A.? It would be fun. I know the meeting won't take up all our time and when it's over we can all go sightseeing."

"I know Siobhan's going to be very emotional, so it would be good if I was there to support her, but, Chucky, I just can't leave

Charlie. He's just too little, and I'm breastfeeding. You know I'll miss you terribly, Chucky darling," Amanda cooed, as she snuggled close until, again, their passion mounted.

Another Mother

Siobhan had been wanting to meet her birth mother for months, right from the time Chuck told her she was adopted. Her mom and dad were still in denial, and every time she mentioned the subject, Esmeralda became hysterical and cried, saying Siobhan didn't love her and was being a cruel and ungrateful daughter. Siobhan hadn't discussed it with Brock; knowing his track record, he would probably leave her anyway. Since she'd known her birth mother actually existed, her ongoing problems with Brock didn't seem nearly as important. She'd long since taken over Amanda's old apartment and intended on keeping it just in case. Siobhan's outlook on life was changing: things that previously seemed very important now seemed less so.

Amanda and Chuck made Siobhan the godmother to their new son, and Siobhan was taking her role as Aunty Siobhan very seriously. She was currently setting up a trust fund for Charlie and also thinking of making some real estate investments in his name. The divorce lawyer she just fired had suggested she buy real estate in the name of a relative. However, up until now she hadn't had anyone she could trust. She intended buying an apartment in Manhattan and putting it in her godson's name. That way it couldn't be touched if she should divorce Brock. It would also give her somewhere of her own to live.

Sadly, Siobhan was slowly realizing she would, indeed, one day need to divorce Brock. She loved him madly, but as a long-term life partner, he was too unreliable. She needed someone she could trust. She'd always thought her husband would unconditionally have her back, just like her own parents did for each other. Living with Brock was like living in a dream one minute and a nightmare the next. She knew she lived for the times that were on occasions quite wonderful. He either loved her more than anything in the world, or ignored and avoided her when he was seeing someone else. She hated the fact he thought her so stupid as to not notice. Materially, she had everything she needed. He never denied her anything, and if he had, her parents would not say no to their little princess. But she needed more. Siobhan was hoping this trip to meet her birth mother would somehow fill the void she had in her life. Amanda was the closest thing to family she had in the world.

They were very close, closer than sisters – they told each other everything. Siobhan thought Charlie the cutest baby on earth, but she also knew now that with Charlie in Amanda's life, Amanda would have less time for her friend. In the last week they had not met for lunch once, and usually they met for lunch at least three times a week. Sure, she'd spent time with her friend at her house, and she knew she could stay as long as she liked. She had stayed for dinner several times, but with Charlie wanting attention and Chuck never allowing her to discuss the case outside his office, she was no longer the center of attention.

Siobhan wanted Amanda by her side when she met her birth mother, but when she asked her, she knew instinctively the timing was wrong and Amanda would decline. However, she told Chuck to also ask Amanda again to join them in L.A., although she was holding out little hope it would happen. The thought of having to go through this meeting on her own scared her half to death. Amanda assured her she was only a phone call away and would carry the phone with her always, but for Siobhan, it wasn't nearly the same. Yes, Siobhan felt jealous of Baby Charlie. And yes, Siobhan felt she had lost a part of her best friend to the newborn.

Siobhan spent hours trying to imagine just what her mother would look like, sound like; would they look alike? Did she have a family, a career, or both? Siobhan Burke had a thousand questions buzzing around her head. She couldn't believe finally this weekend they might all be answered. The question she most wanted to know was, why – why had she given her daughter away to a stranger? Siobhan hoped she would have the courage to ask that one. Siobhan was already packed, and she had repacked her suitcase five times. She didn't know what this woman would be like, so she didn't know what she should wear. Siobhan knew Brock would be home any moment, as they were due to go to a cocktail party for one of the big clients at Banker's Securities. She'd met the client before and remembered him well; he'd made a pass at her. She never told her husband, as at that time he was seeing another woman and she knew he wouldn't care.

Siobhan was dressed in a charcoal gray, chiffon, knee-length cocktail dress. It fitted tightly into the bodice and waist and fell into a full skirt with many layers of petticoats kicking out at the hem. The top layer of charcoal gray chiffon held a slight sheen, while the layers under were black and sparkled as she moved. It showed to perfection her perfect body, and the dark color of the dress highlighted her long blonde hair. She wore high, strappy, black, sparkly pumps. Siobhan Burke knew she looked stunning. Siobhan was restless; she didn't want Brock to see her like this in case he asked why. She quickly fixed herself a double martini and sat in the comfortable white couch awaiting Brock's arrival. Moments later, she heard his car pull into the driveway and quickly finished her martini before moving casually to the door to greet her beloved.

The cocktail party was more fun than usual; she'd met some very interesting people. One man in particular intrigued her, almost as much as she'd intrigued him. He was an entrepreneur from Europe and enjoyed living in his many homes throughout the world. He was tall and very handsome, with dark, smoldering looks and a slight Italian accent. Somehow, she found herself alone with him on the balcony in the moonlight; they had talked for over an hour before Brock came to find her. Siobhan thought he may have felt jealous of the good-looking stranger, but if he did, he never let on. Siobhan was disappointed with his reaction. However, that was not the only reason she enjoyed his company; she somehow felt drawn to him. When he told her he had been adopted by a very rich, aristocratic couple when he was a baby, he immediately held her interest.

Mascoti Vitale was not only attentive and charming, but he constantly smothered Siobhan with compliments, and the way he kissed her hands and held eye contact made her feel hot all over – several times she knew she was blushing. He told her of his easy existence growing up in an influential family as a boy on an Italian vineyard, under the clear Tuscan sky and brilliant sunshine. He told her of his time spent in many different areas of Europe. And then he shared with her his antics at Harvard and the lifetime friends he'd made. He'd learned American football quickly and soon became the captain of his team; he enjoyed baseball, boxing and basketball. He excelled at sailing, waterskiing and cross-country snow skiing, although he admitted to finding it somewhat too cold for his liking. He told her of the restaurants he owned and the properties he had fallen in love with on his journeys, which he had to have. Siobhan slowly became mesmerized with his passion and love of life. Moments before Brock arrived, he gave her his business card, and on the back he wrote his personal cell number.

"I know you are a married woman, my beautiful one. But I shall keep my cell phone close to my heart, should you ever wish to speak to me. It is the same heart that will beat only for you. You have stolen it completely, and should you ever wish to give it back, I desire you to do so in person, my enchantress."

"You've certainly had an amazing life. You make me feel like I have done nothing," Siobhan said, gazing deeply into his hazel eyes.

"Your accomplishments are outstanding, more so than any woman in the room. You are, by far, the most breathtakingly beautiful woman in the world. That alone is your great achievement. It is I who has done nothing with my life. How could I walk this earth and not find you sooner? I look at you and feel my life is wasted. Arrh! Here is your lucky and gracious husband. It has been a pleasure spending time with your pretty wife. Ciao," Mascoti said, not staying to speak further to Brock.

"I thought he may have been bothering you, darling, so here I am on a rescue mission. I know how you hate getting stuck with the bores," Brock said.

Siobhan said nothing as she followed Brock inside and was introduced to more of his clients. Later, as they danced, Siobhan searched the room for Mascoti, but she was unable to find him. Just the thought of not seeing him again made her feel lost inside. She immediately put her vulnerability down to the pending meeting with her birth mother and thought no more of the tall and handsome stranger who had captivated her evening. Siobhan told Brock she was spending the weekend with an old school friend in L.A. She had seen the look of disbelief on his face; however, he said nothing and wished her a safe trip. Siobhan knew that leaving Brock on his own for a whole weekend was a foolish thing to do if she hoped to keep him. Brock Burke was not a man to be left to his own devices, especially during the weekend. However, a weekend with Brock paled in comparison to meeting her birth mother, and Siobhan only briefly thought of the consequences as she got into the cab at four p.m. on Friday afternoon. She would meet up with Chuck at the airport, and she hoped Amanda would at least be there to see them off. Amanda had offered to pick her up, but Siobhan declined in case Brock showed up early from the office. Siobhan wasn't sure if Amanda understood that Brock wasn't going to be told about her adventure in L.A.

"We will shortly be landing in Los Angeles. We ask you to place your seats in an upright position and turn all electronic devices off before landing. It is currently a clear day with blue skies and a gentle breeze from the South; the temperature is a perfect eighty-two degrees. On behalf of the captain and crew, we hope you have enjoyed flying United Airlines, and we hope you will join us again soon," the flight attendant said as they moved fast down the runway toward the terminal. Chuck slept the whole trip, and as he awoke, he apologized for his rudeness. Siobhan was not so fortunate; her mind was racing constantly, thinking of many things. Mascoti Vitale was one of them, and she wished he hadn't been in her thoughts; he had not come into her life at a particularly good moment. Siobhan wasn't even sure she ever wanted to see him again. She'd started to discuss him with Amanda the last time they'd spoken, but then it was Charlie's feeding time, and when Amanda called her back, they talked instead of her impending trip to L.A.

They were staying at the Four Seasons Beverly Hills. Chuck's room was next to Siobhan's suite. It was eight a.m. Saturday morning, and Siobhan had already changed her clothes and redone her hair three times. She'd just Googled Holly Bond on her computer and was surprised to see there were many women with the same name. Without an address either in L.A. or England, it was pointless. In the next room, Chuck was fast asleep – he'd slept all the way over on the plane, and again last night, after he'd spoken to Amanda, he'd slept soundly all night. It was nine a.m. when Chuck emerged from the shower, and he answered the door to room service with a towel around his wet, muscular body. At nine thirty a.m., he was enjoying the last of his large breakfast as he sat back and drank his third cup of coffee. He knew he should get dressed before Siobhan knocked on his door, but he was day-dreaming about Baby Charlie and his beautiful wife, Amanda. He made a mental note to talk to her about birth control and began to get dressed. At ten a.m., Siobhan knocked on his door.

"Well, good morning, Siobhan. Did you sleep well?" Chuck asked, his usual cheerful self.

"No, I sat up worrying and thinking all night; anyway, I hate sleeping by myself," Siobhan answered none too kindly.

"Well, as Brock's not here, I guess you have no choice," Chuck said, laughing and expecting her to do the same.

"There's always choices, Chuck, remember that. Everyone always has choices. It's just that most of us are too blind to see what's right under our noses. Like me and being adopted. I knew it had to be so, but each time I asked my mom, she denied it and seemed shocked that I'd even ask. I just got off the phone with Amanda. She sends you all her love and said for me to give you a big hug, but I don't feel like it right now," Siobhan said, walking briskly into Chuck's room and collapsing in the nearest chair. Chuck stood looking down at her miserable face and felt the anger seeping from her. He knew it was time for a talk.

"Siobhan, firstly, this is not the right attitude or mood to have before you meet your birth mother. The woman doesn't have to see us; she didn't need to reply to my calls. There is no reason to be angry with her, and if you aren't going to lighten up, I suggest we put the meeting off until you can," Chuck said, still looking down at her. Siobhan sat exactly where she was for several minutes as Chuck waited to see what she was going to say. Suddenly, she jumped up, burst into tears and fell into his arms, sobbing.

"I'm... I'm scared. What if... what if she doesn't like me? What if I'm not dressed right? What if I don't like her or she's a diva or a bitch? What if...? What if...?"

Chuck didn't know what to do. He realized he'd been insensitive to her feelings and knew he'd played it wrong. He held her close until she stopped sobbing. Finally, she left the room to fix her makeup, which Chuck thought still looked perfect. When she returned, she stood in the middle of the room, looking about as glamorous as you could get, and said nothing. Finally, Chuck held his hand out to her. "What if we go and find out? There's no time like the present."

For several seconds, she didn't move. Chuck also stayed where he was with his hand outstretched. Slowly, she moved toward him and finally put her hand in his. The limousine was waiting downstairs, and neither of them said anything on the drive to Orange County. They finally pulled into the driveway of a two-story Cape Cod home. The garden was neatly trimmed, the house tastefully decorated. Chuck opened the door for Siobhan, but she seemed unable to move. Finally, he coaxed her out.

"Siobhan, she's probably as scared as you are. Please, just be yourself so she gets to know the wonderful woman we all know and love," he said, trying to sound sincere, even though he thought Siobhan was a mixed up, spoiled diva.

"Chuck, you really mean it? I have never known whether you liked me or not," Siobhan said, giving him her hand as he helped her out. Chuck felt her palms sweating and realized she really was scared. Together, they walked up the pathway to the double white front doors. Chuck rang the doorbell, and within minutes a tall, slim blonde woman with a perfect face and immaculate clothes opened the door. Chuck thought she looked slightly like Siobhan in height and build, although her facial features were not the same. She was a stunner, but lacked Siobhan's femininity.

"Welcome. Won't you come in?" she said, never taking her eyes from Siobhan. They followed her into a well-appointed and tastefully decorated living room where she offered them a seat.

"I'm Holly Bond," she said matter-of-factly, extending her hand to Chuck.

"How do you do? I'm Chuck Hollingsworth, private investigator. I believe you spoke with my secretary, Blue. Thank you for seeing us, Ms. Bond."

"It's Mrs. Bond, actually. So, you're the one responsible for seeking me out, are you?" she asked none too kindly.

"Yes, ma'am, I am. May I introduce you to your daughter, Mrs. Siobhan Burke," Chuck said.

"Siobhan, is it? Then Katie wasn't posh enough for them? I guess you've had a good life?" Holly said, addressing Siobhan for the first time.

"Yes, I have, although I've always thought there was something missing. I only found out a short time ago I was adopted, although I often suspected it," Siobhan said, looking hard into Holly's hardened face.

"And just how could you not know you're adopted, Katie? Your parents are Asian," Holly said, sounding annoyed, before she continued. "Don't expect me to fill the void. You make your own happiness, and I'll make mine," Holly finished as she began pouring coffee from a tall silver coffee pot. Chuck could tell Siobhan was having a hard time holding it all together.

"I think Siobhan would like to know a little about you, Mrs. Bond."

"Like what? I can't be expected to put my whole life into a half hour, young man."

"Well, why did you give me away?" Siobhan blurted out, unable to look at the woman any longer.

"You want to hear the whole miserable story? I already told your nosy girl, Blue; couldn't she pass it on?" Holly said.

"That would break client confidentiality, Mrs. Bond," Chuck said.

"Yes, your discretion is appreciated, although why you needed to find me at all, I can't imagine. You look very well taken care of. Is it money you need?" she asked, as Siobhan finally couldn't hold back the tears any longer.

"No, I don't need money. I simply wanted to meet you and see who you are. But now I've met you, I don't like you at all and I realize I made a huge mistake just like you did. Let's go, Chuck," Siobhan said, getting to her feet.

Siobhan was almost at the front door when Holly spoke again. "I'm sorry, really I am. I've had various emotions, ranging from excitement to dread, in case you didn't like me. I've been worried you'll tear my life apart, and my husband and children will find out. I'm sorry, Katie. Please come back and sit down. I have been dreading this moment all my life. But now it's here, I know I'm behaving badly. I will try not to be so defensive if you can give me your word you won't ever tell my family."

"You have a family?" Siobhan asked, as she moved slowly back into the room and eyed the pile of photo albums on the far coffee table, before again sitting.

"Yes, I have three boys and a girl. I am a grandmother to my eldest boy, who is twenty-three, just five years younger than you, I believe. His baby is just a month old. He called him Charles Bond," Holly said, wiping a dry tear from her eye.

"I have a newborn son and we called him Charles also," Chuck added proudly as he watched Holly's face soften.

"I do promise never to tell your family. I would just like some answers, and then if you don't wish to see me ever again, I won't bother you any-more," Siobhan said, finding her voice.

"All right, from the beginning," Holly said as she sat back and began her coffee.

"I was in my first year at college in Savannah. We partied every night and studied all day – hardly ever slept. One night, I was drunk at a college party and I met a handsome man who swept me off my feet. He was funny, charming and a true gentleman, all rolled into one. That night I was so drunk, he carried me all the way back to my dorm, sneaked me inside and tucked me into bed. Most guys would have tried something, but not him. He was studying accountancy and was due to graduate in just a few months. He seemed the wrong sort of guy to be studying numbers.

"I was taking aeronautical engineering, and he thought it was wrong for me to be doing that – I later learned it was because of all the guys in the class. Even though it was graduation time for him, we couldn't help having a mad, crazy affair; we thought our love would last forever. I came from a poor family and him, I think, a rich one, so I knew the value of a good career. He wanted to marry me, but I wanted us to earn and live on our own money. Anyway, after he graduated, I found out I was pregnant. And when I went to find him he was locked up in jail for holding up a 7-Eleven store or bank or something. I just couldn't believe it; he never seemed the type. Well, the rest is history, as they say. I found a couple desperate for a baby, and they had plenty of money. The adoption was legal and we went through an agency. They gave me the money I needed to finish school and start a career in the Navy, and I gave them the baby they so desired. I knew you'd have a good home," Holly concluded, refilling Chuck's coffee cup. Siobhan hadn't touched hers.

"You sold me. You sold your own baby because you wanted money?" Siobhan said, shocked.

"Well, it was better than drowning you like an unwanted kitten, and I had thought of doing that, too." Holly Bond immediately saw the horror of her words in their eyes, so she quickly continued. "Don't judge me unless you've been there, and you never have," the older woman answered quickly. Siobhan wondered if she'd anticipated the question or was just being defensive. Either way, Siobhan hated being snapped at and quickly wiped the tears from her eyes.

"Can Siobhan/Katie maybe see some photos? It's always a great way to get to know people," Chuck carefully asked, nodding towards the pile of photo albums and hoping it might cheer Siobhan up. Chuck knew this meeting was not going well.

"Yes, I brought some of these all the way from London just to show you," Holly said, retrieving the photo albums. For the next two hours, Siobhan and Holly sat next to each other on the couch and looked at photos. Even Chuck had to admit Siobhan resembled her half-sister. Finally, the two women seemed to run out of things to say and Chuck thought it was time to go.

"I know I said I don't want to see you again, but maybe it would be nice to get to know you a little. All I ask is that you please respect my privacy and my family," Holly said.

"I will always respect your wishes, Mom... Holly... Mrs. Bond," Siobhan said.

"Call me Holly, please; it's easier that way."

"Holly, I would like to see you again, if you would," Siobhan replied, really looking at the woman for the first time since her face had softened.

"Katie, give me your contact numbers. I will be back in L.A. in another four months. If my children or husband aren't here, you can come and stay for the weekend. I would like to know all about your life, I really would," Holly said hopefully, looking hard at her daughter.

"Yes, I'd like that, too, and my name's Siobhan. Here's my card. You can call me any time. My husband doesn't know about you either, so if I can't talk, I will say so," Siobhan said, handing over her card.

"Maybe you'll have more luck with your father. Are you going to contact him?" Holly asked.

"I don't know who he is or where he is, but I'll bet Chuck can find him for me. What's his name, Holly?" Siobhan asked.

"Like me, he was born in Savannah, Georgia. I know now he was the love of my life. I don't know where you'll find him now, as we lost contact the moment he graduated. Anyway, he has an unusual name, his name is Felix Grasshopper."

Realizing There's More

A month later, Amanda realized she hadn't seen Siobhan as much as usual. They still talked daily on the phone, mainly about Holly. On occasion, Siobhan would remember her godson and ask after baby Charlie. Siobhan had been trying to work out what her mother thought of her: whether the older woman liked her, thought she was beautiful, approved of the way she dressed, or if she really did want to see her again. Siobhan kept asking why she had to wait another four months to see her mother. Amanda reminded her she was a pilot with a big airline and that she was flying thousands of miles away; but, somehow, Siobhan did not think it a good enough reason for her absence.

Amanda was beginning to see her BFF as a little selfish and quite self-absorbed. She'd asked her several times to spend the day with her and Charlie at their home, but each time Siobhan had something more important to do. She'd already set up a trust fund for baby Charlie, and was in the process of purchasing a condo in his name. Amanda thought this more than generous, until Chuck had made her aware of Siobhan's real reason for the purchase. Siobhan again complained about the fact that they never had long lunches in the City any more. Finally, Amanda had called Rita and asked her to look after baby Charlie for the afternoon so she could go to lunch with Siobhan. Amanda had hardly left the house since Charlie's arrival, and she liked it that way; in fact, she was exactly where she wanted to be. Rita was thrilled Amanda was going out, mainly because it made her feel needed and she loved the thought of looking after her grandson. Any time with Charlie had quickly become the highlight of her life.

Baby Charlie was almost six weeks old when Amanda got dressed in her designer clothes. It felt strange to be wearing them, and they were still slightly snug, although they did just fit. Amanda looked at herself in the mirror and she felt like an attractive woman again rather than Charlie's mom.

"Don't hurry back now, we'll be just fine. If you want to stay and shop, I will wait until Nanny arrives. Have fun, Mandy!" Rita called after hugging Amanda tightly. Amanda missed her baby the moment she was in the car and alone. It felt strange without him. She saw his beautiful eyes looking up at her as she drove. However, once Amanda got away from the suburbs and neared the Big Apple, she felt differently, freer somehow and more like her old self. She liked that feeling also.

Siobhan talked non-stop about her birth mother. She never stopped analyzing. They enjoyed their first course and then the main course while Siobhan just kept on talking. As they enjoyed coffee, Amanda noticed the absence of Siobhan's five-carat engagement ring and her diamond wedding band. Amanda grabbed her hand.

"Where are your rings?"

"I no longer wear them. They stand for nothing," Siobhan answered.

"What does Brock say about it?" Amanda asked, shocked that Siobhan had never mentioned it.

"He doesn't know. I sold them as a down payment on Charlie's condo. The lease is up on your old condo in another month and by that stage I should be able to move into the new one. I'll take you to see it if you like, but I wanted to surprise you once I had furnished it and moved in," Siobhan said matter-of-factly.

"So where are you staying now?" Amanda asked, again tuning into the conversation.

"I'm still living in your old condo. Most of my things are packed away and stored at my mom's house, and I often go back while Brock's at work and move out more stuff. It's over. I've wasted enough time on Brock. The divorce is happening and I'm seeing someone else," Siobhan finished. Before she could return to the subject of her birth mother again, Amanda told her just how shocked she was and asked why she hadn't said anything about the many changes in her life.

"Why, I thought I had. We do talk every day," Siobhan answered. Amanda thought perhaps she'd told her, but she knew she'd remember something as important as that. Any change in Siobhan's life was a major drama to Siobhan; she was, after all, a diva. They chatted on about the many changes, and Siobhan told her about her new man, Mascoti Vitale. She told Amanda again just where they'd met and said he was one hot guy – they could hardly keep their hands off each other. She felt like a kid again. Siobhan said she was definitely falling in love.

"Siobhan, it's just what you need to take your mind off Brock and also keep yourself from constantly thinking about Holly."

"I know. He's been great. I am very lucky. But when I think of Holly, it drives me crazy. She's in my head nearly all the time. I don't understand who she is or why she is the way she is, or even why she treated me like she did."

"Siobhan, you're a very deep thinker, but you've got to let it go until you can see her again. I can tell you haven't had much sleep. Why, I have a newborn baby, and I look more rested than you."

"It's not all from worrying about Holly. Mascoti keeps me up rather late, too!" Siobhan replied with a big smile and a wink.

"Oh." Amanda was truly happy for her friend.

"Anyway, will you ever meet your birth father, Siobhan? You've never said."

"Well, Chuck found him in a heartbeat. He's very efficient, your husband, as a P.I. I won't be meeting my father for a while; he's a notorious criminal, Amanda. He's locked away in jail. I don't know if I want a jailbird for a dad anyway," Siobhan said, looking at her hands instead of Amanda.

"But you need to understand both sides of the story, and it may help you to know more about your mother," Amanda said.

"Oh, I hadn't thought about it like that."

"Well, getting both sides of the story is important. You wouldn't just read half a book now, would you?" Amanda added.

"My father doesn't even know I exist. He might not want to know me, just like Holly didn't," Siobhan said, about to talk about Holly again.

Amanda quickly continued. "But surely you're going to give him the benefit of the doubt and at least meet him," she encouraged.

"I guess, especially after Chuck was so eager to locate him. I swear your husband's almost obsessed."

Amanda thought that was a very strange thing to say about Chuck. He was a laid back, easygoing type of guy. Sure, he took his work seriously, but obsessed was never a way Amanda would have described Chuck.

"Obsessed... Siobhan? Why, just because he found out where your birth father was so quickly?"

"Yeah, I guess that was an overstatement!"

"Where is your birth father anyway, Siobhan?" Amanda asked, not wanting to talk any further about Chuck.

"He's in Savannah, I think," Siobhan answered casually, but Amanda's ears immediately pricked up.

"Savannah? That's miles away. Do you even know his name?" Amanda asked, her heart beginning to race.

"Sure, I do. It's a weird name, one I won't easily forget. I'm glad I didn't end up with a name like that," Siobhan said, giggling.

"So, what is it?" Amanda asked, feeling more uneasy as the seconds passed.

"It's Felix Grasshopper," Siobhan said, and Amanda's worst fears were realized and her world collapsed around her. She didn't hear anything else Siobhan said for the next fifteen minutes, until she heard herself interrupt her friend.

"Siobhan, I have to go. I don't feel well, sorry," Amanda said, as she got to her feet, taking a deep breath and attempting to steady herself as the room started to swim before her eyes.

"I'll drive you. Leave your car, I'll ask Mascoti to collect it later. I'll call Chuck and let him know. You look awfully pale..."

"No, no, no, I just want to be alone. Please leave me. I'll call you later," Amanda said, rushing for the door. She needed air, but more than that, she needed time to think.

"Amanda, Amanda, wait!" she heard Siobhan call after her, but Amanda drove out of the city much too fast and kept driving until she found a public phone box just inside a park. It was deserted, so she pulled over and placed a call to Savannah.

"Baxter, get me Mom or Dad – it's urgent!"

"Right away, Miss Neve."

"Neve, honey…"

"Mom …," Amanda said, sobbing into the phone. It was the familiar sound of her mom's voice that made her cry even harder.

"Honey, what is it? Whatever's the matter? Hugo, come quickly, it's Neve!"

"Baby Girl, whatever is it, are you all right? What's happened?" Hugo said, sounding concerned as he stared into the phone.

"Oh, Mom, Dad, you were right. I never should have allowed myself to get mixed up in any of this…"

"Honey, I want you to take several very deep breaths. We're having trouble understanding you. Where are you?"

"I'm in a public phone booth in Graves Park, wherever that is. I've just had lunch with Siobhan…," Amanda said, sobbing again.

"Have you had a fight with Siobhan?" Hugo asked, looking at his wife as they waited.

"No…"

"Are you and Chuck having trouble?" Al asked, their concern rapidly increasing.

"No… but this could ruin everyone's life. Everything you've worked for. I'm sorry, Mom and Dad. I'm really so very sorry! It's all my fault!"

"Neve, take another deep breath and just tell us," Hugo instructed.

"I had lunch with Siobhan, and she was going on and on about her birth mother, Holly, so I tried to change the subject and she told me she had a new boyfriend. Anyway, she kept going on and on about Holly. Siobhan's been going over and over it the last weeks and it's driving me crazy. I almost hate it when she calls," Amanda said, taking a breath.

"Okay, honey, go on…," Al urged.

"Well, she was about to start on about her mother again, so I changed the subject and I started talking to her about finding her father. She told me that Chucky had already found him. Then she said Chuck had been obsessed with finding him – I thought that was a bit weird, 'cause Chucky's not like that." Amanda paused.

"No, it certainly doesn't sound like him. But, Baby Girl, why are you so upset?" Hugo asked, as they thought she might never tell them the rest.

"Oh, Dad, I kept talking about her birth father and then she told me he was from Savannah…" Amanda started sobbing again as Al and Hugo shared a look and encouraged her to go on.

"Honey, we're listening…"

"Then I asked his name. Mom, Dad – you'll never guess, never! Siobhan's father is Uncle Felix," Amanda said, sobbing loudly again. Several minutes passed before she calmed down slightly, but the other end of the phone was still silent.

"Mom, Dad, are you still there? I'm really sorry, I didn't know," Amanda said, waiting.

"Baby Girl, don't upset yourself. We'll talk more when we've had time to think. We'll drive down to see Felix in the morning. You did the right thing calling from a pay phone. Remember, a secret shared is a secret halved. Stop worrying, it's our problem as much as yours. Love you, Baby Girl," Hugo said.

Al repeated, "Love you, honey. Stop worrying and go on home to baby Charlie." Al was more concerned than she wanted to let on.

"I'm sorry, Mom and Dad. I guess you'll be putting your visit off for a while now."

"Maybe, honey; we'll call you and use the code word when you are to use the public phone. Love you, Neve." Moments later, the line was dead. Amanda slowly drove home.

"How was he, Rita?" Amanda asked as she burst in the door.

"Just the cutest, most perfect baby ever. Siobhan called, said you aren't feeling well. I called Chuck, he's on his way," Rita said.

"I'll be fine, Rita. I just feel a little sick," Amanda said, hoping she looked better than she felt.

"Mandy, you look very pale. You're not pregnant again, are you?" Rita asked, looking closely at her daughter-in-law.

"How can I be? Charlie's only just over seven weeks old."

"Well, you can easily be pregnant; I hope you and Chuck are taking something, unless you want another one so soon. You make wonderful babies, I must say." Rita was interrupted as Chuck burst into the house.

"Mandy darling, I came as quickly as I could. You look so pale; here, come and lie down," Chuck said, immediately scooping her into his arms and depositing her on the bed.

"Bye, Chuck. Mandy, get well soon. I'll call you tomorrow," Rita called as she put on her coat.

"Thanks, Mom!" Chuck called.

~

It was nine thirty p.m. in the offices of Banker's Securities, on the 7th floor of the Fraser building on Wall Street. All the employees had long since left, and most of the day lighting had been changed to scattered night lighting. Only one worker remained. Saffron Moffit sat behind her tidy glass desk, the lights in her office blazing. The fragrant scent of the tall white lilies filled the room. Saffron Moffit wasn't working, she was just sitting. She had just realized it would be the first time in her entire life she had ever gone home to an empty house.

Cox had suddenly gone on vacation to England. He'd finished his last exam paper at eleven a.m. yesterday and called her at noon to tell her he was flying to London at four p.m. He had mentioned a holiday after his exams, and she had encouraged it, but it was all rather sudden. Saffron wasn't looking forward to going home to an empty house. She would hire a housekeeper, someone to live in. Once she made that decision, she felt happier.

She breathed deeply the fragrance of the lilies, but as she did so, a movement at the far end of the hallway caught her eye. How could anyone be here at this time of the evening, and why hadn't the security guard called up to her? She squinted into the gloom. Yes, it was moving toward her office. She saw the outline of a tall, slim, stealth-like figure, clad entirely in black. Saffron couldn't see a face and then she realized it was because the figure was wearing a black mask. The black shadow was staying close to the wall and remained almost entirely hidden, as it silently continued moving swiftly toward her office. Saffron thought this was someone who had been here before. The black figure moved closer now. Saffron urgently raised the telephone to her ear and pressed the button which connected her directly to the security office…

The solid click of the safety catch being released on the revolver immediately drew her attention. As she looked up, the tall, black figure stood on the other side of her desk. The barrel of the gun was pointed directly at her. At this range, Saffron knew they wouldn't miss. Saffron became aware of another perfume; it was a fragrance she had smelled several times before.

"Don't…," the voice said, and Saffron Moffit immediately hung up the phone. For the first time in her life she felt the icy talons of fear run down her spine…

~

It was later the following night when Amanda again rested in bed. Nanny Bates was looking after Charlie and Chuck was making sandwiches. Sitting down on the bed, he became unusually serious.

"Mandy darling, I have something to tell you. I'm sorry, I should have told you earlier, but I didn't want to disturb your day; you were still looking pale this morning. Anyway, I knew you'd want all the facts first, so I spoke to Special Agent Bow Grismold, who's handling the case, just this afternoon."

Amanda began shaking involuntarily, she thought she may pass out; surely, he didn't know her secret already. She'd hardly had time to think. She didn't answer as all she could do was nod; it felt like a death sentence was hanging over her.

"Darling, I'm sorry to have to tell you this, but your boss, Saffron Moffit, was found shot to death. She was still sitting at her desk in her office. I'm sorry to have to tell you. I know you liked her."

"Oh no," was all Amanda managed to say, as she felt relief flood through her.

"At first, they thought it was a suicide. Saffron left a note owning up to the two murders of Brock's secretaries, Marlene Brice and Floris McKrill, and she also admitted to having a seven-year affair with Brock, said she couldn't live with herself any longer. When they found her, she was still holding the pen tightly in her right hand. However, she was shot with the same gun and in the same manner as the other two secretaries; although, unlike them, she was not mutilated in any way. Suicide would probably be ruled out. Also, there was no gun anywhere. The window behind her was wide open, so they think she may have somehow thrown the gun out, but how, I can't imagine. I'm so sorry, darling," Chuck said, watching her reaction carefully.

"I can't believe Saffron would do something like that. Why, she didn't even care when her husband died. She was so disciplined; she just kept right on working."

"Well, Mandy, everyone has different ways of dealing with grief."

"Yes, but I just know she wouldn't kill herself. I had no idea she was having an affair with Brock. Did you say the pen was still in her right hand, Chucky?"

"Yes, that's what Bow Grismold told me. He was first on the scene after the security company."

"So there, you see, Chucky, it must have been murder. Saffron Moffit was left-handed," Amanda said, as the phone rang. Moments later, Nanny Bates peeked around the door and asked Amanda if she wanted to speak to Siobhan; she said she sounded upset.

"Well, she couldn't have heard about Saffron Moffit because Bow Grismold is keeping it quiet until tomorrow – says he needs to talk to several people first and get their reaction," Chuck said, kissing his wife as he handed her the phone and left the room.

"Amanda, I came home from having lunch with you yesterday and Mascoti was here. He has his own key. He didn't hear me enter as he was on the phone. I wasn't being sneaky, but I was putting my coat in the closet when I realized he was talking to Brock. So, I froze…," Siobhan said, sobbing.

"Siobhan, why would Mascoti and Brock be talking? I thought they were just business partners?" Amanda asked.

"Yeah, well, Mascoti had Brock on speaker phone. He wouldn't have been expecting me home until much later as I said we'd probably go shopping after lunch. I thought they were just business partners also, and they were probably discussing business. Anyway, I was just about to enter the room when I decided to stop and listen some more."

"Yes, and what did you hear?" Amanda asked.

"They were discussing me. Can you believe it, my meeting Mascoti was a set-up. It was a setup by Brock so I would finally divorce him. Mascoti was getting shares in the company when he succeeded in getting the divorce through…," Siobhan sobbed into the phone. Amanda couldn't believe what she was hearing.

"Siobhan, I can't believe it. Brock could have divorced you any time; why now?" Amanda asked, knowing it sounded callous, but hoping Siobhan wouldn't notice.

"Oh, Amanda, it seems Brock wants to marry that bitch Saffron Moffit now that her husband is dead. It seems they've been lovers for years; can you believe it?" Siobhan said, completely stunning Amanda.

"Siobhan, where are you?"

"I'm in my car. I can't go back to the condo while he's there. I just can't. He's called and called, but I'm not answering. I will stay in a hotel; I need time to think. I thought he loved me, I really did. He even told Brock the deal was off because he never cared for shares in a company with so much scandal surrounding it. He said he thinks I'm such a special lady and he told Brock he was a foolish, foolish man for letting me go. Then he asked Brock if he was sure he was letting me go. Mascoti said he'd fallen deeply in love with me and he wanted to marry me. That was when Brock hung up and I left…"

"Siobhan, why did you book into a hotel instead of coming straight here? I wondered why I hadn't heard from you; I know you called Rita after I left the restaurant."

"I thought you were too sick and I know you have other things in your life now. I didn't want to bother you until I'd made my mind up about a few things," Siobhan finished, composed now.

"Siobhan, check out of your hotel now and drive over here – unless you want me to come and get you? We have to talk about this some more before you make any decisions," Amanda said, her head swimming with all that was happening.

Renewing Acquaintances

Amanda

It was moments later when the phone got her attention again. This time it was Amanda's parents and the sign she had been waiting for. She promised to call them tomorrow and hung up as she continued making preparations for Siobhan's arrival. It was late that night before she got to bed. Siobhan seemed upset but somehow strangely calm as Amanda said good night – it was almost like she knew Brock would never marry Saffron. Amanda dismissed the thought quickly, thinking it was her over-active imagination. Although she never told Siobhan what she had just learned about Saffron, she wondered why she had held back.

The next morning, Amanda asked Nanny Bates to stay the day so she could drive with Siobhan into Manhattan. Siobhan had finally answered Mascoti's calls and told him they had to meet. Amanda's first impression of Mascoti was that he was everything Siobhan said he was. He had a sexual magnetism that was undeniable, and he obviously cared deeply for Siobhan. The moment Siobhan met him, he embraced her tightly and she began crying again. It was Amanda who spoke for her friend and suggested Mascoti gave her some space for a week or two and move out of her apartment. The meeting went better than Amanda thought it would. Mascoti readily agreed to do whatever Siobhan wanted. He said he didn't want to be without her and she could have all the space she needed. He assured her he would move out by the evening and he wouldn't call her until she called him. Even though Amanda thought this was a good outcome to the meeting, Siobhan seemed to cry even more. It had a sad effect on Mascoti, as he also had tears in his eyes by the time they left the restaurant.

Siobhan said she was badly in need of retail therapy, and even though Amanda had more important things on her mind, they enjoyed browsing and purchasing from the most expensive stores in New York. It was after five when Amanda headed out of the city. She encountered all the traffic, so it was a slow journey home. She knew Chuck would be working tonight and had wanted to see him before he left, but she knew now it would be much too late by the time she arrived home.

Once outside the city limits, Amanda pulled off the road beside a phone box and placed her call.

"Baby Girl, where have you been? We've waited all day for your call. We were getting rather worried." Amanda clearly heard the concern in his voice.

"Sorry, Dad, Siobhan had some issues and she needed me."

"Honey, we have issues, too," Al said, sounding annoyed.

"I didn't want to do anything out of the ordinary and create suspicion, Mom. You always taught me that."

"Okay, honey, we were just getting worried, that's all. I've begun looking up flights; thought you may need us. Maybe Chuck already knows too much."

"Mom, Dad, I know Chuck isn't going to be a problem."

"Baby Girl, you know nothing of the sort. He will always be a private investigator first and your husband second. It's who he is, it's in his blood," Hugo said.

"You are still in disguise, I hope?" Al questioned.

"Yes, Mom, still waiting on your instruction," Amanda replied.

"The time is not right, honey. Anyway, all the equipment you will need is waiting for you at your local post office under your last alias. Use the scrambler before you enter Chuck's office – he may be your husband and you may have a key, but he's also a very smart guy and his security will be state-of-the-art. Honey, he knows his stuff. I watched him in action at the Dolmans' house, remember?" Al finished.

"I know, Mom. I won't underestimate him just because I love him. And no, he has never given me a key, but I have one. Did you include the key pad activator? I don't know the security code to the office either," Amanda added.

"Baby Girl, it's all there. Have you ever been to his office?" Hugo asked, perplexed by her answers.

"No, Dad, but we've driven past, and I know exactly where it is. I've studied the habits of the inhabitants, also," Amanda replied, clearly proud of her efforts.

"Honey, I know we don't need to tell you, but sooner is better than later. You obviously don't seem to be aware of the urgency," Al said.

"Mom, I am aware of the urgency and I plan to make the visit tonight. There's been a lot going on. Chuck told me Saffron Moffit was murdered last night and she left a note saying she was responsible for the other two murders of Brock's secretaries. But it was a setup."

"Wow, there is justice in this world... if anyone ever deserved it...," Hugo said, as Al cut him short.

"Hugo, you know we have never condoned murder!" Al reprimanded.

"I know, I know. I've just never liked the bitch – she was a piece of work, and I for one think she would easily murder if it suited her, although I can't imagine why she would murder Brock's secretaries."

"But, Dad, Saffron and Brock have been having an ongoing affair for years – the note said so," Amanda said.

"No... I just can't believe it! Not Brock and Saffron. I really thought the guy had better taste!" Hugo said, chuckling.

"Honey, how do you know she didn't do it? What makes you so sure?"

"Well, Mom, several things. Firstly, Chuck said she was still holding the pen in her hand from writing the note when the police found her."

"Yes, honey, go on. So what does that mean? There's nothing unusual there; after all, she'd just written the last note of her life before shooting herself."

"Mom, Chucky said the pen was still clinched in her right hand."

"Well, so what, where was the gun?" Al asked.

"They never found a gun, but, Mom... Saffron was left-handed."

"Well, somewhere close to Banker's Securities, the murderer still lurks free," Al said.

"Baby Girl, I'm so glad you're out of there," Hugo added.

"Mom, Dad, it's almost dark now. I should make a move. I know where every member of Chuck's team will be until midnight, so I must do this now," Amanda said, sounding agitated.

"Okay, honey, good luck. Don't go taking any chances, and remember..."

"Mom, Dad, I've got it. I'll be careful. I'll use everything. Now I've got to get to the post office before it closes at nine. Love you both...," Amanda said, hanging up the phone as an old, rugged, homeless person tapped on the glass at the side of the phone box. She quickly pulled out a ten dollar note and thrust it at him. While he stood looking at it and mumbling, she raced to the car. She looked up to see him walking after her, and quickly she pulled away from the curb and into the traffic.

Amanda made it to the post office with minutes to spare. She then purchased a black tracksuit with a hood from Target. She changed in her car before throwing all the wrapping paper in the car park garbage bin. It was almost ten p.m. when she cruised quietly into a side lane several blocks from Chuck's office. She sat in the car with the black hood covering her head. Using the side mirrors of her car, she slowly checked out the surrounding area. Then she turned on her listening device to see if she could hear anyone close, talking. There was no sound and no movement. Slowly, she got out of the car, placed her car keys in her pocket and zipped it up. The black bag she carried was not large, but quite heavy. She threw the thick straps over her shoulder and tucked the bag under her arm.

The key she had made works easily and the alarm was easily deactivated. Amanda set her scrambler and relocked the door. Chuck had night lights around his office and Amanda had excellent vision. On one wall were large, colored, framed photos under the heading 'The Team'. In the center was a large photo of Charles Arthur Hollingsworth the Second; below his name was a brief description. The second row was comprised of four framed photos, all in color and in the same slim black frame that matched Chuck's. Amanda carefully looked at each face before reading the captions below. Walter Dense she recognized from their wedding, and then there was Fred Blook, Guy Tom, and lastly, a new employee that she hadn't even heard about – Pluto Kisk. According to the caption below Pluto's photo, he had only begun work last week, and as Amanda read on, she realized Pluto was actually a girl. It was hard to tell in the dim light as the person had very short-cropped brown hair and a thin face. Lastly, on a line of her own, was a framed photo of Blue Satine.

Also, in the outer office against the opposite wall were many filing cabinets, each drawer neatly labeled. Amanda immediately went to the letter 'G', but quickly found nothing under Grasshopper. This was not going to be so easy. Next she tried 'H' for Hugo and then 'A' for Alberta. Still nothing. Then she searched under some of their aliases, but she still found no files. Suddenly, she remembered it was Uncle Felix who Chucky would be tracking, so, releasing the breath she'd been holding, she pulled out the filing drawer marked 'F' – she felt sure this was it. But there was nothing there either. Amanda's heart was pounding, her palms were sweating, she had to find out what he knew – it must be here. She then checked Siobhan's file, and flipping through the pages, she finally saw the reference to Felix Grasshopper and beside it a large red asterisk. She had never seen another asterisk in any of the files she had looked in. Amanda stood and looked around Chuck's modern office. It was neat, clean and very organized, but so much smaller than she'd imagined.

Amanda couldn't imagine where else the Grasshopper file would be. Maybe they had been worrying over nothing; maybe it was just a passing thing and perhaps Siobhan wasn't related to Felix after all. Then, Amanda realized Siobhan would be her cousin if she was Uncle Felix's daughter. Amanda wasn't sure what to do next. It was already eleven fifteen p.m. She walked into Chucky's office and sat down behind his desk. She touched it with her gloved hand – she loved him so much, she would have to find a way around this mess. In the dim light, Amanda began opening his drawers. The first drawer held his notepads, pen, pencils, wages and sign-in book. The next drawer down contained the reports of each day and night's work submitted by each employee as they signed off. She briefly began reading one, and it was fascinating: the chase, the cops, everything, it read like a thriller. The next one wasn't nearly so exciting: Chuck's guy Fred had just sat outside in the snow for hours and there had been no action at all.

Amanda hated failure; she felt like she had let her family down. So slowly she placed the wire and set up the equipment for her mom to monitor Chuck. She hated doing it. It didn't feel right; after all, he was her husband and they had to have trust. Then she briefly sat again at his desk. This time, she opened the top drawer on the right side and found more pictures of her and Baby Charlie; she briefly stared at the large picture of herself on his desk. Then she opened the second drawer: it was full of files. Each file had a red stamp that read 'Active'. These must be his current cases, she thought. She flipped through the files, and just as she was about to close the drawer, she saw the corner of a very old, worn file poking out from the bottom of the pile. It was jammed tightly under all the rest on the bottom of the drawer, and in the dim light it was hard to see. She lifted out the files on top and then removed the old yellowed file from underneath; it was the thickest file she had ever seen. The writing was different from all the rest and Amanda used her flashlight for the first time that evening. The handwriting was almost unreadable, it was so old. Holding her flashlight over the words, she managed to read the faded name written across the top.

The moment she saw it, she froze. Maybe she was mistaken, so immediately she flicked her flashlight on again, but some-how she knew just what she'd see. Written across the top of the file in old-fashioned handwriting that was not Chuck's was the name, 'The Grasshopper File'. The file was about ten inches thick and looked like it had been around the world several times.

Amanda didn't know what to do. How could he do this? Had her parents been right all along? Had Chuck only married her because of who she was? As she held the file, the answers to her were obvious. No wonder it all happened so fast; he was an incredible actor. She loved him more than life and he had deceived her and was still deceiving her. Amanda instinctively touched her stomach and the child she thought she was carrying. As she flicked open the top of the file, she read about the cases her parents had been on when she was just a little girl. She remembered those times when they'd gone away and left her and Zax alone for months with the nanny and the staff. By the time they'd returned, she and Zax hardly knew who they were. Then, quickly, her parents would shower them with love and attention and they would again become a close-knit, happy, loving family. Until, in time, they would leave again. Two young children left behind in the huge Grasshopper mansion with two broken hearts. Neve promised herself many years ago that she would never be left behind again – whatever it took, she would somehow stay in their world.

Amanda skimmed through the first case and onto the next one. She remembered nothing of these cases; she had obviously been too little to know what was going on. It was about ten cases later when she vaguely remembered the names her parents had used, and she worked out from the date that she would have been about thirteen or fourteen years old and Zax a year older. It was just as Amanda was about to turn the page that she heard a car softly pull up outside. The small town where Chuck's office was located was almost abandoned at night, so her ears quickly tuned in. Yes, it had stopped outside the office; its headlights lit the office before they went out. She quickly put the file back in the second drawer of the desk and the others on top, hoping they were just as she had found them. Then, she looked around for a place to hide. Everything was so neat, there were few hiding places. As she heard the key in the lock, she prayed it wasn't Chuck and quickly hid under Blue's desk. She was just pulling the chair back into place as the light went on and she heard someone talking on his cell.

"I know, I'll take the night shift, but I thought the medicine was going to make him sleep." Then a pause before the same voice said, "Yeah. Look, I'm at the office now. I'll drop my report on the boss's desk and I gotta use the washroom; four hours is ages without a pee. Then I'll be home. If he's sleeping, you go to bed. The night cavalry is on its way. Bye, sweets." The guy unzipped his fly as he headed for the washroom, which must be toward the back of the office,

Amanda thought. She quietly watched through a crack in the desk. She was hoping he would shut the door, but he didn't. Amanda could see there was a large mirror on one side of the washroom, so the moment he was looking down, she, too, kept her head down and hidden under her hood and moved swiftly to the door. It opened and closed quietly, but he must have seen or heard something as he called, "Is anyone there? Is that you, boss?"

Amanda kept in the shadows close to the buildings and ran all the way to her car. She was just about to turn the corner when she saw the flash of headlights behind her. Once around the corner, she stopped and peeked back around. A second car was stopping in front of the office. Amanda recognized the car as Chuck's. Her heart raced even faster. The moment she was in her car, she pulled off her clothes and drove quickly out of town. Their house was over thirty minutes away. Several miles out of town, Amanda pulled over when she saw a sleeping figure under a pile of old newspapers. She opened her car window and threw the black tracksuit out.

Just under an hour later, Amanda lay in bed in the darkened room, her heart racing as she heard Chuck enter the house. She tried to quiet herself, but her mind and body would not obey. The moment she heard Chuck, her mind seemed to race faster. Once Chuck showered, he climbed into bed and moved closer to Amanda, as always. When he wrapped his warm, protective arms around her and held her close as she slept, Amanda used to think this was the best place on earth, but tonight it was all she could do not to pull away. Several minutes later, she knew by Chuck's breathing that he was asleep. Amanda didn't sleep at all – she'd gotten them all into a potentially life-threatening mess, and she would get them out of it. Amanda Hollingsworth felt betrayed.

As the first light of dawn sneaked into the bedroom, Amanda knew just what she must do. The moment Chuck left for the office, Amanda asked Nanny Bates to stay on another couple of hours as she needed to do some shopping. But it wasn't shopping Amanda had in mind. She spent her morning in the library and all the books stacked in front of her were on one particular subject. And that subject was poison!

Alberta and Hugo Grasshopper

Al and Hugo were worried; they were worried about many things. They felt Neve had no idea the problems that could arise from her actions. Al wanted to fly over and be with her daughter until everything was sorted out. Hugo reminded her that Neve was their daughter and probably smarter than both of them, so he suggested Al sit tight and wait. Hugo hoped it was the right decision. It was after twelve fifteen a.m. when Al finally saw on her computer the connection had been installed in Chuck's office. Now she could monitor most of what went on. The first thing she saw was Amanda dressed all in black with a hood over her head: the lights were on and she was sneaking out the office door. That was too close, Al thought, as her heart raced faster at the thought of what nearly happened. Then she saw a young man having a pee and coming out of the bathroom with his fly still undone as he called, "Is there anyone there? Is that you, boss?"

Then, as Al continued to watch, she saw Chuck enter the office and speak for a while to Fred. Fred said his baby was sick and asked if Walter could fill in for him for a couple of nights. Chuck said he'd be in touch. The moment Fred left, Chuck placed a call on his cell. Fortunately for Al, he sat at his desk with the cell phone on speaker.

"Walter, you'll need to come back tomorrow; Fred's baby is sick and I need you here," Chuck said.

"Well, boss, I just visited with a young girl named Fran Fillimoore, apartment 7B. And it gets better."

"Yeah, go on, Fred, I'm liking this," Chuck said.

"Apparently, Fran Fillimoore lives life in a wheelchair. I knocked on the door and said I was lost and was looking for the Grasshoppers' apartment. She said they'd left many months ago. I then asked her if she knew them. She said no, but she had pictures. Anyway, we got talking like old friends; I think she gets pretty lonely. Then she asks me in. She showed me the pictures all neatly labeled with the time and date. But it's just like you suspected, boss, there were two couples living in the apartment, but you never see them together."

"Great; go on, Walter," Chuck said, sitting on the edge of his chair.

"Well, the times correspond with Alastair Rasnic and his wife, Sylvia. I then took the photos to Banker's Securities and showed them to an old bat named Mrs. Berry Pye… no, boss, I know what you're thinking, and she is definitely not a looker! Anyway, she immediately recognized the guy as Alastair Rasnic, described him as a real peach of a man, too. So, you may have your first photos of a Grasshopper. Congratulations! I'll go back tomorrow and tell Ms Fillimoore you'll be calling. Lonely little thing; not that old either. Maybe still a teenager, but on her own most of the time in that expensive apartment and in a wheelchair. Sad."

"A photo of the Grasshoppers! Walter! Now that would really be something! Are they connected with any of the murders?"

"No, boss, not so far as I can tell, but they're good. As Sheffield always said, never underestimate a Grasshopper."

"If we can get these guys, it will put us in the big league."

"I know it will, but, Chuck, you're already one of the best. You've also got a good reputation amongst the rich and famous."

"Thanks, Walter, but I want this one for Dad," Chuck said.

"I know you do, and so do I. Sheffield was one special guy."

"Walter, we'll have to put this on hold for a few weeks; need you to relieve Fred for a few days, then we've got the job with the rock star. As much as I want to put the Grasshoppers to bed, we need to keep the money coming in. Anyway, I'll be right beside Mrs. Siobhan Burke when she meets her birth father, Mr. Felix Grasshopper. He gets released from the Federal Correctional Institution in Jesup, Georgia, in only thirteen days' time, but who's counting! Talk about coincidence – why, it's almost like Dad's looking down on me and telling me to catch a Grasshopper, and then he's showing me the way. Mrs. Burke was my first case after he died, Walter. Didn't want to take it either; it was just circumstances that kicked it into place. Dad must be giving us guidance from above; who else could make this happen? After all, they were indirectly responsible for his death.

Sorry, Walter, my mind was wandering. Yes, I'd like to see the girl immediately after, unless the case is closed before then."

"You're right, boss, only Sheffield could make this happen. Boss, gotta go, my subjects on the move. Maybe I'll have the name of their next Grasshopper scam by tomorrow."

"Walter, you're doing one hell of a job; sorry I gotta call you home."

"Boss, we've been hunting Grasshoppers for so many years, a few extra days won't hurt. See you tomorrow evening," Walter said, and the line went dead.

Al sat exactly where she was. Was their life over? Were they about to get caught? She couldn't believe it, after all these years. Should she tell Neve and Hugo? That was the question that kept her up until five a.m. By the time she finally went to bed, she'd decided they must all know, and soon. The first order of Al's day was to talk to Baxter.

"Baxter, we won't be taking the limo to Jesup to collect Felix. I want you to find a long, sleek, black car that is built for speed and add bulletproof glass in all the windows and purchase it in someone else's name," Al instructed Baxter as he served them breakfast. Hugo looked strangely at her but said nothing.

"Certainly, ma'am. I know exactly the name to use – how does Jon Riddley sound to you?"

"Quite perfect," Al replied, not seeing the slight smile that played on Baxter's lips as he turned away.

"Darling, what's going on? The limo will do fine, unless you're expecting trouble," Hugo asked.

"I am, Hugo. I am," Al responded, suddenly realizing her appetite was gone.

"Al, what's—?" Hugo began, but she cut him short.

"Let's just finish our breakfast and then I'll place a call to Neve and you can both hear what I heard last night."

"I'm guessing by the look on your face this is not a happy call." Hugo looked at Al and already knew the answer.

It was an hour later when she placed the call.

"Neve, honey, where are you?" Al asked as her daughter answered the phone.

"Just leaving the library. Do I need to call you?"

"Yes, we'll be waiting."

Moments later, the phone rang. They expected it to be Neve on the other end, but instead it was a voice they hadn't expected to hear. It was their son Zax.

"Mom, Dad, you together?"

"Yes, Zax, we're waiting for a call from Neve. Is everything all right?" Al asked, knowing by the sound of his voice it wasn't.

"Well, you've both done it this time, you really have," Zax yelled as a sob escaped him.

They heard Molly in the background say, "Zax, let it go, hang up the phone."

"You've really done it this time. Guys coming around unannounced asking all sorts of questions about the Grasshoppers. They know I'm connected to you."

"What sort of guys?"

"Some private eye from New York. It was all in his letter."

"Whose letter, Zax?"

"Lord Win-Stanley's letter. He said it was the shame. The shame I have bought to the family, to Lord Win-Stanley and his grandchildren. He said shame never goes away, everyone knows about it and they talk behind their hands in whispers. Shame hangs over you and on you and it doesn't leave you for generations – it's scandalous!" Zax stopped to take a breath.

Al asked, "Why did he give you a letter?"

"He wrote the letter before he hanged himself. He said the shame was just too great and that he'd never be able to hold his head up in society again. Thanks to you both for killing my father-in-law," Zax said, sobbing as Molly took the phone.

"He'll be all right. We'll call you soon," she said. As she was about to hang up, they heard Zax yell at her.

"No, we won't. We'll never call them again. As far as I'm concerned, the children don't have American grandparents, and—" Then the line went dead.

The phone immediately rang again. Al answered on the second ring as she tried to stifle a sob. The sight of her so upset tore at Hugo's heart. He had always known children bring so much pleasure and so much pain.

"Sorry I took so long, everyone seems to be using public phones these days and there are hardly any of them around," Neve said, sounding out of breath.

"Hi, honey, it's quite okay!" Al responded.

"Mom, are you all right? You sound… upset," Neve said, searching for the right word.

"It's nothing, or at least I'll tell you later," Al replied.

"Darling, I can't wait to know any longer – please tell us what you know," Hugo added.

"I want to know, too, Mom," Neve replied.

"Well, you two. I'm sorry, it's not good. I laid awake all night wondering whether you should hear this or not."

"I thought we agreed in New York, you would always share good or bad, darling. In the past you've kept too much to yourself."

"I know, Hugo, that's why I'm sharing what I heard in Chuck's office last night after Neve placed the wire and the camera," Al responded.

"Oh," was all Neve added, and then all was silent as Al switched on the recording. They had the same reaction as she did the previous night. Neve started crying on the other end of the phone and neither of them could understand a word she said. Hugo's jaw was open and he said nothing.

"Neve, take a deep breath, honey, please," Al begged.

"Mom, thanks for not saying I told you so, but you did."

"It's much too late for blame, Neve. What we need now is damage control," Al said coolly.

"Mom, I got us into this mess and I'll get us out of it. It's my mess and I'll clean it up. My family is always the most important thing in the world. Mom, Dad, the Grasshoppers are my family."

"Neve, we need to discuss this, please, you're way too upset now."

"Upset? Well, of course I'm upset, Mom."

"Baby Girl, never take action while your emotions are in control," Hugo said.

"I know, Dad, and I won't. But I think you should organize a nanny in case I need to come home."

"Neve, let's talk tomorrow. I know you're very upset and you're scaring me sounding so cool – I've never heard you sound this way before. Let's all sleep on it and talk tomorrow," Al pleaded.

"Just let me handle this. I can't talk about it anymore. Love you. Bye." Neve was gone. For a long time, Al held the phone as she stared at Hugo. He said nothing, but just stared back. They could see the fear they felt mirrored in the other's eyes.

The next ten days flew by. Baxter had a nanny on standby. Hugo made several trips to see Felix and fill him in on what would be unfolding. He was excited by the prospect of meeting his daughter. Felix reckoned he had found Jesus and was a born-again Christian. He saw Siobhan as a sign of his new life. Felix explained she was a grown woman and was very used to the good life. Hugo also advised him not to encourage too much closeness until he was settled in the real world. He told Felix as much as he could of his plan to meet him outside the gates, and also informed him there had been a slight hiccup, so things could get heated. Felix understood most of what was going down, but he ended most of his sentences with, "Jesus rocks," and Hugo was beginning to find it annoying.

Al, Hugo and Baxter were up before dawn on the morning of Felix's release. They'd hardly discussed it with Neve as she wouldn't call them back on a pay phone, so they only talked to her and Chuck at home.

Hugo and Al were wearing heavy disguises, and Baxter also wore a mustache. They had guns. Baxter was not sure whether they were about to bust Felix out of jail or whether he was being released, but he was getting a huge bonus to follow orders and the thought of purchasing more property kept him from asking questions.

They left Southwest Savannah on Route 301. The traffic was light, and they expected to reach their destination in a little over an hour. It was a clear, sunny morning as the red globe of the sun appeared over the horizon, its brilliant rays casting long golden fingers across the land and bathing the new day in a crimson glow. Baxter followed Al's instructions to the letter, as he always did. The car they were in looked older than it actually was. It was a long low Buick specially fitted with bulletproof glass and an extremely fast engine.

The moment the facility was in view, they cruised the block until they found a place hidden from view but where they could see the front door clearly. Within half an hour, a white limo took its place directly outside the front doors. The uniformed driver soon alighted and stood smoking at the rear of the vehicle. Siobhan, immaculate in a cream silk suit and five-inch cream Jimmy Choo's, was helped out of the back seat and proceeded to pace up and down for the next fifteen minutes, before returning to the limo.

With her high-powered binoculars, Al searched the area for Chuck, but apparently as yet he had not arrived. Hugo pointed to a light-colored SUV hidden in bushes to their right, and as Al again used her binoculars, she noticed Chuck. Several other cars arrived, parked and waited to collect the freshly released inmates of The Jesup Federal Correction Institution. No one would be walking through the door for the next thirty minutes at the earliest. Al had the rear window slightly down so she could use her binoculars, and she could feel the anticipation. No one spoke, and they either stayed in their cars with the windows shut or paced the sidewalk as Siobhan had previously done.

Al checked her gun, then she checked Hugo's gun. Baxter did the same. The time was almost upon them and all eyes were on the doors, when Al noticed two unmarked cars quietly slide into position to their left. Al thought she was the only one who had noticed their arrival. She opened the other window just enough to use her binoculars. To her horror, what she saw was someone in the unmarked cars also observing her. She quickly shut the window. When no one emerged from the door and several more minutes passed, she again took a look at the cars. This time she saw what looked like an FBI agent emerging. Al focused her glasses on his face and immediately realized it was a face she knew. Silently, she passed the glasses to Hugo.

The first inmates were emerging through the door. Al checked their faces, but none of them were Felix. The driver opened the back door of the limo and Al saw one of Siobhan's legs connect with the sidewalk, but she stayed where she was. Al saw the FBI agents move closer. Two more inmates stepped out into the world, and one was greeted by family as the other headed off on foot.

Moments later, Felix walked through the door. He briefly looked around as the early morning sunlight hit his face. Siobhan spotted him immediately. Al and Hugo listened; they had Felix wired.

"Are you Felix Grasshopper?" Siobhan asked.

"Yes," replied Felix, looking her over and letting out a long, low whistle.

"Well, I believe I'm your daughter. My mother is Holly Bond," she said, waiting for Felix to acknowledge her. When he didn't respond, she added, "You may remember her as Holly Fletcher," Siobhan said, as, unbeknown to her, the agents moved closer.

"Well, yes, that's a name I haven't heard in many years. What a great surprise. Why didn't she tell me about you?" Felix said, opening his arms to his daughter. Siobhan hesitated only briefly, before moving into his embrace as they hugged tightly. "Can I call you Daddy? Because that's who you are!" Siobhan whispered, she could feel her own body trembling with happiness as she spoke, but she didn't miss the slight hesitation in Felix before he whispered "yes". The FBI agents were now just several feet away. Al saw Chuck also walking over to where Siobhan and Felix hugged. Al thought it a good thing he was out of the car. Several more inmates walked through the doors; each was greeted by someone and quickly left.

As Siobhan and Felix finally released the other and wiped the tears from their eyes, Siobhan asked, "Can we go somewhere and talk?" But Felix never got to answer.

Bow Grismold quickly stepped between them as his partner produced handcuffs and began placing them on an unsuspecting Siobhan. Chuck backed away, unnoticed.

"Siobhan Burke, you are under arrest for the murders of Marlene Brice, Floris McKrill and Saffron Moffit. You have the right to remain silent, as anything you say can and will be used against you."

"No, no, leave me alone, take your hands off me! Felix...Daddy, help me! Do something! Help me, please!" Siobhan screamed, fighting the agents. Felix stood exactly where he was, shocked. He wanted to help his daughter, but he had no idea what to do or what she had done. He had heard the word 'murder', but just couldn't believe it.

"Daddy, help me, please. I had to do it. I'm married to him. He's mine. I had to cut off their hands. I had to, you must understand, they were each wearing a diamond bracelet. He's mine, Daddy, please help me...," Siobhan continued, sobbing uncontrollably. Felix watched helplessly as she fought the two strong men. He hadn't moved. He watched as the agents finally picked her up and placed her in the back of a second unmarked car. It had slowly and quietly moved closer.

Chuck was almost back to his car when Al could wait no longer and instructed Baxter to quickly stop at the curb so Felix could jump in. Baxter was an expert driver. The car glided to the curb and barely stopped as Hugo opened the door and grabbed Felix. Baxter drove like a bat out of hell and as Al watched through the back window, Chuck was only beginning to give chase when they were out of sight. Baxter kept to their prearranged plan and hid the car around the corner as they all sat and watched Chuck speed by. Then he casually turned the car toward Route 301 and headed home.

"Very smooth, Bro. Jesus rocks!" Felix said, as Al hugged him tightly in the back seat.

"Never did like gunfire. I always thought it should be left in the Wild West movies. Did you manage to get those John Wayne Westerns I wanted, bro?"

"Sure did, Felix. Baxter took care of that. I think he managed to find three more also," Hugo said as Baxter nodded from the front seat.

"Now if that was my daughter... she's quite a looker – but what the hell's going on?" Felix asked, as they raised the partition between themselves and Baxter before explaining.

"We're as much in shock as you are. We had no idea. I still can't believe it," Al said.

Hugo added, "We know her quite well. She's Neve's best friend, although she doesn't know Neve as Neve, if you know what I mean."

"You never know what goes on inside people's heads. Some of the guys inside seem quite nice; that's until you really get to know them, then you see the dark side, and, man, can they get dark – their own hatred, it eats away at them – way scary, too!" Felix added.

"I know you'll want to help your daughter. I'll get Baxter onto it. But don't leave a trail, Felix; we can count on you, can't we?" Al warned.

"Sure, I for one never want to be back in there again. If Jesus allows me to live a full God-fearing life, then that's what I'll do!"

"Pleased to hear it, bro, we'll be there to help you all the way." They chatted on until they reached a mall. Al took Felix to get a haircut and then Hugo took him shopping. It was almost evening when they headed home. The moment Baxter dropped them off, he said he was going to dispose of the car and left. Little did they know he would be spending the night with Chartreuse. Baxter had finally met his soul mate. Chartreuse was once a man, but now had all the outward appearances of a woman, except for one important part – and that was just the way Baxter liked it.

Neve

Amanda knew Chuck would be staying the night in New York and she also knew why. He was going to meet with Fran Fillimoore and finally see the first photos of the Grasshoppers. Amanda asked Rita Hollingsworth to babysit so she could surprise Chuck at his hotel. Naturally, Rita thought it a perfect idea. She knew they seldom managed any alone time, between the baby and their busy schedules.

The moment Rita arrived, Amanda asked her to sign a power of attorney.

"Amanda, why on earth would you want me to sign this?"

"Just in case; after all, Rita, we now have baby Charlie to consider."

"And perhaps another on the way, dear?" Rita questioned, not for the first time – and not for the first time, Amanda didn't answer her.

"So Chuck's already signed it? Does he think it's necessary also?" Rita asked, referring to the power of attorney.

"Of course, it's his idea. Surely you don't think I'd ask you to sign it without his knowledge, do you, Rita?"

"No, dear, of course I don't. I just wondered why he hadn't discussed it with me. He usually talks to me about everything," Rita said.

"Too much on his mind, I guess, Rita; we've been meaning to talk to you about this since Christmas," Amanda said matter-of-factly. Finally, Rita signed the paper and Amanda handed her a copy.

At four thirty p.m., Amanda kissed Charlie and Rita, before heading to New York for her big surprise meeting with Chuck. She let herself into his hotel room and ordered champagne and chocolates, along with a lobster salad for two. Then she had a long, luxurious bubble bath and slipped into a sexy red silk camisole, which concealed nothing, the lacy fabric being so sheer. Then she helped herself to another glass of champagne and waited. She didn't have to wait long. She heard Chuck talking on his cell phone as he moved down the hallway toward the room.

"Okay, Walter, I know we will. I'll see you around eight thirty a.m. Bye," Chuck said as his room card clicked the door open.

Chuck was overjoyed at the sight of her lying on the bed, drinking champagne.

"Mandy, darling, I almost asked you to come along, but I didn't know how long it would take. The meeting I was hoping for didn't happen. Something about her old Uncle Tom passing away; Walter said her Uncle Tom was about the only relative she had who visited her, other than her absent parents. I know this isn't making much sense, Mandy. But I'll have to try her again tomorrow. I know I've never told you about any of my cases, but this one's personal. So I can share it with you and tell you everything. It's a very long story, so maybe not right now, darling." He almost forgot what he was saying as he eyed his gorgeous wife.

"Chucky, I ran a bath for you; it's overflowing with bubbles," Amanda cooed.

"Sounds divine. Anything to get close to you, my darling."

"Well, hurry now, don't keep me waiting, lover. After all, we are also celebrating!"

"Celebrating?"

"I'll tell you everything over champagne," Amanda said, watching him quickly undress, his sexy body never failing to arouse her. Tonight, she watched and memorized every move. He strutted naked into the huge marble bathroom and she could see his reflection in the mirror as he climbed into the bath. He briefly glimpsed her watching and instantly became eager and aroused.

Together, they enjoyed the lobster salad, washed down with champagne. They linked arms and looked into each other's eyes as they drank. It was a magical evening.

"So, my beautiful, perfect wife, what is this news we are celebrating? You simply must tell me," Chuck asked, not really caring as he gazed deeply into her eyes; there was only inches between them.

"Well, darling, I hope it's good news for you. It is definitely good news for Charlie, because, I'm pretty sure he's about to become a big brother," Amanda said, still so close to him she could see into his soul. He was immediately delighted and leapt to his feet, before lifting her into his arms and twirling her around and around. Chuck threw his head back and laughed.

"So soon, my darling, how clever you are!"

"Well, Chucky, I feel you may have had something to do with it," Amanda cooed breathlessly.

"Only the best part, my precious lady." Chuck's eyes sparkled, as, looking deeply into hers, he continued to twirl.

"Have you told Mom or your parents?"

"No, darling, I would never tell them before you," Amanda replied, gazing up at him.

"Then let's call Mom now. I know she'll be thrilled." Chuck reached for his cell phone.

"There's plenty of time, lover. Let's just enjoy our time together; we get little enough of it," Amanda cooed.

They both landed on the bed as he continued to stare deeply into her eyes. He still held her lovingly in his arms. He kissed her neck and lingered over her breasts, then gently caressed her stomach with the touch of a whisper at midnight, until she moaned with pleasure. He continued moving downward, caressing, licking, touching and teasing every part of her body, as only Chuck could do. Amanda was completely aroused, and her whole body tingled as she rolled on top of him, kissing him passionately, until she began teasing his already highly aroused body. She knew just what he liked, and she lingered lovingly in each intimate and special place. It was almost an hour later when they could not contain their passion a moment longer, and Chuck slowly pulled her on top of his very aroused body.

She first saw it in his eyes and then watched his desire slowly abate.

"Darling, I know you'll never forgive me, but I feel suddenly very tired. I promise it's not you, and this has never happened before, but I think I need a little nap before we continue," Chuck said, his words already slurring as he finished yawning widely.

"I know, Chucky darling, we have very busy lives and sometimes it just catches up." She quickly turned down the bed and helped him lovingly replace his boxer shorts, before guiding him between the sheets.

"I love you, Mandy," Chuck said for the tenth time that evening, only this time it was hardly audible.

"I love you forever, my darling Chucky," Amanda said, as the tears already flowed. She lifted his arm and wrapped herself in his embrace. The deep of night moved slowly for one that doesn't sleep. Amanda's tears rolled freely down her cheeks; her love for Chuck was so deep, it was beyond words. At three a.m., she dozed slightly, before waking with a start and remembering where she was. Quickly, she changed into clothes she'd hidden in her bag. In the dark of night, she returned to Chuck's office. She let herself in, and, as before, she remembered to use her scrambler. Only this time, she knew exactly what she wanted and where to find it. It was less than five minutes later when she left Chuck's office for the last time. She let herself back into Chuck's hotel room. Amanda felt confident her movements had gone unnoticed.

Chuck had been unconscious now for several hours. Amanda listened closely to his breathing. It was shallow and uneven. She lovingly arranged his arms over his chest. She knew the end was near; it was only a matter of time.

By six a.m., Chuck was barely alive; his pulse was weak and his breathing erratic. Amanda busied herself with removing any trace of her visit to the suite. She washed the tub and wiped every surface. She took with her the extra champagne glass, plate and cutlery. She changed her clothes and packed her bag, before checking to see everything was in its place.

Before she left the suite, she looked down at Chuck for several minutes as she tried to convince herself he was just sleeping. She kissed him tenderly as again she told him how much she loved him. Amanda was finding it hard to hold back the tears.

About seven fifteen a.m., Amanda was seated behind the wheel of her car in the basement car park of the hotel. She was trying to compose herself and was using many different types of justification in order to achieve it. By seven forty-five a.m. she was slightly more composed. She continued to sit, watch and wait. Walter Dense was always on time. He belonged to the old school, and today Amanda appreciated it. The older man carefully locked his car and walked across to the elevator leading up to the guest rooms. Amanda quickly started her car. There was no way Walter Dense was going to come between her and her future. She planted her pedal to the floor and drove straight for him. He tried to run, but he hit the front of her car with a thud as he crumpled to the ground. Amanda then removed the scrambler so the video surveillance cameras would be restored, and drove out of the car park.

"Hi, Rita, did my boy behave himself?" Amanda asked, trying to sound happy.

"You're home early. Yes, of course, he was positively perfect, a true Hollingsworth," Rita replied, yawning, as she buttoned her pink fluffy robe tightly around her waist.

"I know Chuck likes to start early, so I didn't disturb him; he was sleeping like a baby when I left."

"Did you have a nice evening, Mandy? You look a little sad."

"Rita, I love your son so much. I can never get enough time with him," Amanda answered truthfully as she walked toward Charlie's room.

"I know, I felt the same way when he was a boy. He grew up much too fast and left home way too soon," Rita chuckled, heading for the kitchen.

It was lunchtime before the doorbell rang and the two officers delivered the news of Chuck's death. Amanda screamed and collapsed on the floor. Rita tried to hold herself up and somehow managed to thank the officers and close the door. Then she calmly telephoned Nanny Bates, got Amanda to bed and called the doctor. Once the doctor left Amanda, he stopped and looked down at Rita, who sat curled up tightly in the window seat, sobbing loudly. Her cup of tea remained untouched.

"Mrs. Hollingsworth, your daughter-in-law appears to be in deep shock. I have given her something to make her sleep. I am assuming your son and daughter-in-law had a very close marriage. The baby is unharmed, and its heartbeat is strong." The doctor waited for a reply, and when he got none he moved into the other room and spoke briefly to Nanny Bates. Charlie gazed up at the stranger and chuckled happily.

It was Nanny Bates and Rita who placed the call to the Dolmans' house. Of course, the phone was not answered, but the message did get transferred to Savannah. It was much later the next afternoon when the Dolmans arrived. They found Amanda in a terrible state. She asked her mom to do several things, and Ruth followed her daughter's instructions without question.

The funeral was a small, intimate affair in the tiny white church the Hollingsworth family had always belonged to. The church was full and people spilled outside when there were no longer seats. Many of those who had known and loved Chuck sobbed. Amanda stood supported between Rita and Ruth. It was when Chuck's body was laid to rest that Amanda finally collapsed and was carried home to bed.

Rita Hollingsworth managed to stay until the end of the proceedings as she was supported by so many of her dear friends.

Rita never knew it was the Grasshopper file that had now taken all her family from her.

At eight p.m. that evening, Amanda walked into Charlie's room, where Nanny Bates was putting him to bed for the night. Then she told Nanny she would no longer be needing her services, and she handed her a rather large check and asked her to leave. Amanda filled a small bag with photos and memories from around the house, wrapped baby Charlie tightly in his blanket, turned off the lights and locked the door. Together, they walked several blocks, with her parents at her side. The first taxi cab that passed, they flagged down. Hugo and baby Charlie got in. Several blocks later, Amanda took a cab, and soon after that, Alberta did the same.

They met up at a prepaid hotel room at the Days Inn, on the way to the airport. Neve was still not talking, so Al immediately got to work. She partial wig and the hair extensions, cut Neve's long blonde hair to a neat shoulder-length bob, before coloring it to its original light auburn. While the color did its work, Al expertly removed Neve's disguise. Al carefully hid everything from sight under the false bottom of her suitcase.

Neve stared at her reflection in the mirror. Her skin was so blotchy, pale and dry, but it felt good to be out of the disguise she had worn for so long. Al and Hugo soon showered and changed their appearance also.

Several hours later, Hugo, Al and Neve Grasshopper left the hotel room with Neve's baby son. – Left behind in that hotel room was the name Charlie; from now on he would be known as Clarke Hugo Grasshopper. In her new handbag, Neve held all the necessary ID papers for them both. They made the eleven o'clock flight with minutes to spare and enjoyed the comfort the first-class seats offered them. Baby Clarke slept soundly through the entire flight, unaware of the changes unfolding around him. Neve still said very little, but she just sat and stared. Al and Hugo exchanged several concerned looks; the only thing Hugo said was, "Baby Girl, the Grasshoppers look after their own," and he squeezed her hand, but there was no response. Soon, he continued, "We want you to be the first to know that now you are home, the Grasshoppers have officially retired!"

"Mom, Dad, this has to be your decision. You mustn't do it for me," Neve whispered, looking at the floor.

"Honey, this time we're doing it for us all," Al said, kissing her lightly.

Three days later, the Grasshopper mansion was a hive of activity as the preparations for Al's fiftieth birthday party went into high gear. Felix was an incredible asset, as he took charge of the chaos around them. Nanny Snell was a small, chubby woman with an efficient manner and happy nature. Baby Clarke took to her immediately, and she to him.

It was Tuesday morning and Al's birthday celebrations were planned for Saturday. Neve had stayed in her suite of rooms since Baxter collected them at the airport. She had spoken to no one. The staff left food trays outside her door several times a day; they'd knock quietly and walk away. Sometimes the food had been picked at, but usually it remained where they'd left it.

"Hugo, we have to do something. It's been almost four days and all she does is stay locked in her room and cry."

"I know, darling. What do you say tonight, after everyone leaves, we see if she'll let us in?" Later that evening, she did. They were surprised to see Neve looked better than they'd expected her to look. She had obviously been spending time on her balcony in the sun, as her face now held a light tan and matched the rest of her body color.

"Can we come in, honey?" Al asked as Neve finally opened the door a crack and then allowed them through.

"Neve, we have to talk this through, you can't shut yourself away forever. You will break Al's heart if you're not present at her birthday on Saturday, and you haven't even spoken to your Uncle Felix," Hugo said kindly as they sat on the edge of Neve's large bed and held one of her hands in theirs.

"I want to bring Siobhan here. I want to tell her everything. Good friends shouldn't have any lies between them. I thought you might have called her and brought her here. She's my best friend," Neve finally said.

Al and Hugo exchanged looks; they hadn't realized she didn't know about Siobhan. So, very gently, Al told her about her best friend's arrest. Neve immediately broke down into tears again and screamed, "I don't believe it, she wouldn't do that! Not Siobhan, she wouldn't do that!"

Hugo held her close as her body shook with sobs. Not much more was said, but they continued to sit. Finally, Neve asked for her fire to be lit. Even though it was a warm summer's evening, Al quickly instructed Baxter to light the fire in Neve's room. Baxter then served martinis and left the room. They sat looking into the flames, hoping Neve would tell them what had happened. They sat patiently and waited, but still she said nothing.

"Mom, I won't ruin your birthday – I promise," Neve eventually said in a very soft voice.

"Come to the spa with me on Saturday morning, just the two of us, please," Al begged, trying to look at her face as her head remained downcast.

"Sure, Mom, if that's what you'd like," Neve replied in no more than a whisper. It was over an hour later when Neve finally got to her feet and took a file to the fireplace, before throwing it in.

"That was Siobhan's file and this is the Grasshopper file," Neve said, handing them the heavy old file. Both Al and Hugo gasped. They had no idea!

Together, they sat in front of the fire, reading the file, before throwing each page into the flames. They had no idea why they hadn't been caught when Hugo worked at Banker's Securities – it was all here, their many aliases, where they lived, everything. Neither of them had known just how close they'd come to being locked away forever. It appeared Sheffield Hollingsworth was a thorough and meticulous man.

As they came to the last page, the first bird songs of dawn filtered into the room. Neve took the final page and slowly threw it into the flames. Then she tore the old file holder in half, before also placing it in the flames.

"Mom, Dad – the Grasshoppers' motto has always been, 'A Grasshopper looks after its own'. Everything will be all right. I have taken care of it all, as I said I would," she said, pausing briefly as a sob escaped her.

"I had to do it; I had to protect us. Chuck could have destroyed us all. I had to do it. Mom, Dad, I poisoned Chuck!" she said, again collapsing in a heap into their arms. Then, in a mere whisper, Neve continued, "Yes, Dad, I have kept my promise and lived by the Grasshopper motto, 'A Grasshopper always looks after its own'. The Grasshopper file is no more. I sacrificed the love of my life so all Grasshoppers can continue to live and remain free."

The End

The Grasshopper File

Mary Barr has hit another one out of the park – this time for adults. Few authors can move through the worlds of children's, young adult, and adult literature with the ease and elegance of Mary Barr. And few writers consistently turn out well-structured stories and exciting characters that pay off time and time again. *The Grasshopper File* has class, protagonists you love (even if they're naughty), and non-stop action that will keep the pages turning. I loved this book; I love this author; I wait with bated breath for the next book.

– Jeff Lyons, Author, Director, Editor, Founder of Storygeeks.com

About the Author

Author Mary Barr has indulged her passion for writing for several decades. Now semi-retired from a fast-paced and varied career, she is able to focus on her favorite interests: oil painting, renovating houses and designing jewelry. However, her greatest passion has remained storytelling. Creating characters, their lives and destinies proves an exciting and thought-provoking pastime. Bitten by the writing bug at age seven, when she won her first literary award, Mary has enjoyed a lifelong love affair with writing, one that keeps her busy each day. Children's books have recently joined her range of genres. Mary Barr resides in British Columbia, Canada, with her Canadian husband; she has one adult daughter, who lives and works overseas.

www.Mary-Barr.com

Read a sample chapter from Mrs Dolymauchers Daughters

Chapter Two
Bethony Smith

Bethony Smith was tall and slim. Her golden blonde hair cascaded softly down her back. As she walked, the hair around her face gently moved with the breeze. Bethony had a pretty face and bright blue eyes. Once a happy girl, it was the separation and divorce of her parents which changed her outlook forever. Her happy disposition and love of life were no more.

Bethony only completed one term at university and dropped out. She had the brains but not the desire to achieve. Her only regret had been leaving Brett, her boyfriend of four months; she knew he was probably the best thing that had ever happened to her. When she'd told him she no longer wanted to continue with her studies, she was shocked to learn that he didn't want a girlfriend that was uneducated. With that one comment, she knew he was no longer the one for her, although she thought she'd loved him and she still missed his witty conversation and upbeat attitude. Bethony often saw Brett's handsome, laughing face in her mind and wondered what and whom he was sharing his time with now.

Slowly, with her head downward, she walked through the park. Bethony appeared to be intently watching the ground, but she was in fact hiding the tears that ran unchecked down her cheeks before dripping off her chin. Bethony had no idea she was being watched. At twenty years old, Bethony knew she shouldn't be crying, but she had decided long ago that it was all right to cry if no one saw you. Bethony had just spent the last week with her father, Lyndon Smith, in his semi-detached house outside Essex. His girlfriend Lucy drove Bethony crazy with her constant chatter. Bethony knew Lucy saw her as a nuisance; she often hinted that Bethony should get a job and find her own place instead of living off her parents. Bethony knew this was probably correct, but she didn't really care. Lucy finally left earlier this morning and Bethony hoped her father would now have some time for her.

Together, they had sat at the dirty, broken kitchen table and had a short discussion about Lucy. Lyndon seemed to value her opinion, and Bethony was quite willing to share it. Bethony and her father saw eye to eye on most things and the subject of Lucy was no exception. He told Bethony he was quite willing to give Lucy up as he had met a rather interesting girl at the bar the other week, anyway. Bethony was secretly pleased that Lucy would no longer be in her life. She didn't want her father to see the pleasure his comments created, so she merely replied that she was thinking of making tea in the old, blue chipped teapot, when the phone had rung.

It was her mother, but she didn't want to speak with Bethony. Lyndon answered and after they appeared to share a cordial conversation, they started arguing. Bethony knew it was over her, as her father had the call on speakerphone and she could hear every word. They were arguing again over whose fault it was that Bethony had dropped out of university. Their conversation took the same route it always did, and then they started arguing about whom Bethony should live with. It wasn't because they both wanted her, it was actually the reverse. Both her parents had busy lives, her mother was Jess Tonkin-Smith, the famous playwright, while her father had several jobs, none of which allowed him the time to spend with his daughter, as the hours he worked, were varied.

Between his two evenings a week as a bartender, and his two nights a week singing in a nightclub, he also cleaned up after a construction crew each afternoon. Jess, on the other hand, was out at the theatre most nights, and many afternoons. Bethony had heard the same argument many times before. Bethony was already packed and ready to leave for her trip back to her mother's house, so she threw her backpack over her shoulder and left her father's small house, without interrupting his loud conversation to say goodbye. She needed to get away, so she decided to walk the mile and a half through the park to the train station, rather than taking the bus as she usually did.

The air in the park seemed crisper and fresher and as she inhaled, she felt her composure strengthen. By the time she was near the center of the park, she was beginning to feel better. Finally, she raised her head and brushed the hair from her face. She looked ahead at the dappled, winding pathway that led through the fresh, green spring trees. She saw the kids in the grassy clearing, playing rugby, and she heard the birds singing. But what she didn't see was someone watching her. They were not only watching but also following her. They were closer now.

Bethony decided to stop and buy a Cornish pasty from the vendor who always sold his pies and baked goods in the same place; he had been there for years.

"'Ere ya go, Miss. Mind now, it's hot. Fresh out of me oven, it is, an' all," he said, as he handed over the pasty wrapped in crisp brown paper. Bethony paid him and walked on until she found a seat under a shady tree.

Bethony unwrapped her pasty but never got to savour its hot meaty taste. It fell to the ground the moment the unknown stranger approached her quietly from behind and placed a cold wet cloth over her mouth and nose. It took seconds for her body to go limp.
However, it took nearly a week for her parents to realise Bethony was missing and wasn't living with either of them…

Synopsis
Mrs Dolymaucher's Daughters

Sadie Timmons lives in a quiet, upper-class suburb outside London. Nothing ever happens in the village of Winton, and Sadie likes it that way. Sadie lives a quiet life with her middle-class parents: her father, Murray Timmons, once the priest at the local church, and her mother, Maude.

Sadie is a solicitor and works for a large law firm in London. She enjoys her job and her life. Sadie remains blissfully unaware that she is not attractive and, therefore, doesn't miss the attention she has never had. With her career on fast track, Sadie is free to focus on the things she loves most in her life, mainly her friendship with Cassandra and Dexter Morley and the object of her desire, Crispin Huntington the Third. Sadie is obsessed with Crispin and wastes many hours each night watching him in his bedroom through her binoculars. Until one day, Crispin's little brother Clifford observes, by accident, Sadie's nightly antics. Delighted by his observation, young Clifford Huntington sees this as an easy opportunity to earn some fast cash.

While Sadie is trying to remove herself from the situation she has created, she fails to notice that she is also being watched. Mrs. Dolymaucher, the creator of collectible porcelain dolls, stands six feet tall, has a square jaw and a heavy square body, greasy gray hair and a thick German accent. She resides in the basement flat of the Huntingtons' mansion. She has lived there since arriving in England soon after her daughter and husband were viciously murdered. Each year, on the anniversary of her daughter's murder, a girl disappears. It takes several years before Detective Fox Hunter begins to see a pattern unfolding. Many years of questioning and searching doesn't reveal the girls' bodies, nor does it uncover any clues as to their whereabouts.

Each doll Mrs. Dolymaucher creates is perfectly life-like in every way. Every year another doll, complete with birth certificate and a set of designer clothes, is launched. The new doll has the same birthday as all the rest, the same birthday as Gretchen Dolymaucher, Mrs. Dolymaucher's deceased daughter.

Like Mrs. Dolymaucher, Sadie Timmons is a creature of habit. She, too, does many of the same things at the same time each day.

Mrs. Dolymaucher watches Sadie. Sadie watches Crispin. Boris Wainwright watches Clifford.

Will Sadie become Mrs. Dolymachers last and final victim? Will Sadie's face and name match that of the final doll? What happens when the watcher is being watched?

More fiction books you may enjoy – from Mary Barr

Wild Dog Canyon

Hagar's Curse

Browning Amble – The Sect. (similar Genre)

Mrs. Dolymauchers Daughter's

A Rumble in the Attic

Dahlia's Choice

How to Buy a Husband

Ms. Barr also writes:
Short stories
Novella's
Young adults
Juvenile
Children's books

WWW.Mary-Barr.com

'Remember, adventures in life are all around, live in the moment, there are no second chances.'
Mary Barr

Character Sheet
The Grasshopper File

Hugo & Alberta Grasshopper, alias Alastair & Sylvia Rasnic and Harrington & Millington Hoarders and also Sam & Ruth Dolman

Felix Grasshopper – Hugo's brother

Zax (Hugo & Alberta's son) **& Molly** (formerly Lady Molly Win-Stanley) **Hopper**
Their children, **Bobby** (Lord Robert Hugo Hopper – one year old) and **Beth** (Lady Elizabeth Florentine Hopper – one month old)

Neve Grasshopper (Hugo & Alberta's daughter), twenty-four years old – alias Amanda Dolman

Baxter – Assistant/Butler to Hugo and Al

Jon Riddley – Baxter's boyfriend

Fran Fillimoore – Apartment 7B

Special Agent Bow Grismold

Gus Boozeman & Pa – [? Details?]

Uncle Tom – Pa's neighbour and friend

Brock Burke – CEO & President of Banker's Securities

Siobhan Burke – Brock's wife

Esmeralda & Enoch Ginzo – Siobhan's parents

Holly Bond – Siobhan's mother

Marlene Brice – Brock's secretary, deceased

Borg Brice – Marlene's husband

Enid Shillington – Secretary

Saffron Moffit – Vice-President of Banker's Securities

Potter Moffit – Saffron's husband

Cox Moffit – Saffron's & Potter's son

Loot Whimsey-Sparrow – Potter's lover

Aunt Adele – Potter's aunt

Berry Pye – Alastair's secretary

Phil Monkton & Ross Moss – Accounts Department

Sheffield, Rita & Chuck Hollingsworth – Detectives

Blue Satine – Chuck's secretary

Fred Blook – Chuck's assistant P.I.

Walter Dense – P.I.

Mazey Dook – Wedding planner

Ali Singh – Truck driver

Uncle Tom

E.M. Distribution

Colonel Emmett Wiggins – President, CEO & Board member

Colonel Tom Sanders – Chairman of the Board

Flower Patricers – Harry Hoarders' secretary.

Storm – Flower's husband

Angel Wings, Pet Arbry, Lamb Sonny, Trig Smith & Colt Patricers – Flower's children

Carman Finnick – Sam & Ruth Dolman's neighbor

Charlie & Clarke – Neve's babies

Mascoti Vitale – Siobhan's other love interest